DEATH SPIRAL

DEATH SPIRAL

JAMES W. NICHOL

McArthur & Company
Toronto

First published in Canada in 2009 by
McArthur & Company
322 King Street West, Suite 402
Toronto, Ontario
M5V 1J2
www.mcarthur-co.com

Library and Archives Canada Cataloguing in Publication

Nichol, James W., 1940-
Death spiral / James W. Nichol.

ISBN 978-1-55278-792-2

I. Title.

PS8577.I18D42 2009   C813'.54   C2009-904285

The publisher would like to acknowledge the financial support of the Government
of Canada through the Book Publishing Industry Development Program (BPIDP)
and the Canada Council for our publishing activities. The publisher further wishes
to acknowledge the financial support of the Ontario Arts Council
and the OMDC for our publishing program.

Design and composition by Tania Craan
Cover photograph © Mark Owen/arcangel-images.com
Printed in Canada by Webcom

10 9 8 7 6 5 4 3 2 1

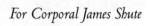

For Corporal James Shute

PROLOGUE

Death Spiral. You have no other choice. You have to let go.

They weren't supposed to be there. Everyone on both sides knew the war was as good as over. Off my starboard wing a flood of Lancasters and B-17s surged along under a brilliant blue sky, light glinting off their wings like off the tops of waves. A slow tide of death over Germany.

It was the Messerschmitts that weren't supposed to be there, hidden in the sun five thousand feet above and dropping down like diving seabirds. The Luftwaffe's last gasp.

Fake your own death. Trust in the Almighty Spitfire. Flutter down like a leaf in October. Don't pass out.

Arcing across the top of our bombers, flashes of gunfire under their wings, slicing through and disappearing into the silver tide. They were below us now. Somewhere.

"Great Jesus in the morning." Wilson Mahoney's voice crackled in my ears, "Wake the hell up."

Two Lancasters began to trail smoke. A B-17 droning beside me rolled its huge white belly. An explosion of flames ballooned out of its side.

Keep your head lolled over. He can see you. Pray he doesn't fire again. Sky spinning like a top. Horizon coming up fast.

Squadron Leader Mahoney slipped his lead Spitfire and headed down. "Everyone pick up your wing man. Don't do anything alone, boys." It was the last five minutes of his life. Soon there were dogfights all over the sky.

Where the hell is he? Where am I? Stick jerking between my legs like a mad thing, eyes popping, brain turning liquid, steaming like porridge on a cold winter day, frost on the kitchen window, late for school. Oh god, I'm going out.

Knocked one down, had another jumping in and out of my sights like a rabbit heading for the bluest blue. Now I had to concentrate as fierce as God on the first day of creation, death could come in all directions otherwise. Had to see everything, think of everything. Otherwise.

I'm dead. The world's turned a kind of fluorescent green, instruments luminous in a sparkling haze, piss warm as a bath running up my belly and trickling across my chest. I'm hanging upside down. I can hear the drone of an engine somewhere faraway. The tops of evergreen trees are rushing past my face.

Going for a second kill, so locked in I forgot my wing man, an amateur's mistake. Nothing now but blue sky and me and a retreating silver streak. Glanced at the fuel gauge. Tried to sneak a look at my watch. How long had I been flying?

And like a shadow falling, like a dream coming to life, the pilot I'd been waiting for for three years dropped in behind me. I threw the Spit into a screaming starboard sheer, fire licking below his wings now, lead tearing into my plane like some vengeful giant driving nails. Put her nose up, scrambled toward heaven, he was there, so close behind I could see his face. Another burst of fire, a final falling loop. Better than me. He was better. Three holes in my canopy. No choice. Play dead.

Brilliant sunlight and a rushing bright forest like green water where the sky should be. I reach out, touch the stick, turn her right side up. Just in time to soar over a rise, just in time to fly into a tumbling mass of the blackest smoke I've ever seen.

Wait to come out the other side. And wait. Dark as a grave. The motor dies. I can hear myself breathing.

CHAPTER ONE

The mayor and other assorted town dignitaries were standing on top of a baggage wagon in the bone-chilling January cold and even though the train was still moving and its brakes were just starting to make a screeching noise, the mayor gave the signal and the band struck up the first series of notes to "Hail the Conquering Hero."

The train shuddered to a stop, a coach door swung open and a black porter leaned out into the music and the steam. Behind him, hesitating for a moment, peering out and looking a bit shocked and more than a trifle chagrined stood the last local soldier to return home from the war.

The crowd cheered, men brandishing their fedoras high in the air, women and children fluttering a forest of tiny Union Jacks and Canadian Red Ensigns. They'd been gathering at the train station and doing just that for over a year.

This particular day was special though, because this was the greatest hero of them all, looking splendid in his light-blue greatcoat, his officer's cap, a black and shiny hospital cane caught by the crook and dangling from his arm. Flying Officer Wilfred McLauchlin. Spitfire fighter pilot. Trained on Hurricanes and Mark 9s. Fought in Mark I Is. And then in 1945, the upgraded Mark 14. Twelve kills.

"Hurrah!"

He began to make his way down the steep iron steps. His left leg dragged behind him. He had to tilt himself to the side to swing it forward. His left arm was trussed up in a black sling under his unbuttoned coat. The porter reached up to help. His father hovered behind him.

It seemed to take a long time to make the descent.

CHAPTER TWO

Wilf pushed himself up with his good arm, turned on the light and sat on the edge of the bed.

He'd been home for a week, a week of house parties and a banquet in his honour and hotel-hopping in crowded cars full of ex-servicemen, everyone laughing, everyone drunk. It sure was good to be home. That's what he'd said when it was his time to stand up in the crammed and steamy community hall and make his thank-you speech.

"You can't imagine," Wilf had said, "just how good it feels to be finally home."

The heavy gong of a grandfather clock rang through the empty house, a clock purchased years ago by his own grandfather, Taylor McLauchlin, Queen's Counsel and Liberal Member of Parliament. Wilf listened as if he'd never heard it before. Two more times.

He picked up his cane and limped slowly over to the dresser mirror. A sleep-deprived man of only twenty-eight years stared back, hair so black it looked blue creeping over his ears, lean sensuous face, deep shadows under his eyes. Once upon a time young women had found him exotic-looking, or so they claimed. Scottish lasses with red hair and freckled faces. And English. And French. To laugh with. To dance with. To tumble into the nearest bed with, the world being on fire, anyway, or so they whispered to each other, they could all be dead the next morning, anyway.

Warm skin and warmer breath, thin girlish arms fiercely around his neck.

Wilf's heart ached for those girls. His body ached.

And what did Chuck the Chopper used to say to all the lads? "Plenty of you left, mate, to do whatever you want." And from deep in their recovery beds, each young face would look up at him with such great hope.

Wilf took a deep breath and smiled at himself, an exercise he'd been doing for close to two years, smiling into mirrors and trying to locate his old optimistic self. He turned away, limped out into the dark upstairs hall, hooked his cane over the back of a chair and with the same good hand picked up the phone.

"Number please," the operator said.

"Two two one."

"Is that you, Wilf?"

"Yes."

"It's Nancy Dearborn. Remember? I was three classes ahead of you."

"Oh, sure. Hi Nancy."

"It's so good to have you home, Wilf."

"Well, thanks."

"I'll put you through. Andy must be working nights, just like me."

"Yes he is."

"I'll ring you through."

"Thank you, Nancy."

A phone rang at the other end of the line. And rang a few more times. After a while it was picked up. "Police station. Creighton here."

"Hi, Creighton."

"Hello there, McLauchlin. Are you still drunk?"

"That was three nights ago. I've been drunk twice since then. So what are you up to?"

"Nothing much."

"How about picking me up? Must be time to go out on patrol."

"Wilf, it's three o'clock in the morning."

"Time to secure the perimeter," Wilf said.

By the time Wilf had wrestled his pajamas back off and his clothes back on, pulled his winter coat over his shoulders and struggled into his galoshes, Andy Creighton was pulling the police cruiser up to the front door.

Wilf made his slow way down the porch steps and through the dark frosty air, opened the passenger door and slid in.

"How's it going?" Andy said.

"It's going fine. I can't sleep."

Andy put the car in gear. A row of street lights glowed faintly in front of them. All the houses were dark. They began to glide down the snow-packed road.

"How are the brats?"

Andy grinned and stuck a cigarette in his mouth. "The brats are great."

Wilf and Andy had been friends all their lives but, unlike Wilf, Andy hadn't signed up at the beginning of the war. He was already the young father of one child and to further complicate matters Linda had gone and put another bun in her oven. Andy had enrolled in police college and joined the local force instead. It was an attempt to apologize for staying home while the rest of his friends went off to war; he was aware of this but it hadn't worked out the way he'd hoped. Dressed in his new uniform for the first time, creases freshly pressed by Linda, a shiny revolver buckled to his hip and patrolling Main Street, he'd felt like a joke.

"Can't get over how tall Davey is," Wilf said.

"Well, he's seven now." Andy, himself, was stocky and just tall enough to make the police force's minimum standard.

"That's what I mean. How could it be seven years?"

"What's it feel like?"

"Seventy. Sometimes it feels like just a few days. It's all buggered up."

Andy and Linda had thrown Wilf a homecoming party. Once the crowd had left and Linda had gone up to bed, Wilf had said that he thought he'd stay the rest of the night on their couch. It seemed a reasonable idea since alcoholically speaking he was in a semi-comatose state anyway.

Sitting on a slant and half-asleep he'd begun to tell Andy about the hospitals in France and in England. It had struck Andy then that Wilf had been waiting all night for just this opportunity. Numerous steel pins and a steel plate were the only things holding his left hip together. Same with his left shoulder. Nerves completely and irredeemably severed up there but the blood flow was still good and so he'd decided to leave the arm attached. "It has sentimental value," he'd told the surgeon, one Chuck the Chopper.

It was his loss of sight that had been the big mystery, though. He'd been found unconscious in his wrecked plane along some country road and his doctors had been telling him all along that there was no direct physical damage to his eyes. His blindness had been most likely caused by a concussion, some kind of trauma to the occipital lobe at the back of his head.

He'd been blind for close to three months and then suddenly there was a slit of peripheral vision one morning. It was as if an orderly had tiptoed into the room and had lifted up a corner of a blanket he'd been huddling under for all that time. Light slid in and lit up his mind with a kind of cathedral glow. By the end of the day he could make out his hospital room and his assembled doctors. Outside his window he could begin to see the world.

Wilf had tapped Andy on his wrist.

"What?"

"About my eyes?"

"What about them?"

"The thing is, I didn't have so much as a bump on my head."

Wilf had stared at Andy for a long moment as if he'd just

told him the strangest thing in the world, and then he'd closed his eyes and fallen asleep.

"Nancy Dearborn is still single, at least she's still using her maiden name," Wilf announced.

They were driving past the high school they'd attended together until Andy had dropped out in Grade Twelve. A lonely light illuminated the front door.

"She's still single," Andy said.

"As I remember, she filled out a sweater in a very admirable way."

"Still does. Twin peaks of unspeakable delights."

Wilf laughed. "Really?"

"She's engaged, though. Some guy from out of town."

"How do you know they're twin peaks of unspeakable delights?"

"I don't. I'm just guessing." The sound of Wilf's familiar laugh reassured Andy. Maybe that was all Wilf had wanted. Or needed. To go for a ride, have a stupid laugh or two.

"I should ask her out. Find out for myself. Maybe she'll break off her engagement."

"Yeah, that's a good idea," Andy said.

They drove by the town's hospital. All the windows were dark except for two brightly lit ones up on the top row. Wilf could see a nurse moving back and forth. Trouble up there, he thought. The breath-pinching pain in his left side surprised him. It always returned, about once every five minutes or so, and it always surprised him. He waited, caught his breath. "Then again, maybe I should just ask out the loneliest girl in town."

"Bullshit." Andy continued to concentrate on his driving, not wanting at that particular moment to look over at his best friend sitting a little askew beside him, his coat sleeve empty.

"My father took a train to North Bay yesterday," Wilf finally said.

"Oh yeah?"

"He's got some property case up there going to trial, he'll be gone the rest of the week. Wants me to go down to the office tomorrow and look like I know something."

"Sounds like fun. When are you going back to Toronto? Law school and all that?"

"I'm hoping by the end of the month."

"I thought you'd stay in town for a while. Ambitious bastard." Andy sounded genuinely disappointed.

"I want to get back into it. Can't wait, actually. I'm excited about it. I need to restart my life."

"Right," Andy said.

Wilf went back to looking out the window. Random flakes of snow were suspending themselves in the passing street lights. Spiralling slowly down. Spiralling. It reminded him of a long time ago. Early morning hockey practice. Trudging down to the arena in the dark, equipment bag slung over his shoulder, a stick in his hand, half-asleep and already full of a soaring anticipation, a boundless joy.

"I'll be all right," Wilf said.

Andy turned to look. Wilf was smiling at him.

It was six o'clock in the morning and still dark by the time Wilf had had enough of driving around the town and drinking murky coffee in the police station. Andy dropped him off in front of his father's house.

Wilf struggled up the stairs and without bothering to take off his clothes fell back on top of his bed. He was trying to find a way to sleep besides taking the sleeping pills his doctors had supplied. Horse pills, all the lads had called them, the size of small white pillows. He didn't want to use them. He was already too dependent on his painkillers.

The large house was silent, sitting far back on its front lawn but still towering above the town's most prestigious street. His home had always seemed silent except for the grandfather clock in the downstairs front hall. He'd been raised by his father and a succession of nannies, his mother having died when he was exactly three months old. He could still remember some of those women if he put his mind to it. He was trying to do that now in an attempt to drift off. All the lost faces.

The flyers he'd known, too. In particular, all the dead ones. All their names. It seemed important to remember their names. It wasn't difficult to summon up their faces, Canadians, Brits, Yanks, each with their own particular tilt of head, the individual way they carried their shoulders.

All ghosts now.

And the Scottish girls. English. French. No names there. Faces, though. Their eyes blurring, so close to his own eyes. Drifting away. And the faint sound of a faraway motor. He could recognize the sound of his own plane anywhere. And the smell of petrol.

Water colder than he'd ever felt before was riding up his face. He was suspended on the crest of a great grey wave, legs scissoring madly, and falling down between chunks of ice. And riding up again, the tilted tail of his plane looming above him. Teeth beginning to chatter. Eyelids freezing together. Heart clenched like a fist.

Wilf woke up. His body felt frozen to the other side of his soul. He lay there gasping for breath.

He looked at his bedside clock.

He'd been asleep for less than half an hour.

CHAPTER THREE

Carole Birley unlocked the front door of *T.W. McLauchlin & C.J. McLauchlin, Solicitors at Law,* turned on the light and surveyed the outer office. She was purposely ten minutes early. Wilf McLauchlin had not arrived.

Carole took off her snowboots, hung up her coat, unwound her scarf and pulled off her wool hat. It was going to be an excruciating situation. What was she going to do with him? She could hardly ask him to file. He couldn't file with one hand anyway.

Mr. McLauchlin had said to keep him busy. She didn't want to ask how. He might have taken it the wrong way, as some veiled reference to his son's physical, physical what? Limitations? No. Frailties seemed a better word. Frailties of the moment.

Carole had attended the banquet at the community hall and that's how his situation had struck her because he'd looked so determined to be normal, laughing and chatting and limping his way through the crowded room, his one arm trussed up in a sling and forever useless or so she'd been told.

Standing at the back of the hall Carole had thought to herself that Wilf McLauchlin had turned out to be not quite as handsome as she'd remembered. Of course it was nine years since he'd left high school and he was no longer boyish. He was a man, a man who had seen things and who had suffered.

Carole had been in her second year when Wilf had been in his last. Most of the younger girls had a crush on him. He was the high school's overall track and field champion, he was the school's debating champion, he edited the yearbook in his final year. It was obvious back then that the local high school and everyone in it were just the beginning for Wilf McLauchlin. He was one of those people who would go on to university and do all kinds of interesting things, and then one day you'd read in the "About the Town" column that he'd become someone really important, and that he and his wife and his two perfect children had spent a pleasant weekend visiting with his father.

Of course it hadn't worked out that way. A lot of things hadn't worked out like they were supposed to over the last few years.

Carole sat down at her desk and looked over a pile of files. A full day's worth of typing.

Take her own life for instance. Donny had wanted to get married and she'd said, "Why don't we wait until you're back from overseas. I think it's bad luck. We should leave something undone, just for luck."

They hadn't left sex undone, that was for sure. But the truth was she just wasn't absolutely certain she wanted to spend the rest of her life with Donny Mason. She loved him but her love felt to her like a shallow lake. Why weren't there deeper wells of feeling, a more ferociously held attachment, a desperate keening edge of passion?

Nevertheless they got engaged just before he went overseas and she knitted socks and bought him underwear and shipped packages to him at the end of every month. Each week she wrote him a letter saying how much she loved him. He wrote back saying he loved her, too. Soon it seemed like she was writing five letters for each one she received. Of course that was to be expected. She was only finishing high school and going to business college while Donny was being shipped all around England and Scotland and then to the frontlines in Europe somewhere. And anyway who could have guessed that the war would take such an incredibly long time? The last note she'd received was in February of 1945. It was a Christmas note but it had been delayed. *Merry Christmas. I am all right. Hope you are, too*, it said. On November 20th he'd arrived back in town accompanied by a Scottish wife and a six-month-old baby.

She'd felt like a fool but that was all she'd felt, she hadn't even cried.

Carole looked up at the clock. She'd already typed her way through a will and two agreements to purchase. It was almost ten thirty but no Wilf McLauchlin.

Actually, the truth was she'd felt more than just a fool. She'd felt discarded. And slightly disoriented. She avoided her friends and walked to and from work with even longer strides than she usually did, holding her head at an even higher tilt than usual and smiling at everyone she passed as if she didn't have a care in the world. She knew what they were all thinking, "Poor Carole Birley."

One day she dyed her hair red. The Scottish girl's hair was a kind of reddish colour. She hadn't realized her terrible mistake until it was too late and she'd already walked out of the beauty parlour.

Carole winced. She could still feel that awful sick feeling in the pit of her stomach, the sudden realization of what she'd just done.

The front door opened and a cold draft and Wilf McLauchlin blew in.

"Morning," he said.

"Good morning," Carole replied.

Wilf struggled with his overcoat. Carole wondered if she should get up and help him. He finally hung it up beside her coat. He had to sit down on the chair by the front door to take off his galoshes.

"I've always wanted to meet a Spitfire pilot."

Wilf kept his head down. "Consider this your lucky day."

Carole reddened a little. In retrospect, it seemed like an incredibly stupid remark to make. "Your father wants you to use his office. For now."

When Wilf looked up, his face seemed surprisingly pale to Carole. There were dark-blue marks under his eyes.

"I know you. You were the Grade Ten reporter for the year-book," he said.

"Was I?"

"You had your pictures and all your material in before anyone else. You helped me with all the layouts. You were great."

"I didn't think you'd remember."

"Oh, I do," Wilf smiled at her and pushed through the little swing gate that separated Carole from clients. "I remember thinking, boy, I wish I was back in Grade Ten again."

"With a line like that you should be back in Grade Ten again." Carole turned to her typewriter and advanced the carriage, making a louder bang than she'd intended. She could hear Wilf laugh, it was a pleasant-enough sounding laugh.

Carole smiled. She felt relieved, things weren't going along too badly.

"Why would I sit in my father's office?" Wilf asked.

"Because your grandfather's office hasn't been used in years and it's jammed full of files."

"What I mean is, I'll be lonely back there."

Wilf sat down at the desk that had been Dorothy Dale's place of residence from time immemorial, until she'd retired three months after Carole had begun, having assured herself that Carole could handle the work but not convinced that her personality lent itself to the peculiar combination of diplomacy and aggression that being an excellent legal secretary called for. She'd told Mr. McLauchlin on her last day that Carole seemed just a touch flighty.

"Flighty?" Clarence McLauchlin peered at her over his glasses.

"Time will tell," Dorothy Dale had said. In her older years she'd become inclined to make ominous predictions rather than conversation.

Carole looked over at Wilf. He was swivelling around on Dorothy Dale's swivel chair. "You can't sit there."

"Why not?"

"It doesn't look right. You're not a clerk."

"No one's here."

"Someone will be here soon."

"You're being stuffy."

"No I'm not."

"Rigid then."

"I'm going to find you something to do." Carole got up and walked over to a row of filing cabinets along the back wall. She knew that Wilf was looking at her. For a fleeting moment she wished she had more to look at.

Wilf looked Carole over. She was tall and too thin, but nevertheless he liked the way her narrow waist and sharp hips flared her skirt out. He liked the way she had her hair swept up to reveal the tender whiteness at the back of her neck, too. Her hair was kind of a peculiar colour though, mostly a brownish blonde but reddish on the ends.

"Why don't you look over the most recent files?" Carole said hopefully, gathering some up in her arms. "That way, if a client calls or drops in you can talk to him."

"And tell him what?"

"That you're familiar with his file, that it's on top of the pile, and as soon as your father returns next week you'll be speaking to him about it."

"What if he asks a question?"

Carole came back and stood in front of Wilf, her mouth tight, the files held against her chest. "Will I put these on your father's desk?"

"No. Put them right here." Wilf tapped Dorothy Dale's desk.

Carole laid them down. "You were halfway through law school, weren't you? I'm sure you can answer most questions."

"I was just entering the law part of law school." Wilf opened up a file with his good hand. "This is what I think we should do. You answer the phone and I'll talk to anyone who comes in. If we're really pressed for an answer we'll just make something up."

"Fine," Carole said and sat back down at her desk. My god, she thought to herself, this is going to be the longest week of my life.

Carole went back to her typing.

Wilf leafed through the first file. Something about a coal truck sliding down the front hill and into the corner of the Arlington Hotel causing considerable damage to both parties. Wilf's father was representing the Arlington Hotel. The coal truck, widening the suit, was claiming that the town had been negligent in not sanding the hill.

Wilf's eyelids began to feel heavy.

He managed to continue his reading until noon, at which time he crossed Main Street and ordered what he'd hoped would be a solitary lunch at The Palms. Several people sat down at his table to tell him how proud they were of him and how pleased they were to see him safely home. Wilf smiled and nodded and said that all he wanted to do from now on was to have a good time and catch up with his life.

Carole ate her lunch at the office.

By two thirty and back at Dorothy Dale's desk, Wilf's nerves were beginning to feel as unstrung as the elastic bands that were trying to escape from the small cardboard box sitting in front of him. This was not an uncommon feeling for him over the last long months.

The pain in his side came and went. Announced itself again. Receded once more.

Carole was relentlessly clattering away on her typewriter. The clock on the wall inched forward.

"I think I'll run some papers up to this client's house. Father's left a note to get them signed p.d.q."

Carole kept up her typing. "Cruikshank, Samuel?"

"That's right."

"He didn't say p.d.q. He said in time for court two weeks from now. I was going to call Mr. Cruikshank this afternoon."

"That's all right." Wilf levered himself out of Dorothy Dale's chair and headed for his coat. He felt immediately better.

Carole stopped typing. "Usually clients come in to the office to sign documents."

Wilf was already at the front door and positioning his galoshes for a quick escape. "Today's an exception," he said.

❄ ❄ ❄

Samuel Cruikshank, as it turned out, lived in a Tudor-style house a few blocks from the McLauchlin house. Wilf got out of the taxi and stared at the tall snowbank in front of him. There'd been a heavy snowstorm a few nights before and Mr. Cruikshank had not got around to digging out his driveway.

Wilf limped along the edge of the road looking for an opening. The neighbour to the one side, apparently more desperate to go somewhere than Mr. Cruikshank, had shovelled out a car-sized passageway. Wilf walked up the neighbour's drive and then pushed his way through a foot of snow toward where he assumed Mr. Cruikshank's front walk should be. He pulled himself up on the small front porch and rang the doorbell.

Somewhere inside he could hear the cheery sound of a four-note chime, two ascending, two descending. He waited for the last note to fade and rang again. Mr. Cruikshank did not appear.

Wilf peered through the small window in the door. A thick covering of silvery frost on the inside of the glass gleamed back at him. He turned to look at the leaded bay window. It was covered on the inside by a sheet of frost, too. It made the house look blind.

"Mr. Cruikshank's at home, ain't he, Ducky?"

Wilf turned to see a woman, almost as round as she was tall and bundled up in a black winter coat, following carefully along his trail so that snow wouldn't fall down the tops of her rubber boots. Her Cockney accent floated toward him on puffs of frost. He hadn't expected to hear one again so soon.

"It doesn't look like it."

"Must be, Darlin'. He always rings me up if he's not going to be at home." The woman came to rest at the foot of the stairs. "I've tramped all the way from Upper Town, I have." She cast her eyes over the surrounding expanse of untouched snow. Worry, if not alarm, began to move across her expressive face. "Just look at these walks. You'd think he'd have called in George by now."

"Who's George?"

"George, the odd job man."

She began to wade through the snow again, making her own trail this time, snow tumbling unheeded into her boots. She disappeared around the corner of the house. Wilf followed along behind her. "Kitchen, the w.c. and a light cleaning through the place every Tuesday. Wax and polish every bloomin' floor the second Tuesday of every month. Windows every other month. That's what he wants, that's his routine. It never changes." She pulled a key out of her pocket, unlocked the side door and poked her head in.

"Yoo-hoo! It's Mary, Dearie, come to do the floors!"

Mary stepped in on the landing, pulled off her boots and shook out the snow.

Wilf came up to the doorway and waited to see if what he'd guessed was right.

Mary climbed up two steps and walked into the kitchen in her sock feet. "Mr. Cruikshank, it's me!" she called out and immediately went up on the tip of her stubby toes. "Jesus bloody Christ, it's colder than a pauper's grave in here!"

"I think the furnace has gone out."

"You think the furnace has gone out?" The expression on Mary's round and ruddy face changed. Her voice dropped to a whisper. "He's got a bad heart, he does." She peered warily through a doorway. "Mr. Cruikshank," she called again but without as much enthusiasm this time. She turned back to Wilf. "Do an old woman a favour, would you? Would you look through the house? There's a gallant chappie."

Wilf had to suppress a smile. He lowered himself down on the stairs and began to pry off his galoshes.

"I'm all talk, you know, that's the thing, bluster and noise, but inside I'm a terrible coward. He's had heart attacks before, you see? Not that I was here. No. Before my time. I don't know just how many."

Wilf braced himself with his cane, made the slow ascent up the steps and moved through the kitchen past the fretting Mary.

"There's a good sport," she said.

Wilf walked through an open door, circled around a large dining room table brought to a high shine by the rigorous efforts of Mary herself, no doubt, and stood in an archway that led to the front of the house.

The sun was still struggling to pierce through the thick frost on the bay window. An array of furniture, elegantly designed and looking as unused as if they'd just arrived from a store were distributed tastefully around the large room. The only exception was a threadbare easy chair covered in blue corduroy and assigned to a far corner. A magazine lay open on a small table beside it.

Wilf moved through the room into the front hall and called up the stairs. "Mr. Cruikshank?" He began to climb, his left leg supporting half his body weight and the cane taking on the other half.

"This ratio will improve in time," a pretty English therapist had assured him, though more out of kindness than conviction it had seemed to Wilf at the time.

"Mr. Cruikshank," Wilf called out again.

As he reached the top of the stairs he could see a four-poster bed through an open doorway. It was empty, the sheets and cover tucked in as tightly as a hospital bed. He took a step inside the room half-expecting to see someone lying on the floor or crumpled in a chair. It was empty.

Wilf came out of the room, stood in the half light and stared at a darkly stained door at the end of the hall. A line of white tiles peeked out from underneath it. "Mr. Cruikshank," he said. He walked down the hall, turned the handle and pushed it open. An old man was sitting motionless in a thin sheet of ice in the bathtub.

Wilf dropped down beside him and drove his fist through to the cold water underneath, shouting, "Get out, get the hell out of it! Get out!" He snaked his good arm around the old man's frozen back and under his arm and heaved. The old man resisted. "Get out, get out!" Wilf yelled again.

Mr. Cruikshank, fringed with ice, began to rise up. Wilf levered him onto the edge of the tub, balanced him precariously there and then lost his grip. Mr. Cruikshank hit the floor with a frozen thump.

Mary screamed, her hysterical screech filling the bathroom, the air, everywhere.

Wilf sat on the floor, looked at Mary standing in the doorway and cradled the naked man against his chest. Mary screamed once more and headed back down the hall. "Hold on," Wilf whispered in the old man's ear.

Mr. Cruikshank looked up at him with half-closed, lifeless eyes.

CHAPTER FOUR

Duncan Getty stood in deep concentration across the street. He had done this many times before, watching the office of McLauchlin and McLauchlin sitting behind its wrought-iron fence and its ornate gate, set back from the other storefronts and boxed in on both sides. It looked like a tiny house sitting there with its own front yard.

His face was surprisingly boyish, his expression open-spirited and hurt and sly all at the same time. At twenty-seven Duncan was as open-faced as any half-man half-boy might be, habitually hurt from years of teasing and sly from listening for far too long to only his own advice. Everybody in town knew Duncan Getty and everybody ignored him.

Duncan continued to stare at the office. On a few occasions he'd even mustered enough courage to stand right by the fence and try to see what Carole might be doing. He felt sorry for her. Everyone knew her boyfriend had brought home a war bride and a baby. It wasn't right. But it had made him feel happy, too. She still lived at home with her parents. Her house was by the river, not that far down from the mill. Her bedroom was at the back.

Duncan loved her, he loved her with all his heart.

This thought propelled him off the sidewalk without a sideways glance. If there were any cars or trucks coming along they'd just have to stop. They always did. He was six foot two and close to two hundred and fifty pounds, his belly pushing out from under his shabby coat, a tumble of curly auburn hair falling about his round weather-reddened face. He stepped up on the opposite curb and looked toward the window. Carole was talking to some man and a woman. She was doing her work. She was busy.

He felt like going in. He felt like saying, "Don't be sad. Donny Mason is stupid. He doesn't deserve a wife as good as you." He felt like saying, "Would you like to go to the movies this Saturday?"

He stood there, indecisive, rocking back and forth a little, and then he thought better of it. He already knew what she'd say. The same thing she'd been saying to him for years. "Hi Duncan," she'd say, and she'd smile so that the world would light up all around him. "I'd like to, but I can't right now." And it was enough. It had always been enough.

Not like the other girls who always laughed when he asked them out to the movies, as if he'd just said the funniest thing in the world. Either that or they'd walked away real quick, like they were really busy and had to be someplace else.

Carole wasn't like that. Carole was perfect.

Duncan thought maybe he'd wait for a better time, when she was alone. He thought maybe he'd go around to her place that night, work through the brush along the river and stand in the freezing dark. Sometimes she remembered to pull her curtains closed, sometimes she forgot. It didn't really matter to him because he loved her so much.

He walked with renewed purpose back toward the feed mill. Just the thought of Carole's dark window lighting up at around eleven o'clock enlivened him. And anyway, it was past time to hitch Babe to the cutter and get back to the shop. He had an order to fill. Twelve hundred running feet of white pine ripped in one-inch boards and cut to sixteen-foot lengths. With any luck he'd have it all finished and stacked by suppertime. And then he'd listen to *Amos 'n Andy*. And then he'd hitch Babe up again, or maybe give Dandy a run instead, and head back into town to his favourite beverage room. Maybe some of the fellows would let him sit in with them. Some of the war vets. But at ten o'clock he'd have to say "S'long," and leave. And when no one was watching he'd slip over to the river.

And one night he knew he'd walk right into her backyard. And one night he'd toss something against her window. She'd lift her window up and put her head out and her hair would tumble down like he always liked to see it, her hands going up and pulling out a bunch of pins and her hair tumbling way past her shoulders.

"Is that you, Duncan?" she'd say.

"I was just passing by," he'd say, "And I was wondering if you'd like to go out with me."

"Yes," Carole would call back down to him, "I would, Duncan."

And the night would light up.

Wilf held Mr. Cruikshank's icy body in his lap and listened to Mary's frightened voice coming from downstairs. He knew she was on the telephone talking to the police, maybe to Andy.

He was beginning to shiver. Beneath his coat, his shirt and pants were soaked through. He pulled himself out from under the old man, fumbled for his cane and struggled to his feet. Mr. Cruikshank lay there in a puddle of water. Wilf leaned against the wall trying to catch his breath. A wave of shame washed over him. A fighter pilot, and he'd reacted no better than a frightened kid. Or a blithering idiot. He walked back along the hall to a smaller bedroom than the first one and stripped the top blanket off the bed. When he came back, the old man's knees were still raised to his chest as they had been in the bathtub, his head still thrown back, his body the palest of blues. Wilf covered him up and sat down on the toilet seat.

There was no bath mat to soften the tile floor. There were no bath towels in sight. A thin ridge of ice gleamed under the baseboard.

Wilf's eyes went back to the tub. Shards of ice were still floating around in it, swishing around and around. He stared at the ice for a long moment. He could still hear Mary chattering away. He'd have to call himself a taxi once she'd finished. He'd have to go home and change his freezing clothes.

He got up and walked back down the hall. A round window the size of a ship's porthole was positioned near the top of the stairs. As he passed it some movement from outside caught his eye. Flames of silvery frost laced the glass and at first he wasn't sure he was seeing what he was seeing. He put his face close up to it and scraped the frost away.

A man was standing in the middle of Mr. Cruikshank's back-yard. His slight body was covered in a dark shabby coat; his feet were wrapped in rags. He stared directly up at Wilf.

Wilf hurried down the stairs. When he reached the kitchen Mary was still holding onto the telephone. "Now don't go any-where, Ducky," she called out.

Wilf waded out into the snow and struggled along the side of the house. A scattering of fruit trees stood throughout the yard, their limbs bare and black against the sky. He looked down a ravine toward a railway line. He waded back toward the house, made a large circle of the yard and stood more or less where he'd just seen the man. There was no one in sight.

Wilf's eyes began to water. His heart raced.

The only tracks in the snow were his own.

※ ※ ※

Carole was still sitting at her desk when Wilf came back in. "What do you mean Mr. Cruikshank is dead?" Her light-grey eyes were quite large at any time but now they grew even larger, her hands suspending over her typewriter keys.

Wilf didn't bother answering. He pushed through the wooden gate and sat down at Dorothy Dale's desk.

"That can't be right," she said.

Wilf looked at her from across the small space that separated them as if he couldn't quite make her out.

"Oh my god," she said, "what happened?"

Wilf began to unbutton his overcoat. She could see that he'd changed out of his suit coat and dress shirt. He was wearing a dark wine-coloured sweater and a yellow-checked shirt. They really didn't go together. Snow was melting off his galoshes, forming a pool of water on the floor.

"Doc Robinson says he had a heart attack. He died while he was taking a bath. He has to do a more thorough examination, though. When the old man thaws out."

"Oh my god," Carole said again, and then she couldn't stop herself from saying, "have you changed your clothes?"

"I soaked myself trying to save an old man any fool could see had been dead for days."

"I'm sorry!"

"Yeah. Poor old guy," Wilf replied, though he knew the concern she was expressing was intended for himself. Which made everything seem worse. He leaned toward her. "Can I ask you a personal question?"

Carole nodded cautiously.

"In all your life, have you ever taken a bath without a towel or a bathrobe in sight?"

Carole stared at him. "Not on purpose."

"Me, either. Not on purpose. No one has. Or does."

"I don't know what that means."

"It means that there wasn't even a bath mat on the floor."

"I have no idea what you're talking about."

"Maybe I'm talking about nothing."

"I see."

"If Mr. Cruikshank was feeling pain in his chest, maybe he thought a hot bath might ease things and in his growing confusion he got into the bath without thinking about a towel."

"That's very possible."

"He'd been dead for a few days. Whatever coal he'd banked in the furnace burned out. The water in the tub was frozen and there wasn't any water on the floor. No water left on the floor, I mean, when I came in, because it would have frozen, too."

"Why would there be water on the floor?"

"Because opposite the bathtub, between the baseboard and the tiles, there was this thin ridge of ice. So there must have been water on the floor, quite a bit of it. But someone soaked it up with the towels. Maybe the bath mat, too. But they missed the water pooling under the baseboard."

"Who would do that?"

"Whoever drowned Mr. Cruikshank."

Carole turned back to her typewriter.

"He was a large man," Wilf was continuing on, "it wouldn't have been an easy thing to do. They slopped water all over the place and so they had to clean it up. But they couldn't leave a pile of soaking wet towels around, could they?"

"Why are you going on like this?"

"Like what?"

"Like you're trying to make something out of nothing. Out of just a series of coincidences. Or something!"

Wilf wasn't actually sure why. These thoughts had just come to him. He hadn't made any effort. But once they were in his mind, they seemed shot through with a kind of urgency. They seemed the truth.

"There must be some other explanation," Carole said.

"Like what?"

"I don't know. Maybe he thrashed around in excruciating pain. Maybe he spilled some water."

"Then it would have frozen on the floor."

"Maybe the floor was slanted. Maybe it ran off somewhere."

"There'd still be a skim of ice on the floor."

"People do not go around drowning people in our town!" Carole's voice rang through the empty office and took her by surprise.

Wilf felt a surge of joy. He hadn't felt so much like his old self in months, but then again, in some way, at its heart, this feeling was nothing like his old self. "Is this the only Cruikshank file we have?" He got up out of his chair.

Carole glanced up at the clock. It was almost five. Fifteen more minutes and she could go home. "No. That's a new one. There's at least two more."

Wilf was leaning over his desk toward her, looking obstinate. "Let's have a look."

"I don't believe anyone drowned Mr. Cruikshank."

"And I'm glad to hear you admitting that your opinion is actually only a belief."

"Don't you think you should wait for your father?"

"No."

Carole began to examine her fingernails. She'd painted them a soft coral colour. She'd been thinking about letting them grow longer but the problem was that even at a moderate length they began to interfere with her typing. She could feel her pulse beating in her wrist, she could see it.

"Are you going to get the files?" Wilf asked.

All she had to do was start typing. Why should she do anything else simply because there was an absence of towels in Mr. Cruikshank's bathroom?

Carole got up and with an irritated sigh she meant Wilf to hear, went over to the filing cabinets and pulled out two dog-eared files. She came back and dropped them on top of his desk.

"Why don't you pull up a chair?" Wilf said pleasantly, sitting back down. He began to leaf one-handed through one of them.

Carole remained standing.

After a while Wilf remarked, "Mr. Cruikshank and his wife seem to be in continual litigation. Against each other."

"Correct," Carole replied.

Wilf continued to read.

Carole watched him. His dark hair, his dark eyes. For the first time since he'd arrived he seemed to be enjoying himself.

"Mr. Cruikshank was the owner of quite a few farms," she said, sounding more collaborative than she'd intended.

Wilf nodded.

"About a thousand acres in all."

He nodded again.

Carole felt oddly encouraged. "A few years ago he left his wife and moved into town. She still lives on the home farm and runs things along with their son. Mr. Cruikshank always paid his son a fair wage and he continues to do so, but he refused to pay his wife anything."

Wilf looked up at her. He seemed impressed.

"Frank Cruikshank, that's the son, he made a formal offer to buy his father out. You'll see it in there somewhere. Mr. Cruikshank refused the offer. He said Frank's mother had put him up to it, it was a ridiculously low offer and if he'd only be patient he'd inherit everything anyway. That's when Mrs. Cruikshank went to court and argued that by virtue of forty years of shared labour she had a proprietary right to a fair portion of the business. She lost that suit so she took him back to court to force him to pay her a reasonable wage for services provided. Mr. Cruikshank argued that he was providing her with free room and board which was the equivalent. The court forced him to pay her a reasonable wage. Mr. Cruikshank sued her, claiming that she was selling calves behind his back, cheating him blind. He lost his suit. She countersued for calumny and libel. She lost. Mr. Cruikshank tried to fire her and have her removed from the property, claiming it was his right to fire and hire anyone he wanted. He lost. And so on. And so on."

Wilf had been turning the papers over, trying to keep up.

"When I first started working here," Carole said, "I had to go through all the active client files and more or less memorize them. Dorothy Dale made me."

Wilf picked up a sealed envelope.

"What's that?" Carole asked.

"It says 'Last Will and Testament, Samuel Marshall Cruikshank.'"

Carole snatched the envelope away. "I didn't put that in there."

"Maybe my father did." Wilf took it back. "It's his hand-writing."

"Well anyway, it's sealed. You can't open it." Carole made another grab but she was too late. Wilf was tearing it open with his teeth.

Carole retreated to her desk. She could see herself being firmly escorted out the front door by Clarence McLauchlin at nine o'clock the following Monday morning. It would give the town something else to talk about. She was becoming a regular freak show.

She glanced back at Wilf. He had pinned the envelope under his sling and was drawing out a handwritten sheet of paper. He unfolded and studied it for a moment.

Carole looked up at the clock. Five minutes to go.

"Who's Adrienne O'Dell?" Wilf said.

"Why?"

"Mr. Cruikshank left everything he owned to an Adrienne O'Dell."

"That can't be right." Carole got up from her desk and with

a surprising display of speed crossed over to Wilf and snatched up the will again.

"Is that Cruikshank's handwriting?"

Carole was too busy reading to answer.

"We've got enough samples of his signature in these files anyway. And a couple of handwritten notes from him to Dad. We should be able to tell."

"This doesn't make any sense." Carole was staring at the will as if it had gone out of its way to personally offend her.

"Why doesn't it make any sense?"

"How would he even know Adrienne O'Dell, let alone leave everything to her? She's just, she's one of those O'Dells!" In sympathetic shock, a soft lock of her hair came loose and fell slowly over her one eye.

"The O'Dells are not ringing a bell."

"Half of them are drunks. Half of them have a new baby every year!"

"Oh, right. Those O'Dells." Wilf had a vague memory of being very young and watching a hopelessly drunk man stop to hug each hydro pole as he made his weary way along the street.

"Adrienne was a grade behind me. Actually she was the only one who ever made it to high school. She tried really hard."

"Where is she now?"

"But that's why it's so strange. She works in a dress shop. How could old Mr. Cruikshank know her?"

"What dress shop?"

"It's just down the street."

"Do you think she'd be there now?"

Carole could feel her face heating up. She tried to speak firmly. "You can't tell her about this will. There's been some mistake. You'll have to wait until your father arrives back home."

Wilf got up on his feet. He began to button his overcoat "What side is it on?"

"What?"

"The dress shop."

Carole put the will back in its envelope. She put the envelope back in its file and carried all three files back to the filing cabinet. She put the files back where they belonged and slammed the cabinet shut.

"I'm not going to tell her about the will." Wilf was pushing his way through the gate.

"What are you going to do then?"

"I just want to have a look at her."

"You think someone drowned Mr. Cruikshank in his bathtub, and now you want to meet the sole heir of his complete estate just to have a look at her. I could be fired, you know?"

Wilf looked back at Carole, at her tall willowy figure standing tensely on the other side of the little wooden fence. For some reason she looked very attractive. "I'll be careful. She won't suspect a thing."

Carole made a face. She brushed back her wayward lock of hair. "It's after five o'clock."

"Meaning what?"

Meaning nothing, Carole thought to herself. Meaning I should just shut up and go home. "Meaning it's time to close the office and since you're going to do whatever you're going to do anyway, well, I suppose I could just show you where the shop is."

Wilf and Carole walked down Main Street together. Wilf glanced over at her from time to time ready to give her a smile of encouragement but Carole continued to stare grimly ahead. She was almost as tall as Wilf, his bad hip had dropped his height by almost an inch, and he could tell by her slight hesitations that she was having difficulty walking in time to his slow halting gait. He tried to speed up.

As they neared the end of the business section Carole pointed across the street to a lighted shop window. Wilf thanked her very much, said he'd see her first thing the next morning and aimed himself through the five o'clock traffic toward the other side. A bell tinkled over his head as he pushed through the shop's door. He could hear a rough voice coming from the back, rising in volume and then falling abruptly silent.

A tall man in a long yellowish leather coat hurried toward him, maneuvering sideways along the narrow centre aisle to brush by the racks of clothes. He passed without a word or a look, yanked the door open and headed out into the dark.

The door slammed shut, the bell tinkled merrily behind him.

Wilf moved along the aisle, pushing through the first phalanx of women's dresses. A wave of warm, faintly perfumed air greeted him. He tried not to entangle his cane, his bad leg, knock anything down. When he looked up he was surprised to see a young woman standing in the middle of the store. She was short and slight, her shiny black hair cut almost as close to her head as a boy's. She didn't seem the least upset over the tall man's abrupt departure.

"Can I help you?" she said.

"Hello," Wilf replied, "I'm Wilf McLauchlin." He rested his cane against the front of his coat and held out his hand.

The young woman smiled and walked up to him. She was at least a head shorter than he was. She put out a small hand. "I'm Adrienne. Hi."

Wilf took her hand. It was small and soft and surprisingly warm.

"Can I help you with something?" she said.

Wilf wondered which it was, either she hadn't heard the news yet that her benefactor was dead and therefore she remained untroubled, or she'd known for days and still remained untroubled. He looked into her eyes. They were a wash of pale violet, endless as a trackless sky. He couldn't tell.

"What are you looking for?"

"Oh. Just a present."

"That's nice. And who's the present for?"

"My girlfriend."

"Well, that's even nicer. Do you have anything in mind?"

Wilf released her hand. "I was thinking maybe a sweater."

Adrienne smiled again and walked between two racks of clothes toward a shelf of sweaters. Wilf followed her.

"Do you know your girlfriend's size?"

"I'm not sure. She's tall. About five ten maybe. A bit skinny."

Adrienne turned to him. "Slim you mean."

"That's it," Wilf said. "Slim."

He couldn't take his eyes off her. He wondered if it had to do with the thick press of women's clothes secluding them in the otherwise empty store. Her frailty, her smallness. And it seemed to Wilf that she knew she was vulnerable in all that crush of clothes and that the thought of it amused her. A distinct message of availability wafted through the warm perfumed air, though it didn't seem to be anything she was actually doing, just an innate part of her. Just palpably there. It struck Wilf as extraordinary.

"We have some really lovely sweaters. Does your girlfriend wear cashmere?"

"I'm not sure."

And it struck Wilf that if only he had the courage to reach out and touch her right then, touch her anywhere, she wouldn't have moved away.

She reached up for some sweaters.

Wilf studied the curve of her lower back where her blouse and her skirt met. And the lift of her taut behind. He could feel cold sweat trickling down his side.

"Here's a lovely one," she said.

He could see Samuel Cruikshank's strong knotted arms in the muted light in the bathroom; he could see his long veined torso.

Adrienne turned back to him. "Does she have a favourite colour?"

"Pink," Wilf replied.

✳ ✳ ✳

Carole was waiting across the street when Wilf left the shop. He could see her dark outline standing in front of a light from a store window, the shadow of her frosted breath rising. He hadn't expected her to be there.

He crossed the street and nudged her gently with his shoulder. He was carrying a gift-wrapped package under his good arm. "Here's a present for you."

"I don't want a present." She was shivering in the cold, but she didn't move away.

"Take it," Wilf said.

"I just wanted to tell you. That man who came out of the shop when you went in?"

"What about him?"

"That was Mr. Cruikshank's son."

"How do you know?"

Carole looked upset. "I know. That was Frank Cruikshank. I've seen him in court enough times."

"I bought you a wool sweater. I thought it was more practical than cashmere."

"I don't want it," Carole said.

CHAPTER FIVE

Three nights a week, Clarence McLauchlin had a woman who worked in the high-school cafeteria come in and cook a hot meal. On the other nights, it was his custom to eat out, usually at a favourite restaurant on the edge of town, though on occasion as far afield as the small cities of Brantford or Galt. This was not one of the woman's nights.

Wilf ate alone in the large kitchen, aimlessly stirring around the canned stew he'd heated up for supper and thinking about the man in Cruikshank's backyard. He tried to concentrate on figuring out how he could leave no tracks in the snow, what the trick was, did it have something to do with the rags on his feet, but he couldn't sustain this train of thought very long. His mind kept going back to what his body had already absorbed, absorbed so well that to think about it at all brought on waves of vertigo. The truth was he'd seen a man who wasn't there.

Some of the lads in the hospitals had seen things. Terrible things, apparently, because they'd end up crawling under their beds or shivering in a corner or worst of all just screaming. Screaming at nothing.

Wilf tried to picture the round window by the stairs, the frost melting away under his breath, the man's stark face looking up, desperate hungry eyes. At the time it had seemed to Wilf that the man had wanted to tell him something, something no one else could possibly know.

A loose window rattled in the side door. Someone was knocking. Mr. Gill, Wilf guessed. Alf Gill was the neighbour his father had asked to keep the furnace going while he was away. Wilf had said he could look after it himself.

"What if you fall down the cellar steps? Who would know?"

"Jesus Christ," Wilf had said with an equal measure of dismissiveness and irritation, but his father had been adamant. While Wilf was staying in the house alone, Alf Gill would have to come in to look after the furnace.

Wilf picked up his cane and opened the door that led to the landing. Andy's face was peering in through the window.

"It's open," Wilf called out. No one bothered to lock their doors in the town. No one but Samuel Cruikshank, Wilf suddenly thought.

Andy was dressed in his police uniform although it was only seven o'clock and his shift didn't start until nine. He untied his boots and came up into the kitchen in his sock feet. "What are you eating?"

"A can-of stew." Wilf sat back down at the table. "It was always canned this or canned that. I'm trying to relive my life as an Air Force hero. Want some?"

Andy looked down at Wilf's plate. "I don't think so." He took off his cap and sat down. "So I hear you went for a header in some old man's bathtub."

"Want a coffee?"

"Sure. I'll get it."

"I'll get it, for chrissake, I can do something!" Wilf was just as surprised as Andy looked to hear himself flare up.

"I wasn't suggesting you couldn't."

Wilf pulled himself up off his chair. "I was trying to see if he was still breathing. It was an accident; I slipped." He limped over to the counter, purposely leaving his cane behind.

"Must have been unpleasant, though."

Wilf filled up a large mug and hobbled back without spilling a drop though his hip hurt like hell.

"Thanks," Andy said.

Wilf eased himself back down. "I've had my share of unpleasant experiences. I've seen lots of dead bodies, son."

Andy had to smile. When Wilf got pissed off at him, he always called him "Son." He'd been doing it since they were twelve years old.

"And not always from ten thousand feet in the air."

"All right," Andy said.

Wilf began to stir his stew around again. Andy sipped his coffee and watched him.

"Have you read the police report?" Wilf finally asked.

"Haven't been downtown yet. Bolton, you remember him, right, Ted Bolton? He's a cop now. Anyway, he knows we're good friends so he called to tell me more or less what happened. You know what this town is like."

"Did he tell you what the housekeeper had to say?"

"More or less."

It was obvious why Andy was heading downtown two hours before his shift started. Wilf could almost hear Linda demanding that he check in on Wilf first just to make sure he was all right. Andy wouldn't have come over on his own volition, he wouldn't have wanted to make a big deal out of it, he wouldn't have wanted to risk embarrassing Wilf. To Linda that would have been beside the point.

Wilf stabbed a piece of beef with his fork. "Did Bolton say anything about somebody forcing their way into Cruikshank's house? Shattered window. Broken lock. Anything like that?"

"No." Andy stared across the table at him. "You know it was an accidental death, don't you? You know the old man had a heart attack?"

"That's what Doc Robinson said."

"That's right. And he's the coroner."

"I just wonder if anyone checked the house. That's all."

"Well, sure. They would have."

"Good."

All these questions. The pursuit of a crime, if there was a crime. It had all felt irresistibly compelling to Wilf and it still did. And dangerous, too, as if he were letting go of some essential part of himself, as if he were feeling his way into a dark place. He had already involved Carole and to have her company felt better. A society of two in the dark. And after all, Andy was a cop.

"There weren't any towels in Cruikshank's bathroom," Wilf said.

Andy just looked at him.

That was all the encouragement Wilf required. He began to tell him everything he and Carole had found out, including walking in on Frank Cruikshank arguing with Adrienne in the dress shop. "I've asked Carole to snoop around a little tonight, see if she can come up with a connection between the old man and Adrienne O'Dell."

Andy had been sitting tilted back a little in his chair. Now he got up and looked out the kitchen window though there was nothing he could see. "Poor Carole Birley," Andy said. "She was engaged to be married to Donny Mason. Remember him? He's younger than us. Anyway, he came back from overseas with a hot little number from Scotland. A redhead. And a baby."

Wilf nodded. That was interesting information actually, but he knew Andy was stalling.

Andy started to search through his pockets for his cigarettes. He took his time lighting one up. "I think you're way out on this whole deal, Wilf."

"Explain the ice on the floor then."

"A pipe burst, water pooled behind the wall, leaked out and froze."

Wilf hadn't thought of that. He felt like he'd suddenly been jerked back about a foot. "Explain the will."

"Well, I don't know, but I bet there's an explanation that doesn't include Adrienne O'Dell and Frank Cruikshank drowning the old bugger."

Explain the man in the backyard, Wilf felt like saying. Explain Adrienne O'Dell's eyes.

The chain slowly drew the squared-off timber into the saw. The saw began to scream. Duncan was getting impatient. The job was taking longer than he'd thought. He hadn't had his supper yet. Neither had Eric, the teenager who lived on the farm next door and helped out whenever Duncan needed an extra pair of hands.

Eric was crouched down watching the taut chain for slippage and pushing at the huge timber with an iron-tipped pole. Duncan was at the other end holding on to an inch-thick plank as it peeled off the main piece of timber. Seventy-five planks in all. Six to go.

Duncan eyed the remains of the timber they were ripping. He could usually get ten 1" x 8" planks sixteen-feet-long out of a good-sized piece of white pine. He was either going to be one plank short on this one, and then he'd have to half kill himself getting another log set in place, or it would come out just right. He'd dress the full order of seventy-five planks down to exactly eight-inch widths in the morning. That was a job he could do himself. He liked working by himself, but some heavier jobs required the help of Eric, and other jobs required a whole crew.

His mother had had no problem getting a crew of men together when she'd needed one, mainly the hired help off the nearby farms. And years before that when his father was alive he'd had two full-time men on the payroll. But times had changed. There weren't many hired men working on farms anymore, for one thing. And the factories were booming; there seemed to be good jobs everywhere. Duncan didn't have the faintest idea how to hire a crew of men.

After Mrs. Getty's funeral all the neighbours had wondered how Duncan would make out being left alone in that tidy frame house with its lumberyard to the one side, the shop, the stable and forty acres of bush at the back. That was three years ago and to everyone's surprise Duncan seemed to be making out more or less all right. His mother's old customers were going out of their way to give him small orders to fill, which he managed either by cutting out a few trees from his own bush or from time to time hiring on to help mark and cut trees out of some neighbour's bush lot, taking half-pay and keeping a few extra logs for himself. It was all working out, which seemed a kind of miracle to anyone who could remember the odd-looking boy he used to be, hurrying along the backroads at any time of day or night, eyes bright as two lights, nose continually running, breathlessly heading toward a destination no one else could see.

His mother had to admit back then that she could never keep Duncan in the house, but that was many years ago. The only thing anyone could say against Duncan these days was that he had a tendency to get drunk in public places. He was a harmless, good-natured kind of drunk though, wrapping his huge arms around anyone who made the mistake of getting within range and seeming to look younger the drunker he got until finally that same little boy's face would shine out of his almost grownup one, a young boy's face full of a dreamy and dazed wonder.

Duncan turned off the saw. He didn't have to set another log. The seventy-fifth board had peeled off successfully, leaving behind only the thinnest sliver of rough timber. Eric took off for his home a mile up the road, walking quickly through the cold night. Duncan went into the back kitchen, kicked off his boots and hung up his saw-dusted coveralls just as his mother had taught him to do.

He pushed through another door into the main kitchen, turned on the light and looked around. And just like every night, he couldn't help but feel proud. Numerous models of airplanes he'd assembled himself hung down from the ceiling on invisible threads. They swayed slowly, spun around in the draft he'd let in. Every available space on the walls was covered with pictures of tanks and warships and planes and artillery pieces and anything at all to do with the war. He'd taped up pictures all through the rest of the house as well. Some were black and white but his favourite ones were in full colour. He had galleries of portraits. Generals. Medal winners. Flying aces. All the local boys, too. Any time anyone in a uniform had their picture in the town's newspaper Duncan would add it to his collection. Even now with the war finished for over eighteen months he still might see something in a magazine or a newspaper he just had to cut out.

Duncan walked through his model planes and smiled to himself. It was like he was flying too, peering into their cockpits, friend or foe, circling around, speeding away.

He opened a cupboard door and stared for a while at the sparse contents. He'd have to eat something sometime but for now he thought he'd have a drink. He picked up a bottle of whisky, took a swig and sat down in his father's broken-down old sofa chair. He turned on the radio. Charlie McCarthy and Edgar Bergen were arguing about something.

Duncan took another drink and stared at a news article he'd recently cut out and taped to the wall. It was all about the banquet given in Wilf McLauchlin's honour. Of all the local warriors, Wilf McLauchlin was Duncan's favourite. Too bad the picture wasn't in colour. Wilf, wearing a suit instead of his uniform for some reason, was standing behind a table full of plates and dishes and glasses and he was making a speech. He looked like a movie star. Only better, Duncan thought, because he wasn't pretending to be somebody he wasn't. Wilf had flown higher than anyone could imagine. Faster, too. He had protected everyone in the town and he had been glad to do it even though he had paid a high price. He was a hero.

And his father was Mr. McLauchlin. And Carole worked for him in his office.

Duncan took another drink. It burned nicely going down. Maybe one day, once he got up the nerve to ask Carole to marry him and she said yes and they had a big wedding, Wilf would stand up and give a speech just like he did at his own banquet.

"I know Duncan," Wilf would say, "and if it wasn't for the fact that he was too big he would have been flying a Spitfire Mk 14 right beside me. I am proud to call him my friend."

And Carole would turn and look up at her new husband, and she'd smile her wonderful smile just as if he had flown an Mk 14, and they'd stand up together and cut the cake.

He'd seen lots of pictures of other happy couples doing just that. He would have his hand on the knife and her hand would rest on the top of his hand, as gentle and soft as a leaf.

Duncan heaved a sigh. How he wanted to be high up somewhere.

Oh god, how he wanted to fly.

Wilf came into his father's study and flicked on the light. All the other rooms had a Spartan look as might be expected in a large house occupied by a long-time widower. No female decorative flair anywhere to be seen, or more importantly to be felt. But at least the study looked more lived in with its two creased leather chairs inviting a friendly conversation, the iron-grated fireplace, the faded but still warmly coloured oriental rug, the tall shelves of well-worn common law and statute books, reference books, novels and histories, Shakespeares and Shaws, philosophies, poetry.

Whenever Wilf had thought of his home, which hadn't been too often, he'd thought of this room. Something had been added though, stacks of transcripts from the trials that were still going on in faraway Nuremberg. His father had become enormously inspired by those proceedings and had been collecting everything he could find. He'd even purchased an oak filing cabinet to house newspaper clippings. It was sitting in the one corner, filled to overflowing.

"Something brand new is happening," his father had announced just as soon as Wilf had stepped into the study for the first time in years. "Thanks to these trials we have detailed records of state-directed atrocities against civilian populations. We can establish precedents in international law. World courts and so forth." His father's eyes were becoming luminous with deeply felt emotion. "The United Nations is open for business now, fifty-one countries in New York negotiating their differences. Just think, Wilf. Never again will we see concentration camps or forced work camps or death camps or the willful destruction of civilian populations because never again will anyone dare to commit such crimes."

Wilf had limped into the middle of the study, his eyes trailing across the familiar books of poetry and philosophy, across the white stacks of transcripts. He'd wished he could share his father's enthusiasm, he knew it was meant as a consolation for his own wounds suffered, but all he could muster then was a perfunctory smile.

"For chrissake, don't start your own investigation," Andy had said, looking at him as if he thought Wilf was still suffering from the after-effects of the war. Wilf should just wait until his father returned and the will was officially read to the Cruikshank family and to Adrienne O'Dell. Everything would come clear at that moment.

"All right," Wilf had said.

Later on, as Andy was heading out the side door to go to work, Wilf had called out, "Have a look at the report for me, will you? Find out what Mary's last name is and give me a call?"

"Who's Mary?"

Wilf leaned against the kitchen door. "Cruikshank's housekeeper."

"Oh, right. The housekeeper."

"I upset her. I should call her sometime tomorrow and apologize."

Andy had grinned at that. "I'll see what I can do."

Wilf eased himself down onto one of the leather chairs. An invisible weight was beginning to bear down. He'd become familiar with it over the last year or so. He'd decided it was somewhat like the weather. He'd even entertained himself with this thought during his long convalescence, perhaps it had even helped. What were the probs? Sometime tonight there's a good chance that it will begin to rain hopelessness. By morning, a possibility that the rain could turn to despair.

Wilf pushed himself out of the chair and began to think everything through again. Unlike all the people he knew in town, Samuel Cruikshank had made a habit of locking his doors. Which begged the question, what or who was the old man afraid of? Wilf felt immediately better. The weight of his depression faded away, the pain in his hip sank below conscious monitoring. He moved around the room.

The housekeeper had a key in her possession. Of course she'd need one if he locked his doors, just in case he was out. But he wasn't out, he was inside the house; but the doors were still locked. He kept his doors locked all the time. No forced entry, according to Andy. Which meant he must have unlocked the door to let his murderers in. Or they had a key.

Wilf hadn't seen any cuts or scrapes on the old man's body. More to the point, neither apparently had Doc Robinson. But if he'd been dragged up the stairs, forced into the tub and drowned, why hadn't he fought back?

Because he was already in the tub, Wilf thought. And it had to be the night of the storm, or earlier. Otherwise, just as Mary had said, the old man would have had George, the odd job man, shovel out his driveway and his sidewalk.

When Wilf had looked through Cruikshank's files it had seemed to him that Frank Cruikshank had tried to stay out of the family fight. That was smart of him, of course, because he'd naturally assume that his inheritance was on the line. It had to be a difficult stance to maintain though, because he was living with his mother and working with her and his mother was making the old man angrier and angrier. Frank Cruikshank seemed angry too, face flushed, pushing through the racks in the dress shop. A tall man. Easily as large as his father.

Wilf leaned up against the stacks of transcripts on the library table. He could see the snow pelting down. He could see a shadowy figure moving through the dark toward the house, unlocking the side door, creeping up the stairs. The bathroom door opens. The old man looks up through the steamy air. To see who? His son? His wife?

Adrienne O'Dell?

The sound of the phone in the kitchen rang through the empty house. Wilf crossed the hall and picked it up.

"Mary Barron," Andy announced on the other end of the line. "That's the name of his housekeeper. Want her phone number?"

"Sure."

"Eight four two."

"Are you looking at the report now?"

"Yeah."

"Did the fellows check for forced entry or not? What's it say?"

"Wilfred, are you questioning the competency of our police force? Yes, they did, and it says, no, there wasn't."

"Okay. Anyway, like you said, I'll wait until the solicitor gets home."

Wilf put the phone down and picked up the phonebook. He leafed through until he found Mary Barron's listing. She resided at 62 Walsh Street.

❋ ❋ ❋

Backing his father's car out of the garage proved to be a more difficult task than Wilf had anticipated. For one thing he had to use his good hand to help lift his bad foot up on the clutch. He tried putting the driver's seat back as far as it would go so that he was half lying down. That allowed him to lift his left leg by force of will only and by bearing the pain, and freed up his right hand to either change gears or to steer, he couldn't do both at the same time.

The new Buick Roadmaster his father had washed and polished at the garage downtown every week come rain or come shine jerked into reverse, barely missed creasing a front fender on the way out, shot across the road and hit the snowbank on the other side.

The big car stalled.

Fighting the pain once more, Wilf depressed the clutch, restarted the car and put it into first gear. He let his foot slip off the clutch and pressed on the gas. The car headed across the road toward the garage again.

Wilf corrected the trajectory, released the steering wheel, jammed the car into second while depressing the clutch and then made another one-handed grab for the wheel. The car jumped down the middle of the icy road, picking up speed. And into third gear. And accelerating. And finally smoothing out, soaring like a low-flying plane under the lights lining the one side of the street.

He drove down the front hill with increasing confidence, cruised past the police station in his half-prone position and thought of Andy, climbed an even steeper hill and came to an abrupt stop in front of an old stone mansion.

The rundown building had been renovated into a warren of small apartments.

Wilf got out, limped up to it and looked for Mary's apartment number beside the front door. He climbed a staircase and knocked at apartment six in a shabby hallway. Mary's plump face peered out, strips of paper rolled up in her hair.

"Hello again," Wilf said. "Sorry to bother you, I know it's late, I know you've had a long day."

"That's not half of it, is it?" Mary's bright eyes widened in a kind of accusatory way.

"No, it isn't."

"I've had the shock of my life, I have. It's a wonder I'm still breathing."

"Me, too," Wilf said.

"I know." Mary's expression didn't seem particularly sympathetic, though. Her eyes searched Wilf's face as if she were afraid he might go mad again right there in the hall.

Wilf leaned against the opposite wall and began to work his galoshes off. "Could I come in for a minute? There's something important I need to ask."

"And what would that be?"

"I suppose you know McLauchlin and McLauchlin?"

Mary shook her papered head.

"No? Well, my father was Mr. Cruikshank's lawyer but he's out of town for the rest of the week. I was delivering some legal papers; that's why I was there. Look Mary, you're the only person I know who knows anything about Mr. Cruikshank.

Unfortunately I need to know who his next of kin are now. And a few other things. I was hoping you could help me. Am I right that he lived alone?"

Mary nodded cautiously.

Wilf moved a little closer. "I'm sorry if I frightened you. I thought Mr. Cruikshank was still breathing and all I could think to do was to get him out of that ice."

"It's a sight I won't soon forget, I can tell you."

"I'm very sorry."

Mary's face softened. "You're a flyer, ain't you? One of the coppers said."

"Yes."

"I'm a fright to look at, I was just doing my hair." She opened the door the rest of the way and backed up a little.

Wilf stepped into a small sitting room crowded with a collection of old furniture, sundry knickknacks and an array of porcelain figurines. A very small person wrapped in what looked like a shroud was sitting in a corner.

"Mother don't say much. Just ignore her," Mary said.

A tiny, wizened face was peering intently into the middle of the room but not at Wilf.

"Hello," Wilf said.

"She won't talk back, Ducks. You're wasting your breath." Mary was wrapped in a faded red kimono, a pair of men's wool socks had collapsed about her stubby feet. She pointed to a wooden chair guarded by two plaster gnomes. Wilf sat down.

"To tell you the truth, I don't know that much about the poor old toff myself." Mary aimed her broad bottom down on a slightly splayed sofa. "He was not a great talker, he was more of an orderer. A regular General, he was. Debbie Banks, that's his old cleaning lady, when she gave him to me she told me that he was a regular dragon, but we'd get on because I was a bit of a dragon myself. 'Just give him back as good as you get and you'll see that he's not such a bad sort,' she said. So that's what I did and we had a laugh every once in a while. We had a glass of scotch every once in a while, too. Truth is, I got to kind of like the old bloke if it wasn't that he was so god-loving particular. A man like him living alone hardly makes a mess but oh, he had to have the bloomin' place cleaned every week. Not that I complained, you see, because it meant more lolly for me." Mary's eyes went sly.

"Right," Wilf said. He glanced over at her mother. The old woman continued to be transfixed by the presence of someone unseen. "What do you know about his family?"

"He had a wife, I know that much. They lived apart and she was always trying to take his money. He called her 'That bloody old cow.' And when we were having our scotch he'd say, 'If we get married you won't try to take my money away from me, will you, Mary?' I think he fancied himself a bit of a lady's man."

"Did he?"

"Seemed like it. He had a son, that's the one thing I know for sure. Tall and good-looking he was. He looked me up because he couldn't get his father on the phone. It was the heart business, you see. His son was worried, which of course he would be, wouldn't he?"

"But why did he come here?"

"To borrow my key, Dearie. He didn't have one. There was some falling out over his mother, he said, and of course I knew all about her, didn't I, and he was very worried about his father so of course I lent him mine."

"And how was his father?"

"The old goat was fine."

"Seems a bit strange, doesn't it? Why wouldn't he just knock on his father's door?"

"Well, I asked him that. He said he had, but the old man hadn't answered, so he was worried. Wouldn't answer most likely.

I felt sorry for him. Families, you know how it is." Mary cocked her head toward the old lady.

"Did he bring the key back?"

"Of course he did, that same afternoon. He's the one you should get in touch with."

"How long ago was this?"

"Oh, two months. Three, maybe."

"Do you know his first name, where he lives?"

"He's a farmer, he is, I remember that much."

"And did you ever see anyone else in Mr. Cruikshank's house? I mean anyone who wasn't a family member?"

Mary looked a little surprised. "Why?"

"It would be someone else I could talk to."

"It was just always himself, Ducky."

"No younger person then? Some young woman?"

Mary seemed to be growing nervous again. "No."

Wilf got up. "I appreciate this. You've been very helpful. There's only one other thing. Since McLauchlin and McLauchlin is Mr. Cruikshank's executor, of course we're responsible for his estate until we can pass it on to his legal heirs. Which means we have to secure his house and all his property. So if you don't mind I'll have to collect your key to his house. It's just the law."

Mary seemed taken back by this and a little dubious. "It is?"

"Yes, it is. But before you hand it over you could call Constable Andrew Creighton down at the police station. He'll confirm what I'm saying. Just to put your mind at rest."

Mary looked up at Wilf. She seemed to be considering the call and then she turned to her mother. "Well, it's not like I'll be needing that key anymore, is it?"

"No, it isn't," Wilf said.

❈ ❈ ❈

Wilf managed to park the car safely back in his father's garage but the familiar weight he'd felt earlier that evening had suddenly descended on his shoulders again.

He walked slowly into the house and turned on the light in the study. The first thing he saw in the flare of light was the Nuremberg transcripts and a thought suddenly struck him that the whole war was somehow contained in that little room. All the mad dreams. The feverish expectations. The Nazi mirage of a new civilization of appalling grandeur. And all the pain.

Wilf picked up a sheaf of transcripts. He was surprised to feel tears in his eyes. It had been a long day. He sat down and let the transcripts fall to the floor. He felt for Mary's key. It was still safely in his pocket. His spirits lifted.

He'd known what Frank Cruikshank was up to the moment Mary said he'd asked to borrow her key. He'd wanted to make a copy of it. But where? If he'd been smart, he would have taken it out of town.

Wilf tried to recapture an image of Frank Cruikshank rushing past him in the store but all he could see was Adrienne. She was standing close to him in the crush of clothes, her small face perfectly still in the warm perfumed air. And now he did reach out and touch her cheek. Her neck. Trailing his hand over her blouse, trying to feel the coolness of the material, the rise of her hidden breasts. She of the fathomless violet eyes. She, who seemed to be waiting.

And so was he. After nearly two years of forced abstinence. Waiting for a miracle to happen, to feel a sudden, familiar tightness electrify his stomach, the delicious push of blood.

He rested his head back against the chair. He was unbuttoning her blouse. Slipping his hand inside. Her skin felt warm. Her dark nipples.

It wasn't happening. His body was refusing to respond. Distracted by trauma. Confused by steel plates and pins and god knows what.

Wilf left the study and struggled up the stairs. He went into the bathroom, swallowed his pain pills and chased them down with a sleeping pill and then took one more. He walked into the bedroom, pulled off his clothes and sprawled out on the bed. Downstairs the grandfather clock was striking twelve. He lay there and listened.

He'd have to stay away from women. That was all he could do. If he didn't want to cause a scene. Embarrass himself.

It was hopeless.

He began to drift. Sleeping pills as big and fluffy as pillows were floating through his mind. No panic in his chest now though. No shadows in any room. He wondered why he hadn't been taking his sleeping pills more regularly long before this. Stupid of him. Stupid.

Drifting, drifting away.

He was standing in a shadowy warehouse. He could see a large wooden tank some distance away. He could hear the hollow sound of water dripping. Dripping. He drew nearer, reached up and pulled himself over the damp slippery edge. Mr. Cruikshank was floating on his back in chunks of ice. He was wearing a flight suit. A tangle of wires were attached to his stomach.

Wilf opened his eyes.

CHAPTER SIX

It was just before nine o'clock the next morning when Carole pushed open the door to the office. It was unlocked, the lights were on and Wilf was sitting at Dorothy Dale's desk.

"Morning," Wilf mumbled. He was looking through a file.

Carole wondered if he'd had any sleep. Or if he'd slept in the office. Anyway, he seemed to have forgotten to brush his hair, parts of it were standing up on end.

"Good morning." Carole took off her hat and coat carefully. She'd been looking forward to seeing him, telling him what she'd found out, but now she wasn't so sure.

"Just checking the date on Cruikshank's will," Wilf said.

He looked feverish. Carole had spent at least ten minutes that morning staring at the sweater Wilf had given her, deciding whether to wear it or not. Now she was glad she hadn't. She pushed through the little gate, took the cover off her typewriter and sat down opposite him. "What's it say?"

"July twenty-third of last year. He must have been head over heels in love."

"Or thought highly of her, anyway."

"Thought highly of her?"

"Yes. And then he died of a heart attack."

Wilf looked over at Carole. She was sitting as erect as a schoolteacher. Her long straight back. If only there were more to her, Wilf thought to himself, she'd be attractive. Not that it would do him any good. Or her, either.

Carole pushed her unruly lock of hair back and began sorting through her work.

"Did you find anything out?" Wilf asked

"Well, yes and no. Do you remember Nancy Dearborn from school?"

"She's a telephone operator."

"She's also my cousin and when I thought about it I realized that my uncle's house is just across the street from where Mr. Cruikshank lived. So I called Nancy and of course it's the talk of the neighbourhood. I got the feeling that no one liked Mr. Cruikshank very much, he wasn't very neighbourly, but everyone's feeling sorry for what happened to him anyway."

"That someone drowned him in his tub?"

"No," Carole replied.

More firmly than necessary, Wilf thought.

She went on. "I told Nancy that he'd been a client of ours and we were just feeling bad about it and she started talking about Adrienne O'Dell without me even having to mention her name. They saw her around there a lot. For the last year or so anyway. She helped him with his garden, took him grocery shopping, took him to his doctor appointments."

"He wasn't an invalid."

"But he was elderly and he had a bad heart and so she was just helping out. That's all. All the neighbours thought that it was a very nice thing for her to be doing, particularly since she was an O'Dell. They never saw any of his own family there."

"And we know why, don't we?"

"So did all his neighbours. Everyone knew there was a big fight going on. The courthouse is in Brantford, but you can't keep a secret in this town. Everyone knows everything. You can't keep anything private."

"Right," Wilf said and remembered. Poor Carole Birley.

Carole glanced toward the front door, looked back at Wilf and dropped her voice. "But the most interesting thing was, my aunt saw Mr. Cruikshank on his front porch arguing with someone. Someone tall and blonde and middle-aged. She hadn't seen him before but with all the swinging of arms around and all the angry talk it was obvious they were really fighting. And then the man went away. That's what everyone's talking about, that it's no wonder poor Mr. Cruikshank had a heart attack after such an ugly scene. My aunt thinks that that man should be charged for contributing to Mr. Cruikshank's death."

"When was this?"

"Last Saturday afternoon."

"It sounds like Frank Cruikshank."

"I know, but even if it was, it doesn't mean what you think it means."

"What do I think it means?"

"You know what you think it means."

"Then why do you think Frank Cruikshank was in the store arguing with Adrienne?"

"They were probably discussing the terms of the will."

Wilf looked out the window, past the faded gold lettering. A car passed by on Main Street. A truck passed the other way. "Carole, do you really think that all Adrienne did was help Mr. Cruikshank go shopping and look after his garden and he said, 'You're such a sweet kid. Here's my whole estate.' Do you really think that?"

Carole's face reddened a little because in her secret thoughts she hadn't thought that. She hadn't thought that at all, but she'd been trying to push them away. Such thoughts seemed to say more about her own questionable state of mind than Adrienne's.

"Saturday night was the night of the snowstorm. And he had a key," Wilf went on.

"Who did?"

"Frank Cruikshank had a key to the house. He borrowed one from Cruikshank's housekeeper because he said he needed to get in to make sure his father wasn't ill." Wilf got up, picked up his cane and headed for the front door. "He was lying. He wanted the key to make a copy."

"Where are you going?"

"To make sure."

"I'm just wondering," Carole called out after him.

"What?"

"Is that your father's car parked out front? Sort of sideways?"

Wilf began to pull on his coat. "As a matter of fact, yes it is."

"Didn't you say that Doc Robinson was going to examine Mr. Cruikshank more thoroughly? Could you do me a big favour? Before you do anything else, could you drive up to his office and ask him what he found out? If Mr. Cruikshank did die of a heart attack then everything's all right. And it's just us. We're the ones going crazy." Carole looked at him hopefully.

"All right. I will," Wilf said and went out the door.

Carole sat there for a moment. She picked up a legal form and rolled it into her typewriter. She looked at it. She'd already typed in the required information. It was already signed.

She pulled it back out and tried to study her notebook. She couldn't think of what it was she was supposed to be doing. There was so much work and Mr. McLauchlin would be back by Monday. The Conacher file. Yes. The business partnership papers. Of course. As she turned to her side table for the file, the front door opened and Frank Cruikshank walked in.

"My father's passed away," he said, his voice hoarse and full of some kind of complicated emotion that Carole couldn't identify. He walked right up to the wooden railing. "Sometime yesterday."

"I'm sorry," Carole said.

"They found him yesterday, I mean."

He was wearing a long leather coat with a dirty wool lining. He looked even taller than he had in court, his face highly coloured from being out of doors all the time, his hands as wide as they were long and permanently swollen from a lifetime of work. Carole could hardly take her eyes off his hands.

"My name's Frank Cruikshank, if you don't know."

The railing was supposed to protect her, separating the public from the rest of the office but it only reached a little above Frank Cruikshank's knees.

"You'd know my mother. McLauchlin's been fighting her for years."

Carole easily resisted the temptation to say that it wasn't Mr. McLauchlin who had been fighting his mother, it had been his own father.

"Did he have a will?" he asked.

Carole found her voice. "Mr. McLauchlin is out of town until this coming Monday. At such time I'm sure that Mr. McLauchlin will deal with everything that needs to be done and he will be in contact with you as soon as possible."

"I just asked if he had a will."

"That's not my job. I have no idea."

"Look in his file."

"I'm sure Mr. McLauchlin will look in the file as soon as he returns."

The man's pale eyes turned hard. "You don't know anything about it?"

"No."

"You'd think he'd have a will."

"Yes, you would."

Frank Cruikshank was beginning to look increasingly upset. He ran his hand through his thinning blonde hair. "What's your name?"

"Miss Carole Birley."

"Well, Miss Carole Birley, maybe you can tell me this. Has anyone else, some young woman say, come in here asking about a will?"

"You mean your father's will?"

Cruikshank just stared at her.

"No."

The man's face went cold. He looked out the window and then turned back. "As far as I'm concerned, his goddamn corpse can stay wherever the hell it is. Goddamn him to hell!" He slammed out the door.

Carole got up from her desk, pushed through the gate and turned the lock on the front door. She looked out the window. Cruikshank had already gone past the wrought-iron fence. He was turning onto Main Street.

❋ ❋ ❋

"This belongs to an expensive lock," Tony Gillo announced, standing in his cluttered shop and holding up Mary's key in his grimy hand. "You see the difference?"

"No." Wilf leaned across the equally grimy counter and looked more closely.

"It's longer than your ordinary key. This is how it works. You put it in halfway, you make a quarter turn to the right, say, if you're opening. Quarter turn the other way if you're locking, see? And then you push it all the way in and turn to the left or the right as the case may be. Do you know why?"

"No idea."

"Because," Tony's watery eyes peered triumphantly over his thick glasses, "if you can't go straight in, you can't pick a lock." A grin spread over his grizzled face.

"I get it."

"Like a woman with a chastity belt, eh?"

"Right."

"Very nice. Expensive. Who would need a lock like that?"

"Could you make a copy?"

"Sure. But I don't have the right blank for this. It needs to be cut special, give me an hour."

"I don't need a copy, Tony, I was just asking if it was possible. Theoretically."

"Theoretically?"

"If you did make a copy of a key like that, say within the last two months or so, would you remember?"

"Now I got to remember?"

Wilf grinned. "So no one's come in here and wanted a copy of a key like that?"

"This is a special job. Take an hour or so. I'd have to explain all that to the customer, why it was special, why he couldn't just wait for it."

"Right."

"Right." Tony handed the key back, "So, mister lawyer's son, I think I'd remember."

❄ ❄ ❄

By the time Wilf had driven back into town it was the middle of the afternoon. It had seemed to make sense that Cruikshank would take the key out of town but Wilf had visited all three locksmith shops in Brantford and two shops in Woodstock, and just like Tony Gillo, no one had remembered.

He pulled the car up to Doc Robinson's home office. He had somehow made it, though his left leg felt like it was on fire from depressing the clutch all day and his shoulders ached from straining to see over the dashboard. He tried to rest for a moment but his mind refused.

Why had Frank Cruikshank been in the dress shop in the first place? Because of the will. Even if Adrienne hadn't known anything about it, Frank had found out somehow. But that didn't make any sense. If he'd known about it the last thing he would have done was murder his father. Unless, of course, he and Adrienne had had an understanding.

Wilf looked down the hill toward the double line of store-fronts, the dress shop hidden in amongst them, and the steeper hill beyond. Everything looked wintery, misty and grey. But what if the thing Frank had found out had nothing to do with the will? What if he'd found out about Adrienne herself, that she was always at the house, always around his father? He'd become suspicious. More than that. Paranoid. That's why he'd asked Mary for her key, and by last Saturday he couldn't stand the not knowing any longer. He banged on the front door expecting that his father, as usual, wouldn't answer, but the old man stepped out on the porch and all the suspicion and paranoia and hurt spilled out of Frank, and his father began to shout back that if he didn't quit haranguing him he damn well would leave every-thing he owned to Adrienne O'Dell, she was the only one who really cared a damn about him anyway. How would Frank like that? Him and his cow of a mother? How would they like that?

Wilf opened the car door. He had to lift his burning leg over the ledge. He sat there sideways, staring up the steps toward Doc Robinson's house and seeing instead the old man on his porch and his furious son and snowflakes beginning to fall all around.

What Frank didn't know, of course, was that his father, in his resurrected passion, in his dotage, had already done exactly that. He'd written out a new will. But Frank was more than alarmed now. His body felt charged. Overcome by something.

Wilf pushed himself out of the car and began to climb the steps. The waiting room was filled to overflowing. After an hour it was Wilf's turn. Doc Robinson was standing in his examining room fixing something with a strip of white tape.

"I just stepped on my glasses."

Wilf eased himself down into a chair.

"How long have you been waiting?"

"Not long."

"If Diane had told me you were out there, I would have brought you in before all those old women. That's why I see them two at a time. There's never anything wrong, they just drop in here for something to do."

Doc, whip-thin, hollow-chested and perfectly bald, tried on his wounded glasses. There was a ball of white tape wrapped around one of the hinges. "How do they look?"

"Like you need new glasses."

"I don't have time." Doc sat down behind his desk and took a long look at Wilf. "I see you've recovered from yesterday."

"It didn't have much to do with me."

Doc nodded but continued staring. Wilf looked away.

"Well, what can I do for you, Wilf?"

"I was just wondering about Mr. Cruikshank. What you thought once you had a better look at him. And I guess the family will need death certificates."

"I was surprised to see that your father put you to work so soon."

"My idea. I want to keep busy. Get back to normal. You know."

"You said the other day you were planning to go back to college."

"Right. As soon as I can. Can't wait."

"And you're connected in with the Veteran's Hospital in Burlington? The doctors there?"

"That's right."

"That's not too convenient though, is it? Anything you need in the way of prescriptions, anything you want to talk about, I'm here."

"I appreciate that, Doc. Okay."

Doc took off his glasses and examined his repair work. "The gentleman in question is resting peacefully in the basement at the hospital. As soon as the family gives the word and he's sent off to a funeral home they'll be able to obtain copies of the death certificate from the funeral director. That's the normal procedure."

"I see. So everything's fine then? Nothing out of the ordinary?"

"Sam Cruikshank had been my patient for some time. Had to hospitalize him twice. So a full stop myocardial infarction was not too surprising. He struggled though. It wouldn't have been a pretty death."

"What do you mean?"

"Just the amount of water coming out of his lungs. A major heart attack can sometimes paralyze you. It's like being in a vice. He must have slipped under the water."

"You mean he was still alive when he went under?"

"For a gulp or two. Not a pretty picture, is it?" Doc put his glasses back on and refocused on Wilf's face.

"No."

"He probably lost consciousness before he slipped under the water though. Let's hope that's the way it went."

"Did you do an autopsy?"

Doc looked a little surprised. "There was no need for an autopsy, Wilf. I know what happened."

"All right." Wilf got up out of the chair.

"You're feeling reasonably well, are you? Not too much discomfort?"

"No. I have pills, Doc. I'll bring them in to show you."

"I feel bad about it."

"I'm all right."

"Not you. Cruikshank."

"Why is that?"

"Why? Because I talked to him on the phone the day he died. The snow was already coming down to beat hell. That's why I didn't want to make a house call. He said he was out of his pills and he was having some pain. I said I'd send a bottle of his pills around by cab. Told him to call if things didn't settle down and to be sure to come in and see me the next day anyway, it wouldn't matter that it was Sunday. He said he would."

Doc turned and stared out his office window as if he expected to see the snow begin to fall again. "I sent the pills. He didn't call. And I forgot." He pushed away from his desk and stood up, "I should have got in my car and drove through the goddamn storm. That's what I should have done. Put him in the hospital."

"You didn't know, though."

"What didn't I know?"

"That he'd have a full-scale heart attack."

"Why didn't I? I'm supposed to." Doc got up, walked over to the sink and began to wash his hands.

"I'm sorry about it, Doc."

Doc nodded.

Wilf let himself out the door. He drove the car by his father's house, past the high school and the hospital, and all the while he could see Old Man Cruikshank laying on a stainless-steel table in the basement, water pooling darkly inside his gaping mouth, trickling out. It drove him on.

This time he was travelling north toward Galt, the last town of any size within a half-hour's drive. The wind had come up and snow was beginning to blow across the road as high as the hood of the car. The car rocked a little. And it all fit. The Cruikshanks, father and son, had had their fight on the porch. The old man went back into the house and looked for his heart pills. He called Doc. The cab delivered them and the pain settled down. Maybe he ate a light supper, read a magazine in his easy chair. Couldn't concentrate, decided to have a warm bath instead. He eased himself down in the hot water. The wind was whistling outside, the snow closing off the house, wrapping it around like a giant white curtain. And his son was standing at the side door with a copy of Mary's key in his trembling hand.

"Hey Tommy, you work on a key like this?"

The owner of the first shop Wilf walked into held up Mary's key. A young man, wearing a pair of tinted goggles on the top of his head and an exasperated expression on his face looked up from his bench. "How would I know, Pop? I work on all kinds of things."

"Come here. It's a special lock. A Chelsie Star. Double action."

The young man came over and took the key from his father. "Are you a cop?"

"Just a lawyer. Asking questions for a client."

"Is that right?" The young man grinned and looked at the key more closely. He looked back at Wilf. "Yeah, I made a copy of this baby."

Wilf was surprised to feel himself ambushed by tears. A rush of relief. He fought them back. "When? About two months ago?"

"Shit, no. First of last week maybe. Something like that."

"What did he look like?"

"You mean, she. Short, young and sweet. A regular little fox."

"Now, now," his father said, "have respect."

"I'm just wondering," Wilf said, "could you tell me the colour of her hair?"

"Upstairs or downstairs?"

The older man shook his head and retreated to the back of the shop. "If your mother was alive."

"Upstairs," Wilf said.

"Probably just the same as downstairs. Black and shiny."

"Was it cut short?"

The young man grinned again, his face a happy mask of oil and grime. "Hell, yes, it was cut short. Shorter than mine."

Wilf left the cluttered shop and stepped back out into the side street.

He could hardly breathe.

❄ ❄ ❄

The light in the dress-shop window was still on when Wilf pulled the car up with a jolt. Adrienne must be working late, he thought to himself, it's past six.

He turned off the engine. It had been a dark flight back. In and out of cloud cover. No visibility. He'd had to fly by instruments and the seat of his pants.

Wilf rested his head on the steering wheel and tried some deep breathing like he'd been taught to do. Take an inventory of your body. Relax every muscle. Empty the mind. Concentrate on infinity. What would it look like if you could imagine it? It would look like nothing at all.

The light across the street blinked off and an older woman came out, followed by Adrienne O'Dell. The older woman locked the door. They said something quickly to each other and Adrienne cut across the street. She was wearing a dark coat and bright white mittens and a white wool hat. Easy to see in the dark.

She's showing off, Wilf thought somewhat hysterically, the only murderess in town.

Adrienne passed in front of the car without a glance at Wilf and turned up the street. When he looked in his rear-view mirror she was already half a block away. He got out of the car and followed along. Adrienne hurried across a side street and pushed through the *Ladies & Escorts Only* door into the Arlington Hotel.

The men's side was crowded and steamy, not unlike an English pub full of safely returned and grateful flight crews. All warmth and laughter. Wilf walked up to the bar, ordered himself a beer, called out hello to a few fellows he knew and before anyone could beckon him over to their table hobbled out into the hall. He had to hook his cane over his sling to hold his beer, but even so it slopped all over his hand. He crossed over to the *Ladies & Escorts Only* side and sat down at the first empty table he saw.

A burst of laughter came from somewhere. The room was crowded with couples and hazy with smoke. Teddy, a waiter who was approximately the same age as the old hotel winked at Wilf as he went by. "Will I bring you one for your lady friend?" he said.

"Too much commotion on the other side."

"You do whatever you want." Teddy knew who Wilf was and the price he'd paid. He could have the run of the place, as far as Teddy was concerned.

Wilf glanced around.

Adrienne was sitting behind a table at the back of the room. She'd taken off her white mittens and white hat but had left her coat on as if she wasn't planning to stay long. Teddy walked over and set two draft beers down in front of her. Not bothering to look up at him, she picked up one of the glasses and took a drink. She stared off into the drifting smoke.

She's waiting, Wilf thought, waiting to be surprised by the contents of the will. "Who, me?" she'll say.

Wilf sipped at his beer.

A young man carrying what looked to Wilf like a Navy pea jacket over his arm crossed the room from somewhere and sat at her table. She barely glanced at him. He was slightly built, round-shouldered. He picked up the other beer and took a sip, staring off into the half-distance with a mournful pair of eyes.

One question had been buzzing around Wilf's mind all the way back from Galt. How could Adrienne have managed to drown Samuel Cruikshank? She was too small. The answer seemed to be his son Frank. But not now.

Wilf got up from his table, hurried down the hall to the back of the hotel and fumbled a nickel into a payphone.

"Number please." It wasn't Nancy Dearborn.

"I don't have it. I need to call Carole Birley."

"Address, please?"

"I don't know it."

It didn't matter, a Carole Birley was not listed, anyway. Three other Birleys were. After a discussion as to what Carole's father's first name might be and a wrong call made and a very short conversation with her mother, Carole came on the line.

"Who's Adrienne O'Dell's boyfriend? It was Adrienne all the time!" Wilf said. "She was the one who made a copy of Cruikshank's key. And I was wrong. It wasn't Mary's key that got copied. Do you know whose it was? It was her own. Of course she had her own key. So she could come and go whenever Cruikshank wanted her, whenever the neighbours were asleep, with no fuss or bother. She had a key of her own!"

"Please calm down," Carole said.

"So who do you think the extra key was for? It was for her boyfriend! And I've got them, I've got them both here. He's sitting right here, right beside her, right here in the hotel!"

"Who is?"

"The guy who helped her drown Old Man Cruikshank!" Wilf dropped his voice. "You see, that's why I'm calling, Carole. Who does Adrienne go out with? Who is this guy? Look, I've got to go."

"Wilf!"

Wilf hung up and half-stumbling, half-running back down the hall came to the open doorway again. Adrienne and her friend were still sitting at their table, still lost in their own thoughts. Wilf stood in the hall and watched them.

He could feel some faceless, formless panic flying around in his chest. Growing. I have to calm down, he thought.

Adrienne seemed to be gathering her strength for the coming storm. Terrible gossip sweeping over the town. Frank Cruikshank and his mother going berserk. Perhaps a fight in court. But the will was safely filed at McLauchlin and McLauchlin, dated and signed. And any number of people would probably testify that Sam Cruikshank was as sharp and clear of mind as he'd always been until he'd unfortunately died of a heart attack.

Adrienne looked like she was preparing herself, stony and resolute. Her friend looked sick.

Wilf felt ravenous. He went into the men's side and bought himself two pickled eggs. A couple of fellows came over and started up a conversation. He couldn't get away. They bought him a beer. They'd been part of a Lancaster crew, they'd fought from the first bombing runs over the Ruhr Valley to the last over Berlin, it was a miracle they were alive. It was a miracle anyone was alive.

Wilf had to be courteous. He downed his beer in three gulps. "Look, I have to take a leak," he said and hurried back into the hall. Adrienne and her friend were gone.

Wilf stood there staring at the two empty glasses they'd left behind. Teddy was circling around the tables picking up glasses, carrying his tray like a hungry old hawk. Wilf hustled over, stuffed the glasses in his overcoat and, expecting to hear Teddy call out after him, hustled back toward the hall. He pushed through the outside door into the night. A car was passing by. Three people were walking toward the bridge that spanned the larger of the town's two rivers.

Adrienne and her friend were nowhere in sight.

❋ ❋ ❋

Prosecutor: The experimental subjects used in the freezing experiments were political prisoners. Is this correct?

Witness: There were a number of political prisoners and also a number of foreigners, but there were also prisoners of war and inmates who had been condemned to death.

Prosecutor: So these people were not volunteers?

Witness: No.

Prosecutor: Suppose you describe to the tribunal exactly how these freezing experiments were carried out.

Witness: The experimental basin was built of wood. It was two metres long and two metres wide. It was filled with water and ice was added until the water measured three degrees centigrade. The experimental subjects were either dressed in flyer aviation suits or placed in the ice and water naked.

Wilf hadn't intended to read when he'd driven back to his father's house. He'd pulled the beer glasses out of his coat pocket, put them carefully down on the library table and poured himself a tall shot of rye. That's when his eyes had fallen on the sheaf of transcripts that had dropped from his lap the previous night.

His father had placed a hand-printed card under the metal clasp that was holding them together. No one in the world was more organized than his father. He'd made the notation *DOCTOR EXPERIMENTS* and under this heading he'd compiled a list. Beside C) he'd printed *FREEZING WATER–INDUCED NARCOSIS*.

Wilf had stared at those words for a long moment.

Witness: The temperature was measured rectally and through the stomach by a Galvanometer apparatus. It took some time until so-called freezing narcosis set in. The lowering of the temperature to zero degrees centigrade was terrible for the experimental subject. At zero degrees the experimental subject lost consciousness. These persons were frozen down to minus four degrees body temperature.

Prosecutor: What was the purpose of such experiments?
Witness: The purpose was to develop techniques to revive air crew who had been shot down and recovered in the North Sea and in other cold waters.
Prosecutor: Out of a total of three hundred prisoners used, approximately how many died?
Witness: Approximately eighty to ninety subjects died.

Wilf couldn't get it straight.

He could see Old Man Cruikshank frozen blue in his tub. He could see him awash in his dream, a tangle of wires attached.

Wilf stared across the room at the two empty glasses. He'd stolen them.

He stared down at the transcript again. And he thought of the man standing in the snow who wasn't there.

There was only one explanation for all of this. For everything.

I'm going insane, Wilf thought to himself.

CHAPTER SEVEN

Duncan felt half-frozen. He was standing in the grove of trees behind Carole's property for the second night in a row. Her father's property actually.

He knew Carole's father, at least to see him. He worked at the mill that made kitchen cupboards and counters up near the railway tracks. He'd delivered lumber there when his mother was alive. Whenever he saw Mr. Birley, he always seemed to have a scowl on his face like he somehow knew the bad thing Duncan did behind his house.

Duncan stamped his feet around in the snow to try to keep them warm. Carole's window remained dark. She was later than usual. She was on time the night before, that's what had brought him back so soon. Her long naked back, her tumbling hair, a quick glimpse of her beautiful breasts.

He leaned against a tree. He felt a little drunk after a long evening of sitting in the men's room at the Empire Hotel. The fellows at the table he'd sat down at had been friendly enough. They all knew him. Everyone knew him. They even bought him a few beers but just after nine o'clock they had to leave.

Duncan sat alone at the table drinking glass after glass of draft beer like someone else might eat their way through a bowl of peanuts. He didn't want to bother with the two remaining men who were sitting at their own separate tables. He knew them both. He knew that they lived in separate rooms upstairs and preferred to be left alone, which was all right with him. They weren't much to talk to, anyway.

He made himself sit there and watch the clock until the hands reached ten thirty and then he pushed out the side door.

At first it felt warm outside. He walked down the dark street to where it came to an abrupt stop above the river, hauled himself over a pile of snow and half-slid down to the river's edge. You couldn't see the river of course, just more snow but you could hear it gurgling underneath somewhere, the water running swift and dark.

The first time Duncan had dared to do this he'd worried about the trail he was leaving behind but no one seemed to notice. That was a few years ago. Now he just bulled himself along, urgent to get there in time, not thinking about anything else but Carole, his heart full of pounding blood and a compelling excitement.

Carole was really late tonight, though.

Duncan felt cold all the way through. His great arms were beginning to quiver with cold. So was his chest. His teeth would be rattling soon.

Maybe she wasn't feeling well, maybe that was it. Maybe she'd gone to bed early. She'd done that before. Or stayed overnight somewhere. At a girlfriend's, maybe.

And poor Dandy would be standing in the feed mill's open stables shivering with cold and wondering what the hell had happened. He had his blanket on, of course, he had oats in his bucket but still he'd be half-frozen by now.

The light in Carole's bedroom turned on and the electricity went straight into Duncan's heart. He shuddered from head to foot.

And now he could see her.

And then she went away again.

❄ ❄ ❄

Wilf heard the grandfather clock striking somewhere, striking insistently, one drawn-out gong. He swam up into consciousness and realized that it wasn't the clock, the phones were ringing.

He was still sitting in a chair in the study, the transcript on his lap. Moonlight was coming through the window. The snowstorm he'd driven through earlier had disappeared.

Wilf hauled himself up from the chair and went out to the kitchen. Everything seemed to be floating in front of him.

"I hope I didn't wake you," Carole said at the other end of the line.

"No."

"Did you just get in?"

"What time is it?"

"Ten after twelve."

Wilf's eyes went up to the clock drifting above the refrigerator. "What took you so long?"

"I've called you twice before."

"When?"

"At nine. And at ten. I was just going to go to bed and then I thought I'd give it one more try."

"I must have fallen asleep."

"Some sleep. I had to explain to Nancy why I was calling you all night long."

"Why did you have to explain?"

"All I said was that it was urgent business that had to do with the office."

"Is she listening now?'

"No, of course not. She wouldn't."

Wilf wasn't so sure.

He remembered the transcript, he remembered drinking. And drinking some more. He felt sick.

"You didn't give me a chance to tell you something," Carole was saying. "Frank Cruikshank came in just after you left. He wanted to see the will. I told him he'd have to wait for your father. He was very unpleasant. And he looked upset. But then, his father had just died."

"I don't care about him anymore."

"You don't?"

"I'm interested in Adrienne O'Dell's boyfriend."

There was a pause at the other end of the line. "What did Doctor Robinson say? Did you go see him?"

"Yes."

"Are you lying?"

"No."

"What did he say?"

"He said that Cruikshank had a lot of water coming out of his lungs, like he'd been fighting for his breath."

"Oh."

"He still believes he died of a heart attack, though."

"Oh."

Wilf rested his forehead against the kitchen wall and tried to remember. Was that exactly what Doc Robinson had said. He wasn't sure. "What did you find out about her boyfriend?" Panic was moving around in his chest again.

"His name is Tom. I don't know his last name. He's from Brantford. He's a sailor. He was Adrienne's boyfriend before he went overseas. He got back a few months ago."

"Who told you this?"

"A girlfriend who called a girlfriend who knows Adrienne a lot better than I do."

"Where are they living?"

"They're not married."

"Some people live together when they're not married."

"Not here."

"Okay. So where's Adrienne staying? Is she still at home?"

"You know that butcher shop on the corner in the Junction?"

"I think so."

"There's an apartment at the back. Adrienne's been living there."

"That's not too far away from Mr. Cruikshank's house. Is it?"

"No."

"Just down the tracks."

"You know what I think? I think you should wait for your father, he'll know what to do." Carole's voice was sounding a little tremulous.

"Thank you for all your help, Carole."

"It's so awful."

Wilf could almost feel her light breath coming down the line, the warmth of it.

"You're welcome," she said.

※ ※ ※

By the time Wilf pushed Mary's key into the lock he was shivering in the cold.

Tony Gillo had been right. Partway in and a quarter turn to the right. The rest of the way and a full turn to the left.

The door pushed open and Wilf stepped into the landing. The air inside the house felt even colder than it had the day before. He climbed up the steps into the kitchen. Moonlight poured in through the window, spidery x-ray shadows moved on all the walls.

This is what Adrienne would have seen, Wilf thought to himself, night after night. Bringing in the heady smell of the night air. The little saint of the garden. Little saint of groceries. And Cruikshank would make sure she locked the door behind her. And he'd touch her face. And she'd wait, just as she had that day in the dress shop. Inviting his touch. His trembling fingers. His faltering body.

And her body, passive, quiet, white as snow.

Wilf made his way down the hall. Moonlight filled the round window at the turn of the stairs. He began to climb, wondering if he'd have the courage to look outside. He scraped the frost away. Light lay like a blue haze across the backyard. He could see the railway tracks glinting faintly in the ravine. The fruit trees were holding their dark arms up to the moon. And that was all.

Wilf felt his way along the darker upstairs hall and found the bathroom switch. The light flared on. Everything looked harsh and bleached. Someone had let the water out but there were still splinters of ice lacing the bottom of the tub. And a smear of excrement.

Wilf crossed over to the sink and looked at himself in the mirror. "Having fun?" And once again, inexplicably, he felt on the edge of tears.

He opened the medicine cabinet and looked inside. A frayed toothbrush. Hair tonic. Combs. Aftershave. Stomach tablets. Bandages. Two small pill bottles, one empty, the other half full.

He closed the cabinet, walked back to the master bedroom and turned on the light. Everything looked the same as it had the day before. Tidy. Shipshape. The made-up bed. Who would make a bed with the blanket as tight as that? It had a familiar look, a military look. He could hear Adrienne's voice. She was calling down the hall. "Make the bed, Tom." She was down on her hands and knees soaking up the spilled water. She wouldn't want the bed left messy, not still rumpled and stained from where she and the old man had snuggled together against the wind outside, against the sandy sound of the pelting snow.

Had she drawn him a warm bath afterwards? What an angel of mercy she must have been. And the old man had settled down in the hot water. And she'd taken a cloth and washed his back and he'd closed his eyes and he hadn't heard a thing. Nothing until he'd felt another pair of hands on his shoulders, colder, more muscular.

Wilf moved around the bed. He could see what he'd come for on the top of the dresser, a pill bottle, larger than the other two. Doc had scribbled a note across the label recording the name of the pills and the date. The date of the storm six days before.

Wilf sat down on the edge of the bed and listened to the commotion coming from the bathroom. It would have taken both of them to manage it. Adrienne grasping for his legs. Lifting. The boyfriend swarming over his head, pressing down. And now Adrienne was screaming at the old man, her face ecstatic, screaming something dark and terrible. Her body on fire. Wild. Beside herself.

Wilf could hear her.

❄ ❄ ❄

Andy stared at the two beer glasses and the amber-coloured pill bottle Wilf had just fished out of a scarf. It was two in the morning and as usual at that time of night he was sitting alone in the police station.

"What the hell is this?"

"Proof that Samuel Cruikshank was murdered."

Andy got up and distanced himself a little from the evidence that was now sitting on his desk. "I told you to let everything alone, didn't I? I told you to wait until the will was read."

"I couldn't wait."

"What the hell's the matter with you?"

"Nothing. It didn't have anything to do with Frank Cruikshank anyway. It was Adrienne O'Dell."

"Is that right?"

"Yes." Wilf eased himself down onto the nearest chair and tried to look relaxed, in control of himself. "I found out a few things today. There's this locksmith in Galt. Adrienne came into his shop a few days ago to make a copy of the old man's key."

"And that proves what?"

"That she already had a key to copy. Do you know how she

came to be the sole heir to Cruikshank's estate? Because, in the middle of the night, while the neighbours were asleep, whenever the old man wanted her she'd let herself into his house."

"Wilf, for chrissake, he was old enough to be her grand-father."

"He was a tough old bastard, that's what he was. Rich, too. That's what Adrienne knew. He was rich. And who knows? Maybe he wrote out that will just to make sure she'd keep show-ing up, and maybe he thought someday he'd get around to destroying it. Big mistake. Do you know why she needed that extra key? She couldn't drown the old buzzard herself. She needed her boyfriend's help."

"Oh yeah?" Andy looked less than convinced. "What's all that stuff on my desk?"

"The pill bottle was sent over to Cruikshank by Doc Robinson late in the afternoon on the day he died. The glasses came out of the Arlington tonight. The one with the lipstick will have Adrienne's fingerprints all over it."

"And?"

"Since Adrienne was Cruikshank's little friend maybe she helped him take his pills, too."

"You're dreaming."

"Are you sure? If she gave the old man everything else, including warm baths, why not his pills? A late-night pill."

"Right," Andy said. He squared his stocky body toward Wilf and spread his stance a little as if he were about to write out a ticket. "I can guess how you got those beer glasses but I'm a bit stumped on how you managed to get that pill bottle?"

"After you gave me Mary's number, I went over to see her and talked her into giving me her key to the house."

"Fucking Christ! So what are you, a plainclothes detective now? Did someone deputize you? I thought you gave me a promise."

"You know what Doc told me? When Cruikshank thawed out water was running out of his mouth."

"I don't care! Entering private property without permission, removing private property! Jesus Christ!" Andy began to pat his pockets down looking for his cigarettes. After a while he spotted them lying on a windowsill. He walked over to them and took his time lighting one up. He looked back toward the glasses, the pill bottle. "What are you after, as if I didn't know?"

"Test them for fingerprints."

"We don't do that kind of thing here."

"Then who does? Where would you take them?"

"Nowhere. That's where. If this was a legal investigation, and I emphasize the word *legal*, this so-called evidence of yours would be transported into Hamilton. They have a lab there. Not the municipal cops. The Ontario Provincial Police. That's where everyone around here goes with their forensic work."

"Could you?"

"Are you kidding? The way you acquired that pill bottle?"

"There's no way to do it then?"

"Look Wilf, I'm just a constable."

"Constable First Class."

"An ordinary everyday flatfoot. It's not what I do."

"Okay."

"I could lose my job."

"I don't want you to lose your job. You have to think of Linda and the kids. You have a family. Responsibilities."

"We have certain rules around here."

Wilf smiled. "Sounds like the Air Force."

"Yeah well, I was never in the Air Force."

Wilf nodded sympathetically.

"Not that I didn't want to be."

Wilf nodded again. And sat there and waited.

Andy took a deep pull on his cigarette. "There's someone I

know. He works in the lab but he lives in Brantford. I don't know what shift he works."

"Right," Wilf said.

"I guess, maybe, I could find out."

Wilf kept his expression neutral.

"He was just a guy I knew at police college. He ended up going with the OPP."

"I don't want to get you in any trouble."

Andy grinned. It was the first time he'd felt the least bit adventurous in years.

"Yes, you do," he said. "Welcome home, asshole."

Wilf pulled his father's car into a service station that was closed for the night, circled around the gas pumps and came to a stop. Across the road the butcher shop and the two-storey brick house it was part of looked isolated and lonely sitting on its corner. A street light, leaning over a little, cast a faint light on the walls. Someone had built a wooden extension on at the back with an open staircase leading to a door on the second floor. A large window by this door was lit up. All the other windows were dark.

Wilf sat in the car and stared up at the window. A shadow moved behind the blind and disappeared. After a while two shadows appeared and disappeared. Wilf smiled to himself and thought of Carole. Everything felt just right. Everyone was where they were supposed to be. Andy in his office trying to make a connection with his friend in the lab. Cruikshank lying in the dark in the basement of the hospital feeling like the world's biggest fool, no doubt. And Adrienne and her boyfriend pacing the floor at two in the morning haunted by desperate remembered images and by dark premonitions of disaster.

Wilf opened the car door and pushed himself out into the

frigid air. The sensible thing would have been to go straight home after talking to Andy. Try to get some sleep. He needed sleep. But he was too wound up. High on something.

He limped along the snowy road past the butcher shop, turned at the corner and followed this street toward a series of wooden planks that crossed a double set of railway tracks. He walked up onto the crossing and looked toward Old Man Cruikshank's house. He could almost see Adrienne walking along the path beside the tracks. All it would take was a turn to the left, a short climb up out of the ravine, slip past the fruit trees and in through the side door. For half a year. Or a year. And who in all the sleeping town would have been the wiser?

The road Wilf was standing on continued down a steep hill into a river valley. A line of street lights far below were blinking back at him. Carole was asleep down there somewhere according to the telephone operator. And now he could almost see her body stretched out long and skinny under a fluffy pink quilt, a frown creasing her brow, her mouth a bit skeptical as it always seemed to be.

Wilf had to smile to himself. Despite her small-town conservatism and at some cost to her peace of mind she was trying to help.

She was helping him.

Wilf looked over the town and suddenly he felt like an alien standing there in the dark. A refugee from far lands and foreign disasters. The air felt ten degrees colder. A sharp pain rippled down his left side, lingered for a second.

He turned back to the car and as he trudged along he could see that the light in the window was off. Retreated to their bed, exhausted from discussing all possibilities, rehearsing every response, Wilf thought to himself. Adrienne with all the answers, the sailor following along. And now two pairs of eyes staring into the dark. Sleep impossible.

Wilf opened the car door, eased himself in and was about to turn the ignition on when he caught sight of a shadow passing quickly in front of him. The passenger door opened and Adrienne slid in.

She closed the door. The interior light went off again. They sat there together staring ahead for a moment as if they were hesitating before embarking on a long-planned trip.

"Hello," Adrienne finally said.

"Hello."

"What are you doing?"

"Nothing."

"Yes you are. You're watching me."

Wilf turned to look at her, her face floating in some faint reflected light. "Is that what you're thinking? No. I have a difficult time sleeping, that's all, so I drive around."

"I know who you are."

"I introduced myself the other day. When I bought that sweater. Is that what you mean?" Wilf waited. "Or do you mean, you know who my father is?"

There was no discernible reaction.

"I'm not blind." Adrienne turned toward him. Her eyes were hidden in two dark whirls of shadows. She looked blind.

"What do you mean?"

"I saw you watching in the hotel."

Wilf glanced toward the extension across the street. The blind had been pushed aside, a pale face was pressed up against the shadowy window.

"And now here you are again," Adrienne said.

"I guess I'm not as inconspicuous as I thought."

"Are you curious? Is that what it is?"

"Curious?"

"Yes. Curious. About me?"

Yes, Wilf thought, Jesus Christ, yes.

Adrienne turned her small body toward him. She'd only taken the time to throw her coat loosely over her shoulders and as she moved it pulled open a little. In the dark there was no telling what she had on. Or didn't have on. "Is it true?" she said.

"Is what true?"

"About that crazy will. Did Sam actually give that will to your father?"

It was all Wilf could do, to keep his eyes on her face. "Yes."

"But I thought it was a joke. It was supposed to be a joke. I told him to throw it away."

"Why?"

"Because I don't want anything!"

"You don't?"

"No! That's what his son was going on about, too. He'd gotten the idea from somewhere that Sam had left everything to me. He was really being nasty about it. And then you came in pretending to be interested in buying a sweater."

"And that's when you knew it had to be true."

"That stupid will! I couldn't believe it. I just thought it was another one of his jokes!"

Wilf looked up at the window again. Her boyfriend was still there. "Was that the first time you'd heard he'd died, Adrienne? When Frank Cruikshank came into the store? You were putting on a brave face."

"You were the one who found him. Weren't you? You were putting on a brave face, too."

"So I suppose you don't want to be the beneficiary of his will?" Her eyes were still hidden. His hand ached to slip inside her coat.

"Can I refuse to accept it?"

"You could sign everything back to his family, I suppose. Probably there'd have to be an exchange with some kind of reasonable value. Otherwise you'd be contravening his last will and testament."

Adrienne smiled her quiet smile. "You've become obsessed about something. Do you want to tell me what it is?"

"It seems an exceptional will, that's all. You're not a relative. And it's a large estate."

"Is there something wrong with it, I mean legally, besides that it's going to an O'Dell? Is there anything else wrong?"

"It's not wrong. That it's going to an O'Dell."

"Do you know what I think?"

"What?"

"I think that you, Wilf McLauchlin, have a dirty mind. It's all in your filthy dirty mind, what you're thinking."

"You don't know what I'm thinking."

"Yes, I do."

Adrienne pulled back from him a little, her eyes moving out from the shadows now. Wilf was surprised to see that they were red and swollen. She looked like she'd been crying for days.

"I'll tell you what it was since you're so curious. And then maybe you'll stop following me. He was kind. That's all. Like a father. More than my own father ever was. And I ran errands for him and I did all the little things I could think of just to make his days easier and happier. Because he actually cared for me. And that was all there was. There was nothing else. There was nothing wrong! Have you ever heard of Christian love? Pureness and sweetness and thankfulness? Have you ever heard of that?"

The light flashed on as Adrienne pushed the door open, the door slammed shut and she was gone.

Wilf watched her run across the road holding her coat tightly against her small body.

He looked up at the window.

The face had disappeared.

CHAPTER EIGHT

There was no light on in the study. Wilf left it that way, felt for another bottle of rye he knew was in the liquor cabinet, tucked it under his arm and made his way up the stairs.

He sat down on the edge of his bed, snapped the light on, opened the bottle and took a drink. He looked around the room. He took another drink.

This was the real world. Maybe he should try to stay in it. Cling to it with all his might. Two chairs. The dresser. The outside wall. It was three bricks thick. His father had told him that a long time ago. To keep the cold wind out. The elements. They seemed to be clawing outside right now.

Wilf took another drink.

It wasn't beyond the realm of possibility that Adrienne was innocent. Maybe the old man had asked her to make a copy of his key for reasons of his own and she was going up to Galt anyway, it was just another errand to run. Another one of her Christian errands. That was all it was.

Wilf thought about his sleeping pills. They were waiting for him, sitting inside the bathroom cabinet. Maybe he'd try three.

She could hardly have stopped the old man from making a will, if that's what he'd wanted to do.

Wilf began to pull off his clothes, struggling one-handed out of everything until the only thing he had left on was the sling that supported his arm.

He could see Adrienne's eyes, fresh tears shining.

Dirty filthy mind, she'd said. He should be ashamed.

He did feel ashamed.

Wilf stood in the yellowish light from his lamp and looked at his reflection in the mirror. He unbuttoned his sling, his arm dropped limply to his side. His left shoulder and his left hip and leg were rippled with scars. Some places were shiny as silk, some veined and scaled and faintly blue.

"Hello, monster," Wilf said.

✳ ✳ ✳

"Wake the hell up. Come on!" Andy seemed to be pleading. He seemed to be pushing Wilf on his shoulder. "Jesus, you must have tied a good one on last night."

Wilf opened his eyes a little. The morning light hurt. His head hurt.

Andy looked to have a suit on under his overcoat. Wilf could see a multicoloured tie dangling down inches from his face. He could see the half-empty rye bottle nestled on the pillow beside him.

"Mmmm," Wilf said and struggled to sit up. He held his arm against his chest so Andy wouldn't have to see it flopping around.

"I knocked. I yelled. Nothing worked," Andy was saying, looking a little embarrassed now. Or shocked. He walked over to the bedroom window and peered out as if he'd just remembered that something of extremely compelling interest was going on outside.

Wilf dragged his legs over the edge of the bed.

"I came to tell you about that pill bottle," Andy said.

"What time is it?"

"Almost noon."

"Why are you dressed up?"

"Well, there's lots of excitement. Some bigwigs are in town." Andy couldn't contain himself, he turned back to Wilf. "Jesus, don't you want to know about that pill bottle, for chrissake?"

Wilf reached for his underwear. It was lying on the floor.

"Wilf, you were right. They found prints on it that matched up with her prints on the glass. She had to be there that night. She was there!"

Andy's face had gone bright red. Wilf hadn't seen him look so excited since grade school.

"It only proves she was in the house." Wilf's throat felt raw. "It doesn't prove anything else." He tried to measure his own feelings but he couldn't reach them.

"Wilf, after she went to work this morning the OPP picked up her boyfriend. He's already crying his eyes out. He says she made him do it. It was all her idea." Andy headed for the door. "I just had to tell you. You're a hero, Wilf. I'm a hero, too. The Chief wants me downtown to take part in everything."

"What about Adrienne?"

"She doesn't know anything yet." Andy disappeared into the hall.

Wilf sat there and listened to him clumping down the stairs.

There goes a happy man, he thought to himself.

❄ ❄ ❄

Adrienne was looking after a customer when Wilf came into the shop. She glanced his way, actually smiled a little and then went back to talking to a very large woman who was asking about a winter sale.

"We've already had our sale," Adrienne was telling her.

"But it's still January," the woman countered.

Wilf circled the racks of clothes. He had to push through to make any headway. A sea of women's dresses and skirts, slacks and jackets. The warm smell of perfume. He could see Adrienne keeping an eye on him. She was telling the woman that she should come back the next day and talk to the owner. She was almost certain something could be done about the price of a certain winter coat.

The woman finally seemed satisfied. She left the shop. The bell over the door tinkled behind her.

"Hello again," Wilf said. All he could see of Adrienne was her face and her shoulders. She looked frozen there, marooned, standing among the racks of clothes.

"Hi," she said.

"I just came to apologize for last night."

"That's all right."

"I just wanted to see you again." And now he knew what he felt about her and about what she'd done because the feeling was familiar to him. The same feeling he had felt himself after a victorious sortie. An engagement. A kill.

Despair.

Adrienne looked at him more closely. He was making her uneasy. She glanced toward the door. "I'm working," she said.

She knew something was wrong. Wilf could see it in her eyes. Something had gone terribly wrong.

"I'll get out of your way." That was all Wilf could think to say. He pushed himself back through the clothes and went out the door. He walked along Main Street. The air felt warmer than it had for some time. A real January thaw. Rows of icicles swayed precariously down from the eaves above the stores. Water was dripping everywhere.

He could see an OPP cruiser sitting in front of the town hall. The Chief of Police and two men he didn't recognize appeared out of a lane that led back toward the police station. They began to cross the street.

Wilf cut across the street, too, going the other way. He made himself wait until he'd reached the far side before he turned around. The Chief was opening the front door of the dress shop. The three men disappeared inside.

Wilf had to lean against a wall to steady himself.

Some young man was sauntering down the sidewalk toward him, dishevelled-looking, workboots toed out, his hair a wild auburn mop. He grinned at Wilf as he walked by just as if he knew him.

Wilf looked back across the street.

The dress shop and the stores to either side seemed to rise up off the ground and move in a gentle, undulating wave.

And all of Main Street swam in his eyes.

CHAPTER NINE

Several weeks had passed by and Wilf was feeling better. Having his father back in the house had helped. Avoiding as much as he could the town's congratulatory attention after the arrests had helped. And regular exercise, lots of cold air, walking up and down the snowbanked and sun-blinding streets as far as his bad leg would allow. His physiotherapist back in Southend-on-Sea would have been proud.

But mainly it had to do with accepting the obvious, that he was one of the unlucky ones, one of those who had been affected too deeply by the war. It wasn't like it was such a rarity, there were enough of them around but still it felt like a shameful weakness. Which was only pride talking. And ignorance. But he was over that now.

The man he'd seen in Cruikshank's backyard had been nothing more than a hallucination, no matter how vibrant he looked, no matter how much more there he seemed than the trees and the snow and the railway tracks. And Cruikshank sitting frozen in his tub had nothing to do with any freezing experiment that had taken place in Germany. He'd obviously read about that experiment somewhere else and everything had gotten jumbled up in his mind.

Wilf continued his walks and tried not to think about Adrienne. He couldn't manage it, though. He kept seeing her walking along the railway tracks, letting herself in through the side door, standing in the kitchen as quiet as a dream. And why wouldn't the old man write out a will to sustain those nights of trembling, to feel once again her hands moving over his parched body, her cool breath against his skin? A gift from God. Angel in the moonlight. Miraculous midnight drug.

And what had been going on in Adrienne's mind? A growing anticipation of the final act that no second thoughts could derail, an anticipation that began to turn into desire that began to turn into lust to see the old man's face floating under the water, his white hair streaming, bubbles of amazement flying out of his mouth.

"Guess what the Chief showed me?" Stuffed from his Sunday dinner, Andy leaned back in his easy chair, king of all he surveyed. The town council had presented him with a glowing commendation for his outstanding role in the Adrienne O'Dell case and the Chief had moved him up in rank and pay. He was Sergeant Andrew Creighton now.

"What's that?" Wilf had eased himself down on the carpet in Andy and Linda's living room and was beginning to help Carmen put together her *Jack and the Bean Stalk* jigsaw puzzle. As soon as Andy's promotion had been announced Linda had put her arms around Wilf's neck, kissed him and told him that she owed him a lifetime of suppers. He'd just collected on one.

"The official statements."

"What statements?"

"The ones Adrienne O'Dell and Tom Elbee made."

Adrienne and her boyfriend were being held in the county jail some distance away and their trial wouldn't begin until late summer at the earliest. Whenever it did convene Wilf knew he'd be one of the Crown's main witnesses testifying to all he'd observed and all the bizarre actions he'd taken.

He continued to help Carmen search through the puzzle pieces.

"She's saying more or less the same thing that her boyfriend said, only the other way around. The idea to murder Cruikshank was all Tom Elbee's idea, she only went along with it because she was afraid of him. Afraid for her own life. He was a murderous son of a bitch, according to her. She was terrified."

"Andy," Linda said, "will you please remember that there are two pairs of little ears in this room?"

Six-year-old Carmen didn't seem to be listening, she was too busy trying to find a piece for the giant's nose. Davey, a year-and-a-half older and alerted now by his mother, looked up from his comic book.

Andy lowered his voice. "Elbee says as soon as he'd returned from overseas she was all over him about that will Cruikshank had written out, telling him exactly what they should do and how easy it would be, how the old man had treated her so badly, how he was still taking advantage of her, how he deserved to die, going over and over it day and night until he was half-crazy, until he couldn't think straight."

"Andy," Linda said. "Stop it."

"Sorry, Dear," Andy winked at Wilf and began to pat himself down in search of his cigarettes. "Anyway, you can see there seems to be a large difference of opinion."

"I can see that," Wilf said.

"Makes you wonder whose idea it really was."

Wilf found the missing piece for the giant's nose, handed it to Carmen and kept his silence. He knew as well as he knew his own name whose idea it had been. He was carrying her around inside himself now, feeling everything she had felt every step of the way. It had been Adrienne's.

By the end of February Wilf had talked to the Dean at the college of law he was planning to attend and to the Registrar's Office. It seemed that rejoining his law studies in mid-semester was not out of the question. At the very least he could monitor some classes. Managing to get this much finally organized put him in an exuberant mood. On impulse he asked Carole out for supper and a movie. As usual, Carole was typing.

"When?"

"Well, I don't know. How about tonight?"

"Tonight?" She continued on with her typing.

"Unless you've got something else planned." Wilf sat down at Dorothy Dale's desk. As was often the case he'd been late coming in to work. "Or we could go out Saturday night instead."

Carole continued to finish the paragraph she was working on; it gave her more time to think. She assumed he was talking about going to Brantford since they didn't have a movie theatre in town and she was wondering how they'd traverse the seven miles. On several occasions she'd overheard heated conversations between Wilf and his father concerning Wilf's continued use of the car. Apparently Mr. McLauchlin didn't think that driving with just one arm and a damaged leg was such a good idea. Not to mention the absence of a licence.

Carole stopped typing. "Okay."

"I'll pick you up at six. The movie doesn't start until eight. That should give us lots of time."

"What's playing?"

"I have no idea. I should have looked it up."

Carole smiled. "Sounds like fun," she said.

They ate supper at a busy restaurant just around the corner from the theatre. Carole had recovered more quickly from the Adrienne O'Dell affair than Wilf had, though she'd been deeply shaken by the thought that someone she actually knew could do such a thing, and that what Wilf had surmised was going on between old Mr. Cruikshank and Adrienne, what she herself had half-suspected, was apparently true. Everyone was still talking about it. She was trying to put it out of her mind.

Carole took off her coat in the crowded dining room. Wilf could see that she'd worn the pink wool sweater he'd given her.

Her cheeks coloured a little.

"It looks good," Wilf said.

"I don't usually wear pink. It makes me look five years old."

"No, it doesn't."

They sat down in a booth facing each other. Sooner or later I'll have to try and see if I work, Wilf was thinking to himself, and I might as well try with Carole as with anyone else. He smiled at her. Carole smiled back. She picked up a menu and began to read through it.

Her grey eyes are beautiful, anyway, Wilf thought to himself. He did an inventory. Cheekbones assertive but at the same time as delicately arched as a small bird's wings. Long ascetic face in a battle with her lips that were nicely rounded and sensuous when they weren't being skeptical. And yes, promising things that being a proper girl her mouth would never say.

Wilf could feel a ripple of excitement tickle across his stomach. It seemed faint though, more like a memory of good times past than anything else. It felt more like fear.

Anyway, Carole would be understanding if things didn't turn out the way they were supposed to, that was the type of person she seemed to be. And whatever disappointment ensued she'd be discreet about it, no one else would ever know. She'd been well trained by Dorothy Dale.

Wilf smiled a little to himself.

"What are you thinking about?" Carole asked over her menu.

"Nothing. How nice this is, being with you. We should have done this before."

Carole regarded him with her light-grey eyes. Wilf had no idea what she was thinking. Possibly about her soldier fiancé. And betrayal.

"I'm really looking forward to the movie," she said.

After they'd had their supper and were lining up outside the theatre, Carole observed that most of the people who'd been eating in the restaurant were lining up for the same movie.

Apparently this was a good sign. Wilf had paid for supper and was going to treat her to the movie and so Carole insisted on paying for the popcorn and the soft drinks. They climbed up the carpeted stairs to the loges and as soon as they sat down Wilf pulled out a flask from inside his winter coat and spiked her drink. He topped up his, as well.

They'd made the trip down to Brantford without too much difficulty. Wilf had perfected a method of shifting gears while bracing his sling against the steering wheel. It began to snow on the drive back home. Carole watched the large flakes race through the headlights and tried not to look too concerned. They discussed the movie. Carole thought Deanna Durbin was terrific. Wilf thought she was a little put on.

"She's supposed to be put on. It's a comedy."

"A comedy, a mystery and a musical. A weird combination. I don't know," Wilf said.

"And a romance. It was very romantic."

"If you believed it."

"I believed it." Carole began to fiddle with the radio, spinning the dial through all the talk searching for some music. "I think you really enjoyed it. You just don't want to say." She settled on a live broadcast from a ballroom in a fancy hotel somewhere in the United States. Lots of saxophones. "Men don't want to be seen liking anything that's romantic."

"Hold the steering wheel, will you?" Wilf said.

Carole held the wheel. Wilf pulled out his flask and offered her a drink. She took the flask and Wilf grabbed the wheel again.

"This is illegal, you know. Your father would be very disappointed." She took a healthy sip. "Anyway, she's a great singer."

"Who?"

"Deanna Durbin."

It was almost twelve o'clock by the time Wilf parked the car in front of Carole's house. A few doors down and through a curtain of falling snow he could see three rows of lights. One of the several large textile mills in town was running a full night shift.

On the way back they'd stopped at a restaurant to share a plate of fries. Wilf talked about going back to college, that it was all settled now, he could resume anytime. And he told her that once he'd finished his studies he wasn't too keen about returning to McLauchlin and McLauchlin. He'd been thinking instead about working in the city for a while and then travelling.

Carole told him that she'd been thinking about travelling, too. She liked the idea of being an independent businesswoman making her solitary way in the world. She'd been mulling over the possibility of applying for a job in Montreal. Or maybe New York City.

"Not Toronto?"

"No."

They'd sat there by the window watching the odd car go by and they'd agreed that settling down wasn't for either one of them, that they'd probably turn out to be a pair of rolling stones.

"I had a nice time," Carole said, addressing the rows of lights in the mill.

"So did I."

"Are you coming into the office tomorrow?"

"Maybe."

Carole's home was sitting in darkness on the edge of the smaller of the two rivers that ran through the town. Wilf reached over and touched her hair. Her eyes seemed to wince a little as if it hurt her to be touched. She met him halfway when he leaned forward, though. Her lips were soft and just as warm and inviting as he'd anticipated. She opened them a little.

She's done this before, Wilf thought, amusing himself. His hand trailed down her cheek. The back of his fingers touched her soft neck.

"Good night, Wilf," Carole said, and smiled at him and got out of the car.

Carole's bedroom light flared on.

Duncan pressed against the tree he'd been standing behind. Darkness swirled around and around. Snow fell down and hissed false insinuations in his ears.

Everything was wrong. Everything was muddled up. He pressed his forehead against the bark of the tree until it hurt. He couldn't go home.

He knew who he was. He was Duncan Laurence Getty. He was just like all the soldiers who'd come back from overseas. He was just like all the men who worked in the bush.

Duncan looked back toward the house and thought of his own house in the country sitting like a giant ghost in the dark. There was a light in a window out there, too. As he thought about that light, he trembled.

He wanted to see Carole, her reassuring face, her slim familiar body. He knew exactly what most of her sweaters looked like. Her blouses. Her dresses and skirts. He knew them all off by heart.

A branch cracked sharply somewhere. Ice creaked on the river. What if someone was coming?

It didn't matter. He had to stay.

He had to watch Carole for as long as he could.

As soon as Wilf came through the front door of the office the next morning Carole stopped typing.

That's an improvement, Wilf thought.

"You're late," she said.

"How do you know you're not early?"

"Because I can tell time."

Wilf sat down on the chair by the door and struggled to take off his galoshes. Despite her tone of voice he could see she was smiling to herself. "I think we should go out Saturday. What do you think?"

"This Saturday?"

"Sure. Why not?"

"Where?"

"Well, we could go to a dance."

"Oh?" Carole tried not to look too surprised. Or alarmed.

"We could go up to Preston. Andy says they have dances up there every Saturday night. He and Linda go up there all the time." Wilf took off his coat. "What do you say? Want to cut a rug?"

"Okay." Carole tried to do a fast calculation. When was the last time she'd been to a dance? Nineteen forty-one.

"They play all the big band music up there. Miller. Dorsey." Wilf limped toward her. "You'll be all right."

Carole, looking slightly alarmed, glanced toward his father's office as if to warn him.

Wilf could see his father looking over some papers through the open office door. His dark hair was peppered with grey now and he was beginning to stoop just a little but nevertheless, Wilf thought with some pride, he still radiated the same precise and scholarly vigour he always had. Wilf walked into the hall.

"Good morning," he said, leaning through the doorway.

"Is it still morning?" Clarence McLauchlin replied. "Why don't you move into Grandpa's office?"

"You keep asking me that. It doesn't make any sense, I'll be leaving soon."

"But until you do. I don't like you sitting out in front. You're not a clerk."

"Carole doesn't like me sitting out there, either."

"Carole's got good sense."

"Anyway, I just came in to say that I think I'll work up at the house today. I want to call Admissions again and I need to track down some people I know and figure out where I'm going to be staying."

"Isn't it too late for this semester?"

"No, it's not. I told you that. You know I told you that."

"Did you?" Clarence sat down at his desk and put aside the papers he'd been examining. "I guess you did. But I've been thinking, Wilf, maybe a little more rest wouldn't be the worst idea. It's been great to have you back and there's no need to push things, is there?"

"I've been resting for a year and a half."

"Why don't you start in the fall? Makes a lot more sense. Besides you've got all that nastiness in court coming up this summer. We should start talking about that."

"It's okay. I'll just be one of a dozen witnesses. I know what I'm going to do."

Clarence leaned back in his armchair. "What?"

"Give my testimony as clearly and simply as I can and get back to Toronto."

"Adrienne O'Dell's lawyer might have a few thoughts about your 'clear and simple and getting back to Toronto' plan."

"Dad, they confessed. It's over."

"Is it? It's never that simple, Wilf." His expression looked a little pained. "Anyway, whatever you think is best. I mean, about going off to Toronto."

"I'll keep thinking about it," Wilf said and forced a smile. "I'll see you up at the house."

The rest of that day and the following day Wilf busied himself organizing his move. On Friday morning he dropped in to the police station to ask Andy if he and Linda were going up to that Saturday's dance. Sergeant Creighton was working days now.

"Having trouble getting a babysitter." Andy was sitting at

his desk entering something in a ledger, "My mother's refusing to come over since Davey swore at her."

Wilf sat down at Ted Bolton's empty desk. "How about Linda's parents?"

"They're going away. Why? Do you want to babysit?"

"No. Carole and I thought we'd go up to the dance."

Andy's face broke into a grin. "Carole Birley?"

"Anything wrong with that?"

"No. That's great. Carole Birley. She has a nice way about her. Terrific legs."

"Oh?"

Wilf and Andy looked toward the doors. A clatter of boots was coming down the hall stairs. Two boys pushed through the swinging office doors, came up to the counter and peered over it. Their winter hats were on crooked, their faces flushed, sweat was trickling down their cheeks, snot bubbling out of their noses.

"What's the matter, boys?" Andy said. "Somebody trying to give you a bath?"

The two boys stared back at him.

"Is there a bear chasing you? Did you hold up a bank?"

"Cline's bush," the taller one finally blurted out.

"What about it?"

"We found something."

"Annie got sick," the other boy chimed in. He looked a little sick himself.

"His sister puked. Because of all the blood."

Something jarred, came loose in Wilf's chest. He pushed out of the chair.

"Is she hurt?" Andy asked. "Is that the problem?"

The boys shook their heads. "There's a man out there. He's in Cline's bush."

"Well, who the hell is it?"

"He's under the snow," the taller one said.

"Is he dead?" Wilf heard himself ask.

"Yes," the boy said.

Andy hurried across the street to inform Constable Bolton, who was eating lunch at The Palms, that he was taking the one and only cruiser out to Cline's bush to do some investigating. Meanwhile Wilf stayed with the boys.

"Are you fellows from around here?" he asked.

The two boys were perched on wooden chairs now, fidgeting around and looking uncomfortable. They nodded.

"From out in the country or from here in town?"

"Town," the taller one said, eyeing Wilf's trussed-up arm, his bad leg.

"This man you found, you said he was lying under the snow?"

They nodded in unison.

"Could you see his face?"

"No," the taller one said.

Wilf rode beside Andy. The two boys sat in the back. It had occurred to Wilf that he could have refused to go. In fact Andy hadn't even asked him. He'd left it open. It was Wilf's decision. And once again, just the same as with Adrienne O'Dell, he'd felt compelled to go.

They drove toward the sun, passed by a snow-filled gravel pit and turned on to a narrow side road that looked more like a frozen stream as it wound its way through high banks of snow. Once over a slight rise it straightened out and shimmered off into the distance.

Andy inched along toward a dark block of trees. A few youngsters were standing in a tight cluster in the distance. "Want to stay in the car? The snow will be deep here."

Wilf shook his head.

The cruiser slid to a stop. Wilf opened the passenger door and got out. A sharp wind, unnoticed in town, was blowing across the fields. It caught Wilf and skidded him back against the car. The young girl and two boys standing at the side of the road looked half-frozen. The only thing they seemed able to move were their frightened eyes.

"Okay," Andy's voice went flying away in the wind, "I only want one person to show me where this man is. And that person will be you." He pointed to the taller of the two boys who'd been sitting in the cruiser. The other children didn't look too disappointed.

"Are you okay?" Wilf asked the girl. Though she was shivering, she set her little jaw and nodded yes. "The kids should sit in the car. It's warmer," Wilf called out to Andy, who was already wading through the snow toward the edge of the woods.

"As long as they don't break anything," Andy shouted back.

Wilf opened the back door and the youngsters piled in. "We won't be long," he said.

Despite the bright sun, the air seemed gloomy once Wilf was in amongst the trees. He struggled to catch up, following Andy's and the boy's tracks, blundering into branches and bushes, stumbling over hidden logs. After a short distance he had to sit down on a snow-covered stump to rest.

Treetops creaked high above his head. Empty corridors were leading off in various directions. An abandoned house, Wilf thought. Windowless and roofless. He looked up through the tossing branches into a high blue sky. It looked familiar.

Wilf walked on, circling around a large brush pile, half rolling himself over a massive log, breathing hard again. He could see the boy a short distance off, and then he could see Andy, too. They were standing motionless on top of a little rise.

Wilf worked his way closer. The snowy slope looked like it was speckled with red paint. He walked past branches jewelled with drops of frozen blood. He could hear Andy telling the boy to wait at the cruiser. The boy walked by without a word and then began to run.

Andy was standing in the centre of a dark crimson circle. He was staring down at a protruding hand. "The snow's not that deep here." He seemed puzzled.

Wilf didn't reply.

"They were trying to bury him, I guess." Andy knelt down and pushed the frozen hand with his gloved hand. The surrounding red crust heaved and cracked a little. He took it by the wrist. A detached arm came up out of the snow.

"Jesus H. Christ," Andy said, standing up quickly but keeping his grip.

A piece of frozen red muscle and white sinews hung stiffly out of the severed end, the rest of the arm was wrapped in a dirty coat sleeve.

"I shouldn't have picked it up. Shit! Where the hell's the rest of him?"

Andy began to peer through the trees as if he expected to see a one-armed man looking back at him. There was no one in sight. He crouched back down and laid the arm as carefully as he could back into its outline in the snow.

"That's two," Wilf said.

"Two what?"

"Homicides."

"We don't know that yet. Do we? Back up, for chrissake, you're making a mess."

Wilf backed up a little, though he wasn't the one making the mess.

Andy began to circle around the rise. "Look at this," he called out. He was standing near a deep trough through the snow. It looked like a wide red ribbon winding its way through the trees. There were boot tracks in the middle of it.

Wilf pointed his cane off to the side. "Two more sets of tracks over there."

Andy hurried along the trough's edge like he thought he might catch up, running through the brush and the trees. Wilf limped along behind. After a while he could see that Andy had come to a stop. He walked up to him.

A man was curled up asleep, at least that's how it looked to Wilf. His overcoat was pulled up around his ears and the small hollow he was lying in seemed to be a perfect fit. Andy crouched down and lifted his head a little. The face, grey and covered with crystals of frost, sparkled up at them.

"Never seen him before," Andy said.

He looked about thirty to Wilf, a small man, almost tiny. The stump of his right arm was hidden beneath his chest.

"Not much blood around here," Andy said.

"He didn't have much left."

"Split lip. Nose flattened, too. One eyelid swollen. Whoever they were, they laid one hell of a beating on him." He looked up at Wilf and grinned. "I guess that would have been before they chopped off his arm. A bit redundant, afterward." He turned back to the little man. "Jesus, another homicide. Can you believe this? When did it snow last?"

Wilf could hear the trees creaking high over his head again. A familiar panic was flying around, flying around. "Two nights ago. It snowed the night Carole and I went to the movies."

"There's no snow on this guy, though."

"No."

"But his arm was under the snow. I mean, his other arm."

"Because of the blood. It was warm. It melted the snow. The arm sank down, the blood froze over it."

"Yeah, right," Andy said.

There I go again, Wilf thought to himself. It seemed the most obvious observation in the world to make and as soon as he'd made it, he began to feel calmer.

Andy eased the man's head back down in its place. "Don't mess anything up," he said.

He had to report to the Chief of Police. The Chief, in turn, would be calling in the Ontario Provincial Police. Once again.

Wilf said he'd wait until Andy drove all the kids into town and then returned with Ted Bolton to cordon off that part of the woods. The crime scene. "I'll be standing guard somewhere between the body and the arm."

Andy looked at him. Wilf smiled. Andy disappeared through the trees.

Wilf turned and stared down at the little man. He looked even more deeply asleep than he had before. Was he already dead when he was dragged to this spot, Wilf wondered to himself, or did it take some time for him to die? Quivering all alone here like a leaf in a wind. Looking up to the sky?

Wilf stared at the three sets of tracks leading off through the snow. He decided to follow them.

After a short distance they made a right turn and headed back toward the road. Wilf came to the edge of the trees, slid down a steep slope and struggled up onto the gleaming strip of ice again.

He looked back to where Andy had parked the cruiser. It was gone. The three men's tracks had disappeared, as well. He walked along the road for a little while but there were no more tracks to be seen in either direction. They could have climbed into a parked car. Or walked along the icy road for miles.

Wilf walked back to where he'd come out of the woods, struggled up the slope again and began to retrace his steps. There was something unconvincing about the trail of boots he'd been following. He'd felt it all along. When he reached a small clearing where the tracks were particularly distinct in the snow he crouched down to have a closer look. He examined the indented mark of each heel. The depression of each toe. He looked up.

A young boy was standing just outside the ring of trees watching him.

"Hello."

The boy didn't reply.

"Didn't you go back with Andy?" Wilf said, although he knew he wasn't one of those children.

The boy began to move away.

Wilf got up and followed, trying to close the gap. Somehow the boy was maintaining the same distance between them. And then the boy began to run. Wilf ran, too, hobbling through the trees, black trunks flickering by, dark and closed like doors. Faster. And faster.

Wilf stumbled and fell. When he looked up the boy had stopped and was watching him again. And now Wilf could see for certain what he'd thought he'd seen. The boy had hardly anything on at all, only a light striped jersey and torn striped pants. His feet were bare. He was standing on top of the snow.

Wilf groaned and turned his face. And crawled away.

Prosecutor: And what was the purpose?
Witness: The purpose was to develop procedures to facilitate the regeneration of bones, muscles and nerves during transplant operations. This was in the interest of our severely wounded soldiers.
Prosecutor: And how were these experiments conducted?
Witness: Inmates were selected from the general camp population. Arms were removed, including the shoulder blades, legs were removed at the hips, sometimes sections of bone or just muscles and nerves were also removed.
Prosecutor: And what happened to these experimental subjects afterwards?
Witness: If the donor inmates survived their operations, they were killed by means of Evipan injections.

Wilf stared down at a grainy black-and-white photograph at the bottom of the transcript. A metal bin with rubber wheels was sitting in what looked like a hospital corridor. It was full to overflowing with severed arms and severed legs.

He'd known right away who that boy was and therefore he'd known who the man in Cruikshank's backyard must be, too. Like everyone else he'd seen enough pictures in newspapers and in *LIFE* magazine to last a lifetime. Inmates escaped from some camp. In Germany. Or Poland. Somewhere.

Except they hadn't escaped. They couldn't have. They weren't real.

When Wilf had been dropped off in front of his house he'd gone straight into the study. It was the sight of the boy that had sent him back to the transcripts. It was the sight of the hapless arm in its sleeve in the snow. His father had listed the experiment under *E).*

Wilf walked out to the kitchen and picked up the phone.

"Number, please," Nancy Dearborn said.

"I want to call long distance."

"Oh hi, Wilf. How are things?"

"Hi, Nancy. Good. How are things with you?"

"Well, nothing much new. You know how it is."

Obviously she hasn't heard about the body in the woods. Amazing, Wilf thought. But then it hadn't been more than a half an hour since the Chief of Police had arrived at the murder scene and Andy had driven him home.

"I hear you and Carole went to the movies the other night."

"Did you?"

"*Lady on a Train*, wasn't it? I haven't seen it. Is it any good?"

"So so."

"Just so so? The movie or the whole evening?"

Wilf braced the phone between the wall and his ear, refused to answer and fished out his wallet from his trouser pocket.

"I think I'll go down and see it for myself," Nancy said.

Wilf plucked out a worn piece of paper and let the wallet drop to the floor. "I want to call long distance."

"I'll have to connect you to the long-distance operator then."

"All right," Wilf said and wondered if she was going to mention the upcoming dance in Preston. Instead she connected him with long distance, who connected him to Jersey City, New Jersey. A woman's voice came on the line.

"Hello?" She sounded exasperated.

Wilf could hear a child crying in the background. "Is Michael Pascani there?"

"Michael Pascani?" More exasperation.

"Well, Mick. Mick Pascani. I'm a friend of his. From the Army. Not the Army, exactly. The Air Force. The Canadian Air Force?"

"I thought you were a salesman."

"No, ma'am."

"You're not Wilf McLauchlin, are you?"

"I guess I am."

"Really? No! My god, I can't believe it! It's so good to hear from you!"

Wilf felt such a wave of gratitude it almost overpowered him. "I'm glad to hear you say that."

"Well, of course. Mick talks about you all the time!"

"I think about him a lot. He saved my life."

"God, he's going to be so sorry he missed you! He's working out of town, Wilf. He'll be calling tonight. Can I give him your number?"

"Sure. You bet. By the way, he talked about you all the time, too. Peggy this, Peggy that."

"Oh, I'm sure he did!"

"He did. You and Mick Junior. I guess that would be Mick Junior making all the noise."

"That's him all right. And believe it or not, there's another Mick or Mary on the way."

"No kidding? That's great!"

"Yes, well actually it is. It is great."

"He came to visit me in France too, just before he was sent home. Did he tell you?"

"Sure. He told me everything. You two must have hit it off."

"He has lots of stories."

Peggy laughed. "I know!"

"And I had lots of time to listen."

"A captive audience, he would have loved that! How are you anyway? Can you travel? Can you come down to see us? I mean, that wasn't the right word. Sorry. You know what I mean, though."

"My eyes?"

"Yes. I'm sorry."

"No, they're fine. That's part of my news. They got better. In fact, not long after Mick left for home I could see just as well as ever."

"My god, that's a real miracle."

"Yeah. Seemed like it. I don't even know what Mick looks like. I'd recognize his voice anywhere though."

"Well, you'll just have to come down here and see his ugly puss for yourself."

Wilf gave her his number and Peggy told him to stay close to the phone, Mick would be calling him sometime that night for sure.

Wilf said he would and hung up.

He sat down at the table and stared at the wall. It wasn't just that he was seeing people. The more he thought about it, the more certain he was becoming. He'd seen the man in Cruikshank's yard and that boy before.

Wilf looked over at his wallet. The contents lay strewn all over the floor.

CHAPTER TEN

It was just before noon when Wilf called a taxi and headed downtown. For some reason he wanted to see Carole. He didn't know why exactly. He knew it wasn't to tell her about that boy. Or the man. And he wasn't sure how much he'd tell her about those three tracks in the woods either. He just wanted to hear her voice.

He got off in front of the office. He could see his father through the window. He walked past the iron gate and stood out in the tiny yard. His father and Carole and two clients were discussing something. When Carole looked up he gave her a little wave. He could see her eyes widen in surprise.

He smiled and walked away.

He felt somewhat better. Lighter, anyway. He felt light.

Constable Ted Bolton was sitting at his desk.

"Hi there, Ted." Wilf walked around the counter, "Where's Andy?"

"Over at the newspaper office getting some photographs developed."

"Great." Wilf sat down behind Andy's desk and tried not to look strange, though he was feeling a little strange.

"Another one, eh?" Bolton said.

His long bony face looks like a sad horse, Wilf thought to himself, a horse with sliding eyes, a horse not to be trusted.

"What are the odds against two homicides in the space of one month?" Bolton asked.

"High," Wilf said.

"There's a forensic team driving in from Hamilton this time, as well as a couple of detectives. We're becoming quite the centre of attention."

"Yes, we are."

Bolton began to search through some papers. "Since you're here you might as well fill this out." He got up from his desk and put a form down in front of Wilf. "You know the routine by now."

Wilf stared at it. A place for his name, address, phone number, occupation, birth date, and below a large empty space with the heading: *Explain In Your Own Words Exactly What Took Place.*

He'd seen the form before, when he'd written out his statement concerning Adrienne O'Dell. He'd used four extra sheets of paper that time.

Wilf picked up one of Andy's pens and wrote his name, his father's address and his father's phone number across the top.

"We're all waiting," Bolton said. He was settling back down at his desk.

"For what?"

"For you and Andy to solve this one, too. Maybe Andy will make Deputy Mayor this time. Or fall flat on his face. Just kidding," Bolton said.

There was a clattering on the stairs and Andy came hurrying in carrying a large yellow envelope. "I really should have been a photographer," he said, spreading out a series of shiny photographs along the length of the counter. "They're still a little damp. I thought you said you wanted to have a rest."

"I changed my mind."

"Don't get too excited," Bolton spoke up. "The OPP's been called in and that'll be that for the Hardy Boys. Right?"

Andy gave Bolton a look as if he were thinking of pulling his newly acquired rank and giving him a dressing down, but then he seemed to change his mind. "I know all about the Ontario Provincial Police," he said.

"Let's see what you've got." Bolton got up from his desk and ambled over to the counter.

Wilf followed him over.

"The Chief and I figure all his clothes are hand-me-downs. Looks like it, anyway. Bad teeth. And skinny as a starved rabbit," Andy said.

"You should have opened up his eyes," Bolton remarked.

"Why?"

"If you want someone to identify him. It would look more natural."

"The Chief didn't want to mess around, not any more than we already had." He glanced at Wilf. "He was kind of pissed off."

Wilf looked along the line of photographs. The little man looked less comfortable now than he had before, startled, surprised by the flashbulb in his sleep.

"I taped one up on the front window over at the newspaper office and they're going to run this one in the next edition," Andy tapped a photograph, "Which I think is my best one. Maybe I can get it in the *Brantford Expositor*, too. I already know who this guy is, though."

Wilf looked up. "You do?"

"One of two possibilities. A hobo, and how many hoboes do we see wandering around here in the middle of the winter? Or one of the DPs out at that camp by the railroad."

Wilf stared at Andy.

Bolton looked more interested, too. "Could be. That's not so far from Cline's bush."

"About a mile away."

"Anything in his pockets?"

"Not a thing."

Wilf knew about that camp, everybody in town did. Hammered together by foreigners, refugees from the war, worn-looking men who'd been travelling across the country searching for any kind of work. They'd decided to spend the winter just outside the town's limit, building huts out of large wooden slabs that were unwanted by the mills and cast-off pieces of tin dragged from the dump.

"You think he was a DP?" Wilf asked.

"Most likely."

Wilf thought of the boy in the woods. The man in Cruikshank's backyard. DPs? Was that it? Was that possible? His eyes stung. He felt like he'd just received a reprieve.

"I'm going out there now." Andy started to gather up his photographs. "Show them this dead guy."

"You'll be tipping your hand," Bolton said.

"I want to tip my hand. I want to make them nervous out there. If they get nervous, maybe someone will talk."

"I'll go with you," Wilf said.

"I don't know," Bolton began to whine, "I wonder what the Chief's thinking is on all this?"

His question went unanswered.

Andy and Wilf were already out the door.

❋ ❋ ❋

"No telling what the hell goes on out here." Andy and Wilf were walking the last hundred yards toward the camp, trudging slowly along a rough trail beside the railway tracks and heading out of town. "Could have been a fight over anything. Maybe he stole somebody's clothes or some food. Maybe he was always stealing. They got sick of him, they had to deal with him. What do you think?"

"Maybe," Wilf said. His legs were strong enough from all his walks but a general kind of weakness seemed to be overtaking him. He pushed himself on, not able to trust putting too much weight on his cane because of the ice underfoot.

"This is my point, Wilf." Andy was continuingly getting too far out in front and had to turn around to talk. "These guys are not going to come into town and say 'Dear Mister Policeman, would you look after this trouble we're having?' They're scared of us, scared of our uniforms. I've seen it in their faces. And given what they've been through, who could blame them?"

"I don't blame them," Wilf said.

"Or maybe it was a grudge," Andy went on. "Something happened in one of those refugee camps over in Europe. Maybe he'd betrayed someone. Or a lot of people. And he shows up here in Canada. Someone recognizes him. The guy is as good as dead."

"He is dead," Wilf said.

"They drew names. You, you and you. Take this son-of-a-bitch out into the woods somewhere and deal with him."

"Three men were chosen you think?"

"Yeah, you saw the tracks."

The man in Cruikshank's backyard hadn't left any tracks. The boy was barefoot and standing on top of the snow. Wilf had been blocking out those uncomfortable facts as best he could. He couldn't any longer. He began to wrestle with them. Yes, they were from the DP camp all right but he'd seen the man just after he'd found Cruikshank dead in his tub and the boy after messing with all that blood in the snow. It was the stress, his mind distorting what he'd actually seen, his imagination playing tricks.

"Heads up," Andy said.

A few men were collecting in a dark knot beside the tracks, their unshaven faces, their eyes aiming a barely muted hostility toward Wilf and Andy, particularly Andy dressed in his long blue coat and shiny officer's cap.

"Let me do the talking," Andy said.

A short man with a large moustache and bulging, bloodshot

eyes took a step forward. He was dressed against the cold in nothing but a business suit that had seen many better days. "I am Joe. I am Head Man here."

"Hi, Joe. Seen you in town lots of times. Sergeant Creighton." Andy shook the man's hand. "And my associate, Wilf McLauchlin."

Wilf shook Joe's hand and studied the small band of men. No one looked like the man in Cruikshank's backyard. "Nice to meet you, Joe."

Andy started passing out his photographs. "Anyone recognize this fellow? You do the telling for me, Joe."

Joe took one of the photographs. "Telling what?"

"Tell them that this man in the photograph was murdered not too far away from here. Right over there as a matter of fact." Andy turned and pointed up a long snowy rise. The tops of the trees in Cline's bush looked like a soft pencil line along the edge of the sky. "I want to know if he lived in this camp. Is this dead man one of yours?"

Joe pulled a sour face and shook his head. The other men took their cue from Joe and shook their heads, too. They handed the photographs back.

"You haven't told them anything yet," Andy said.

Joe spoke in a language neither Andy nor Wilf understood. The men shook their heads again, shuffled their feet, glanced back at Andy.

Andy looked disappointed. "I'll show them to the rest of the men." He turned sharply and hurried toward a huddle of rough shacks. Joe and everyone else began to follow after him.

"Where are jobs?" Joe asked, pulling a tattered piece of paper out of his jacket pocket. "The King of England has signed. The Prime Minister of Canada has signed. See? Right here."

"Doesn't mean shit to me," Andy said.

"We have promised!" Joe shouted.

"That's not my business. That's not why I'm here."

As they approached the shacks some other men began to appear in the gloomy doorways. Andy handed out his photographs. "Who knows this fellow? I know damn well someone knows him."

Wilf limped into the ragged camp and looked over all the faces. He didn't recognize anyone. "Are there any children here?" he asked the Head Man. "Any boys?"

Joe turned and stared at him.

"Why the hell are you asking him that?" Andy said.

Joe's reddened eyes seemed overwhelmed by something, his wild grey hair began to tremble. "Children? Our children?"

"There are no children here, Wilf," Andy said.

"I'm sorry," Wilf said. Joe's face was radiating an anguish so deep, so beyond words Wilf had to turn away.

Andy began a search around the camp's perimeter looking for a trail of three tracks leading back down the long hill from Cline's bush.

Wilf wandered around looking for the man in Cruikshank's backyard. After a while Andy trudged back into the circle of huts. When he saw Wilf he shook his head.

"I'll be back," Andy called out to Joe.

Joe shrugged his shoulders. It didn't matter a damn to him.

❄ ❄ ❄

"They recognized that guy, I know they did." Andy pulled the cruiser up beside the police station and came to an angry stop.

"I think you're right. Looked like it." Wilf pushed open his door.

"The bloody OPP will take over now. You know what pisses me off? They treat us local cops like a bunch of morons."

Wilf headed along the alley toward Main Street. He was hoping Carole might be alone in the office.

Carole's hand rested on the telephone for the third time in as many minutes. She still couldn't decide whether to make the call. There were several operators on duty during the day, but with her luck she'd be sure to get Nancy, not that it should make any difference, and particularly not in these circumstances but it did, anyway. And besides, she wasn't exactly sure what she'd say to Wilf if he did happen to answer the phone.

She took a deep breath, picked up the receiver and just as someone other than Nancy said, "Number, please," Carole saw Wilf approaching through the front window.

"I've changed my mind," she said and hung up.

Wilf came in the door. "Hi."

"Hi."

He pushed through the wooden gate without removing his coat or his galoshes and sat down on Dorothy Dale's chair.

Not a good sign, Carole thought to herself. "Nancy called."

"Nancy?"

"Nancy Dearborn."

"Oh," Wilf said.

"About that man in the woods. It's all over town."

"Is it?"

"You and Andy found him?" Carole asked it as a question, as if she were hoping that Nancy's information might be incorrect.

Wilf looked toward his father's office. The door was closed. "Some kids found him. We just went out there to have a look."

"To have a look? Nancy said his arm was chopped off."

"Is there anything Nancy doesn't know?"

"That couldn't have been a good thing to see."

"He looked like he was sleeping. He looked peaceful."

"I was worried."

"Why?"

"I don't know. I was going to call your house. I thought you might be up there all by yourself."

"It was just a body, Carole."

"Anyway, Nancy says that the OPP are in town again. No one can believe it. Everyone's upset."

"What's the solicitor doing?"

"He's not here. He's in Brantford. He went off to lunch with some clients. I don't think he knows yet."

"I really appreciate the fact that you were going to call the house. I appreciate that very much, Carole."

"I saw you through the window. Earlier. Remember? When you waved. You looked, I don't know, just a little bit in shock. Anyway. . ." Carole trailed off.

"I'm fine."

"That's good." Carole smiled.

It was her unguarded and unskeptical warm smile, the one Wilf had been wanting to see all morning. "You know that Displaced Persons camp out along the railway?"

"Yes?"

"Do you see those men in town very often? I mean, do they wander around much? I don't remember seeing any of them but I must have."

"They hang out around the mills. They're looking for work. Our church has been giving them food and clothes all year. I don't know how they survive out there."

"It's been cold."

"I know."

"And they've been out there for a while and there's quite a few of them. They must pop up in the oddest places and at the strangest times. For instance, would it be exceptional to see one of them standing in your backyard?"

Carole gave him a long look. "Yes, it would."

"How about a boy? Have you ever seen a boy, say about twelve years old, who looks like he might live out there? Maybe you've seen him walking along with one of those men?"

Carole shook her head.

"It doesn't really matter."

"Then why are you asking?"

"I know something, at least I think I do but I haven't told Andy yet."

Carole resisted the bait for as long as she could. She looked away. Her unruly lock of hair began to slide down her forehead. She pushed it back up. "What?" she finally said.

"Did Nancy tell you that it was three men who murdered that man in the bush?"

"No." Carole sat up even straighter than usual and stared out the window. "I don't want to know anything about it. I don't want to get drawn in again. All right? One murder was more than enough for me. And if I were you I wouldn't try to get involved in another one, either."

"I'd like to tell you at least one thing."

"Why?"

It sounded more like a cry than a question but Wilf couldn't stop himself. "Because there's no one else I feel close enough to tell." He hadn't meant to say that, but now that he had, it at least had the virtue of being more honestly felt than anything else he might have said. He knew it wasn't a measure of their closeness though—they'd only gone out to one movie, kissed once. It was more a measure of his dislocation.

Carole's vagrant lock of hair began to fall down.

She has a lovely forehead, Wilf thought. If he'd been his old self he would have gone over and kissed it, and kissed both her cheeks. Her lips. He was positive she would have kissed him back.

"I feel close to you, too," Carole said. Her eyes began to shine. "For some reason."

Kiss her, Wilf thought to himself, go over there and kiss her. But instead he said, "We could see by the tracks in the snow that three men had led him into the woods. Only one of them did all the work, though. The other two just watched from the sidelines. But there was something wrong."

"I don't want to know."

"As soon as Andy went back into town I took a closer look. The one who'd used the axe..."

Carole got up quickly and walked back to the filing cabinets.

"He'd left tracks that were almost smooth except for a circle of small indentations. Hobnails, I thought, on an old pair of workboots. Another one was rippled with tread marks and a thick heel like a new pair of rubber boots. And the third was featureless, almost perfectly smooth like a worn-out pair of galoshes. But the thing was, Carole, they were all approximately the same size and the distance between each stride was the same, and the way each man lifted his feet and left drag marks in the snow were all the same. It was just one man, the same man, and once it was all over he'd walked through the woods twice again."

"Thank you," Carole said. She began to look aimlessly through some unfiled papers. "That makes it worse somehow. That one man could be so crazy as to do that. It makes it worse. Have you told Andy what you've figured out?"

"Not yet."

"I'm sure the OPP can tell the same thing. If it's right there in the snow."

"Yes," Wilf said. Right there in the snow. As plain as day. And what had he done when he'd seen that boy standing in the trees? He'd turned away in a panic. That's what he'd done. He'd crawled, blundered blindly away.

Wilf got up and moved toward the door.

"Where are you going?"

"Dad's car's outside. I think I'll drive up to the house."

"What's your father supposed to do without a car?"

Wilf was already pushing through the wooden gate. "I'll come back for him. And if I don't tell him to call a cab."

The outside door slammed shut.

Carole didn't bother to watch Wilf hurry away down the walk; she could see him vividly enough in her mind. She stood there in the empty office and tried to sort out her feelings.

She knew what she felt. The same thing she'd felt when she'd looked up earlier that morning and he was waving at her from outside the window.

She felt unnerved. Frightened.

The sun was lower now and hanging right over Cline's bush as Wilf drove his father's car along. He could see two OPP cruisers and an OPP truck parked by the edge of the trees. He drove by them slowly on the icy road. There was no one in sight. He continued on until he came to the place where the three tracks had left the woods. And his own track too, the easiest one for the OPP to sort out, the only one whose owner was punching holes in the snow with a cane.

Wilf pulled the car up and got out. The wind had died down; the trees were silent now. He peered into the shadows. It wouldn't be difficult to find the spot where he'd first seen that boy. All he had to do was backtrack to the clearing.

He could hear voices coming from deep in the woods. He'd had an excuse to be there earlier in the day but what could he say now? That he had to find some boy's tracks from the DP camp? And that if he could see them right there in the snow plain as day, then nothing else would matter? Everything else would be gloriously all right?

Wilf worked his way up the slope, hoping the officers would stay at the crime scene, busy with the body, with the arm. The farther he went into the trees, the louder their voices became. They were shouting about something, calling back and forth.

He hurried into the clearing. He could see where he'd knelt down to examine the three tracks more closely. He could see his own single set of tracks leading away. He followed along until he came to the spot where he'd lost his footing and fell.

Wilf walked slowly toward where he'd last seen the boy, and everywhere he searched the snow was as smooth and untouched as the day it had fallen. Specked here and there with tiny bits of bark and rusty cedar leaves. Everything hushed and pristine.

The men seemed closer now, their voices filled the air.

Wilf backed up and began to push his way through the brush toward the road again. He got turned around, and blundering on through a wall of thickets, came out some distance behind his father's car. Something round and dazzling was shining in front of him. As he came closer, it began to look as if a large crystal plate had been left on the side of the road. And now he could see that it was an impression that something had left in the ice, something that had been circular and heavy enough to melt into the surface a little. Two letters in the centre glinted up at him. A reversed *F* and a *J*.

Wilf looked up the road. A man was walking toward him, the sun blazing behind him, his elongated shadow as black as spilt ink. Wilf put up his hand to shade his eyes. Joe, the Head Man from the camp, came into view.

Wilf couldn't think of anything to say. They looked at each other for a moment and then Joe turned and peered into the trees. He glanced at Wilf again and then moved away, crossing the road and beginning to wade through the snow in the ditch. Wilf could see the railway line glinting far below and a grey wisp of smoke rising up from the camp. Joe continued on toward it down the long slope.

Wilf began to hurry toward the car. He snatched the tire iron out of the trunk and scurried back down the road, went down on his good knee and began to chip away. Ice flew, his arm ached, his hand slipped and cramped, and finally the plate of ice reluctantly began to lift off the gravel road. He tipped it up on its edge and tried to stuff it inside his coat. It was too cumbersome. He braced it against his chest, hobbled back to the car and eased it inside the trunk. He slid back to get the tire iron and his cane.

A police officer, toting a canvas bag over his shoulder, was coming out of the trees some distance away, heading toward the OPP truck.

Wilf got back to the car, only half closed the door so he wouldn't make any noise and started up the motor. He looked in the rear-view mirror. The police officer was standing in the middle of the road watching him.

Wilf began to drive away.

He glanced down at the sleeve of his overcoat. It was covered with chips of ice. His hand was wet with melting ice. He could feel chips of ice melting all over his face.

I'm mad as a hatter, Wilf thought to himself.

Wilf wandered around the empty house waiting for his father to arrive. He could feel his heart racing.

The boy had left no tracks.

A severed arm. The bin overflowing. Experiments and murders.

Perhaps Adrienne and her boyfriend were innocent after all. Perhaps a mad man was loose in town thumbing through Nuremberg transcripts and committing homicides in some kind of macabre matching game.

Wilf pressed his forehead against the cold glass in an upstairs window. He had to stop. He had to calm down.

Maybe he should tell Andy about the tracks after all. He'd told Carole. For some reason he didn't feel vulnerable around Carole. But he had to be very careful. How could he tell anyone about all the things that were happening? What would they think? They'd think about calling men in white coats, that's what they'd think. He had to be very cautious, discreet.

Wilf came downstairs and decided, since it was the part-time cook's night off, that he'd make supper for his father as a kind of unspoken apology for not returning the car to the office. Pork chops, mashed potatoes, canned gravy and canned peas.

It was dark by the time Clarence climbed out of a cab and came into the house.

Wilf thought he looked tired, but after his customary two rye and waters he seemed to perk up. He began to ask Wilf about the man he'd found in the woods. Wilf answered all his questions in a calm and detailed way while occasionally flipping the chops.

"What did you want the car for, anyway?" Clarence finally asked.

"I went for a drive. Not that I was bothered by what I'd seen out there. Just restless, I guess. Once you've gotten used to flying at four hundred miles an hour it's tough to stand still." Wilf smiled in his father's direction.

"Right," Clarence said, "So the thinking seems to be that three men from the DP camp killed one of their own."

"That's Andy's thinking, anyway."

"It's the talk downtown, too. Seems to be the OPP's slant on things."

"Is it?"

"Seems to be. As a matter of fact I ran into the lead detective an hour ago, which wasn't too difficult because he came into the office looking for you."

"Wanted to know what my tracks were doing out there, I suppose?"

"Andy had already explained that part. But he needs a statement."

"It won't be any different than Andy's statement. But anyway I'm not hard to find. For now."

"Until you head off to Toronto you mean?"

"Moving has nothing to do with you. It has everything to do with getting on with my life."

"I was just thinking that you could use a little more time. But then again, seeing a man with his arm chopped off and blood all over the place is not particularly restful."

"Not particularly."

"Who'd ever have thought we'd be facing another homicide."

"No one."

"Anyway, you're probably right. Keep on with your plans. The bustle of the big city, the camaraderie on campus, compared to what's happening around here I'm sure it will all seem like a breath of fresh air."

"I think that's what I need," Wilf said.

Wilf and Clarence shared a quiet supper and afterwards Clarence went into the study to do some work. Wilf followed him in and began to read the evening paper. Everything began to feel surprisingly familiar. After a while Wilf closed his eyes and listened to his father turning over pages, the scratch of his fountain pen. This was how it used to be, he thought to himself, me sitting on one of the leather chairs, my feet hardly touching the floor, reading a book or playing with something and listening to my father working away.

When he heard the clock strike eight Wilf said he thought he'd go upstairs and stretch out in his room.

Clarence looked up. "All right," he said.

Wilf climbed the stairs and took his pain pill, but resisted the sleeping pills. He was waiting for a call.

He lay down in the dark. Whenever a car passed on the road behind the house, a light would travel up his wall, cross the ceiling and disappear. It didn't seem to take long until he heard the phones ring out in the hall and down in the kitchen. He remained motionless. The ringing stopped. A moment later his father was calling from downstairs.

"It's long distance! For you, Wilf!"

Wilf sat up and reached for his cane. "I'll take it up here then." He walked into the hall, lifted the receiver and waited to hear his father hang up.

"Hello?" Wilf said.

A familiar voice came crackling down the line. "Well, Jesus Christ, if it isn't that crazy plane jockey from the frozen north."

"Hello, Mick."

"God, it's great to hear your voice! I couldn't believe my ears when Peggy said you'd called. Jump on a train. Jump in a plane. Get down here as fast as you can."

"Hey, whoa up." Wilf tried to put a laugh in his voice and send it all the way down the line. "I can't come see you just yet. Soon, though."

"Soon isn't good enough. How are you? Are you all right?"

"Yeah, I'm fine. I'm fine." Wilf slid down the wall and sat on the floor.

"Peggy said you got your sight back."

"That's right. It just came back."

"That's a miracle. You know that, don't you?"

"Peggy said the same thing."

"You have no excuse now, Pal. You've got to come see us. You've got to meet Peggy. And little Mick."

"And the baby."

"That's right. You've got to come down to Jersey, Wilf."

"I will. Maybe this summer."

"July. I get holidays in July. And the baby will be a couple of months old by then."

"July, it is. That's a promise. I promise. Jesus, Mick, it's great to hear your voice. Peggy says you've been working out of town."

"I'm sitting in my gorgeous hotel room right this minute. It's the lap of luxury. About ten feet by ten. I've been in bigger foxholes."

Now Wilf did laugh. "What kind of work are you doing?"

"Prefab houses. You know the kind, they come more or less ready-made? We just knock them together. As long as the foundations are in we can work in any kind of weather. And the thing is we're busy as hell."

"That's great, Mick."

"How about you? What are you doing? Are you back to school yet?"

"I will be soon."

"Bloody lawyer."

"Listen, if you ever need one I'll be there. Pro bono."

"I hope that means for free."

"Of course it means for free. Of course it does. Listen, I've got a question for you. I know it'll sound kind of dumb after all this time."

"No it won't."

"Well, it's just that I've been wondering a lot lately about what happened way back then. I don't even know exactly where you and your buddies found me. I know you said I was still in my plane and it looked like I'd tried to make a landing on some road."

"You were in the ditch, Pal. One wing broken off. Canopy ripped off, tail gone and sleeping like a baby. Another Jesus miracle. Someone's been looking after you, I hope you're grateful."

"I'm grateful to you."

"Stop that shit. Just a few dog faces, dead tired and walking along hoping we wouldn't run into any suicidal Germans. That's all."

"Where exactly, though? I must have asked you this before but I can't remember."

"I can't remember you asking. You weren't too chatty about all that. You were in some dogfight and got the worst of it, that's all you ever said. Still mad about having your ass kicked, I figured, so we talked about lots of other things."

"There was a wall of smoke."

"What do you mean?"

"That's all I remember. The last thing. I flew into all this smoke. But I don't know where."

"Near Weimar, Wilf. Out in the country some bloody place. We were about five miles in front of the main advance, scouting around, radioing back anything we saw that might be trouble. And there you were."

"There must have been an artillery bombardment going on. Somebody must have hit something."

"No. We didn't have to call in anything. The Wehrmacht had pulled out a week or so before we got there. It was a walk in the park. If you don't count the camp."

"The camp?"

"Yeah, this godforsaken camp. No resistance there either, though they'd waited until the very last moment to leave."

"Where was this?"

"Right near Weimar. Buchenwald. You must have heard of it. It's famous now. What we saw in there, you wouldn't believe. It stays with you, you know?"

"Yeah. Mick...from the road where you found me, how far away was the camp would you say?"

"A couple of miles maybe. Not far. Jesus. You know that smoke? They'd been running crematoriums twenty-four hours a day in there, but even at that rate they couldn't get through them all before they had to abandon the place. Bodies were still stacked up like cordwood when we got there. Some of the poor bastards who'd survived told us that the air got so black they couldn't tell whether it was day or night. They had to feel their way around; they had to lie on the ground to breathe."

"How many days between the time you found me and you found that camp?"

"The next day, I think."

"When did they stop the furnaces?"

"I don't know."

"I flew through human ashes," Wilf said.

Mick fell silent for what seemed like a long time. "Why the hell are we talking about this?"

"We don't have to. Not anymore."

They went on to talk about Wilf's imminent return to college and how Mick was planning to open up his own prefab construction company. Wilf promised once again to get down to Jersey that coming summer, said goodbye and hung up the phone.

He got back up on his feet and walked into the bedroom. He stretched out on the bed and fell asleep. When he woke up he could hear his father snoring gently down the hall. Wilf crept down the stairs to the study, switched on the light and turned to look at the stacks of transcripts. Buchenwald. It was almost a relief. At least it was something real he could concentrate on. Buchenwald was anything but a mirage.

He began to leaf through his father's papers looking for a reference to the camp. He couldn't find one. He opened up the new filing cabinet and looked through the files. Near the back of the top drawer his eyes fell on a tab Clarence had neatly labelled *"Final Statements: the doctors' trials."*

Wilf pulled it out.

"It is immaterial for the experiment whether it is done with or against the will of the person concerned. The meaning is the motive, devotion to the community. Ethics of every form are decided by an order or obedience."

His father had made a neat handwritten note in the margin: *"Dr. Karl Brandt, Adolf Hitler's personal physician, chief architect of the inmate experimental programs."*

Orders and obedience, Wilf thought to himself. It sounded all too familiar. But why obey such heinous orders at all? Out of fear of one's own death. That was the usual claim reported in the newspapers, coming from everyone throughout the German hierarchy. Heard everywhere.

And that had been Adrienne's claim, too. Hadn't it? She'd been afraid of her boyfriend. He was threatening her life; she had to do it.

Wilf read the passage over again. Dr. Brandt was actually articulating an interesting variation, carving up some poor soul not from fear of losing one's own life but for the common good. A person's ethics defined by an order from someone else.

It would certainly simplify one's inner conflicts, Wilf thought to himself, if one had any inner conflicts.

"In my life I have never followed egotistical aims and I was never motivated by base instincts. For that reason I feel free of any guilt inside me. I have acted as a soldier, and as a soldier I am ready to bear the consequences."

So said one Dr. Fritz Fisher.

"Never motivated by base instincts."

Wilf couldn't take his eyes off that phrase. No base instincts flickering under the mind that designed the freezing experiment, no quickening of the blood in the one contemplating the feel of the scalpel on healthy arms and legs, no growing anticipation walking through antiseptic halls, no arousal at the first sight of the helpless experimental subject, no pounding of heart, intake of breath.

Just doing one's duty, as determined by someone else.

And Adrienne was so small and her beauty was so frail and her voice that night in the car was so persuasive. "Christian love," she had said.

"Researching something?" Clarence was standing in the doorway in his pajamas and slippers.

"Just trying to put myself back to sleep actually." Wilf returned the file to its place and shut the drawer. "Nothing like legal documents to induce somnolence. Works every time."

"That could be a problem when you go back to school." Clarence came in and sat down on one of the leather chairs. "It's quarter after four."

"I'm sorry, Dad. I didn't mean to wake you."

"You didn't. I went for a leak and saw your door was open. Looking for anything in particular?"

"Not really. Just browsing. I was reading about the doctors' trials."

"Quite a group, aren't they?"

"Not exactly Doc Robinson."

"No. That's for sure. They were infected."

"You think so?"

"Indoctrinated with all the rest. Fell into line. They thought they were doing advanced science, that's the strangeness of it, and in circumstances that allowed the acceleration of knowledge without the usual restraint on human experimentation and so on."

"And do you think they were?" Wilf moved to the doorway. He had to lean up against it.

"Doing advanced science? I could care less. The international community should destroy everything they did, breakthroughs be damned, they should burn all their notes."

"It stinks. Doesn't it?"

"I guess so. Are you all right?"

"I just have trouble sleeping. You know that. It's nothing to worry about."

"You're not going to wander around the streets of Toronto if you can't sleep, are you?"

"I'll go into the stacks at the library, fall asleep in there. I think I'll go back to bed. How about you?"

"Do me a favour? Stay away from Andy and that business in the woods? You don't need it."

Wilf smiled at his father as he moved into the hall. "I'm a war vet, Dad."

Clarence pulled himself out of the chair and crossed the study. "You're more than that. You're a genuine hero. And that means you don't have to prove anything to anybody!"

Clarence stood in the dark hallway and watched Wilf limp toward the stairs.

CHAPTER ELEVEN

Duncan looked at the photograph taped up in the window. A few other people were doing the same thing. He pushed in closer. Now he could see crystals of frost clinging to the man's dark eyebrows.

Do You Know This Man? Contact Sergeant A. Creighton at the police station or phone 221.

Though his nose was clearly broken and his lips were swollen and split, it was the frost that seemed to Duncan to be the most pitiful thing. It was the frost that proved that the man was dead. Otherwise he could just be sleeping.

"He looks like he's asleep," a woman to Duncan's right said.

"He's dead," Duncan replied.

A man snorted into the cold morning air.

"I know that, Duncan," the woman said.

Dead. Never to come back into that body. Disappeared somewhere. In the wind. Blowing across the countryside. He'd seen the souls of dead people lots of times. Flying through the moonlight, tangled in branches, dark shadows in the swirling snow. They were everywhere.

Bodies were left behind though. The little man's body had been left behind like a dead mouse turned out of his burrow in the middle of winter. Duncan smiled at that. There was a poem. His mother used to recite it to him all the time. "Wee timorous beastie." Which was curious because his mother hated mice and went on a regular rampage every fall when they started to come into the house. She said they carried all kinds of disease. Nothing would drive her crazier than uncovering a writhing pink nest of newborn mice under her bed or in her sock drawer. All the walls in the house would have to be washed. All the bedding bleached. Utensils in the drawers dipped in boiling water.

You could never tell. That was the thing. Even the most gentle, smallest creature could be the most dangerous. That man could be dangerous. With his closed eyes.

Duncan wondered if maybe they'd put that picture in the newspaper. He hoped they would. He wanted to cut it out and tape it up on his wall. He surveyed the town. It was early Saturday morning and there weren't many people in sight. He thought he'd treat himself to breakfast at the restaurant at the other end of Main Street. It was the only one open in the mornings. It was the dingiest one, the one where the people who didn't have any family went to eat. The man and woman who owned the place, whether he was drunk or sober, whether day or night, always made Duncan feel welcome there.

He strode along feeling light of spirit. He thought of his mother again. He knew she was somewhere close by. Perhaps she was sitting up high in the hydro wires or flitting like a shadow along the icicles shining in a long row over his head. She'd always called him her good boy and she'd always told anyone who came to their place that he tried hard to do his best.

Duncan's heart overflowed with a mix of feelings. She could see how he was running the lumberyard and the shop, she could see how hard he was trying to live his life. To be a good man. To do his best.

She knew everything.

Andy stood in the McLauchlin garage and hoped no one would walk past the open garage doors and see him standing there. He turned to watch Wilf crouching beside an old orange crate, rummaging through some rags.

"The Chief is all over me for going out to the DP camp," Andy said.

"I know. You told me."

Wilf had called Andy earlier that morning to tell him that he had some crucial information concerning the murder in the woods but that he couldn't say what it was over the telephone, for fear of Nancy Dearborn. He knew that what he had hidden in the orange crate was an unlikely piece of evidence. His conjecture about the boot prints seemed stronger. But the phone call to Andy wasn't so much a call to action, anyway. He just needed him to confirm that they were possibilities that anyone would have to consider, that they existed in the real world, that he wasn't too far gone.

"Do you know why he's all over me? Because the OPP are all over him," Andy was saying.

"You told me that part, too."

"It was a gross breach of protocol, that's what it was. Messing with that arm. And the body. Getting our tracks all over everything. Once you've established a homicide has occurred you're supposed to desist from any further investigation and call those bastards. And then we went out to the DP camp."

"I was just keeping you company." Wilf reached deep inside the crate and wrestled out the circle of ice.

Andy looked a little startled. "What the fuck is that?"

"What's it look like?" Wilf balanced the ice on the crate's edge.

"Like a piece of ice with a ring grooved in it."

"There's two letters in the middle."

Andy came closer.

"Foundry marks, I think. If you reverse them, they read *JF*. And there's a spidery ridge of ice running here. Another one running from there to there. It's a cast of something and those ridges are cracks in the thing itself. It's like a fingerprint." Wilf looked up and smiled.

"Of what?"

"I don't know. I know what it's used for, but I'm not sure what it's called. Take it."

Andy flinched back a little. "I don't want it."

"Just for a minute. I need to stand up."

Andy lifted the ice up, bracing it against his chest and looked back toward the open doors again.

"I think it's one of those things people tie their horses to when there's nothing else around," Wilf said. "A piece of iron with a ring on the top. They put it on the ground and loop one of the reins through. You've seen them."

"They're called tethers. Weight tethers." Andy was sounding more irritated than enthralled. He lowered the ice back into the crate and covered it up with the rags. "I can't fool around any more, Wilf. If I make one more wrong move I'm going to get my ass fried."

"I found it on the side of the road close to where those three men came out of the woods. And runner marks, too. A cutter had been standing there."

"But that doesn't mean anything. Anybody could have stopped beside that woods. They could have been doing anything."

Andy strode over to the open doors and closed them. The only light left inside the garage was struggling in through a small side window.

"There was just one man," Wilf said.

"What do you mean?"

"Out there. Three men didn't murder that man. There was only one."

Andy leaned up against the doors. "Oh yeah?"

Wilf told him his theory about the similarity in the tracks

and then he said, "The sun was warmer and the ice on the road was melting a little when he came back."

"Why the hell would he come back?" Andy had his arms wrapped stolidly across his chest by this time.

"Because he didn't get the idea to lay down two more tracks until afterwards. He had to go home to get his extra boots."

Andy had to smile. "Some mastermind."

"It must have been Thursday. It was milder on Thursday. It had snowed a little Wednesday night because Carole and I drove through some snow. It turned windy and cold by Friday."

"Everyone knows he was probably killed on Thursday." Andy could feel himself getting drawn in again. He began looking for his allusive cigarettes.

"Have the OPP talked about the tracks?"

With the doors closed Wilf was only a dark presence at the other end of the garage. Andy could hardly make him out.

"Yeah. A lot. Our tracks. Yours and mine. Particularly yours. They said your tracks were all over the place. How did you manage to get that thing anyway?"

"I drove back out there later. I chipped it out of the road."

"What the hell were you thinking? You know you can't do that. Even if it doesn't mean anything, and the chances are it doesn't, you can't remove possible evidence from a crime scene!" Andy found his cigarettes and lit one up. "You know why I came over here? Not because you said you'd found something interesting. It wasn't that. It was because of the way you sounded."

"How did I sound?"

"Well, different. Sort of, like you were kind of afraid of something."

"Nancy Dearborn?"

"And that's another thing. Why would you say Nancy Dearborn might be listening?"

"She might have."

"She wouldn't listen. She couldn't. She'd be fired."

Wilf walked over to the window and looked out into the yard.

"You sounded a bit strange, that's all."

"You thought I was out of my head when I showed up that night with those beer glasses and a pill bottle."

"True enough." Andy could see Wilf's face more clearly now. He looked calm enough.

"Once these things get started they're hard to stop. Adrienne O'Dell could have told us that."

"What things?"

"These kind of things."

"Listen Wilf, I'll forget I saw that piece of ice and you'll forget you ever told me about it. All right?"

"All right."

"And later tonight you could get rid of it somewhere."

"I don't think so."

"I would. Anyway, I've got to get downtown. I'll keep your one-man theory in mind, though. You'd think the OPP would have come up with the same thing by now, with all their men."

"Maybe they have."

Andy swung open the garage doors, looking too eager to leave.

Carole looked through the clothes in her closet. She wasn't sure what she wanted to wear to the dance that night. She wasn't even sure they were still going. She hadn't heard a thing from Wilf since the day before. When Mr. McLauchlin had arrived back from his business meeting he'd already been told that Andy and Wilf had found that poor man in the woods. He seemed alarmed about it. His face was flushed. And then that detective had come in looking for Wilf.

Carole took out her three best dresses and laid them out on her bed. She didn't like any of them. Why was Wilf always in the middle of these terrible things?

She looked at herself in her dresser mirror. She was only wearing a slip and she didn't particularly like what she saw. Her hair was still announcing the mad blunder of that dye job to anyone with eyes, for one thing. Her neck was too long for another, her collarbone stood out like she was half-starved, her breasts only hinted at a possible cleavage and she was sure they were asymmetrical, though Donny had never noticed, or at least he'd never complained.

The only thing she liked about herself was her legs. When her seams were straight they could look quite smashing. She didn't even want to think about her sallow complexion, her colourless eyes, her thin nose.

She made a decision. The emerald dress would have to do because it was the only one with matching shoes that might be comfortable enough to dance in all night, not that she could imagine dancing with Wilf. What would they do? Sit out the fast numbers and just sway in the same spot to the slow ones?

Probably.

As Carole thought about that, she could see everyone watching them, the tall thin girl and the wounded soldier. Everyone would know he was a soldier even though he'd be wearing a suit and tie.

She could feel her face touching his face, his arm about her waist, drawing her close. She wondered where his arm in the sling would go. Against her breasts, such as they were, that's where. Pressing against her breasts.

She hung the three dresses back up in her closet. It was hours before she needed to get ready. She didn't even know if they were going to go out to dinner first. She didn't know whether to eat at home or not. He hadn't even called.

Wilf McLauchlin.

The more she'd gotten to know him, the more it seemed that she didn't know him at all. It was as if he were standing in shadows half the time, as if he were keeping a secret, but of course that wasn't true. If anything he talked too much and told her too much and he wanted too much from her. Those two murders. Wanting her to be involved, or needing her to be involved, she wasn't quite sure which it was, but it didn't matter anyway because she didn't want to get involved. Why would she? Since yesterday all she could think about was how strange it was for one man to take another man into a woods and chop off his arm. Somehow it seemed less crazy if there'd been three of them.

And why his arm? Surely if he'd wanted to kill the man, he would have taken the axe and aimed for his head. It just didn't make any sense.

She turned to look at herself in the mirror again. Her face looked a little flushed. Wilf was obviously obsessed with such things. Such terrible things.

You see what he's doing to you, Carole thought to herself.

✳ ✳ ✳

The phone rang.

Wilf wasn't sure he wanted to answer it. His father had left earlier that morning for another Brantford meeting and since Andy had retreated from the garage Wilf had been thinking once again about what Mick Pascani had said.

And once again he could see the dark billowing clouds. What had come next? The American field hospital.

"Are my eyes bandaged?" he asked. His body felt like it was still buckled into his plane, he felt like he was still flying.

"No," a voice answered.

"They feel like they're bandaged," Wilf had said.

The phone rang once more. Wilf stood motionless in the downstairs hall and listened. He'd just come out of the study after looking through his father's files again, after finally finding something on Buchenwald. The date the first US troops had walked through the gates, the day after Mick had pulled him out of his wrecked plane. Wilf stared down at it for a long time.

April 11, 1945.

He'd climbed into his Spitfire for what was to be his last sortie on April 7th, not April 10th. He was missing three days.

The phone rang once more.

Madness feels like this, Wilf thought to himself. Afraid to move. Afraid to take on anything more. Even a wrong number.

He walked into the kitchen and picked up the phone. "Hello?"

"I think we have a safe line," Andy said. "I just saw Nancy Dearborn crossing the street to go to lunch."

"That's amusing. And what are you up to, tormenting the weak of mind?"

"I don't think you have a weak mind, Wilf." Andy dropped his voice, "As a matter of fact, I don't think your mind is weak at all. It might be right on the money."

"Oh?"

"This gangly farm kid just came in. He'd been looking at that photograph I taped up in the window and he thinks he might have seen our man."

Wilf looked toward the kitchen window. A smoky shaft of light had transfixed it in gold. The sun was shining all over the town. "Where?"

"Working at a sawmill. He said he works there himself every once in a while, and the other day when he was heading for school he saw a stranger sorting lumber out in the snow. He took a second look because he was surprised, he didn't think Duncan had any help."

"Duncan?"

"Duncan Getty. Drunken Duncan. Remember him?"

"No."

"No? Always wandering around drunk at hockey games or anywhere else for that matter? He's a devil to work when he's cutting timber, though. That's what people say. First one up to his ass in the snow in the morning, the last one to quit at night. He's a bit of a simpleton, though."

"But he runs a sawmill?"

"More or less. And Wilf, he has horses out there. I've seen them. He uses them for drawing logs out of the bush. And he drives a cutter around."

"Does he?" Wilf stared through the golden haze in the window toward the garage. "What do you want to do?"

"I don't know. I told that kid to keep what he'd just told me under his hat. He probably will, for a day or two. We don't have much time."

"No." Wilf could hear Andy breathing.

"If we screw this up, I'm dead."

"And if we don't you'll be a hero again. Just think about Linda, she'll be over the moon."

"No she won't. She'll kill me anyway. I should just report this. We don't have much time."

Wilf could see Andy sitting at his desk just as clearly as if he were sitting at the kitchen table right in front of him, clutching the telephone receiver, his knuckles turning white.

"You're a sergeant now, you can take some initiative, can't you?" Wilf said. "It'll be all right."

When Duncan looked out he couldn't believe his eyes. Wilf McLauchlin, fighter pilot and the greatest of all the local heroes, was climbing out of a car and standing right there in his side yard. He scraped away the frost on the shop window to get a better look. Wilf was facing the house. Then he turned to look toward the shop.

Duncan began to brush at the sawdust stuck to the tattered front of his old work jacket. Wilf was staring straight at him now or so it seemed. Duncan took a last swipe at the sawdust clinging to his sleeves, opened the shop door and came out.

Wilf limped toward him. "Mr. Getty," he said.

Duncan grinned. Just to hear Wilf McLauchlin say his name was special. To be called Mr. Getty was special, too. He hadn't been called that in a long while, maybe never.

"I'm Wilf McLauchlin," Wilf said, resting his cane against his coat and extending his hand.

"I know," Duncan said.

Wilf watched Duncan's huge hand engulf his own and expected to feel some pain, but instead he hardly felt the big man's hand at all. "Then you probably know the law firm of McLauchlin and McLauchlin?"

Duncan could see Carole behind the gold lettering sitting in her typing chair. "Twelve kills," he said. "You flew the Mark 14 the last year of the war. That's the Spitfire you crashed."

"Right." Wilf smiled, "Fortunately the Air Force didn't make me pay for it."

"You paid for it," Duncan said.

"I guess you could say that." Duncan had tawny eyes like a cat's, soft and watchful, Wilf thought. They seemed to go with his wild head of hair. A huge matted cat. He looked somewhat familiar too, but Wilf couldn't remember from where.

"I'll show you," Duncan said, apropos of nothing and started off across the yard toward the house.

Wilf watched him go, the roll and length of his stride, his big shabby work boots leaving large tracks in the snow.

"Come on," Duncan called back.

The kitchen was full of planes. They spun around and nodded and seemed to give Duncan a warm welcome as he moved in amongst them and identified each one for Wilf's benefit. He reached out with his big hand and touched a plane painted in ragged rings of red and orange. It was hanging from the light in the centre of the room. "A Mark 14 Spitfire."

Wilf walked up to it. The long elegant tilt of its nose, the wide elliptical wings sweeping forward, it was unmistakable and it was beautiful. Duncan turned on the light and the plane's gaudy colours shone.

"That's it all right," Wilf said.

A broad grin spread across Duncan's huge cherub face. In his excitement he'd forgotten to take off his work coat and his boots, contrary to what his mother had taught him.

"Never saw one painted like that, though. A real circus plane."

Duncan's tawny eyes retreated somewhere. "It's your plane. The one you crashed in. That's why."

"Oh, it's on fire. I get it."

Duncan's grin reappeared. He walked over to the cupboard, pulled open a door and took down a bottle of rye and two glasses that looked like they hadn't been washed for some time. "I glued every one of them together. Lots of different parts. Painted every one. Hung them all up." He filled the glasses half full.

"You've done a great job." Wilf looked over the walls of newspaper clippings, some yellowing with age and curling up at the corners, some new. He pulled out a photograph of the dead man from inside his winter coat. "Duncan?"

Duncan turned around with the two glasses in his hands.

Wilf held up the photograph. "Have you ever seen this man?"

Duncan didn't make an indication either way. He put the glasses down on the kitchen table and then he sat down himself. "You can have one," he said, shoving one of the dirty glasses across the table. He picked up the other one and took a drink.

Wilf placed the photograph in front of Duncan and sat down.

"I seen him in the window," Duncan said.

"That picture downtown in the newspaper window, you mean?"

"People say he was killed by a lot of men."

"Who says that?"

"People everywhere. People at the Comet. I ate my breakfast there."

"This morning?"

Duncan grinned. "Aren't you goin' to drink?"

"Sure." Wilf took a drink. "Hits the spot. Thanks, Duncan."

Duncan kept grinning. "Are you a flyer or a lawyer now?"

"I haven't been a flyer for a long time."

Duncan nodded. "How come a dead man needs one?"

"Dead people still have certain rights under the law. And so do the heirs of their estates."

Duncan leaned forward, his boy's eyes lighting up. "What's it feel like?"

"What?"

"Flying?"

"Well, let's see. The first time I took off I guess it felt like something had just sucked all the breath out of me. They sit you up on top of this massive engine, they wrap you around in a little piece of tin, cover your head with a sheet of glass and all you've got is a stick between your legs to keep her nose up and pedals under your feet to bank her left or right. It's scary as hell. And then you get used to it. And then you think you can't live without it. But you're always scared."

"Why?"

"Your friends keep dying. And every day you feel like it's your turn, this is the day when you won't come back."

"I wish I could fly but I'm too big."

"You wouldn't fit, Duncan."

"You killed twelve men."

"Yes I did. I'm not proud of it."

"They would of killed you."

"Yes. As quick as look at me. By the way," Wilf tapped the photograph, "someone downtown was saying that he thought this fellow worked here."

Duncan looked surprised. He stared down at the photograph again. "Who said that?"

"Someone who saw him sorting lumber out in the snow one day."

"Oh?" Duncan sat back and scratched the sandy bristles on his round face. "I wonder who that was?"

"It doesn't matter, does it?"

"Well, yes it does, Wilf, 'cause he wasn't telling the truth." Duncan shoved the photograph back. "He never worked here. Not even one time." Duncan drained his glass. "I work here all by myself since my mom died. And anyway, she just kept the books and stuff. My dad, he had lots of men to help out but that was a long time ago."

"I thought some young fellow who lives around here helps you out from time to time."

"Eric, you mean? Sure. But that's different."

"Why?"

"Well shit, Eric wasn't killed in no bush. Do you want to see the shop? You can see it if you want." Duncan stood up.

"That would be great, Duncan." Wilf picked up the photograph and put it back inside his coat.

When Wilf had first driven up in Andy's old Ford, a thick

plume of smoke was rising from the metal chimney on the shop roof. That's why he'd guessed that Duncan was in there. But now, as they crossed the side yard, Wilf could see that the smoke had thinned out to almost nothing.

"I burn more wood in that goddamn stove than I sell." Duncan turned back to Wilf as they trudged along, his face breaking into a grin.

It sounded like a well-used joke to Wilf, maybe one his father used to tell. The men lounging around the shop would laugh at it one more time. And Duncan, standing at the back on a pile of lumber and looking like a stranger's boy, would laugh, too.

Everything was covered with three inches of sawdust except for the cutting blades on the various machines. Heavy chains hung down from pulleys on rails set in the rafters, a tumble of hand tools were piled up high on a long workbench, axes of all shapes and sizes were tossed carelessly into a corner.

Duncan opened the stove with a poker and threw a few pieces of wood inside. "This is the finishing room," he said.

Odd bits of wood hidden under the sawdust made walking difficult. Wilf made his way to the middle of the large room and looked around. Some planks were piled up beside a sliding freight door. "It's impressive, Duncan. I didn't realize you had such a big operation out here."

"It keeps me goin'," Duncan said.

"You've got a good-sized woodlot at the back. I noticed it driving along."

"It's mostly worn out." Duncan slammed the stove door shut. "Scrub bush mainly now. That's the trouble."

"So you'd have to work in some of the other woodlots around, would you?"

Duncan straightened up and stared across the room.

"If you were running short on your own timber, I mean."

"Sometimes," Duncan said.

"Well, it's quite a life you've got out here. A lot of men would like this life."

Duncan's face began to glow again. "Would they?"

"Sure. Working with all this machinery. And working outside, too, it's a good healthy life. And working with horses."

"Babe and Dandy."

"I saw one of them standing out by the barn."

"That would be Dandy. Babe had a run into town this morning. I'm keeping her warm."

"Anyway, it's well beyond me, this kind of life. With one arm and a bum leg what good would I be?"

"I seen you come home that day on the train."

"Oh yeah?"

"You don't need to do nothin', Wilf. You've done all you need to do."

Duncan was looking across the room at Wilf with such earnestness and with such a high regard Wilf had to turn away. "Thanks, Duncan. Of course, I have to do something with the rest of my life."

"I'm getting married," Duncan said.

"You are? Well, isn't that great?"

"To Carole Birley. You know her. She works in your dad's office."

Wilf walked over to the pile of newly trimmed boards and began to examine them more closely. "To Carole Birley?"

"That's right."

"Does she know?"

"Not yet. I'm going to ask, though."

"Have you known her for very long?"

"All my life."

Duncan crossed his big arms and shoved his hands into the sleeves of his tattered coat. It looked to Wilf like he was hugging himself.

"She's beautiful," Duncan said.

"You think so?"

"Yes I do. You can come to the wedding."

"If there's a wedding I'll certainly come to it, you can bet on that."

"Do you want me to start up a saw to show you?"

"I don't think so."

Duncan looked around. "That's all that's out here then. This is about it."

"Do you think we can have a walk out to the barn? I've always had a soft spot for horses."

"If you want. Sure."

As they approached the barnyard Dandy began stamping a large hairy foot and snorting steam into the cold air.

"Hey there," Wilf said softly.

The horse raised his big head over the top board to get a better look. Wilf rubbed his nose.

"How old is he?"

"Just seven. He's real good most of the time."

"A gelding?"

"Shit yeah. He'd be nothin' but trouble if he wasn't."

"How old's the other one?"

"Almost twenty-one. She'll be twenty-one this summer."

Duncan pushed open the stable door. Babe was standing quietly in her stall. She was two hands shorter than Dandy, according to Duncan, but still a good size, content to stand there quietly and munch on the armful of hay Duncan dropped in front of her.

Wilf rubbed her wide flank; he could hear her teeth grinding away.

"I've been meaning to get a driving horse," Duncan said, "but then Babe and Dandy wouldn't get any work in the summer and then they'd break down in the winter. It's heavy work hauling out timber."

"A smaller horse for the cutter, you mean?" Wilf had seen a heavy wagon on wooden skis pulled up beside the barn. A small cutter, its red paint faded and peeling, was sitting behind it.

"And the buggy in the summer." Duncan nodded toward a buggy shape standing farther off in the dark shadows of the barn.

"When you get married you'll have to get yourself a car," Wilf said.

Duncan began to scratch Babe's haunch. He grinned. "I know."

Carole was right about the dance.

They did more or less sway in one spot to the slow numbers and sit out the fast ones. And Wilf did press his cheek against her cheek and she did feel her breasts pushing softly against his wounded arm. And she did feel his lips against her hair, her ear.

They left the dance early and fifteen minutes later Wilf was renting a tiny cabin from a commercial establishment just south of Galt. It was well-known for renting out its tourist cabins for just such an occasion. Cabin Three sat on the snowy bank of the same river that some miles farther on passed through their town.

Wilf turned on the light and set the electric heater to high. Carole looked out the window as if she'd just become fascinated by the dark stretch of frozen river, even though, once he'd turned on the light she couldn't see a thing.

How did they arrive at this decision, she wondered? She couldn't remember saying yes.

Wilf had kissed her, she'd kissed him back and his lips had felt delicious and warm and boozy, and she'd hoped hers had felt just the same way to him, and then he'd taken her hand and they'd gotten up from their table, even though the dance was far from over, and without a word they'd walked over to get their coats.

It was the holding of hands, she thought, because Wilf had refused to use his cane all evening, asking the attendant to hang it up with his coat, and now he was holding her hand tightly and limping deeply beside her, and she wanted so much to turn to him and tell him that his situation, his condition, didn't matter to her, wanted to tell him that so much that she could hardly see where she was going.

That's the moment when I said yes, she thought to herself.

But it wasn't out of pity. It certainly wasn't that.

These things were always awkward, though, at least at first. Pulling up to this dubious establishment with its stupid neon rainbow sign and not saying a word to each other was certainly awkward. And watching Wilf go into the office and come back with a key.

"Got it," he'd said.

What was she supposed to have replied, "Hurrah?"

So she'd remained silent and she supposed, though she hadn't really intended it to be that way, inscrutable.

When the light went on in the cabin, she'd taken one quick look at the painted iron bed with its faded quilt and questionable pillows and she knew that she had several choices. She could stand there at the window like a dummy and have Wilf go through the ritual of taking off her hat and her coat and her boots, coaxing her every inch of the way, or they could do this thing together. She and Donny had done everything together.

She watched Wilf's reflection in the window. He seemed to be taking a long time with the heater. Or she could say she'd changed her mind. Three things she could do.

Wilf stood up and turned the light back off. "Is that okay?"

"Yes," Carole said. When she turned she could hardly see him.

"I haven't done this for a long time," Wilf said.

Carole almost said "Me, either" but she caught herself. Not that Wilf would think she was a virgin. She wondered what he did think, or know. Lots, she thought, everybody knows.

The excruciating thing, though, was that Donny had been her one and only lover if she didn't count Michael Cooper's hand. Sometimes she could hardly remember what it had been like being with Donny. At other times, lying in her room at night, she remembered only too well, as if he were right there beside her. Her body remembered him. But it had been five years of abstinence.

A world record, Carole thought.

Wilf came over to her and she could feel his lips on her lips. It had been such a long time. She could feel his hand unbuttoning her coat, touching her breasts through her dress. Not good for a person. He moved against her. She could feel his hips press against her hips. She could feel something else.

"Oh god," Wilf breathed in the dark.

Wilf had wanted to thank her afterwards, lying beside her on the narrow bed, the sheets cold when they'd begun but warm now, her beautiful face visible in the moonlight, her beautiful breasts, waist, curve of her hip faintly visible. Everything was beautiful, but he knew it would be the worst thing he could say, something no woman wanted to hear in that particular situation. Thank you.

But that's how he felt.

He'd been broken, his side alternately ridged with scars or smooth as glass, his arm hideously out of its sling. She'd touched it and he hadn't felt a thing, but it hadn't mattered. Nothing had mattered but her exploring, tender touch, as if she were the one who'd gone blind, as if she were concentrating on discovering every part of him.

Wilf drew close to her. Her body felt warm and cool all at

the same time. It felt sublime. He pressed his face against her watchful, intelligent, gorgeous face. Her secretary's face. Her typist's face.

And he'd touched her like a blind man, too, and her breath had become a little cry and a moan, and when he couldn't support his own weight over her she had moved to the perfect place and they had soared together and they had clung together, and they had become amazed.

"Thank you," Wilf whispered. He couldn't help himself.

Carole kissed his cheek. "Don't be stupid. Shhhh," she said.

CHAPTER TWELVE

Though Carole didn't say anything she worried about the state of her clothes all the way into town. It wasn't quite eleven o'clock, which meant her mother and her ridiculously old-fashioned father might still be sitting up talking about their only child. They knew she was going out with Wilf McLauchlin again because she'd told them. Her mother would take one look at her wrinkled dress, and it was certainly wrinkled because it had somehow landed underneath Wilf instead of on the floor, and she would know. How could she not know?

This was annoying and frustrating because she was twenty-five after all, but still her parents knew her private history only too well and she didn't want them to think that she was going to become one of "those women," of which the town had a few, out of disappointment or disillusionment or some such thing.

Wilf hadn't had a condom with him, or at least he hadn't taken the time to put it on and she hadn't asked him, either. It just didn't seem a very positive thing to mention and then of course it was too late. She didn't want to worry about that, though. It was better to distract herself by worrying about her dress.

When they reached the edge of town Wilf said he'd like to stop in at the Arlington Hotel for a nightcap. He wondered if she might, too. Carole said yes. Her parents almost never sat up past midnight. They went in on the *Ladies & Escorts Only* side. Carole ordered a rum and Coke and Wilf asked Teddy for a draft beer, since he had something important to do later and didn't want to get too fuzzy-minded.

"What do you have to do later?" Carole asked.

She smiled a funny smile and Wilf's heart felt instantly warm, though the situation seemed both surprising and slightly ridiculous. He hadn't made any plans to fall in love and he could feel himself resisting the idea now. It was just gratitude he was feeling. And sheer happiness because, against great odds, his body had worked.

"What's so important?" Carole asked again.

"What do you know about a fellow called Duncan Getty?"

Her smile faded and her grey eyes widened a little. "Why?"

"Some kid was talking to Andy today. He thinks our murdered man worked out at Getty's sawmill."

"That's not possible."

"What isn't?"

"That Duncan had anything to do with that man. I've known him for years."

"I went out there earlier today. He mentioned you. Actually, he spoke very highly of you."

"Why did my name come up?"

"He knows you work for my father."

"Yes, well I guess he would. Anyway Duncan is just this big, gentle, not-quite-bright teddy bear. As far as I know he's never done anything wrong in his whole life. You went out there today?"

"Just to have a casual conversation, I didn't say anything."

"Well, he might look kind of scary but he's harmless. When I was about ten, he nearly killed himself one day."

"How do you mean?"

"He was showing off in a playground, swinging on this swing, standing up on it and going higher and higher. He was trying to impress me. That's why. And then he went right over the top and fell. He was just lying there on the ground as still as anything. A woman came running over. My whole body felt like it was full of pins and needles. I just got up and walked home. I still feel guilty about it."

"What else could you have done?"

"I don't know. Something."

Teddy arrived with their drinks and winked at Wilf. Apparently he was still an admirer despite or perhaps because of the theft of the two glasses. After he went away Wilf said, "I took a photograph of our man in the woods out to Duncan. He says he never worked for him."

Carole looked a little frightened. "Isn't that what the police are supposed to do, run around with photographs?"

"Remember those tracks I was telling you about? The thing is, who'd be more likely to think up a trick like that than Duncan? And the murderer used a horse and cutter. And Duncan knows all the bush lots around here and there's not a farmhouse any-where near Cline's bush so it was the perfect spot. And of course, there's the question of the axe."

Carole closed her eyes. "Why are you taking this upon your-self?"

At that moment Wilf realized how much he wanted to tell her everything. Everything. About the man who wasn't really there. And the boy. And Buchenwald. "It's Andy. He wants me to help him out."

Carole opened her eyes again. She looked around the room. There were only a few other couples in the place. A quiet night. "I don't want to talk about this anymore."

"Carole?"

"What?"

"All right then." Something had caught Wilf's eye. Joe, the Head Man, had just passed the doorway and was heading down the hall.

"It just makes me feel sick," Carole was saying.

"Could you excuse me for a second?" Wilf got up from the table.

By the time he'd reached the men's washroom Joe was standing unsteadily at the urinal splashing copious amounts of urine into the long metal trough. Wilf stood at the other end and added his own flow to the floating cigarette butts and the discarded wads of gum.

"Hello again," Wilf said.

Joe didn't look at him and didn't reply.

"Remember me? We met at the camp yesterday. And later on we saw each other out by the woods."

Joe teetered a little.

"By the way, that man who was killed? We think we know who he is now."

Joe shook himself off and began to button up his trousers.

"And we know who did it. It had nothing to do with you. Nothing to do with your men."

Joe turned slowly and looked at Wilf with enormous bloodshot eyes.

"He came from your camp, though."

"Basil," Joe said. His voice sounded thicker than it had the day before.

"Yes, Basil." Wilf turned away and trying to look nonchalant stared at the grimy wall in front of him.

"Nothing but trouble. All his life. I should have said no. That's all."

"No to what?"

"No!" Joe bellowed, "No to Basil. No to his goddamn nonsense. No to stirring up trouble all the time. No!"

Wilf could hear Joe staggering off, opening the door. He zipped himself up.

"Go to hell, Basil," Joe was mumbling. "Take your tricks down the tracks. Bother some other people. We know who you are." He was leaning heavily against the door frame. He swung his head up and looked back at Wilf. "How he escaped the ovens, no one knows. Yes, ovens, Mr. Policeman. Ovens for men like Basil. For men who made love with other men. Didn't you know this? And there was our Basil , every day trying to be like a woman. He'd never stop bothering the other men."

Joe turned and blundered out the door.

Wilf crossed to the sink and ran some water. He could see the little man lying in the snow. He could see the lonely house out in the country, its shop and barn standing in a sea of wintery fields.

He could see Duncan.

❄ ❄ ❄

Andy was already standing at the end of his driveway when Wilf picked him up. It was one o'clock in the morning. Andy slid in beside him and closed the door.

"What did you tell Linda?"

"That you were having trouble sleeping again. That you wanted to go for a drive."

"What did she say?"

"Tell Wilf hello."

Wilf pulled away down the narrow back street. "No, she didn't. What did she really say?"

"'What are you two up to?' and then, when I didn't answer she said, 'Jesus Christ.' How was the dance?"

"It was good."

"How good?"

"Let's just say it was good."

"Okay." Andy grinned and started patting himself down.

When Wilf had come back to the beverage room he hadn't told Carole what Joe had said, but he'd suddenly found himself going on about the impression the iron tether had left in the ice and the plan to meet up with Andy later that night to go out to Duncan's to search in his cutter for the same tether. He even went

169

so far as to pull out the folded piece of paper he was carrying where he'd traced the stress cracks.

"It's like someone's fingerprint," he said, opening it up and showing it to her.

Carole hardly looked at it and she didn't say anything in response.

"What are you thinking?"

"I should go home now," Carole said.

They drove in silence over to her house with a tortuous space between them and it was Carole who closed the gap to kiss good night. Wilf held her tightly to him. "I love you," he said, though it was the last thing he'd intended to say.

"I love you, too," Carole had replied all in a rush, as if the words had been torn right out of her.

Andy found his cigarettes. He lit one up and filled the car with a cloud of smoke. They were approaching the north end of the town. "Duncan should be fast asleep by now."

"I threw a flashlight in the back. How about you?"

"What do you think I am, an amateur?" Andy drew a flashlight out of his coat pocket. "Just remember. If it is a match, we bring it back into town. Nothing more."

"Yes, Sergeant."

"And pray we don't get a sudden thaw that melts that goddamn piece of ice in your garage." Andy grinned at him.

It looked to Wilf like he was enjoying himself.

Carole's bedroom window lit up. Duncan had been waiting a long time and felt frozen but it was worth it. It was always worth it. Besides, tonight was going to be a special night. He could feel his heart beginning to spin like a flywheel.

He stepped across the backyard and reached for one of the

small pieces of ice he'd stuffed in his coat pocket just for this very moment. He knew he should catch Carole's attention before she started taking off her clothes. That way she wouldn't suspect that he'd ever stood in her backyard before. It would seem like the first time.

And he had to be careful not to wake up her father, but then again he really didn't care anymore. He'd just say what he had to say anyway. Nothing could stop him now. He had to do it.

Duncan tossed up the first piece of ice that came to hand and to his surprise scored a direct hit. The glass rattled. Carole came to the window and looked out. He stepped into the rectangular patch of light on the snow. Carole shaded her eyes. He waved up at her. He motioned for her to open her window.

Carole continued to stare down at him but she didn't move. Then he realized why. There was a storm window covering the outside. He'd forgotten about that. She could raise the inside window, but it wouldn't do any good. She still wouldn't be able to hear what he was about to say.

That wasn't part of his plan.

Carole disappeared.

I'm in trouble, Duncan thought. He took a few steps back toward the trees and was about to break into a run, but he stopped himself. He was a man, after all. He was going to act like one.

He stood there bracing himself, waiting for Mr. Birley to come out and call him bad names. The back door opened and Carole stepped out instead. She looked really small standing there on the stoop in the cold. She didn't even have a coat on.

That's how much she wants to see me, Duncan thought to himself.

"What are you doing?" Carole whispered.

"Hi, Carole," Duncan said, and though he felt warm inside, burning up really, he noticed that he was beginning to shiver.

"It's late, Duncan." Her breath made plumes of gentle frost in the air delicate as little clouds. "Where's your horse and cutter?"

"Over at the feed mill. I'm going to buy a car."

"When?"

"When we get married." Duncan walked toward her through the snowy dark. He'd said it now and now he was really shivering. "Please marry me, Carole!"

Carole's face didn't look happy, not like he'd always imagined her face would look once he'd finally gotten around to saying it. She looked sad.

"Oh god, Duncan, I'm not planning on getting married just yet. I have to stay here and help my parents. You know how it is. With some things."

"Wilf McLauchlin came out to see me today. He's a friend of mine."

"Oh?"

Duncan reached the bottom step. He put his boot up on it. "He said he'll come to our wedding. I'm going to ask for him to make a speech."

"Are you on your way home right now then? Is that where you're going right now?"

Duncan could see that her hand had gone behind her back and she was feeling for the door. He had to think of something to say. "It's okay to get married if Wilf McLauchlin's going to come to the wedding. Your parents won't mind. He's a war hero."

"I know."

Duncan began to climb the steps. "What's the matter? You were going to marry Donny Mason."

"That was different, though. Things have changed."

"What's changed?"

Carole opened the door—she wasn't going to answer.

"We don't have to get married right now," Duncan blurted out. He'd reached the top step. "When, though? When?"

"I have to ask you a question," Carole said.

Duncan couldn't stop shaking, she looked so beautiful standing there in the moonlight.

"That man they found out in Cline's bush. Did you hurt him?"

Duncan was struck by a bolt of lightning. He fell down on his knees. "No! God, no! I wouldn't hurt no one. Oh, Jesus Christ!"

"You wouldn't?'

"No! I wouldn't hurt you!"

"I know you wouldn't hurt me. I know that." Carole's face had turned as pale as the moon. "Good night," she said. She went into the house and closed the door.

Duncan remained where he was hoping she might come back. When it was obvious she wasn't going to, he got up on his feet again. Try as he might he couldn't figure out whether he'd won or lost.

He walked slowly back toward the trees.

At least she knew what he was thinking about and what he wanted, he'd spoken up like a man, and that part felt good. Asking about the dead man didn't feel so good, though. The part about trusting him not to hurt her did, it felt especially good.

It was all mixed up.

Duncan wanted to keep walking like any respectable grown man would, move through the dark grove of trees, slide down the bank to the edge of the river and retrace his steps. But he couldn't.

He looked back at the lighted window and stopped. He could see Carole again. She looked more beautiful than she'd ever looked before. Ever.

"Don't," Duncan whispered.

But she did. She reached up and pulled the curtains closed.

❋ ❋ ❋

The cutter was missing from its place beside the stable and so was the gentle Babe. Dandy had been left behind, snorting and stamping around in his dark stall, unhappy with flashlights blinding him, unhappy with two strangers sneaking in through the door.

"It's all right, Dandy. There's a boy," Wilf said.

"We should have checked the hotels first. Jesus." Andy beamed his flashlight around the stable and out into a larger, cavernous barn. A buggy flashed by in the light. "He'll be drunk as a skunk by now."

"That should make it easier." Wilf circled around Dandy's stall and turned his flashlight off. He ran his hand along the big horse's neck. He could feel Dandy's hot breath on his face. He was settling down a little now that he'd had a good smell. Wilf felt sure that the horse remembered him from before.

"Maybe I'll go over to the shop and look around," Andy said.

"When I was out here earlier I got the impression that Duncan's more than smart enough in his own way. There's a ton of axes over there, all shapes and sizes, though I doubt the one he used on that poor bastard will be there."

"Not likely." Andy stuck a cigarette in his mouth.

Wilf was about to tell him that perhaps he shouldn't smoke in a barn, but relented. Andy was being a faithful friend, particularly given what he was personally risking. Wilf decided to keep a close eye on him instead.

"You know what bothers me." Andy was trying to manage his flashlight, his cigarette and strike a match all at the same time. "Motivation. You've been away a long time, Wilf. It's quite the sight sometimes, when Getty's had too much to drink and he's lurching around like a big steamboat down in the hotels. The boys have their fun, some of it more than a little mean-spirited too, but he just smiles and goes around hugging everyone. I don't think he's ever raised his hand to anyone in all his life. So what was his motivation?"

Wilf felt for Dandy's velvety nose. The horse jerked his head away.

"Even if that piece of paper matches up, all it proves is that he was on that back road in his cutter at some time. Nothing more."

"Shhh," Wilf said, reaching out again for the horse's head, but slower this time. All the way out from town he'd been on the edge of telling Andy what Joe had said, but finally he'd ended up remaining silent. He wasn't sure why. Maybe because Joe seemed to be leading him back to where he didn't want to go. Ovens and death camps. In the light of Buchenwald it seemed uncanny. "Are you getting cold feet?"

"No."

"We have more than the weight tether. We have that kid who says the man in the photograph worked here."

"Right. But you told me Duncan denied it." The beam of Andy's flashlight fell on a dusty window. He went over to it, turned his flashlight off and looked out toward the dark house. "I should have passed what that kid told me over to the OPP. That was a mistake. I'm in trouble again."

"I crashed my plane near Buchenwald," Wilf said.

In the faint moonlight coming through the window he could see Andy turn to look at him.

"It's a work camp in Germany. They executed thousands of people in there."

"Oh yeah?"

"So I'm just wondering, what do you suppose their motivation was? It went on for a long time. No matter what drove them to it in the first place you'd think they would have sickened of it after a year or two. Or three or four. Wouldn't you? What kept it going for so long?"

Andy turned his flashlight back on. He was looking uncomfortable. "Beats me."

"I wonder what Adrienne O'Dell's motivation was."

Andy flashed his light on Wilf for a moment and then flicked it away. "Money. Property. Wasn't it?"

Wilf could see Adrienne's pale eyes again. "I don't know," he said.

They sat in the buggy waiting for Duncan to return. Wilf didn't talk about Buchenwald or Adrienne O'Dell anymore. He began to talk about moving to Toronto. Arranging a place to stay. Organizing his lectures. Getting a reading list.

Andy talked about wanting to take on a few administrative responsibilities from the Chief of Police, now that he was a sergeant, but the Chief was not inclined to share. Afraid to share most likely. Not even the most routine ones.

Dandy was the first to hear Babe's sharp hooves clipping along the frozen road. He whinnied and began to bob his head. Wilf and Andy scrambled out of the buggy, retreated into deeper shadow and listened through the cracks in the barn wall. The cutter jangled into the yard and pulled up. After a moment an outside light and a light in the stable flashed on. They could hear Duncan clucking to Babe as he led her out of her traces, took off her stiff leather blanket, her heavy harness. The stable door swung open and the steaming Babe and Duncan came in. He swung the big animal around and began to rub her legs down with an old flannel towel. He picked up a wool blanket, tossed it over her broad back and cinched it up.

Wilf could see Babe lift her head up over Duncan every once in a while and stare straight at him. Duncan didn't seem to notice. He led her into her stall, carried a pail of water to her, topped up Dandy's water bowl, gave them both a dipper or two of oats and went back out the door. The stable light and the outside light went off.

Andy crept through the dark to the window again. "He's heading toward the house. In a straight line. He must be sober."

Babe was thrashing her head around.

"It's okay," Wilf called softly to her, "there's a girl." Though he couldn't see her, he could feel her eyes rolling. "Shhh, Babe." Dandy was complacently munching his oats. Wilf walked up to her. "You remember me. Sure you do."

"He went inside." Andy said and moved toward the stable door. "Come on."

Wilf liked the smell of the stable, the rich, earthy warmth of it, and the fleshy reality of the horses, all that indisputable living weight. He wanted to touch Babe's great neck, rub her nose a little. It seemed to him to be the most important thing he could possibly do. And stay there forever. And everything else would fall away.

Andy was already rummaging around in the cutter by the time Wilf came out. A light from the kitchen window was shining across the yard.

Andy poked his head up. "Look in the back," he whispered.

Wilf walked around to the back of the cutter, lifted the top of a wooden box fastened there, stuck his flashlight in and turned it on. The inside of the box lit up like a jack-o'-lantern. He could see a pile of rags, a clutter of tools and chains, a coil of rope. And a round iron tether. "It's here."

Andy scrambled over the front seat, peered in and reached inside. "Goddamn thing weighs a ton."

"It needs to be heavy because of the size of the horses."

"Thank you, Professor," Andy said, his spirits on the rise. He jumped down to the ground and tried from there, finally managing to haul out the weight with a minimal amount of grunting and banging, and bracing it against his stomach, staggered off toward the barnyard to be out of sight of the house.

"Be sure not to drop it on your foot," Wilf said.

"You're a pain in the ass," Andy replied. He eased it down on the snow and tipped it over.

Wilf shone his light on it. "*JF*. Right there in the middle."

"I see it," Andy said.

Wilf was checking his piece of paper. "That big crack matches up. So does this one. And the little ones. It's perfect."

Andy looked up at him. "We forgot something."

"What?"

"That we have to carry this bloody thing all the way back to your father's car." Andy surveyed the situation. "Maybe we don't. I'm going to drive right in here with the headlights off. Give me the keys. If Duncan notices it won't matter. We'll be gone before he can do anything about it."

"He'll know something's up."

"So what? Where's he going to run? He's got nowhere to go."

Wilf watched Andy skirt around the barnyard, wade through some deeper snow to the road and begin to jog toward a hill some distance away. The car was parked on the other side and as close to a deep ditch as Wilf had dared to go. It was facing the wrong way, though, and the road was narrow.

Wilf turned away from the weight tether. The light was still on in the kitchen. Strains of dance music began to waft across the yard. A shadow glided by the kitchen window.

Wilf stood there for a moment and listened. The shadow glided by the other way. Wilf began to limp across the side yard. The music grew louder. He peered in through the window. All the fighters and the bombers were dancing together on the ends of their threads, swinging to and fro, spinning, tangling. Underneath them Duncan was sprawled out in the old sofa chair, his head tilted back, a bottle of rye propped up between his thighs.

Wilf moved along the side of the house to the back kitchen and unlatched the door. The music was even louder inside. He crossed to the other door and pushed it open. The planes were still moving of their own accord. Now he could see that Duncan's eyes were closed.

"Hello, Duncan," Wilf said.

Duncan rolled his head to the side and looked at Wilf for a long time. "I was dancin'. Just now."

"Were you?"

"Wanna see?" Duncan put the bottle on the floor, got up and began to spin, slow and ponderous and stately, ignoring the fact that the beat of the music was moving twice as fast. He put his arms out and closed his eyes. The planes began to speed up. The whole house seemed to tilt a little, lift up off the ground.

Wilf had to lean against the wall.

Duncan pinwheeled around and around. "Look at the monkey dance," he called out. "Look at him dance!"

Wilf crossed the room and turned off the radio.

Duncan came to a stop. His matted curls were hanging down, shiny with sweat. His heavy smell filled the room. "I'm practisin' for my wedding. I'm marryin' Carole."

"Are you?"

"Well shit, Wilf, I don't know!"

"Did she say yes?"

"You know what she said? She asked me that same question you asked me this afternoon. It was just exactly the same. I guess you must think I'm stupid."

"You're far from that, Duncan."

"I'm the monkey in the middle."

"No, you're not."

"She works for your father. So do you. You work together. Don't you?"

"Not really."

"You fucked up every fuckin' thing!" The planes were still soaring in the air between them. "Why did you make her ask me that question? You ruined everythin'."

Duncan was looking as sorrowful as anyone Wilf had ever

seen. "Duncan, she was just trying to help you. That's all. We're both trying to help you."

"You don't need to do that though, do you? Because I didn't do nothin'."

"No?"

"No!"

"You mean, you didn't do nothing really bad? When you were with Basil? Is that what you mean?"

Duncan's cat eyes darted toward Wilf. The Spitfire with its red and orange flames was slowing down, circling over his head.

"This is what I know," Wilf said. "Basil worked here and he must have bunked in here too, because it would have been too far to walk all the way back to the DP camp every night. Where did he sleep?"

"Is that what you told Carole?"

"No. She doesn't know anything. Look at it this way. We're all soldiers in life, you just as much as anyone else and sometimes soldiers have to do things."

Duncan's tawny eyes blinked.

"You're like me," Wilf said.

Duncan looked away.

"When you said I'd killed twelve people earlier today because I'd shot down twelve planes, some of those planes had crews of two or three. One had a crew of six. Just to let you know who you're talking to."

"You're a hero."

"Because I had to be. We're the same in that way. You and me. Both haunted, too."

Duncan ran a huge hand through his sweaty hair. He scratched at his head. He began to wander around the room.

"I'll be your wing man, Duncan. I'll watch your back. I'll keep you safe. But in order to do that I need to know what happened."

"Nothin' happened," Duncan said.

"You went home and got two more boots and walked

through the bush twice again. That happened. And then you burned them, and all your blood-splattered clothes, too, maybe in that stove in the shop. That happened. And you hid the axe in a special place."

Duncan blundered into the kitchen table and came to a stop. He hung his shaggy head down. "My mother keeps me safe. She keeps me safe."

"Duncan, why did Basil have to die?"

"Because."

"Because?"

"Because. He was putting bad thoughts inside my head."

"What kind of thoughts?"

Duncan lifted up his face and looked at Wilf, his eyes as wide and bewildered as a child's. "The kind you go to Hell for. But I didn't. Not even when he came up the stairs, not even when he laid down on my own bed. I was scared, though. I was scared to move, Wilf. But after a while he went away and the next morning I got up and I said to him, "Guess what? We've got to go over to Cline's bush and mark out some trees today." That's what I said because I had to teach him I wasn't like that, I wasn't like that at all, and then when we got into the trees I grabbed his scrawny neck and I began to beat on him. I was just goin' to show him that I was just like everybody else, he could act any way he wanted, it didn't mean nothin' to me. And he was lyin' on the ground and I got a boot on his chest and I had the other one squeezin' down on his hand and I got this feelin'. It was like runnin' through the dark, it was like being really, really drunk, it was like seeing Carole, even. And then I knew I was going to do what I'd been thinkin' about doin'. Thinking about it! Oh Mommy, I took up the axe! "

"Duncan," Andy said. He was standing by the kitchen door. He'd come in so quietly and Wilf had been so riveted to Duncan, he hadn't noticed him.

Duncan hadn't, either. He swung around.

Andy pulled a service revolver out of his coat and pointed it at Duncan's head.

"Wilf, call the station. Where's your phone, Duncan?" He took his eyes off Duncan just long enough to glance around and in that instant Duncan crashed through the kitchen window. It was the fastest move Wilf had ever seen.

"Oh Jesus, shit!" Andy yelled and disappeared back out the door.

Wilf looked through the shattered window. He could see Duncan staggering off toward the shop, picking up speed, plunging out into the deep snow, wading out into the moonlight.

Andy knelt down on one knee and took a long careful aim.

Wilf waited.

Andy lowered the revolver. He turned around to the gaping window. "He's heading for his own woodlot. Call down to the station!"

Wilf looked around the kitchen. He could see a phone hanging on a wall just inside a hallway and half-hidden by newspaper clippings. He hurried over and picked it up.

"Number please," Nancy Dearborn said at the other end of the line.

❋ ❋ ❋

Ted Bolton and Charlie Wilson arrived from the town's police force and soon afterward an OPP cruiser came tearing into Duncan's yard.

Wilf stood to the side and listened to Andy explaining to a pissed-off detective that he'd just learned that night from Wilf McLauchlin, the fellow with the cane standing right over there, that he had an important piece of evidence pointing to Duncan Getty, and so he'd decided to act as quickly as possible, he was a Sergeant of Police after all. With that, Andy gave Wilf a desperate look over the detective's shoulder.

Andy became part of the search team. Wilf went home alone.

He drove slowly into town, eased the car into the garage and turned off the lights and the motor. He sat there for a moment. He didn't want to go into the house, he didn't want to face his father.

He got out of the car, crouched down in front of the wooden crate and felt under the rags for the circle of ice. It was still there.

The detective out at Duncan's had introduced himself. "I've been meaning to talk to you before this, Mr. McLauchlin. I met your father the other day."

"I know," Wilf had replied.

"So this evidence Sergeant Creighton's referring to, something about an impression left in some ice?"

"That's right."

"And could you tell me just how you came across this piece of evidence?"

"If you want to see it, it's in my father's garage."

The detective had stared hard at Wilf for what seemed like a long time. "Tell you what. We have to round this fellow up. Why don't I drop by first thing in the morning?"

"All right," Wilf had replied.

Wilf put the rags back in place and climbed into the passenger side of the car. The car was cooling off. Soon it would be below freezing. A familiar sensation. It was always cold in his Spitfire. And when he'd return to base and pull off his flight suit, his body would be gleaming in all its naked glory bathed in sweat.

Anxiety. Continually rolling the plane from side to side, watching three hundred and sixty degrees. Death could come from any direction. Anytime.

Wilf tried to stay off his bad hip and stretch his legs out. He couldn't. He closed his eyes. He could feel the roll now. Back and forth. Back and forth. He could see the countryside passing far below.

Twelve kills. Maybe twenty-five men in all, though some had parachuted out. He'd been tempted to swing around and strafe them to bloody ribbons. Oh god, how he'd been tempted.

Twenty souls, say, in total. Twenty. An unthinkable number. Better to think in planes. I killed a plane today.

And the water was churning and Adrienne was holding the old man's legs up as high as she could manage and she was screaming down at his startled eyes and his hair was floating under the water and the last bubble of his life was climbing up toward her, and Adrienne's feelings were climbing too, an ecstatic shuddering climb, a soaring infinite release.

Wilf knew this. It was just as Duncan had said.

Duncan and Adrienne had felt the same thing.

CHAPTER THIRTEEN

The train swung away from the river and moved into the city, rattling over rusty overpasses, beside factories, past rows of houses with wrought-iron staircases and balconies, and finally came to a steaming halt in a large downtown station. Wilf gathered up his overnight bag.

He was supposed to be in Toronto, at least that's what he'd told Carole and his father, but instead he'd only disembarked there long enough to switch to another train. He was in Montreal, three hundred and fifty miles further east.

Wilf walked over to the first public phone he saw and checked the address. It was the same as the information operator had given him a few days earlier: Dr. Michael Chasson, Orthopedic Surgeon, 355 rue Sainte-Catherine. He wondered about calling Michael now. He'd intended to put through a call when the operator had first looked up the phone number but within a heartbeat he'd changed his mind.

Don't give him a warning, he'd thought to himself.

Wilf closed the phonebook, climbed a long flight of stairs and looked around for a cab.

It had been a week since Duncan had been arrested. He'd spent the night hiding in his own woods, as if no one would look for him there. It was a simple enough job to follow his tracks at first light. When he'd finally been flushed out from where he'd been hiding, he was so cold he could hardly move.

Andy had told Wilf all this, and Wilf and Carole had made love later that same day, in Cabin Three alongside the frozen river. If the first time had been exploratory and gently escalating, the second had been the opposite, urgent and careening. He kissed her so hard Carole could taste blood in her mouth and his eyes seemed not so much full of a reasoned passion but panic. She had to hold him to her as tightly as she'd ever held anyone in all her life, pressing his face down against her face, refusing to give him any space until his body struggled and shuddered against her for the final time, until he slowly grew still, pressing her down into the thin mattress, his body suddenly as heavy and motionless as lead.

She stroked his hair then and she forgave him his craziness. He'd gone out to Duncan's in the middle of the night and he'd found out the truth. About the man in the woods. About the severed arm. Everything that was terrifying and awful. She could see Duncan standing below her in the light from her bedroom window and she clung to Wilf in the dark of their little cabin and she kissed his ear and she made a vow to herself not to think about her wrinkled clothes or the continued lack of a condom or anything.

Over the next few days Wilf seemed embarrassed about what had happened but they didn't talk about it. He had to endure being questioned by two detectives from the Ontario Provincial Police as well as by his father, who found himself defending Wilf's vigilante actions once again and fighting to prevent him from being charged with unlawful interference in an ongoing investigation. At the end of the week the legal questions were still hanging in the air and so it didn't surprise Carole at all when he announced a three-day trip to Toronto to arrange a place to stay. It didn't surprise her, but it hurt.

They did talk about Duncan, about how Duncan had said she'd asked him that very same question. Had he hurt the man in the woods?

Wilf wanted to know how that had come about and so she told him.

"After we'd talked? You were all alone in your backyard with Duncan Getty?"

"I still trusted him," Carole had said.

The cab pulled up to a new blue-glassed building cramped between two stately and very old ones. Dr. Chasson's offices were in Suite 204. Wilf took the elevator and stepped into a waiting room full of people with various limbs wrapped in casts and holding onto large envelopes that Wilf knew contained their x-rays. Suddenly he felt right at home.

"I wonder if I could see Dr. Chasson," he said to the middle-aged receptionist who looked harried and whose eyes seemed to be set slightly too close together.

"Do you have an appointment?"

"No. But I'm a patient of his. A hospital in France. During the war."

"You have to have an appointment."

"If he knew I was here I'm sure he'd take a minute."

"I'm sorry. But as you can see, Dr. Chasson has overbooked himself and he has to be at the hospital by two." She made a tight smile, not unlike the ones Wilf remembered Dorothy Dale making. Her phone rang. "All I can do for you is to suggest you make a future appointment."

"I'm just in town for the day."

She picked up the phone. A door at the far end of the room opened and a patient on crutches swung out followed by a tall man wearing a faded lab coat. Wilf could see that Chasson was still sporting his extravagant and, according to rumours that had circulated among the nurses, infamous handlebar moustache. "Who's next?" he called out.

"Captain," Wilf said.

Michael Chasson looked Wilf's way. At first there was no sign of recognition and then his eyes came sharply to attention, there was a slight hesitation and he smiled. "Well, I'll be back in the army again. Wilf McLauchlin!"

"Hi, Doc."

"Look at you. How are you?"

Wilf spread out his one arm. "I'm fine. Perfect. You did a great job."

"Mr. Ducette is next in line, Doctor." The receptionist was holding her hand over the telephone and looking more than a little fierce. "I'll give this gentleman an appointment."

"Joy, this is Wilf McLauchlin."

"How do you do?" Joy sighed deeply.

"RCAF. Fighter pilot." Chasson grabbed Wilf's hand and then apparently not satisfied, gave him an energetic hug. "Just one moment, Monsieur Ducette. *Un moment, merci.* An old friend. I'll just be a moment. Everyone. Thank you." He ushered Wilf into his office and closed the door. "Jesus, McLauchlin, it's good to see you!"

"Same here."

"Damn it all. It's been what, two years, I guess."

"Almost."

"So how are you feeling?" He put both his hands on Wilf's bad shoulder and then ran them slowly down his arm. "I mean, really?"

"I have some pain now and then. It comes and goes. Nothing I can't handle."

"Where?"

"Just in my side here."

"Above your hip?"

"Just above. It's nothing."

"And everywhere else is fine? You're feeling well? I mean, generally?"

"Everything's fine. But I didn't come here for an examination. I wanted to ask you a question. I should have phoned first. I apologize."

"Why apologize? Are you kidding? We spent enough time together."

Chasson walked over to his desk and lit a cigarette.

"You and Dr. Windemyer."

Chasson smiled. "Chuck the Chopper."

"And lots of other docs."

"And a ton of patients, unfortunately. We were all in that mess together."

"And nurses."

Chasson smiled. "And nurses." He held out his cigarettes.

"No thanks." Wilf took a deep breath. "Michael, I want to ask you about my eyes."

"You've got the wrong doctor, Wilf."

"But I knew where you were practising after the war. I couldn't remember about the others."

"Chuck's in Melbourne. Jason Charles, your eye doctor, he's in Vancouver."

"You were with me all the way through, though, from when they flew me out of Germany until I left for England."

"I suppose I was."

Wilf eased himself down on a chair. "I've got lots of questions."

"Have you?"

"Why was I in isolation?"

"What do you mean?"

"I was in a room of my own for over two months. They said they wanted to keep me as still as possible because of my eyes. I said I'd keep myself as still as a rock in the general ward. I was going crazy, I needed company."

"It was because of your eyes, Wilf. And it worked."

"You were operating on me all through that time, though."

"Had to. You would have smelled real bad, otherwise."

Wilf had to smile. "There's something else, Michael. That last sortie of mine. It was on April the seventh, and you know I've always assumed I was found on the day I was shot down. But I wasn't."

Chasson leaned on the edge of his desk and regarded Wilf through a cloud of drifting smoke.

"I was found by some American troops on April the tenth, the day before those same troops stumbled on to Buchenwald. You've heard of Buchenwald."

"I'm not following."

"There's a gap of three days. I was lying in my smashed-up plane for three days only a mile or two from Buchenwald. Unconscious. Bleeding. No treatment. No water. I couldn't have lasted that long, I would have been dead."

"Obviously you weren't."

"Michael, why was I being held in isolation?"

"I told you why. And you know why."

"There's more to it than that. Isn't there?"

Chasson butted out his half-finished cigarette. "Look Wilf, I'd like nothing better than to spend more time with you, but you've seen that circus out there. Are you in town? Can I get in touch with you?"

"I want to see my medical records. All of them."

"Who's looking after you?

"Doc Kerry. He's in the military hospital in Burlington. I've seen the records he's got. They're mostly orthopedic and there's only a few."

Chasson walked back to the door. Wilf stayed sitting stubbornly where he was.

"I think you'll have to talk to the War Office in Ottawa then. If I were a betting man, and I am, I'd have to say the chances are slight that they've kept all the medical records of every casualty in all the services over five years of war, but if they have they'd be up there."

"I was wondering if you could help me do just that. They'd listen to you before they'd listen to me."

"You're the patient."

"You're the doctor. We could do it together."

Chasson reached for the door. "How long are you in town?"

"I could stay a few days."

"Knowing the military it'll take a lot longer than that. Tell you what. Give me your phone number. There's a pad on my desk. I'll call if I have any news."

Chasson swung the door open. "Monsieur Ducette, come in now please. *Entrez*," he called out.

❋ ❋ ❋

"Good afternoon. McLauchlin and McLauchlin," Carole's voice came down the line.

Wilf hesitated.

"Hello?" Carole said.

"Hi."

"Oh. Hi."

"How are you?"

"I'm fine. How are you?"

"Good. I got back late yesterday."

"I know. Your father told me."

"I was going to call but I made the mistake of going upstairs and lying down first. I guess I was more tired than I thought."

"Well, I'm sure you were busy in Toronto."

"Yeah. Well, no."

"No?"

"I didn't stay with my friends. As it turned out. I got a room in a hotel instead."

"For three days?"

" I didn't feel like the usual college stuff. I guess."

"Oh."

"Dad left today."

"I know."

"For Windsor. Until the end of the week. Litigating some property case. He was hired on at the last minute."

"I work here. I know."

"Carole?"

"What?"

"I don't suppose you'd catch a cab and come up here. Would you? I mean, after work?"

"Why?"

"I'll make you supper."

"And then what?"

"We can talk. I'd like to talk."

"If I take a cab up there everyone will know."

"I'd come and get you but I'm a bit shaky. I don't know why." Wilf was standing in the upstairs hall. He tried to control his voice. "I'm not having that great a day. I don't think I can drive."

It was only three thirty in the afternoon but Carole took it upon herself to close the office early. Fifteen minutes later she was rapping on the loose window in the side door.

Wilf came down the steps. He was smiling and looked normal enough. He opened the door.

Carole came in on the landing, a sprinkling of snowflakes on her hat and coat. "It's snowing," she announced.

Wilf took off her hat and kissed her.

"Did you lie?" she said.

"About what?"

"About not feeling well?"

"No. I might have exaggerated a little."

"If someone calls the office or drops in you can explain this to your father." They kissed again and she could feel her body leaning up against his. She couldn't help it.

Wilf helped her take off her coat, hung it up for her and led her along the front hall.

"This isn't a good idea," Carole said.

They started up the stairs.

As soon as Wilf led her into his room he realized, not for the first time, that his bed looked like a kid's bed. It was a reddish-brown colour and the finials were as big as bowling balls. His father had bought it for him when he'd turned thirteen and was just entering high school. And it seemed too narrow for two people. And he'd forgotten that when he'd dragged himself out of it shortly before noon he hadn't bothered to pull up the covers.

Carole looked the bed over in the faint light coming in from the window. She was wearing a smart-looking sweater-and-skirt set. He could see that she'd freshened up her makeup before she'd come up the hill. Her unruly lock of hair was still in place.

"I missed you," Wilf said.

Carole looked at him.

The bed turned out not to be too small, after all. Wilf made love as slowly and gently as he could, remembering the last time. As lovingly as he could.

Carole responded, gently, lovingly.

And once again they told each other that they loved each other.

Afterward they lay curled up together under the covers. Soon there was no light left and Carole fell asleep. Wilf could hear her soft breathing, feel it feathering across his cheek, and the touch of her naked belly pressing gently against his belly with each breath. Her absolute trust filled his heart.

Carole woke with a start. She gathered up her clothes, held them in front of herself and phoned her mother from the upstairs hallway just to say that she wouldn't be coming home for supper, that Wilf was taking her out. Instead they stayed in and made supper together.

Carole had been in the McLauchlin house several times before, but only long enough to drop off or pick up some work. She knew that what she was doing was not proper behaviour for a legal secretary, she knew it was foolish and childish and stupid beyond belief. And she watched Wilf chopping onions. And she watched him steal glances at her stealing glances at him and then they'd both smile. And she'd never felt so happy in all her life. After supper Wilf built a fire in the study and turned off the lights. The reflection from the flames made the shadows dance. He spread a blanket over the rug and they sat there together as if they were camping. He touched her hand, her hair, her cheek. They made love. When they were finished they rolled themselves up in the blanket and rested. Carole kissed his forehead, his nose, his eyes.

"I went to Montreal," Wilf said.

"When?"

"Before I went to Toronto."

Carole moved back a little. Half of Wilf's face was hidden in shadow, the other half seemed to glow from the fire.

"Why?"

"To see this doctor. A friend of mine. I was wondering if he knew what had happened to my eyes?"

"What had happened to your eyes?"

"I was blind for close to three months."

Carole propped herself up on an elbow. "I didn't know that. From when you crashed?"

"I'm trying to figure something out."

"What?"

Wilf could see the piles of Nuremberg transcripts stacked up behind her. From his perspective their shadows looked huge on the wall. "There's something going on."

Carole leaned over and touched her forehead against his forehead, as if she didn't want him to say anything more.

"Mr. Cruikshank. And the man in the woods. Not so much the way they were killed, but how they looked after they were killed."

"Don't," she whispered.

"There's these doctors being tried in Nuremberg. For experimenting with prisoners in the work camps. Freezing people to death. Cutting off their arms."

Carole kept her forehead against his but she didn't respond.

"I think there's a connection. Somehow."

She still didn't respond.

"I'm the connection," Wilf said.

Carole lay back down and stared up at the ceiling.

Wilf watched her for a moment.

"Carole," he whispered. He kissed her cheek.

"That doesn't make any sense."

"I know. That's why I got jumpy earlier today. I was sitting in this room and it struck me right down to the very bottom of my soul that it didn't make any sense."

Carole turned to look at him. "But that's good."

Wilf smiled. "Is it?"

Carole rolled over and wrapped her arms around his head and held him to her. He could feel his left arm slide over his hip and down his back. Flop uselessly there.

I'm a wreck, he thought.

"I'm not going home tonight," Carole announced.

"Of course you're going home. I'm all right now."

"How can you be all right now?"

"Because of you." He could feel her intake of breath. Her arms grew tighter. "I won't talk about this anymore." He could feel her tears, warm and slippery. "It's gone," he said.

Wilf drove Carole home at two o'clock in the morning, driving as smoothly and in as straight a line as possible to prove that he was a man in full possession of himself. Before she'd even get into the car she made him promise to come into the office that morning. She had to be there by nine o'clock. Wilf promised he'd be there shortly thereafter.

They pulled up in front of her house. The porch light had been left on. It looked like both a forlorn and a hopeful signal from her family. Wilf's heart filled up again at the sight of it. At the very least, he'd taken on the responsibility to be kind.

He glanced over at Carole. She was staring at the light, too.

❄ ❄ ❄

Wilf came into the office just before noon, carrying two take-out lunches he'd purchased at King Sun Lao's Canadian Chinese Restaurant. They ate in Clarence's office.

During that afternoon Carole was relieved to see Wilf chatting in a friendly manner with the few clients that dropped in, though she did notice that the clients seemed more curious about Duncan Getty and what went on out at Cline's bush than the disposition of their own files.

What Wilf was noticing was a certain wariness creeping into people's eyes, not that they blamed him in any way for Adrienne and her boyfriend or Duncan Getty. It was more that he'd been too close to those scenes of mayhem not to have picked up something disquieting and fearful along the way. And then of course, there was the astounding fact that he had some kind of eerie instinct for sniffing out and solving these things.

At five o'clock Carole and Wilf locked up the office and walked out toward Main Street. As they passed through the wrought-iron gate, Wilf suggested that this might be a good night to drive to Brantford, have a leisurely supper and then think of something else they could do. Carole said that she knew exactly what that something else was that he had in mind, and though it was a tempting offer it would be better if she went home and had supper with her parents. Though her mother wasn't saying anything she was giving her funny looks. And her father seemed angry and grim, harrumphing about the house.

"Harrumphing?" Wilf said.

"I just should stay home tonight. I'm going to talk to mom about it."

"About what?"

It was the middle of March and the weather had turned mild. Ice was melting off the roofs of the stores and streams of water were splashing down on the sidewalk and the days were lasting longer.

"Just that I don't want her worrying about me. And that I want to be free to come and go. Just so she'll understand. She just wants me to talk."

"How about your dad? Does he just want you to talk?"

"Mom will talk to him."

"I think you need your own place."

Carole blushed a little. "I think you need your own place."

"Okay."

"I'm only talking. You're going to Toronto soon. Remember?"

Wilf looked above the stores. The sky was turning red. "I'm not sure how keen I am on that anymore." Or how capable, he thought to himself.

Wilf came into the office the next couple of mornings and stayed all day. Apparently Carole and her mother had had a woman-to-woman talk and all was quiet on that front. Wilf had been sleeping reasonably well with the help of his sleeping pills. And no more disturbing dreams.

"I think I'll walk over and get this signed. It's too nice a day to stay cooped up in here." Wilf got up from his desk.

"That's a little unfair, don't you think?"

Carole had been pounding on her typewriter all morning but the piles of legal drafts surrounding her seemed to be growing rather than shrinking. And his father had called Wilf the previous evening. If everything continued to go well in court in Windsor he'd be back in the office by late afternoon the next day.

"I could type and you could walk over."

Carole kept typing. "Can you type?"

"No."

Carole had the idea that if she could only catch up with all her backlog of work Mr. McLauchlin wouldn't know that she'd been in his house and was having an affair with his son. She knew there was a fatal error of logic in there somewhere but her fingers kept flying across the keys nevertheless.

"I'll tell you what's not fair." Wilf was pulling on his coat by the front door.

"What's that?"

"The lousy benefits these war widows are getting. Their husbands go off to serve their country, lose their lives doing it, and then the government is so damn parsimonious their benefits wouldn't keep a mouse in cheese for a month. No wonder she's had to sell her house."

Carole kept typing. "Who are you talking about? Sylvia Young?"

"Her house closes at the end of the month. She probably needs the money to buy groceries."

"At least she has a house to sell."

"That's a bit small-minded."

Carole stopped typing and looked over at Wilf. He was leaning against the door with a disapproving expression on his face. They'd decided that this was the night they'd drive to Brantford for supper. Carole knew that that meant a hotel room afterward, and the truth was she'd been looking forward to it. Now she felt hurt and wasn't sure. "I just mean there are lots of women in town worse off than Sylvia Young. She stays at home with one child, right?"

"I don't know."

"Well, she does. And she has a house to sell. There are lots of women with two or three kids, they're working six days a week in one of the factories and have nothing to fall back on."

"I stand corrected," Wilf said.

"It's not that I don't think they should get more money. They should all get more money."

Wilf smiled. "I find it difficult working with you."

"Why?"

"I can't keep my mind fully on my work."

Carole wasn't ready to let go of her pique just yet. "Then a little fresh air might help," she said, turning back to her typing.

The river was high and muddy and full of ice. The beginning of spring breakup. When Wilf was young he and his friends used to hang over the downtown bridge and watch the water rush under their feet. If they did this long enough and didn't think of anything else, it would feel as if the water had come to a stop and the bridge was beginning to churn its way up the river.

Wilf leaned over the railing and stared into the water. It didn't work. His eyes kept focusing on the pans of ice rushing by.

He walked on. As he approached Sylvia Young's house he could see a boy standing on the veranda. He was a chubby kid and seemed a little cold standing there in just a windbreaker, light pants and bright white running shoes.

Rushing the season, Wilf thought to himself. It was all coming back. Every kid in town thought it was summer as soon as the snow began to melt. Time to get out the bicycles and the baseball bats. Wilf limped up the front walk. "Hi there," he called out.

The boy remained standing by the front door. He looked frightened.

"Are you Mrs. Young's boy?" Wilf climbed up on the porch. "Is there anyone home?"

The boy shook his head. Then he backed up, put his head over the railing and began to retch.

A smell like rotting eggs wrapped around Wilf, scouring his

eyes, searing his nostrils. He rang the doorbell. The smell was even stronger by the door. "Mrs. Young! Mrs. Young!"

The boy retreated down the steps.

"Hey! Where do you live?" Wilf called out.

The boy pointed down the street.

"Tell your mom to call the fire department. Hurry up!"

The boy took off in a waddling run across the melting snow. Wilf gulped a fresh breath and tried the door. It was locked. He hurried off the porch looking for a side door. There wasn't one. He rounded the back corner. Some rickety steps led into a small enclosed porch. He climbed them, pushed through the door into the fume-filled porch and immediately felt like gagging. "Mrs. Young!" he blurted out.

He grabbed for the inside door and pushed it open. A woman was sitting in an armchair, her head slumped over. Wilf took a chest-jolting breath, dropped his cane and moved across the kitchen toward her. She seemed to be sitting there under water; he couldn't make out her face. As soon as he touched her, she slid off the chair.

Wilf had to breathe again, and when he did his lungs caught fire. He made a grab for the woman's wrist and began to drag her across the floor. He reached the porch and fell down the outside steps. The woman slid down after him.

They sprawled out together in the puddled snow. Wilf turned to look at her. She lay there staring placidly back at him.

"I'm sorry," Wilf said, panting for breath, taking air in as deeply as his aching lungs allowed. He struggled to his feet and climbed the steps again. Carole had said something about a child.

He crossed through the kitchen and started down a hall, caught sight of a banister, touched it and knew that he either had to breathe and most likely pass out, or he had to turn around. He lurched back through the kitchen and now he could hear the stove hissing at him. He glanced at it. The oven door was gaping wide. He reached the small porch and half slid down the stairs again.

The woman hadn't moved. Wilf sat on the ground and lifted her head into his lap. Her eyes were just as glassy and calm, her arm just as stiffly outstretched as when he'd let it go. Wilf's eyes were running, glycerine-like water was streaming down his cheeks and everything around him looked elongated and smeared. The garage, the melting snow, the trees.

He looked into the backyard.

The boy in his striped uniform and the man with the rags on his feet were standing there.

CHAPTER FOURTEEN

Wilf held on to the woman he assumed was Sylvia Young and waited for someone to help him for what seemed a long time after the barefoot boy and the man had disappeared. He'd looked away, looked back and they were gone.

The first person Wilf saw who he knew for certain was not a mirage was the chubby kid peering around the back corner. A woman, looking distraught, came hurrying up behind him. "Is Sylvia all right?"

"No."

"Don't move," the woman said to the boy. She came a step closer. She clasped her hand to her mouth. "Oh my god! Where's Bradley?"

"Did you call the fire department?"

"Yes! Where's Bradley?"

"I don't know."

The woman looked up toward a second-floor window. "Oh my god!"

"I couldn't make it. I couldn't get up the stairs," Wilf said.

The woman turned, grabbed her boy's hand and disappeared. After a while Wilf could hear a fire truck coming down the street and pulling up out in front. Two of the town's volunteer firemen came rushing around the corner of the house wearing masks over their faces and tanks on their backs. They went in through the back door. The same woman, accompanied by another fireman, came up to Wilf. She was carrying some blankets in her arms. The fireman took one of them and began to cover Sylvia.

Wilf got up and, caneless, limped toward the front of the

house. The windows, one after another, began to shatter and shower down. The firemen inside the house were breaking them. One of them with his mask dangling over his shoulder came hurrying up from behind. He was carrying a boy in his arms. He went rushing past, laid the body down beside the fire truck and began to press on its chest.

The police cruiser pulled up and Constable Ted Bolton got out. Wilf reached the cruiser, opened the back door and crawled inside.

It didn't take long for a crowd of people to assemble, standing along the sidewalk and around the perimeter of the yard. Every once in a while someone would come over to the cruiser and peek in where Wilf was lying down. An ambulance arrived and took the boy away. Doc Robinson arrived. The ambulance came back and took Sylvia Young away.

After Wilf felt like sitting up he found that he couldn't take his eyes off the house. It was gaping open now, curtains blowing out of broken windows in a freshening wind, the front door flung wide.

Bolton crossed the yard swinging Wilf's cane around in his hand and got in the car. "I guess this is yours," he said, handing it over the back of the seat. "This is a rough one. The mother's dead. The kid's dead, too."

"Is he?" Wilf replied almost too softly for Bolton to hear.

"Why the hell would she do such a thing? I can see her taking her own life. I mean, I can't see that either, but at least it's her own decision. She's a grownup, right? But to take her own kid's life."

Bolton turned to look at Wilf as if he might know the answer. Wilf thought the man seemed shaken by it all, his long horse-face the colour of ashes. "You were delivering legal papers to her. Is that right?"

"Who told you that?"

"Your secretary." He nodded toward a knot of spectators.

Wilf could see Carole standing a little way down the street looking back at him. She'd forgotten to put her hat on; her hair was blowing around in the wind.

"According to Doc they've been dead for a while. Most of the night, anyway. There was nothing you could have done."

Wilf opened the back door.

"Wilf. I don't have to tell you, do I?"

"You'll need a statement," Wilf said.

He walked down the sidewalk toward Carole. People moved back a little, opening the way for him as if he might be carrying something contagious. He kept his eyes fixed on Carole's face. When he came up to her, she leaned against him and put her face close to his.

"I'm sorry," she said.

"Not for me."

"No. Not for you." She put her arm through his good arm and held him. The woman who'd brought the blankets was standing a short distance away staring at the pillaged house with the same dread and fascination Wilf had felt. Or so he thought. "I tried to get to the boy, but I just couldn't breathe," he said in her direction. He felt as if he had to apologize.

The woman looked his way, her eyes teary. "Oh god, why didn't I say yes?"

"To what?"

"To Sylvia! She asked me if Bradley could stay overnight with Tommy, but Marsha had just gotten over the measles and I didn't think it was such a good idea. And I was tired. And so I said no!" Her hand went back to her mouth and stayed there trembling.

"You couldn't have guessed what she was going to do," Carole said. "You couldn't have known."

"She didn't look like she had a care in the world. She just said, 'Well, that's all right, then.' That's all she said. And she walked away!"

"That's what I mean," Carole said.

"But I could tell she'd been drinking!"

Wilf turned away and walked down the sidewalk. He crossed back over the bridge. It seemed to him that he had to lean hard into the wind just to reach the other side. The office door was locked. By the time he'd found his key and had unlocked it, Carole was standing there behind him. Sylvia Young's file was still open on his desk. He walked over and sat down. "What's happening?"

Carole remained by the door. Her hair looked hopelessly tangled. "What do you mean, what's happening?"

Wilf began to look aimlessly through the file. "They experimented with various gases at the beginning, you know. On selected inmates. Of course they did."

"Stop it," Carole said, "or I'll leave right now."

"But don't you see the pattern? Don't you know what it means? She was murdered. Not by some mad scientist and not by some copycat, I'm not saying that. But by someone."

Carole turned and went back out. She closed the door.

Wilf continued to look through the file.

She'd had on what looked like a party dress. A pretty dress, anyway. Earrings. Nylons. More proof, not that he needed it. Who would get dressed up to commit suicide?

He could hear Carole now. Her lovely, slightly adenoidal voice. "Because when she was found, she'd want to look nice."

He smiled to himself. He missed her already.

Wilf manned the office until five o'clock, locked up and drove his father's car up the hill to the house. He went into the study only long enough to raid his father's liquor cabinet. He didn't bother to look through the Nuremberg papers. He didn't have to anymore.

With a bottle of rye tucked under his arm, he climbed the stairs, went into the bathroom and opened his bottle of sleeping pills. He wondered if he should call Carole and apologize. But for what?

The weather pattern was changing. Carole was gone. He studied himself in the mirror. What was the forecast? A drizzle of hopelessness followed by gusts of despair.

A great, raging, spiralling hole.

Duncan looked out the window. He thought he might recognize something but all he could see was an alley right below him and a windowless brick wall on the other side. He thought he might see the market square. He and his mother had taken the bus to Brantford when he was young to go shopping in the farmers' market there. That was one of the most exciting things that had ever happened to him. Until now.

That was a long time ago though.

Duncan wrapped his meaty hands around the bars and thought about Babe and Dandy. They were his biggest concerns, had been since that first morning out in the frosty, freezing bush when he'd been hunted down. Who was going to look after them? Feed them? Get them out into the air? Run them? Who was going to rub them down?

Duncan sat down on the cot to calm himself and looked around. At least this place was quieter. The jail in Hamilton had been much larger, a clanging and raucous place crowded with a wild gang of men. The first day he'd been put in there they started calling him Jumbo. The slick young man he had to share a cell with came up with that name right away and it spread down the range of cells and flew from table to table in the mess hall and ricocheted around the walls in the exercise yard. Jumbo.

One of the men leaning up against the wall in the yard where it was warm in the sunshine told him that it was an elephant's name. A famous elephant that had worked in the circus and had got itself killed crossing a railway track.

Duncan smiled when he knew that this is what the men had meant. He grinned at all the men and shook his mass of matted hair and laughed. He'd done this all his life. His mother had told him that that was the best way to stop people from teasing. Later that same day two of the guards led him to a room in the basement and shaved off all his hair.

This place in Brantford was a lot better. For one thing he had the cell all to himself. It wasn't going to be for very long though. If he'd understood his lawyer correctly he'd be taken to a court in the morning for some kind of hearing and then he'd have to go back to Hamilton and then he'd come back to Brantford for his real trial later. Maybe not for months and months.

He'd get out for sure, he wasn't worried, anyone would have done what he'd done, any man would, but it might take too long a time. And by then what would happen to Babe and Dandy?

He'd asked his lawyer that question but he didn't seem to know.

"Maybe Wilf McLauchlin will help," Duncan said.

His lawyer's eyes went big. "Help what?"

"Help look after my horses. He's my best friend, anyway."

His lawyer looked disgusted then, not unlike his own father used to look just before spitting out a stream of tobacco and calling him one of his breath-stealing names.

"Jesus Christ, get this straight, will you?" his lawyer said. "It's important. Wilf McLauchlin is not your friend. He's your enemy. He just pretended to be your friend so he could trick you into telling him things you never should have said. Why did you say those things? Because you were trying to impress him. Because you didn't know what you were saying. Because you're slow. And when I get Mr. Hero into a court of law I'm going to make him look like the grandstanding, conniving, lying, low-life little bastard he is."

"Yeah, okay. I get it," Duncan said.

But he hadn't really gotten it.

Wilf had told him that he was a soldier, too, and that sometimes soldiers had to do bad things to protect the world. He'd said they were just the same. He'd even said that he'd be his wing man.

He really wished he hadn't told Wilf about Basil, though, lying down beside him on the bed. His eyes all glittery. Talking away. Couldn't understand a word of it. And smiling. His head on the pillow, almost. His face right there. And he could see that Basil had put charcoal all around his eyes. And a frightening thing had begun to happen. He'd begun to feel the same rush of excitement that he'd always felt below Carole's window.

"Go away. Go downstairs," he'd said.

Basil had left for his cot in the kitchen and Duncan had lain there in a torrent of confusion. He'd had to touch himself just to calm himself down. And the worst thing of all, all the time he was touching himself, he'd wanted Basil to come back up the stairs.

Of course he hadn't told Wilf all that.

His lawyer had been going on lately about Andy Creighton, too, but Duncan couldn't remember exactly what that was all about, either. It was funny, though, when he thought about it, the way Andy had just appeared that night.

And Carole said to him, "Did you hurt that man in Cline's bush?"

She was just trying to help him though. That's what Wilf said, they were both just trying to help him, and in order to do that they needed to know the truth.

But what if Carole knew that Basil had come into his room and that he'd laid down on his bed? What if Wilf told her? What would she think now?

Duncan got back up and looked out the window again.

It was hard to keep everything straight. Andy standing in his kitchen that night like he'd just dropped out of the sky. Wilf telling him that he'd be his wing man. Carole asking him such a question. He used to be able to keep things straight.

And what if Wilf told her the biggest, scariest secret of all, that having to take Basil out to the woods, having to deal with him like that, having to teach him a lesson, was the most exciting thing that ever happened to him in his whole life? Better than going to the market. Better than watching Carole even.

Because it had been.

But what if Wilf told Carole that? What would she think of him now? She'd hate him now.

Duncan closed his eyes.

He could see Wilf lying on the ground, helpless as a baby. It was like seeing a picture in a newspaper. Or maybe he dreamt it once, it was so clear. His one arm limp and useless hanging out of its sling. The brave hero crying to be let back up. Just like Basil had. Tears and moans and screams.

Duncan was standing over him now.

At first Wilf thought his father had arrived home one day early. He heard the side door close. He heard footsteps coming along the hallway downstairs.

He was sitting on the edge of his bed having taken three sleeping pills but resisting for the moment the urge to take the top off the bottle of rye.

Someone was climbing up the stairs.

Wilf got up and waited. The door pushed open and Carole was standing there. He thought it was quite probable that he wasn't making a good impression, bottle in hand and dressed in nothing but his underpants.

Carole looked stunningly beautiful. Her cheeks were glowing from her trip through the cool March wind. She walked across the room and with her back held characteristically straight, sat down in a chair. It reminded Wilf of something, maybe some old Dutch Master's painting, she was sitting so still in the thick yellow light.

Woman in Chair, Wilf thought to himself.

"I'm ashamed of myself," she said.

"Why?"

"Leaving like that. I can't believe I did that."

"I thought you showed very sound judgment."

"It was the last thing I wanted to do. It was against everything I was feeling." Her eyes began to glisten.

"Not everything you were feeling," Wilf said. "And once again I have to say you exhibited sound judgment." He undid the top on the bottle of rye, "Would you like a drink?"

"No. I want to talk."

"About what?" Wilf screwed the top back on and sat down.

"About what you were saying. About what happened to Sylvia Young. And those experiments in Germany. Germany is over there somewhere and we're here. So that can't be true. I mean, physically. It's impossible."

"I know."

"And you told me the other night that you somehow thought that you were the connecting link. But Adrienne O'Dell had been planning to kill Mr. Cruikshank long before you arrived home, so how could you have anything to do with that, and you didn't even know who Duncan was, and you don't know anything about what happened to Sylvia Young. You have no connection to her at all."

"You've been doing a lot of thinking."

"Yes, I have. But I didn't come here to tell you that. I'm sure you know all that. I came here to tell you it doesn't matter."

Wilf could feel his chest tightening. He looked away.

"We both know what it is, don't we? I don't know how I could have left like that."

He could hear her getting up; he could feel her sitting beside him on the bed.

"It's the war. All the terrible things that happened to you. It's only been a year or so. What could anyone expect? What could you have expected from yourself? Wilf?"

Wilf glanced her way.

Her lips were trembling. "I'm sorry."

"Don't be sorry."

"But I am. And I wanted to come here and tell you, I'm hopelessly in love."

"With who?"

"Shut up. And I won't leave again. Unless you throw me out."

"I won't throw you out."

Carole took off her hat. Her hair came tumbling down. She looked irresistible. She broke his heart. When he kissed her, her lips felt cold.

"I've just taken three sleeping pills," Wilf said.

"Then you're not drinking." She took the bottle out of his hand and walked back into the hall.

He could hear the phone being lifted off the receiver and Carole giving the operator a number. After a moment he heard her speak again. "I just wanted to let you know, I won't be coming home tonight. No. No. Wilf McLauchlin." A long silence. "Bye, Mom," she finally said.

Carole came back into the room.

"I think you just did it," Wilf said.

"I know."

"We'll have to find someplace to live."

Carole began to unbutton her coat. She looked flushed of face and a little bewildered.

CHAPTER FIFTEEN

Carole shook Wilf awake early the next morning.

He had a vague memory of her sitting beside him after she'd taken off her coat, of them holding hands, lying down close together, talking, and then the sleeping pills had kicked in.

She was leaning over him in her slip, so apparently she'd stayed the night. She was saying that he had to get up right away and drive her home so she could change her clothes in time for work. And he had to prepare himself for his father's arrival later that day. She was looking a little hysterical.

Wilf ran his hand up her leg to the top of her nylon. She removed his hand as if it were a wayward kitten. "It's past eight o'clock already," she said.

Wilf drove her home. Carole sat in silence beside him until the car turned on to her street and then she began to talk about a friend of hers who'd been renting a country house, but now she and her husband had just bought their own place in town. If Wilf wanted her to, she could speak to her friend and find out if that house had been rented again and if not, how much it might cost.

"It's not very big. It has a small bedroom, a small living room, a kitchen and a really tiny bathroom, but I was out there last summer and it's made out of field stone and it overlooks the river and there are wild vines climbing over this old rail fence and there were birds and butterflies all over the place." Carole paused to catch her breath. "I think it would be really peaceful out there."

Therapeutic, Wilf was about to reply but he cut himself off.

There was no question that Carole was the best thing that had happened to him for some time. He didn't want to think, since forever. He still wanted to cling somewhat wistfully to the allusive ghost of that other Wilf McLauchlin, the one who'd been sound of body. And mind. And heart.

He knew she was right though. The thought of a cottage and Carole and the sky miraculously full of birds and butterflies seemed the correct choice. The safe altitude. The perfect air speed. And Nurse Carole with her long, lean, acrobatic body ministering to him every night. And more than that, of course. The whole of herself. The sound of her throaty voice that always made him want to smile. Her watchful grey eyes, relentlessly and restlessly moving from tenderness to quizzicality and back again. Her unasked for, her undefended love.

Wilf smiled at her. "Sounds like a great idea," he said.

Clarence McLauchlin disembarked from the train at a little after two that afternoon. He'd phoned ahead and Wilf had driven up to meet him. As soon as his father had settled himself in the passenger side of the car, having grudgingly reconciled himself some time ago to Wilf's continued insistence on driving, Wilf began to tell him that there'd been another incident in town and once again, unfortunately, he'd found himself in the middle of it.

Clarence swung around to look at him, his sharp eyes already alarmed and searching. "What incident?"

"A client of yours. Sylvia Young."

He told his father the few details he knew and with some effort restrained himself from calling Sylvia's apparent suicide a double homicide. All he really wanted to do was get to the other side of his father's inevitable barrage of questions. And his father's palpable anxiety, his searching sideways glances.

"Why, though?" Clarence was saying. "My god. What would have driven her to do such a thing?"

"I don't know. Maybe the police know. I've been staying away from Andy. He's still in hot water from the last time we got involved."

"You're not involved in this one though. You just found her."

"That's right."

Wilf kept his eyes on the road.

Carole was sitting primly at her desk when they came through the door. "Welcome back, Mr. McLauchlin," she said with a pleasant smile.

"Thank you, Carole. It's always good to be back."

Wilf peeked at her from behind his father and wiggled his eyebrows up and down like Groucho Marx. Carole blushed and went back to her typing. Clarence walked through to his office. Usually he would have spent a moment or two exchanging pleasantries with Carole and then asked to be brought up to date with anything that might have happened in his absence. Wilf sat down at Dorothy Dale's desk.

"Just another day at the office," Wilf said.

Carole whispered, "Did you tell him anything?"

"I told him about Sylvia Young."

"Anything else?"

"No."

"Oh." She resumed her typing.

Five minutes later Clarence came out of his office and went back out the front door without a word.

"I know where he's going," Wilf said.

"Where?"

"To the police station. To see what I've got myself into this time."

"He has to ask some questions because she was a client of his."

"He was acting for her on the real estate deal. That's all. She doesn't have a will with us. Nothing else on file. I looked."

"Anyway, I'm glad your father's back. Everything just feels

better when he's here." Carole played with her typewriter keys. "When are you going to tell him?"

"About what?"

Carole's eyes narrowed. "Never mind."

"I'm teasing. Tonight."

"Really? Oh my god. Don't."

"When do you want me to?"

"I don't know!"

That evening Clarence invited Wilf out for a decent restaurant meal. He didn't discuss Sylvia Young. He didn't bring up Wilf's continuing problem with the Crown attorney's office in Brantford concerning the evidential piece of ice he'd unlawfully removed from the scene of the crime in the Duncan Getty case. He talked about the trial in Windsor and afterward he asked about Wilf's plans for returning to college. Wilf replied that he thought he'd take his fatherly advice after all and not worry about rejoining his law studies until the fall semester. Clarence nodded. Wilf could tell that he was doing a fast calculation. Delaying to the fall. Was that a good sign or a bad sign?

"How are you feeling? I mean, generally?" Clarence asked. Though he had a number of positive attributes, he was not famous for subtlety.

"Good. I'm really feeling better than I have in a long time."

"Even after having dragged a dead body out of a gas-filled house?"

"Yes."

"That's great," Clarence replied, though his voice seemed to trail off at the end.

They returned home and sat in the study and had a couple of drinks. Two or three times during a gap in the conversation Wilf thought of telling him about the amorous adventures of his legal secretary. Those moments passed by. Carole was supposed to be finding out about the availability of the cottage that night. Better to wait. And anyway he didn't feel up to having that particular conversation, or any conversation of substance for that matter. He felt more comfortable just staring politely into the middle distance, listening to his father's voice, letting his mind go. He felt adrift.

When the grandfather clock struck ten Wilf yawned extravagantly and excused himself, climbed up the stairs, chased the drinks he'd had that evening with two sleeping pills and fell almost immediately into a deep and dreamless sleep.

The next morning he was standing on the bridge staring down at the racing water below his feet. The flood level had crept higher overnight. Store basements were getting wet. The dam a few hundred yards up the river had all but disappeared. Only a line of frantic waves marked its place.

Tree branches swept past him, disappearing beneath the bridge. Blackened logs reared up, sped by. Not so many pans of ice as the day before though. Wilf could feel the heat of the sun on the back of his neck. He let his eyes go glassy, his mind empty out. The water slowed to a stop. The bridge began to make its way through the muddy water, churning upriver in search of the dam.

Wilf stood across the street from Sylvia Young's house. It looked almost the same as it had the day before, windows broken, shattered pieces of glass clinging to the frames. The front door had been closed though. He crossed the street and walked along the side of the house. The puddles had grown larger and patches of grass were showing through. The snow that had been left behind crunched under his feet.

He turned the back corner. No one was waiting for him in the backyard. He stood there, mesmerized by nothing, his thoughts spooling out. Carole had been absolutely right, of course. Her logic unassailable. He was ill.

That was all.

Something shuddered deep inside him. He turned away.

The chubby boy from the day before was standing out on the front sidewalk. He was still wearing his windbreaker and running shoes, but then the weather was warmer than the day before.

"Hello," Wilf said.

The boy started walking away.

Wilf watched him go, and as he did he realized that regardless of Carole's peerless logic he knew for an absolute certainty that someone had murdered Sylvia Young and her son. It had to do with the vulnerable way in which this boy had turned his back, the weakness of his slightly waddling walk, the emptiness of the street. It had to do with a tremulousness in the air. It had to do with a tremulousness in himself.

"I guess Mrs. Young's son was a friend of yours," Wilf called out, walking up behind the boy.

The boy looked nervous. "Yeah."

"What was his name? Bradley?"

"Yeah." The boy walked faster.

Wilf walked faster too. "And I've forgotten your name."

"Tommy."

"Right. Tommy. Is your mother home, Tommy?"

"No."

The boy crossed the street toward a small park squeezed in between two houses. Wilf could see a woman pushing down on one end of a teeter-totter, giving a ride to a small child who was perched on the other end.

Tommy hurried across the park. Wilf followed along. He had to skirt around a puddle the size of a small lake. "Hello again," he called out.

Tommy's mother looked a little surprised. "Hello."

"This must be the brave girl who had the measles."

"Marsha, say hello. She wouldn't stay in today. She just had to come out."

"Well, it's too nice a day to stay in. Hi, Marsha."

The little girl, suspended in mid-air, stared back at him.

"My name's Wilf."

Marsha continued to stare.

"She's shy."

"The reason I was at Sylvia's yesterday, she was selling her house. I had some papers for her to sign."

"Your father's the lawyer."

"That's right."

"I'm still in shock." The flesh around the woman's eyes looked puffy and bluish. "It's been hard on Tommy."

Tommy, hearing his name, looked away.

"I'm sure it has."

"Someone was saying you've had a run of bad luck yourself," she said.

"Oh?"

"Or maybe it's good luck. I don't know. That old man that was killed by Adrienne O'Dell and her sailor friend? And then weird Duncan Getty?"

"I don't know what to call it either. Good luck or bad. I'm sorry. I don't know your name."

"Catherine. Cathy Shepherd," she smiled.

"Wilf."

"I know."

"To tell you the truth I feel a little bit in shock myself. I wouldn't mind talking about it, unless you'd rather not. We could sit over there."

The woman hesitated for a moment. She glanced toward the street. "Tommy, take Marsha over to the merry-go-round and give her a push, would you? Don't let her get her feet wet."

Tommy pulled his sister off the end of the teeter-totter and they headed toward a small merry-go-round.

Wilf began to walk toward a bench on the other side of a flooded sandbox. "He's a good big brother."

"Yes, he is. He's great with her."

Cathy hesitated a moment longer and then followed along. The wooden seat looked dry enough in the sun. Wilf was standing there, waiting. She sat down, pulled a package of cigarettes out of her coat pocket, took one and held the package out for Wilf.

"No thanks," Wilf said, sitting down.

"That's unusual."

"Why?"

"Just that all the vets seem to smoke."

"Well, I never did take to it. And now, with one hand, it just seems like too much work."

"I'm sorry."

Wilf smiled. "I didn't mean it that way. Some of the fellows with one arm, or none, smoke like chimneys. I'm just too lazy."

Cathy smiled back at him. She was pretty in a plain sort of way. Thick tangle of dark hair. Wide nose. Freckled face. She lit up her cigarette.

"I've been wondering if I knew Sylvia Young from somewhere. Met her somewhere. I mean, since I've been home."

Cathy looked toward the street again. She turned to watch Marsha and Tommy. "I wouldn't know."

Marsha was sitting on the floor of the merry-go-round. A pool of water gleamed underneath it. Tommy, running with his head down, was pushing it around and around.

"Not so fast!" she called out.

"We don't know quite what to do with the disposition of the house. There were a few things left unsigned. And no will, as far as we know. My father was wondering, did Sylvia have any relatives?"

"Not around here. Her husband did, but I think Sylvia had a falling out with them a few years ago, just after she got the news that Kyle had been killed. She was never the same. She just kind of let everything go. She had a good job in the general office at Parson's and then one day she just up and quit, and after that she stayed to herself. She wasn't an easy person to get along with."

"Maybe she was just angry about the war, what had happened."

"Not so much angry though. More just, not really there. It was hard to have a conversation with Sylvia, you were never sure if she was actually listening. And she could be abrupt."

"I think you said she'd been drinking when she asked if Bradley could stay over?"

Cathy nodded. "I heard there was a bottle on the kitchen table too. I suppose you saw it."

Wilf tried to remember. He could see Sylvia slumped over, her face barely discernible. He could see the gaping stove. Hear it hissing. Could feel his lungs on fire.

"I think I missed seeing the bottle," Wilf said.

"And a full ashtray, Ted Bolton was telling everyone. She was a chain smoker. It's a wonder she didn't blow up the place. Maybe that would have been better. If the gas had blown up right away, maybe Bradley would have survived somehow." Her eyes were looking puffy again. "I'll never forgive myself for saying no."

"That's the strangest part, isn't it? Not that she'd go through with killing herself, but that she'd turn on the gas when she knew her son was in the house."

"Because she was too drunk by that time. And depressed. I think she must have been depressed for a long while but she covered it up with that 'I don't give a damn' attitude of hers. And maybe she thought the gas wouldn't reach him because he was upstairs. There was one of those old-fashioned grates in her kitchen ceiling, she must have forgotten about that."

"How could she have forgotten that?"

"I don't know, but she must have. My husband hates her now.

He didn't have much good to say about her before but now he really hates her. I can't talk to him about any of this. He's really upset. Because of Bradley." Cathy examined the end of her cigarette. Tears were balancing themselves on the rim of her eyes. "After Bradley lost his father, Ivan kind of took his place. He said it was the only decent thing to do. They were quite the pair. He was a nice kid, lots of fun, one of those kids everyone likes. Ivan treated him just the same as Tommy. Even better than Tommy sometimes, if you ask me. God help me if I ever said anything about it though." One of the tears tipped over and began to slide down her freckled cheek. "Ivan was always over there."

"I thought you said he didn't like Sylvia?"

"He did, and he didn't, I guess." Cathy was kneading her one hand and twirling her wedding ring around and around.

Wilf made a little square in the mud with the tip of his cane. He felt surprisingly calm now. As light as the sun-filled light in the park itself. A romantic entanglement, then, was that it? That ended badly?

"Ivan will kill me if I tell you." She was looking back toward her two children. Tommy had gotten tired of running in circles and had jumped on the merry-go-round himself. Both children were lying on their backs looking up at the bluest sky.

"Tell me what?"

"I saw someone that night."

"Who?"

"Some man I've never seen before. I don't think I have, anyway. Marsha was crying out in her sleep and I picked her up and I was standing by the window and he came hurrying along from the direction of Sylvia's house. There was this fancy white car parked around the corner. I hadn't noticed it before. He got in and drove away."

"It could have been anyone though," Wilf said, "doing anything."

"That's what Ivan says. And that I should mind my own damn business. But it was three o'clock in the morning. And the man was in such a hurry." Her face froze.

A man in workman's coveralls was walking into the park.

"That's my husband," she said.

He strode by the swings and picked Marsha up off the merry-go-round. He was a small man. His face was so dark, covered with a few days' growth of beard, that Wilf could hardly make out his expression. He held his child in his arms and stayed where he was halfway across the park, boots dug into the wet ground.

Tommy got off the merry-go-round and stood a little apart from his father.

"I've got to go," Cathy said.

CHAPTER SIXTEEN

Duncan hadn't really planned it out. It just happened. The judge said there'd be a fifteen-minute recess, maybe he had to take a leak or something, and he got up and left the court. His own lawyer walked over from the table he'd been sitting at and said he had to go and make a phone call. He went out another door.

Duncan had noticed that there were three doors in all, the one the judge had come in, the one at the back behind the empty spectator benches that his lawyer had just used, and the one the young policeman had led him through from his cell down the hall.

There were three people left, too, the lawyer for the Crown who had been saying bad things about him, a woman who sat below the judge and had been writing everything down, and the policeman. After a moment the lawyer for the Crown walked past the spectator benches and out of the courtroom.

Duncan remained sitting in the prisoner's dock. He had chains on his wrists but they'd taken his leg irons off the day before, just as soon as he'd arrived in Brantford from Hamilton. He snuck a look at the policeman. He was reading the funny pages. The older woman was still writing in her notepad. Duncan got up and walked out.

He heard the policeman yell something just as he went through the same door the lawyers had used. He was free now and moving just as quickly as he had the night he'd dived through his own kitchen window, racing down a hall, turning a corner and banging out a door marked Fire Exit. He came out on a rusty iron platform. A pair of wooden warehouses were listing against each other across a muddy lane. He swung down a ladder that didn't even reach as far as the ground, jumped the rest of the way and made a run for the narrow gap between the buildings.

Duncan could hear the creak of the fire-escape door opening just as he plunged into the dark space. He had to maneuver sideways now, his face up against one of the buildings, shuffling over bits of wooden crates and pieces of rusting eavestroughs, stumbling over odorous mounds of soft and miscellaneous debris. The ground pitched downwards. He began to see massive posts, rotten-looking and mouldy, trying to hold the whole building up. Light began to stream into the narrow alleyway.

He came out the back into the sun and stood there blinking down a steep bank to the same river that ran through his own town. The familiar dank smell of it filled his nose. It was in flood, rampaging along in a wide, muddy boil.

Duncan slid down through melting snow and thick brush. When he reached the water's edge he looked back up expecting to see the young policeman standing at the top of the slope. All he could see were the roofs of the two warehouses. He began to make his way up the river. Sometimes, where the bank was low, he had to wade into a waist-high and ice-cold swirl of water. Other times he had to crawl along on his hands and knees through almost impenetrable thickets, his chain dragging along underneath him, hanging up on jagged pieces of ice sometimes and throwing him down hard on the sopping ground. He could hear his own breathing now, high and harsh, over the rushing sound of the river. He could feel his chest heaving under his thin shirt.

He came to a place where he had to sneak past the backs of brick buildings. He could see fire escapes and trucks parked behind a row of stores. He could see some people walking along a sidewalk. Luckily they were paying no attention. Soon he was screened behind the tall winter-seared grass again.

He bumped against the rusting hulk of a car. He parted the grass and peered inside. The seats were bright green with slime and they had holes so big he could see rusty coils of wire. He stood there for a moment thinking about forcing the door open and hiding inside, but the old car seemed unsatisfactory some-how, the first place that that young policeman would look.

He continued on following the river upstream until he stum-bled into a clearing beneath a railway bridge. He scrambled up to the top of a concrete abutment and wedged himself under some iron struts. He couldn't find any comfortable way to rest there though. The concrete was harder than anything he'd ever laid on in his whole life and his wet clothes were pressing his skin and felt as cold as winter. A train rumbled across. He could see the gaps between the freight cars flickering right over his face. Everything shook; bits of rust and live cinders showered down on his bald head, the noise hurt his ears.

Duncan waited for the train to pass and then slid down off the abutment and moved on. He walked into a cluster of pine trees and noticed a large wooden box sitting on the far edge of a shadowy ravine. He had to wade across a cascading stream to get to it. The top was covered with leaves and moss and when he lifted it he could see a pump sitting at the bottom of a shal-low hole. It was crusted with orange rust. Duncan could tell at a glance that it hadn't pumped anything for a long while.

He walked along the ravine and began to break off pine boughs in what he hoped were places the policeman wouldn't notice. He carried them back and stuffed them down the hole, weaving them around the pump and then over it. It took him three trips before he had the box filled close to the top. He hauled his huge bulk inside, sunk down in the boughs and lowered the lid.

This was a perfect place, the kind of place he'd always man-age to locate when he was a boy. It wasn't that dark, either, once he got used to it because of the cracks between the boards.

When he put his eye to one of them he could see the river just down the slope from where he sat. He could hear it too, slipping along like the sound of a giant snake moving through dry grass. Duncan curled up as best he could and for the first time since he'd been arrested he felt peaceful. His old self.

Except he knew it had been a lot longer than that since he'd felt his old self. A long time ago. From before Basil first knocked on the shop door looking for work. He'd pronounced it "wirz," standing there in oversized hand-me-downs like a boy dressed up in his father's clothes. It took Duncan some time to figure out what he was saying. "Wirz pliz," he'd said, in the strangest accent Duncan had ever heard.

He felt at peace now though. Finally. For one thing he knew his mother was close by somewhere. She always was. Somewhere.

He decided he'd wait until it grew dark. He knew there was a busy car bridge ahead of him, he'd seen it at the same time he'd seen the box. It had appeared so low it looked to be resting on the flooding river itself. He hoped that there'd still be room enough to crawl underneath. And then he should be close to the edge of the city. It seemed like he'd been travelling for a long time.

Duncan imagined the river valley would get broader once he was out in the countryside. More thickly wooded, too. He'd continue to follow along the shore, the water roiling by in the moonlight. And even if there wasn't any moonlight, it wouldn't matter. He was used to making his way through the dark. It was one of his most favourite things to do. And as he moved, he'd just keep telling himself that each step brought him that much closer to where he had to go. Soon he'd hear Babe whinnying a welcome. And Dandy stamping his feet and banging up against the stall the same way as always. And he'd run up to the stable and lift up the latch and push inside and they'd be standing right there smiling back at him as always, ears up, eyes bright and soft.

And he'd rest his face on Dandy's nose. And on Babe's nose.

And feel their breath, sweet with hay.

And he'd be home.

More fortunate townspeople were standing at the edge of the smaller of the two rivers watching the water creep over other people's lawns and cascade into basements. It did this almost every spring. Filled to its brim and unable to enter the larger river at a quick enough rate, it would invariably back up a hundred yards and then overflow.

Wilf limped along the edge of the flood. He could feel people shifting their gaze away from the muddy water as he passed by, watching him with a mixture of fascination and fear.

Wherever he went, there was death.

He wondered if Carole had arranged for the cottage yet. He wondered if her family's basement was getting wet. She lived about three blocks farther along but at a higher elevation. He wondered whether Cathy Shepherd, seeing her husband coming into the park, had changed her story at the last moment.

It was too horrible to tell the truth. How could she have found the words? "I saw my husband hurrying home from Sylvia Young's house that night." And then what? "I think he murdered her."

"Why?"

And she would have shaken her head. Shaken it. She wouldn't have been able to find the words. Was that it?

She'd almost told him and then at the last moment she'd made up a story about a man in a fancy white car.

Wilf climbed up to the top of a bank that was managing to stay dry and looked across the river. There was a park for children on the other side, a much larger park than the one he'd just been sitting in with Cathy. It was under water too.

Cathy hadn't really said anything about her husband though. Had she? Wilf stood there for a long time watching the river race by. Everything in his life seemed to be racing by. He turned away and started the long walk up the front hill.

It was past noon by the time he came back in through the side door. Clarence had moved from the study where he'd been working earlier in the morning. He was sitting at the kitchen table with a kind of half-bemused, half-startled look on his face.

"The river's flooding," Wilf said as he pried his muddy galoshes off.

"I just had the strangest visit."

Wilf took off his coat and climbed into the kitchen. "With who?"

"Millie Telfer."

Wilf walked past his father, crossed the hall into the study, picked up a half bottle of rye that was left from the previous night and carried it back into the kitchen.

"It's only past noon," his father said.

Wilf opened the bottle with his teeth, took down a glass from the cupboard and poured himself a shot. "Want one?"

"If you insist."

Wilf got down another glass.

"This whole town's going nuts," Clarence said.

Wilf filled his father's glass to the one-third mark and turned on the cold water. Clarence was a rye and water man. Wilf liked his rye neat. "Why do you think that?"

"It's all these deaths the last couple of months. People don't know what to think, so they're thinking the stupidest, wildest things that could ever enter into their heads."

"About me, you mean?"

Clarence looked genuinely shocked. "No. Not you."

"Who then?"

"I mean Millie. What she said. What she's thinking."

Wilf handed the glass to his father, took a drink from his own and thought of his sleeping pills. His supply was dwindling. He'd have to go see Doc Robinson soon, not an encounter he was particularly looking forward to.

"She thinks Scarfe is having an affair. Jesus Christ, can you imagine that?"

Wilf couldn't imagine that. Another affair. Just like Cathy Shepherd's husband. Affairs all over the town.

"Is there a man on this earth less likely to be having an affair than Scarfe Telfer?"

The half-bemused, half-surprised expression settled back on Clarence's face. "All he's ever done is work all his life and go to church every other Sunday."

Wilf took another sip and thought about taking an afternoon nap. One more glass of rye, complain that his hip was hurting, climb up the stairs and swallow the last two or three sleeping pills.

"It gets worse," Clarence said, "much worse."

He could lay there in a semi-haze. He could think of Cathy Shepherd's husband standing there in the park like a dark hole in the world.

"She didn't have anywhere else to turn," Clarence was going on. "'You're an old friend, you know the law,' she said to me."

It was obvious that Cathy was afraid of her husband. Of course she was.

"She thinks he's trying to poison her."

Wilf looked at his father.

"Isn't that the goddamn limit?" Clarence said. He got up from the table, drink in hand, and crossed over to look out the window into the backyard. "Wilf, what made you say people would be thinking about you?"

"Just my curious association with all these deaths. Haven't you wondered?"

"No." Clarence didn't turn to look at him though. "They're just coincidence."

"Right."

"And that's my point. Everyone's getting so goddamn jumpy in this town, they can't accept coincidences. Scarfe was away on business the other night. Millie called, he wasn't registered at the hotel he was supposed to be in and she noticed that half her sleeping pills were missing. Ergo, Scarfe is having an affair and is planning on slipping some pills into her nightcap and smothering her to death with her own pillow."

"Is Scarfe still the secretary-treasurer at Parson's?" Wilf asked.

"Sure."

"Then he works in the general office."

"That's right." Clarence turned to look at Wilf now.

Wilf didn't notice. What he was seeing was Sylvia Young's house. The gaping windows. The front door ajar. "What night did Millie call?"

"What?"

"The hotel."

"I think she said Wednesday."

"Of this week?"

"What's it matter? Yes, I guess so."

"And some sleeping pills were missing?"

"That's what she said."

"There must be more to it, for Millie to tell a story like that."

"There isn't, believe me. All she said was that Scarfe hasn't been himself for a long time. Short-tempered. Brooding. I tried to tell her that it had to do with his age. He's in his mid-sixties, after all—he'll be retiring soon and I think Scarfe's the same as a lot of men. When their life work is over they think their lives are over. And then they discover their colleagues don't give a damn whether they retire or not and neither does the business they poured their lives into. They turn bitter."

"Did Millie buy your explanation?"

"No. She asked me if I would please, please invite Scarfe out somewhere for a drink, talk about old times and see if he'll tell me what's really going on."

"And you said?"

"That I'd call him first of the week. Pure nonsense. But I never could say no to Millie Telfer." Clarence sat back down at the table. "She was your mother's best friend. We go back a long way. The four musketeers."

"I used to caddy for Scarfe."

"Yes, you did. And I remember why. Because he'd pay you more than I would and filial affection didn't seem to come into the picture."

"Money's money."

Clarence smiled. "So it is."

"I seem to remember that Mr. Telfer always drove a fancy car."

"A Cadillac man. Always has been. He's still driving his old Fleetwood. Nineteen thirty-seven or thirty-eight. Something like that."

"What's the colour?"

"A kind of cream colour. White leather interior."

"Yes. That's it," Wilf said. He laid his drink down as carefully as he could. It rattled on the counter.

"God, can you imagine such a thing? Scarfe having an affair? And contemplating murder? Poor dear Millie. I had to feel sorry for her. The whole damn town's spooked, that's all I can say."

"I told Andy I'd drop around this afternoon."

"I thought you said you were keeping your distance. The Duncan Getty mess. All that."

"I bumped into him this morning. He said to drop around."

Wilf began to make his way down the steps to the side door. He took his coat off its hook.

"Don't you want any lunch?"

"I had a sandwich downtown."

"Well, take the car."

"It's such a great day. I think I'll walk."

"But you've already had a walk."

Wilf opened the door. He didn't seem to hear.

The morning sun had disappeared behind a misty layer of clouds and the light had turned to amber as Wilf hurried along toward the Telfer house. The air felt wet to breathe. A winter's worth of moisture was beginning to seep up from the ground. Mist shrouded the houses, hung in the trees.

Scarfe Telfer and Sylvia Young were having an affair, Wilf thought to himself. Was that even remotely possible?

He could see an earring lying against her neck again, a round silvery disc like a winter moon. And her face at rest on the melting snow.

How long ago had she left her job in the general office at Parson's? What had Cathy said? Five years? Four?

A bottle was sitting on her kitchen table. In his haste he hadn't seen it. Smelled it. Tasted it. Laced with sleeping pills?

The oven door flung open.

And Bradley sleeping somewhere upstairs.

Wilf came to a stop.

He was standing at a corner. The Telfer house towered in the mist across the street. If he remembered correctly there was a lion's face on the front door. He'd reached up for the iron ring attached to its nose on occasion, knocking for his father to come home or selling tickets for assorted raffles or fundraising for high school projects. But what if Millie came to the door? What would he say?

And if Scarfe came to the door, what would he say?

"I know who you really are."

Scarfe was his father's lifelong friend. That's who he was. And who was he, braced against his cane and standing there? Who had he become? One wrong question to Scarfe Telfer, one outrageous accusation and he'd pull his father's world down around his head.

Something across the street caught Wilf's eye, a kind of flickering in the backyard between the slats of the board fence. He felt a rush of panic, turned to leave but he couldn't. He moved across the street instead, stepping up on the curb and looking through the fence. Scarfe was crouched down in the middle of his sopping garden.

There was a gate a few steps away. Wilf stared at it and then pushed it open. As soon as the hinges creaked Scarfe stood up.

"Well, my goodness. Look who's here. Wilf! It's so good to see you."

"Hello, Mr. Telfer." He moved through the gate and limped into the garden along a wet sandy path. "I was just passing by so I thought I'd drop in to say thank you. You know, thanks to you and Mrs. Telfer for attending my welcome home banquet. I didn't get a chance that night."

"Well, actually you did, Wilf. You were quite effusive actually. But it never hurts to say thanks twice."

Now Wilf could see what Scarfe had been crouching over, a small pond with a slab of ice floating around in the middle. Water bubbled up on one side.

"Just cleaned the filter. One of the first signs of spring." Scarfe didn't look down at the pump though. He kept his eyes, watery and blue and wary, aimed straight at Wilf's face. What was it that his father had always said about Scarfe Telfer? "Scarfe has class, even though he doesn't come from class." Which in his father's eyes seemed to make it all the more admirable a trait. A natural-born elegance.

He was still handsome enough, Wilf thought to himself, in a silver-haired, older sort of way. And he seemed very concentrated, very alert. But why wouldn't he be? He had to know who had found Sylvia Young. Everyone in town knew.

"Are there goldfish in there?" Wilf peered down into the murky water.

"Close to a hundred at last count. They're still sluggish though, hugging the bottom. If things keep warming up they'll start stirring around."

"They stay in there all winter?"

"A kind of miracle. I can't tell you how many times I look out my window during a winter, snow blowing around out here, everything bleak and dead, and I think about this little niche of life. Flashes of gold under the snow. Spring will come, I think to myself."

Scarfe's voice seemed to catch in his throat and now Wilf could tell that the fierce light in his eyes was simply pain. A radiant pain. It was apparent everywhere, in the misty air, in the sag of his shoulders, in his clenched hands.

"Nice of you to drop around, Wilf. I should go in now. I have things to do. Say hello to your dad for me, will you? I haven't seen him for a while." He started moving off.

"Mr. Telfer?"

Scarfe stopped on the other side of the pond. "Yes, Wilf?"

"Did you see yesterday's paper?"

There was a slight hesitation, hardly anything at all. "Yesterday's paper? I'm not sure. I was away on business. Didn't arrive back until late yesterday."

"About Sylvia Young's death?"

"Oh, that. Yes well, I did see that, actually."

"Then you must know that I was the one who found her."

"Well, I did. But I didn't want to say anything. Ask you about it. I'm sure it was very upsetting."

"You knew her, didn't you?"

"No. I don't think so."

"She worked at Parson's. In the general office. She left a few years ago."

"People come and go, Wilf. I don't keep track of everyone. I might have known her. It doesn't really matter, does it? It's a tragedy either way."

"I didn't realize that the general office at Parson's was so large."

Scarfe's thin chest seemed to expand under his light jacket. "I don't know what your point is. Do you have a point?"

Wilf couldn't stop himself. "My point is, someone saw you coming out of Sylvia Young's house the night she was murdered. She recognized you. She recognized your car."

Scarfe Telfer went absolutely rigid. For a moment Wilf thought he might fall down.

"That's a lie." Whatever colour had been in his face was gone. Grey as slate. Even his lips. As grey as Sylvia Young's face. "The woman committed suicide."

"The woman was murdered."

"You must be out of your mind. My god! Coming in here and saying something like that to me. I have no idea what you're talking about. I don't know what to say."

"I'd like an explanation, that's all. I'm not accusing you of anything."

"I wasn't there!"

"I'll have to go to the police."

"What do you mean, you'll have to go to the police? Are you bloody-well insane?" His face was flushing now. Patches of flaming red. He took a few steps back around the pond. "You can't run around saying things like that. Have you any idea of the damage you could do, just to mention such a thing? My reputation in the town. My business reputation. Think of my wife, for godsake!"

"Perhaps your wife could vouch for where you were on Wednesday night."

"Of course she can," Scarfe screamed. He glanced toward his neighbour's house. "But as long as I have a breath I can assure you that no one is going to ask her. You're a disgrace to your father." He jutted his jaw out so far it looked like he might dislocate it, then he turned on his heels and walked around the pond again. He spun about and came back. "Out of respect for Clarence and out of respect for what you've been through, because obviously it's had an enormous effect on you, I will not press any charges. For uttering this horrible lie, this deformed and outrageous calumny." He pointed a shaking hand toward the open gate. "Now get the hell out of my yard!"

"It's too late," Wilf said. And he knew it was. Too late for everyone and everything. "I've already talked to the police. Not about you though. Just in general terms. Would you like to hear what they had to say?"

"No!"

"They found traces of a sedative in Sylvia's blood. They suspect sleeping pills but they couldn't find an empty pill bottle anywhere in her house. No prescription from her doctor. No records at the drugstore. This seems to have put them on edge. Of course if she'd wanted to make doubly certain she'd kill herself she could have taken an overdose of sleeping pills. And there's no trace of the sedative in the remains of that bottle left on the table. But then, if a clever person such as yourself had put her to sleep, he'd have taken that bottle away and replaced it with another one. And the glass she was using too. Hidden them somewhere."

Scarfe had been standing a little distance away staring at Wilf like a man standing at the side of a road watching his own automobile accident. "You're babbling. Pitiful sight. You'll be drooling next. I feel sorry for Clarence." He swung away and with a display of icy resolve and a squared-off back headed around the pond again.

"Has Mrs. Telfer returned or is she still out?"

Scarfe kept going.

"She dropped in to see my father earlier this morning. Told him you weren't in the hotel where you were supposed to be on Wednesday night. She was missing a half-bottle of sleeping pills."

Scarfe's shoulders flinched, he looked like a condemned man taking fire, but he refused to stop or turn around. He kept heading for the back of his house.

Wilf stood up. "Your wife is very frightened."

Scarfe kept on. He walked up the sloping lawn. He made it to a flagstone walkway. He was almost at the back door when he came to a stop. He stood there for what seemed a long time to Wilf. "My wife's not home." He turned and smiled a weak smile across the soaking garden. "Come on in the house, Wilf."

Scarfe pushed open the door and disappeared inside.

Wilf stared at the open door. He tried to think of any other option he might have. He knew there were no other options. His body knew that for a fact. His soul knew it absolutely. He began to walk through the garden toward the house.

The back room was full of winter boots and coats and snow shovels and assorted garden tools. A flight of wooden steps led up to another door that had been left half open too.

Wilf pulled off his galoshes, took his time lining them up beside Scarfe's muddy pair of boots and began to climb the stairs. He entered a narrow hall. He stood there listening.

A thick yellow light was moving at the other end of the house, moving and rippling, as if the flood had crept up the hill and entered under Scarfe's front door.

Wilf walked toward it and came to a stop at the entrance to a wider hall. Light was seeping in through a large fan of brandy-coloured glass over the heavy front door. He could remember that fan of glass, he could remember standing below it waiting for his father to appear or for Mrs. Telfer to reappear, watching the light creep over the walls, move in syrupy ripples across the parqueted floor.

"Wilf?"

Scarfe was standing behind him. "Please," he said and disappeared from sight.

Please what, Wilf thought to himself. Please what?

Wilf retraced his steps. A short side hall led off toward an open door. He eased himself down a step and into a panelled room.

Scarfe was standing at a window looking out over his garden. "Did you say that Millie went over to your father's place this morning?"

"That's right."

"And she was telling Clarence about not being able to reach me the other night? And about missing sleeping pills?" He turned and looked at Wilf.

"She doesn't know."

"Know what?"

"That you were seen coming from Sylvia Young's place. You and your white Cadillac. My father doesn't know either. I didn't tell them."

"You didn't?"

"No."

"Then why was Millie there?"

"Because she thinks you're having an affair with some mysterious someone. And because of that she thinks you might be planning to murder her."

Scarfe cast his eyes upward as if he thought God might materialize from out of the ceiling and help him out. He walked unsteadily over to a chair and sat down behind a desk. He began to rearrange some pencils and pens. "This is a nightmare."

"I know it is," Wilf said.

"So you haven't told the police? Or anyone?"

"Only you."

"And the person who mistakenly thought she saw me, you did say a she, didn't you?"

"Yes."

"Has she told anyone else? I mean, besides yourself?"

"No."

"Just the two of you?"

"Yes."

Scarfe fell silent for a moment. "The thing is, a false accusation will do almost as much harm as if it were actually true. You understand that, don't you? You see my situation." He looked up at Wilf with a faint smile.

Wilf nodded.

Scarfe seemed reassured. He reached down and opened a drawer.

Wilf gripped his cane and waited to see what instrument of Fate might show itself. After all the sorties, all the rounds of thumping ammunition given and received, cold sweat running, icy fear, was it to end in this quiet room? One short, sharp sound and it would be over. He tried to touch his feelings. He wasn't sure that he actually cared.

Scarfe's hand came up holding a bulky envelope. Wilf could feel a shiver move through his body from somewhere.

"This happens to be most of my life savings," Scarfe said. "Fifty thousand dollars in bearer bonds. You know what bearer bonds are, don't you? As long as you're in possession of them, you can cash them anywhere. No questions asked." Scarfe set the envelope down on top of the desk. "There it is, the rest of your life, Wilf. Just like that. Go wherever you want, do whatever you like. I'll leave it up to your good judgment how you might want to divide it up with that person who said she saw me the other night. Mistaken as she was." He pushed the envelope across the desk.

Wilf stood motionless.

"Don't you see? It's all for the two of you. All of it. Take it."

Wilf shook his head.

"Government of Canada bearer bonds. Absolutely guaranteed. No questions asked. One-thousand-dollar denominations." Scarfe ripped open the envelope and began to pull out a thick stack of certificates. "Fifty thousand dollars. Fifty of them. All yours." He got up and came around the desk, fanning them out in his hands like a deck of large playing cards. "Look at them, goddamn it! Will you look at them? Goddamn, take them!"

"How am I going to take them?"

Scarfe came to a stop. He looked down at Wilf's cane. "Oh, I'm terrible sorry, I'll get a bag for you." He began to wander around the darkly panelled room as if he'd never been there before. He stared at some shelves on the wall and at a side table for any possibility. "Something with a handle, I guess. Something you can carry."

"I know what went wrong," Wilf said. And he did know. It was written all over Scarfe's body, all over his face.

"Nothing went wrong. I'm protecting my reputation, that's all."

"Bradley went wrong. It's Bradley, isn't it? He wasn't supposed to be there."

And Scarfe's face went dead white. It broke. "Oh, that fucking harridan. Oh, that fucking whore. Oh, that goddamn fucking whoring pig! Oh my God! Oh Jesus God!"

Tears sprung into his eyes. He walked back to the window. Wilf thought he might walk right through it but instead he slid down the glass and came to rest on the sill. He slumped his head between his knees. His shoulders began to heave. Sobs ripped out of him. Short strangled cries. The bonds slipped from his hands and slid across the floor.

"I knew I couldn't buy you, Wilf. Not you," he was mumbling. When he lifted his head, his eyes looked drowned and blind. "I apologize. I have no regret about Sylvia Young though. None whatsoever. She was an entirely worthless human being. Bloodsucker to the core. But Bradley. I killed a child!"

Scarfe shot to his feet as if the horror of that accusation had lifted him up by the scruff of his neck. He reached out and held on to the window. Behind him, out in the garden, Wilf could see a silvery fall of mist.

"Millie and I. We don't have any children," Scarfe was saying, "Couldn't have them. Tried. Well, the fact is we don't have anything now. I'll be plucked out of here." He began to jam the back of a hand into his eyes. "I killed a child!"

Wilf refused to move, to say anything, comfort him, touch him.

"Bradley was never in the house when we met. In case he overheard, you see? Never there. I asked her. Of course I asked her. She said he was staying with a friend." Scarfe made his way back to the desk and sank down in the chair. He picked up a pen. Looked at it. He put it back down. "You're kind of an agent of retribution these days, aren't you? I suppose it's the war experience. Is that what it is? That's what gives you an instinct. Is that it?"

Wilf didn't answer.

"I'm just wondering. Could you do something for me? Could you explain to my wife? She should know. In private, of course. Just the two of you. And in a calm and considerate way. Could you do that for me? Because I won't be able to, you see, not once the police, once they have me."

"I don't know what to explain."

"No? Well, you could begin by telling a story. She knows most of it anyway. She knows the Saskatchewan part anyway." Scarfe forced a weak smile. "About this young man who came from a ridiculously poor family. You could tell her about the part she doesn't know, though, the part about how poverty works, that even if such a young man makes something of himself, studies hard, is hired on by a bank, meets the right people and finally becomes a secretary-treasurer of a large and prestigious firm, it will make almost no difference. He'll still be afraid of ending up where he started. He'll still smell the smell of poverty everywhere he turns, he won't be able to wash himself enough, won't be able to get rid of it. And so, to make himself feel better, he'll steal. Oh, not right away. No, he'll resist for years because it makes no sense whatsoever, but then he will. And he does. And this is where a certain Sylvia Young enters the picture. Not from any intelligence on her part. Christ no. But simply because one day she spilled some ink on an invoice. That's all she did. That's the irony of it. That's where God comes in, I suppose."

Scarfe pushed himself up out of the chair and felt his way around the edge of the desk like he'd just aged twenty years. "That was part of her job, you see, trotting upstairs to my office for my initials. When she came back to pick up that particular invoice she noticed something peculiar, that bit of ink she'd spilled earlier had miraculously disappeared. And so, being the kind of person she turned out to be, what do you suppose she did? She put a small spot of ink on that same company's invoice the next month and lo and behold, the exact same thing happened. The ink had disappeared." Scarfe knelt down on his bony knees and began to gather up the scattered bonds. "That's how she stumbled on my arrangement. Every month this certain bulk wool supplier submits an invoice to our company. Our woollen mill checks it, initials it, and then when it comes to me for final approval I replace it with an identical one, except that the new invoice has been calculated at a slightly higher price per pound. I fake everyone's initials and a cheque gets cut. This supplier, my friend and I, we split the overpayment. Nothing extravagant of course, easily within the margin the company can absorb and since I do the budgets and work with our accountant on the year-end reports, nothing I can't lose in a flurry of figures. I always intended to stop. Every month. But once she began to blackmail me I needed the money even more. Or thought I did. These bonds were her final payment. She made a promise to sell her house, move away, never bother me again. All I had to do was pay her fifty thousand dollars." Scarfe struggled to his feet again.

"So why didn't you?"

"Well, as you can see I was about to. But then I thought, she'll just come back. She'll want more. I'd been paying her off every month for the last five years. I knew her very well."

"She'd even dressed up for the occasion."

"Yes she had. And I'd brought along a celebratory bottle of booze. I always brought her some booze on the few occasions when she wanted to meet with me, when she'd invariably jack up the price. I tried to keep things amiable, you see. She knew the spot she had me in. She could see my fear; I think she could see it all the way back to Saskatchewan. People like her can smell such things, you know. Not like the rest of us. I was wracked with guilt about everything. She had no conscience whatsoever. Do you know what her mistake was? She thought I was too much a gentleman, too meek a soul, to ever do her any harm."

The bonds fell out of Scarfe's hands and fanned out all over the floor again. "I believe we can call your father now. Would you do that for me, Wilf? I can't think of a better lawyer or a better friend." He began to move toward the door. "Tell him that we're on our way over. I don't want to be here when Millie comes home. I'll get a few things. I don't know. A toothbrush. Pajamas. And then I suppose, once we've had our chat with your father we'll have to go down and see the police."

Scarfe stopped at the doorway. "There's a phone in the corner. Would you call? And when you see Millie for your little talk, would you tell her that there was never any other woman. Never in all my life."

He disappeared into the hall.

Wilf could see the telephone sitting on a table in a far corner. A bronze statuette of a cowboy riding a bucking bronco sat on a pedestal next to it. Except for the bonds there was nothing in Scarfe's study that seemed messy or out of place.

All class. Neat. Precise.

A secretary-treasurer's office.

Wilf looked out the window. Despite the blowing mist he could see that the garden was neat and precise too, laid out with a pleasing symmetry. The several flower beds. The adjoining paths. A pair of balancing trellises. The goldfish pond placed at the very centre. Countless hours spent down there. A great deal of care.

He tried to imagine Scarfe when the snow was blowing all around looking down at that spot of life. Hidden flashes of gold. "Spring will come," he had said.

Wilf crossed the room and picked up the phone. He had no idea what he was going to say to his father, he'd just have to trust that something intelligent and halfway apologetic would come out.

"Number please," Nancy Dearborn's familiar voice came down the line and at that same instant the air in the room buckled and the house filled with a thunderous roar.

Wilf dropped the receiver and ran stumbling for the doorway. As soon as he reached the side hall he could smell an acrid all too familiar smell. He turned the corner into the main hall. A cloud of grey smoke was floating in front of him. He walked through it toward the yellow pool of light. He could see the bottom of Scarfe's stocking feet.

Wilf leaned against the wall. The smoke began to sting his eyes. A thick ruby liquid was moving swiftly toward him across the parqueted floor.

CHAPTER SEVENTEEN

Wilf wasn't able to use the phone in Scarfe Telfer's house. He didn't want to deal with Nancy Dearborn. Instead he went next door and asked the neighbour to call an ambulance though he'd seen enough to know that there was no real urgency for one. And then he asked her to phone the police.

Wilf remained standing in the distraught neighbour's vestibule for what seemed a sufficient amount of time to show appropriate concern and then he started walking back toward his own house. He felt numb and that was all. He passed the ambulance going the other way. A block and a half farther along Andy pulled up beside him in the police cruiser and rolled down the window.

"Wilf," he called out.

Wilf crossed over to the car.

"It was you who found Mr. Telfer, wasn't it?"

Wilf leaned against the car and stared off down the street.

"The man who just blew his head off? Jesus, you should have stayed there. You should have waited. Better get in the car. We'll go back."

Wilf bent down and looked at Andy through the window. "I've got some news for you. Last Wednesday evening, sometime in the middle of the night, Scarfe Telfer turned on the gas that killed Sylvia Young and her son Bradley."

Andy stared at him, "Oh shit, Wilf."

"I can't help it," Wilf said. His legs felt like they were about to give way.

"Will you get in the car?"

"I'm going home. Talk to me later."

Wilf started down the sidewalk again. Andy pulled the cruiser into someone's driveway, turned around and sped back the way he'd come.

What am I going to tell the old man, Wilf thought to himself.

It didn't turn out to be too difficult a task. By the time he'd reached the house he'd decided he wasn't going to feel anything anyway. No more pain, his or anyone else's. No more shock. He just had to retreat somewhere. A concrete bunker.

His father, as usual, was in his study. Some of his Nuremberg transcripts were sitting on his lap, or perhaps they were brand new ones he'd had his law society forward to add to his collection.

Wilf stood in the doorway. "Scarfe Telfer is dead."

Clarence's head snapped up. "What? God! What happened?"

"He's at his house. The ambulance might still be there. But he's dead."

Clarence took one moment to search Wilf's face, one terrible moment, and then he rushed past him and out of the house.

Wilf looked at his watch. It was past two o'clock and he hadn't had any lunch. He walked into the kitchen and began making himself an omelette. He grated some cheese, cracked some eggs into a bowl and switched on the stove.

Pieces of Scarfe's brain had redecorated the front hall, a rainbow of fleshy pink arcing across the flowered wallpaper.

Wilf was feeling light again. Breathless. He added a little milk to his eggs and began to whisk them around. He looked in the fridge for some green onions. Pepper.

Scarfe had had himself all figured out. Oh yes, he certainly had. An impoverished childhood. Irrational fears. Stole to make himself feel better. All neat and precise and tied up in a bow. He'd tied Sylvia Young in a bow too. She had no conscience and therefore he had no limits. She'd suck him dry, wouldn't she?

There was nothing else he could do, he was simply defending himself.

Wilf dropped a dab of butter in the heating frying pan.

Did Scarfe really think his wife would understand what he'd done? Did he really think she'd feel sorry for him? Anyway, it was all a convenient lie.

"In my life I have never followed egotistical aims and I was never motivated by base instincts."

Who had said that? It was resonating as clearly in Wilf's head as if Scarfe himself had just whispered it in his ear. He poured his eggs into the pan. He could hear them sizzle but he couldn't smell a thing.

Egotistical?

Of course not. His embezzlement was all psychological. He couldn't help himself.

Base instincts?

Perish the thought. A logical conclusion followed by a dispassionate, intellectual decision. There was nothing else to be done.

Wilf flipped the omelette. He could see Scarfe sitting at his desk. Mist was blowing past the window. He was holding a pen in his hand. Working it out. Precisely. Neatly. Dispassionately.

Option One: give her the bonds, hope she keeps her word.

Option Two: don't give her the bonds, call her bluff. Riskier.

Option Three: if she actually is going to go to the police out of sheer bloody-mindedness, no matter the consequences for herself, renegotiate.

Option Four: and if she still won't disappear after renegotiation and payment, if it looks like she intends to keep this going on forever, disappear myself. Sell the house. Move to the United States. The Caribbean. Mexico. Millie and I have already discussed just such a retirement and she won't need to know the real reason why.

Option Five: go to the company myself, before Sylvia has a chance, and try to make some kind of restitution in as private a manner as possible. Beg for forgiveness. This is a difficult one, though.

Option Six:

He was writing this last heading down with a trembling hand. He didn't dare fill it out. Option Six already felt too good. His heart was pounding crazily. It felt like a release. It felt like ecstasy.

At four o'clock Clarence returned to the house. Wilf was sitting in the front parlour reading the Saturday paper. They rarely used either of the two front rooms. The one was dominated by a grand piano that had rarely been played, and only many years before by his young and beautiful mother. At least that's what Wilf had been told. The other room had a stiff formality to it, still full of the overstuffed and dated furniture his grandfather had purchased the first year of his marriage.

It took Clarence some time to locate Wilf. When he did he sat down on the other side of the large room, his coat and fedora still on. "I've talked to the Chief of Police and I've made it absolutely clear that we'll be happy to discuss anything and everything first thing Monday morning, but I wanted the rest of today and Sunday to be undisturbed. I insisted on it. A little peace and quiet. Time to muster our reserves for the onslaught."

Wilf looked over the top of the newspaper. "That sounds like a good idea."

"I can't imagine what you were doing over there."

"I had some information."

"What information?"

"I thought we were going to have peace and quiet."

"You're in serious trouble."

"Why?"

"Because you were with him when he died. That's why!"

"I killed Scarfe Telfer?"

"Were there any other witnesses?"

Wilf resumed his reading. "Not that I noticed at the time."

"Look Wilf, I'm not saying you killed him. Of course I'm not saying that. But what I am saying is that I can't control these things and if the forensics aren't clear, the Crown will make up their own mind. They always do. There was just the two of you, wasn't there?"

"Yes."

"It speaks to motivation."

"What does?"

"Why the hell would Scarfe Telfer kill himself?"

Wilf had never seen his father look quite so shaken. His face was trembling with a thousand questions.

"Because he was stealing from Parson's," Wilf said. "Sylvia Young was blackmailing him. Scarfe killed her. I found out. And so he killed himself."

He'd just struck his father a mortal blow. Clarence's eyes bulged out, his mouth moved but Wilf couldn't hear any sound.

"You're right, Dad. We should leave it until Monday morning. I've already told Andy, anyway."

His father somehow found his voice. "Do you mean to say that Scarfe had something to do with that woman's death? Her son's death? That's preposterous!" He stood up and started unbuttoning his coat as if the room had suddenly become too hot. He walked out into the hall. He took off his coat. He took off his hat. He bundled them up in front of his chest like a shield and walked back.

He's not going to leave this alone, Wilf thought to himself.

"How do you know that, Wilf? How do you know?"

"Because there was a witness. Not today. But Wednesday night. She saw Scarfe coming from Sylvia's house. She recognized him. Well, not him exactly, but his car. Well, not his

Cadillac either, but she saw a fancy white car. And as you'll recall, Wednesday was the night Millie couldn't locate her husband. Or her sleeping pills."

"You went over there on the basis of that less than overwhelming information?"

"Yes."

"What the hell did you say to him? What did you do?"

"I lied. I told him I knew more than I actually did."

"And then he shot himself?"

Wilf nodded his head.

Clarence stood there clutching his coat and his hat and staring at his son. "I need a drink." He went into the hall again and disappeared.

Wilf looked back at the newspaper but he couldn't concentrate. Hunker down in a concrete bunker without even a slit to peek out of, that was all one required. That was the thing.

Eventually Clarence came back carrying two drinks in his hands. He gave one to Wilf and sat down where he'd sat before. They sipped their drinks.

Wilf could tell that his father had resolved for the time not to ask any more questions, but the strain on his face was more than evident. He looked overwhelmed. Before he was half through his drink he had to excuse himself. He disappeared down the hall again.

Wilf remained where he was and waited.

After a moment Clarence returned. "I'm the one who talked to Millie this morning. I'm the one who's been friends with Scarfe since the day he moved into town. I'm his solicitor, for god sakes, and I'm your father. Why didn't you come to me if you thought you had some information tying Scarfe to Sylvia Young's suicide? We could have talked. We could have decided the best thing to do together. Why didn't you come to me?"

"Just because of that, because you are his friend. I thought it would be more respectful of Mr. Telfer, his privacy, if I went alone. He might have had a reasonable, straightforward explanation."

"If you'd handled it differently, it might have turned out differently."

"He broke down. He confessed to everything."

"If you'd handled it differently, he might not have shot himself."

"It was because of Bradley. He didn't mean to kill Bradley."

"But he shot himself!"

Clarence looked bereft. He looked lost.

❄ ❄ ❄

Carole waited until her father had left the house. She could still hear the sewing-machine treadle going up and down, up and down, right above her head. Her mother was occupied, mending something by the light of the window at the back of the upstairs hall.

She picked up the phone.

"Number please," Nancy Dearborn said.

"Six four one."

"I was wondering what was taking you so long. Isn't it just awful? Let me know if you find out anything more."

"Will you please just connect me?"

Nancy's voice tightened. "That's what I am doing."

Carole listened as the phone at the other end of the line rang and rang. It rang five times before it was picked up.

"Hello," Clarence said.

"Oh." Carole's heart sank. "Hello, Mr. McLauchlin. It's me. Carole."

"Yes, Carole."

"I just heard about what happened. I mean, today."

"Yes?"

"About Mr. Telfer."

"Yes. Well, thank you for calling. It's very thoughtful of you. It's been quite the shock."

"Yes. It is."

"He was an old friend, you know. A dear friend. Anyway, everything's as fine here as might be expected and thanks again for your call. I'll see you in the office on Monday."

"Mr. McLauchlin?"

"Yes."

"Is Wilf there?"

"Wilf? Well, yes he is but he's resting. I don't know how much you know about the events of today, Carole."

"I know he was there."

"I suppose the whole town knows. Anyway, I'll pass on your kind concern, and thank you for calling."

"Mr. McLauchlin?"

"Yes, Carole?"

"I want to talk to Wilf. Please."

There was a pause at the other end of the line.

"I'm not sure he's in the mood to talk."

"He'll talk to me. I need to talk to him. Please."

She could almost hear Mr. McLauchlin thinking out loud, thinking it all through. He was so smart. He'd been away on business for days. His house had been empty.

"Just a moment," he said.

Oh god, Carole thought to herself. But it didn't matter, she wanted to hear Wilf's voice. And anyway it was only fair. Her parents knew what was going on between them. Her father wasn't even talking to her.

"Hello," Wilf said. He sounded a long way away.

"Hi."

"Hi, you."

"Nancy called. She told me what happened. The ambulance and the police and all that. And that you were there."

"Did she tell you that he's dead?"

254

"Yes. A suicide. He shot himself."

"He was a client of ours."

"I know."

"At this rate my father won't have any practice left."

Carole wasn't sure whether she'd heard Wilf laugh or not. Some kind of weird sound. Her chest felt as tight as if someone were squeezing it. "Are you all right?"

"Sure. I'm just trying to figure out things. I don't know what to say."

"No one knows what to say. Another suicide."

"To add to Sylvia Young's, you mean?"

"Yes. But that's not why I'm calling. I just wanted to let you know that the house in the country, the stone cottage, it's still empty. We could have it."

"When?"

"Whenever we want. If we still want it."

"How much?"

"Fifty dollars a month." Carole waited for what seemed like an endlessly long time. "Maybe it's too much money. Maybe it won't work out. We could think about it, anyway. Or not."

"This one was different," Wilf said.

"What do you mean?"

"Because he wasn't dead before I went over there. And if I hadn't gone over there he'd still be alive."

"You know something, I just want to see you. Can I see you?" Silence again. "Wilf?"

"Why don't you call your friend back. Or whoever owns that cottage. And tell them we'll take it."

"From when?"

"From now. From right now. What do you think?"

"Well, I don't know. Okay."

"Why don't you give me the rest of the day. I'll talk to Dad. I'll get my stuff organized. I'll see you in the morning."

"I guess so. I guess that will be all right. If you're sure about the cottage?"

"Thank you, Carole."

"For what?"

Wilf had already hung up.

Carole sat down in her parents' kitchen, the kitchen she'd grown up in, the kitchen she'd known all her life.

Soon she'd be sitting in her own kitchen.

What have I done, she thought to herself.

❄ ❄ ❄

At six o'clock Mr. and Mrs. Wellesley from three doors over rapped on the McLauchlins' side door. They'd brought over a hot chicken dinner complete with a tureen of soup and dinner rolls. They said how sorry they were to hear the news. Clarence thanked them and they went away.

"That was strange," Clarence said. "You'd think we'd had a death in the family."

"Nice of them, though." Wilf eyed the steaming tomato soup his father had just placed on the table but avoided looking at all the rest.

They sat down and ate in silence.

Wilf sipped at a bowl of soup and poured himself another rye.

Clarence picked at the chicken. He didn't seem particularly hungry either.

"Her name's Catherine Shepherd," Wilf finally said. "Cathy. If you want to know. She lives just down the street from where Sylvia Young lived. That's the person who saw Scarfe in the middle of the night." And to hell with her miserable-looking husband, Wilf thought to himself, circumstances have changed, his wife will have to get herself involved now.

Clarence nodded carefully.

Wilf thought about telling him that he'd be moving out of the house soon. Into the country. With his secretary.

He glanced across the table. His father looked reduced somehow, his shoulders more drooped, his face smaller, his hands veined and defenceless-looking.

I'm sucking the life out of him, Wilf thought to himself.

He decided to leave the conversation about Carole until later. Maybe Monday evening. By then, after a day of dealing with Doc Robinson and the police and all the possible implications and complications under the law it would seem like a trifling thing. It might even come as comic relief to his father. At least his son wouldn't be living with him, he'd be out of his tortured sight.

After supper Clarence announced that he hadn't seen Millie that afternoon when he'd gone over to the house. She'd been intercepted downtown and taken directly to her sister's. God only knew when she might want to go back to her own house. Probably never. He said he'd like to go over to Millie's sister's place and see Millie for a little while. Would that be all right? He'd only be gone from the house for an hour or so.

Wilf was back in the front room still trying to read the paper. "What do you think I'm going to do? Of course you should go over there. Stay as long as you want."

"I'll only stay an hour. At the most."

"As long as you want. And tell Millie..." Wilf couldn't finish the sentence.

"I know. And I will," Clarence said.

"Dad, I'm sorry," Wilf managed finally to blurt out.

"I know."

Wilf continued to read. After a few moments he heard the side door close, the loose glass rattling in its frame. He listened to see if he could hear the car pulling out of the garage. He couldn't. The walls of the house were three bricks thick.

Wilf looked around the room. He wondered how he might pass the time. He could read the Nuremberg papers from beginning to end. He thought not. He could begin to pack. But what would he take? He'd take everything he owned. Every scrap. As if he'd never lived in that house at all.

Of course his father was right. Of course he should never have gone over to Scarfe's. And why hadn't he talked to his father? It wasn't because he'd wanted to save Scarfe from embarrassment, or himself, if he'd been wrong. That wasn't it at all. He couldn't have stopped himself from going over there even if he'd tried. And he had. Hadn't he? He'd been compelled to go, the absorbing sense of moving toward something fateful and eternal one limping step at a time.

When the phone rang Wilf was wrestling his suitcase out of his bedroom closet. He wondered if it was Carole. Perhaps she'd changed her mind. He felt a slight stab of panic. He walked into the hall and picked up the receiver.

"Hello?"

"Is this Wilf?" A familiar voice came down the line.

"Hello, Michael. That was fast."

"Well, I still don't have your medical records. I didn't need them."

"Oh?"

"Wilf, I'm sorry but I thought I'd better check out something first. That's what serving in the army does to you. Proper authorization. Chain of command. All that."

"You never used to give a damn."

"I still don't. But Wilf McLauchlin has always been a special case and I needed a clearance."

Wilf clung tightly to the telephone. "For what?"

"First of all, you have to know that you're fine. That was determined a long time ago. So don't worry. Understood?"

Wilf could see Chasson's tired and thoughtful face as plainly as if he were standing right there in front of him. He'd seen it enough times hovering over his recovery bed.

"Understood."

"Then why don't you ask your questions again."

"Michael? What was wrong with my eyes?"

"No idea. If it was a symptom it was the only one you had. Other than that, the bacterium had no measurable effect at all."

"Uh huh," Wilf could hear the sound of his own blood pounding away inside his ear. "What bacterium?"

"That's what got everyone so excited and why you ended up in isolation, Wilf. You had typhus, but with a significant difference. It showed up in your bloodstream first, just as normal typhus would, but then it migrated to your lungs. That was brand new. Typhus isn't supposed to do that. And it scared the fuck out of us."

"Why?"

"Because it meant the little bastard had the potential to become airborne, which meant we were looking at the potential for a catastrophe. You could have spread it by sneezing, coughing, talking. "

"I don't know what all this means."

"Well, one of the things it meant to us was that you didn't pick up that kind of mutation by accident. Remember those three lost days you were talking about? We think someone did take care of you. They were experimenting with typhus in Buchenwald."

"Oh?"

Wilf wondered if he could stop now. If he did, if he just hung up the phone, he knew Michael would understand. He knew he wouldn't call back. Ever.

"Are you all right?"

"Uh huh."

"Kind of a shock?"

"I guess."

"You either came down near Buchenwald, or for all we know you crashed right inside its perimeter. It's large enough. They stabilized you over a day or two and then we think they injected you with this altered bacterium. You have to remember that the American army was only about twenty miles away by this time and those scientists, doctors, whoever they were, were feeling desperate enough to try most anything. And it almost worked. They trucked your plane outside the compound. They put you back inside. And just as they'd hoped, some American troops found you and took you behind the lines. Perfect. Fortunately for us though, you failed to go off. As a secret weapon you were a bust."

"Michael, if this thing was in me, why wasn't I put in isolation right away? Why wasn't everyone around me put in isolation?"

"Because it didn't show up in your blood work until you were in France. Some clever person in our lab identified typhus, which is bad enough, and then they had a closer look and said, 'What the hell is this?' Shortly thereafter that blind Canadian pilot in the general ward on our third floor became a very special patient."

"Why didn't it work?"

"Well, it did, partially. It had worked, in that it had migrated from your bloodstream into your lungs, just as certain types of infections that cause pneumonia can do, but from there it was supposed to become an airborne contagion similar to tuberculosis only ten times as fast and twenty times as deadly. Instead it seemed too susceptible to your own body's defences; it could move around in your system but it couldn't get a sufficient foothold. Once we'd cultured it in the lab we killed it off with the usual antibiotics."

"You're telling me, I was meant to cause a plague." Wilf tried to sound matter-of-fact about it, as if he was just remarking that he was meant to practise law, or meant to fly a plane.

"And that it didn't work. They were desperate enough to try but the science wasn't there. What you have to remember is that you're fine. It's almost two years ago now and you were clear of that thing within a few months. You were monitored long afterwards, of course. Nothing is going to come of it now."

"Right."

"That's an absolute guarantee."

"Right."

"We should have told you long before this but germ warfare is top secret these days. Individual sacrifice for the greater good. All that."

"Sure."

"Any time you want to come down here again, we can go out for a drink. We can talk about it some more. We can talk about it until the sun comes up."

"I appreciate that, Michael, but you know what I'm like. Thirty thousand feet. Steady at the controls."

"That you are, my friend."

"I'll be fine."

Wilf put down the phone.

When his father arrived home a half-hour later, Wilf was still standing in the upstairs hallway.

CHAPTER EIGHTEEN

The cottage didn't look quite like Carole remembered it. It was empty of furniture and stripped of curtains for one thing, which made the rough plaster walls look grimy and the windows bleak and in dire need of a wash. And for another it was raining outside and it had turned cold. The rooms were even smaller than she'd thought. The bedroom seemed scarcely larger than her mother's clothes closet.

"What do you think?" she said.

Wilf was still standing in the living room looking out the window. "I like it."

"So do I."

He turned to look at her. "We'll probably need some furniture."

"I have some furniture. I mean, I bought some out of my own money so I guess I can take what's in my bedroom, and there's a settee my grandmother gave me."

"We won't need much."

"Do you think it's too small? It's really small, isn't it?"

Wilf crossed the room, gave Carole his cane and put his hand on her shoulder. "No." His hand touched the back of her neck, it moved to her hair, trailed gently across her face.

"Don't get any ideas."

"I don't have a thought in my head."

He kissed her so gently she could hardly feel his lips.

"I don't know about my body, though. Sometimes it gets up to things all on its own."

"We'll have lots of time for that out here."

"So you say."

Carole handed him back his cane. "You'll see. Country people do it all the time. That's what I hear anyway."

Wilf laughed. Carole adored his laugh. She moved toward the kitchen. She could hear the rain pattering just above her head. She'd regretted all the way out to the house that they weren't driving through sunshine. The rolling countryside had looked bleak and forlorn. She'd kept her hand on Wilf's leg all the way.

"I have to tell you about Sylvia Young," Wilf said.

Carole's heart sank. The whole purpose of the move was to get him away from all that. "What do you mean?"

He began to tell her all the things she didn't know. She could never have guessed, dreamed in a thousand years what he was telling her, though he had said something on the phone about having been the cause of the shooting. It had sounded crazy—she had closed her mind off to it.

As Wilf talked he sat down on the window ledge. He's going to go on and on, Carole thought. And he did. Sylvia's connection with Scarfe Telfer and the unthinkable thing that Scarfe had finally done. And how he'd tricked Scarfe into confessing. And how that had led to Scarfe picking up a shotgun.

Wilf finally finished his story and just sat there in the grey rainy light.

Carole turned away and went into the bedroom. "There's no closet in here. Of course, if there were a closet there'd be no room for the room." And she said, "You were right all the time then. They were murdered."

She could hear Wilf getting up, crossing the floor toward her.

"She was," he said, "drugged and gassed. Bradley's death was a mistake."

Carole wasn't feeling frightened exactly. Not of Wilf. But there was something that felt cold and foreboding. She'd felt it when she'd got up first thing that morning, like a presence in her room, she'd felt it driving along the river and turning into the half-hidden lane. "What's happening?"

"I honestly don't know," Wilf said.

Carole turned to look at him.

He was resting against the doorway. His eyes were closed. "This will be good out here. Listening to the flowers grow. The beat of butterfly wings. I need to get away from people. I just need some peace now."

"You're tired," Carole said.

"Yes. I think so."

Carole crossed the small room and put her arms around him.

"All right," she said. She pressed her face against his face. "All right."

❋ ❋ ❋

Duncan trudged along the road past Eric's home. The light near the barn was on but the windows in the house were dark. It was the middle of the night.

Eric's stupid dog began to bark even though he must have known who it was that was passing by. Duncan hurried on. He felt sore and cold and half-starved. He came over the top of the last hill and saw the top of the roof on his own barn. He laid down in the ditch. He had to be very cautious now.

Duncan had seen the police two days before, lined up on a narrow iron bridge somewhere between Brantford and his own town. There were police cars and trucks. There were dogs. He'd had to wade through a swamp deeper into the woods and hide himself under a log. He'd had to lie there for the rest of the day.

Once the light had faded he'd retraced his steps and looked out at the bridge again. The cars and trucks were gone but he couldn't be certain that they hadn't left someone to watch. He circled around and came out on the edge of the gravel road some distance away. He could just make out the bridge at the bottom of the hill. He continued to wait until it grew dark and then he made a dash for the other side. No one yelled. No dogs pursued him.

Early the next morning he snuck into a henhouse and stole some eggs. An implement shed was standing nearby. There was someone's oil-stained winter coat hanging up on a nail inside the open door. He stole that too. The eggs tasted good but the coat wouldn't work because he still had his chain on. He had to wear it thrown over his shoulders like an old woman wearing a shawl but at least it made him feel warmer. He only had a shirt on and the temperature had dropped below freezing every night. His feet were continually wet. His body was shaking all the time.

It had taken him four days of mostly hiding and four nights of mostly walking to cover the ten miles of river that led to the town, and then he'd snuck across the river on the town's high level railway bridge and had hurried toward the sawmill.

Duncan crawled out of the ditch and up the embankment. He could see the barnyard now, and the stable door and the shop beside the barn, and across the side yard he could see his home. Everything looked shadowy in the moonlight. Abandoned. But he couldn't know that for sure. Someone could be hiding in the barn or watching from a window in the house. After all, every cop in the world seemed to know he'd escaped and where else would he go? Duncan couldn't resist any longer. He began to run across the intervening field.

As soon as he reached the barnyard he knew something wasn't right. He pushed open the stable door. "Dandy," he whispered, "Babe!" He walked into Babe's empty stall. And into Dandy's. He sank down on the straw. Everything was quiet. Quieter than in the deepest heart of the woods. Quieter than in his own most secret thoughts. He closed his eyes and stretched himself out. He could feel the touch of Dandy's nose on his cheek. His moist warm breath. "Let's run in the pasture," Dandy might say. "Let's go into town," he'd say.

And Babe would complain. "It's always Dandy," she'd say.

Duncan knew one thing for sure. He'd known it all his life. If he'd been someone else the neighbours would have helped. They always did when people got sick or had to go off some-place because there was an emergency. But he was different. There was lots of hay in his mow. Lots of oats to keep Dandy and Babe fed so they could stay right where they belonged. But no one had helped.

Duncan rubbed his eyes with his swollen and chained hands. He had to find Babe and Dandy. He had to see them. They had to be somewhere.

Wilf McLauchlin hadn't helped. Wilf McLauchlin hadn't done anything.

Duncan felt around in the straw until he found one of Dandy's horse buns. It was cold and dry and hard as a rock. They'd been gone for days. Days and days. He tried to think of where they might be. He couldn't think. He stretched out in the straw again and closed his eyes.

When Duncan woke up a faint light was coming in through the stable window. He got up and looked out. There was no police car pulled around to the back of the house. There was no smoke coming from the chimney. No sign of anyone stirring around.

He tried to think things through. If he was going to find Babe and Dandy he'd have to get rid of his chain, he knew that for a fact. Who would talk to him if he was standing in chains? Who would tell him anything?

Duncan snuck out of the stable and hurried over to the shop. As soon as he turned the corner he could see the door was off its hinges. It was lying there flat on the ground. He stepped over it and looked inside. All the table saws had disappeared and so had the big rip saw. He could see where they'd been unbolted from the floor and pushed through the deep sawdust toward the freight door. The freight door had been left wide open.

Duncan circled around the near-empty room. All the power tools were missing. So were all the good hand tools. He circled around again, as if they might appear if he did it enough times and then he turned back and went through the open door. He'd had a terrible thought. He ran across the side yard toward the house. He barged in through the outside door and through the kitchen door.

All his planes had been ripped down from the ceiling. They were lying all over the floor, broken-winged and crushed, floundering in a sea of newspaper clippings that had been torn off the walls.

Duncan crossed the room. Hidden beer bottles hit up against his boots and rolled emptily away. There were more empty bottles on the counter and on the table too. Someone had tipped over the refrigerator. Someone had wrenched the cupboard shelves half off the wall.

He climbed the stairs and went into his mother's room. The drawers in her dresser had been pulled open as far as they'd go, her clothes that were hanging in her closet since the day she'd died had been strewn all around. Somebody's muddy boot prints marched across the quilt on her bed.

A word was written in bright lipstick on the mirror. *FREAK,* it said.

Duncan began to rock back and forth. The floor creaked under his weight.

Sticks and stones will break my bones, sticks and stones will break my bones.

"Ohhhh," Duncan said. "Ohhhh."

❄ ❄ ❄

Wilf could see Andy draped over the fender of his rusty old Ford, his head hidden under its raised hood. The car's motor was chugging away.

He took a deep breath, tried to summon up some measure of his old self and walked into the garage. He poked Andy in the ribs with his cane. Andy lurched up and hit his head.

"Jesus Christ, don't do that!"

"What are you doing?"

"Trying to save a few dollars and asphyxiating myself at the same time. Shut it off, will you?"

Wilf leaned through the window and turned the key. "Maybe you should work outside."

"It's snowing." Andy put his screwdriver down and began wiping his hands on an oily rag.

"I have a favour to ask."

"My carburetor is sucking too much air. Or not enough. I don't know."

"I need a truck."

"You need a truck?"

"Carole and I were looking at this cottage out on the East River Road, we think we might rent it but we need a small truck to take out some of her furniture. I thought you might know someone."

Andy's face broke into a smile. "Let me get this straight. A cottage? You and Carole Birley?"

"There's no fooling you, is there?" Wilf circled the car. "I would have asked the first of the week but my father's been keeping me busy the last couple of days."

"Right. Scarfe Telfer. The OPP again. All that."

"All that."

"I think we could locate a truck. Have you heard my news? I'm back to being a constable again."

"Are you kidding?"

"Demoted."

"Jesus, Andy, I'm sorry to hear that."

"You should be. You and that goddamn piece of ice."

"Maybe I can talk to someone."

"After Scarfe Telfer, I don't think so. Aw shit. I didn't mean that, I'm just pissed off."

"That's all right. But look, don't just take it. Put up an argument with the Chief. And maybe the mayor. You acted on sound information. You took charge. If it wasn't for you Duncan might still be running around."

Andy looked at Wilf. "He is still running around. Didn't you know? He escaped Saturday."

"What?"

"I'm not kidding. He just walked out of the courthouse in Brantford. Good old Drunken Duncan. He's probably hiding in some woods again."

"Saturday?" Wilf leaned up against the car. "My father hasn't been telling me anything. He's been tiptoeing around me like I'm breakable."

"Yeah...well," Andy said.

"Why didn't Carole say something? She'd know by now, Nancy Dearborn would have told her."

"There you go with Nancy Dearborn again." Andy headed out of the garage. "I'm supposed to be babysitting."

"Where's Linda?"

"Don't ask."

Andy stopped at the open door. A wet curtain of sleet was pelting down, covering up the grass again. "Riding around with one of her girlfriends because our car won't go and she doesn't think we can afford to get it fixed. She's looking for a job." He put his head down and ran for the side door. "Come on!"

Wilf followed him across the slippery lawn and into the house. Andy brought him a kitchen chair. Wilf had dispensed with wearing his galoshes. He sat down and began to untie his shoes.

"Davey, where are you?" Andy shouted.

"I'm upstairs," Davey yelled back.

"Where's Carmen?"

"She's up here, too."

"I'm up here, Daddy!" Carmen yelled.

"Okay." Andy opened the icebox. "Want a beer?"

"I feel bad about you losing your stripes, Andy."

"Maybe it's a good thing. Not making less money but for Linda to get a job. She might not worry so damn much about everything." Andy pulled out two beers. When he turned around Wilf was smiling at him. "What?"

"Nothing. Just thinking about the glories of domesticity. And who might have a small truck. Do you know anyone? I'll pay for the rental and the gas."

Andy flipped off the tops and handed Wilf a beer. "And the help? I suppose you'll need some help."

"I might need a little help."

"I'm happy for you, you know. I'm happy for you both." Andy raised his beer in a toast. "Here's to Carole. Here's to Wilf."

Wilf raised his. "Thanks. We're hoping it might be a little more peaceful out there."

"It would have to be, wouldn't it? What's she think about Scarfe Telfer?" Andy was leaning up against the table and looking innocent enough.

"Do you think she should be frightened or something?"

"Of course not."

"I didn't plan them. All these things. I didn't want them."

A heavy silence descended on the kitchen.

Wilf looked away. He took a sip of his beer.

❋ ❋ ❋

"You know, this is the first time I've ever driven in the back seat of my car," Clarence remarked. Wilf was behind the driver's wheel. Carole was sitting stiffly beside him. Clarence didn't want to sit in the front; he said he'd prefer the back. It would feel more like he was being chauffeured.

Carole was looking a little feverish, Wilf thought, her face shiny and slightly flushed in the passing street lights. They were going out for supper at the fancy restaurant on the edge of town. Clarence had insisted. Wilf glanced in the rear-view mirror and caught a glimpse of his father. He seemed surprisingly relaxed.

The previous evening Wilf had told him that he and Carole were seeing each other and that they'd made a decision to live together. Clarence was sitting at the kitchen table reading over a copy of the statement Wilf had given to the OPP and looking increasingly concerned. When Wilf began to talk about Carole, he didn't turn to look at him. He just stared at an invisible point on the opposite wall.

"I think the world of her," Clarence finally said. "I hope you know what you're doing."

"What do you mean?"

"You don't just live with a girl like Carole and then decide not to live with her. You don't do that."

"I'm not intending to do that."

"Are you engaged?"

"No."

"Are you planning on getting engaged?"

"I'm not sure. I don't think we've thought about it."

Clarence turned then to look at Wilf. He smiled. "I'm sure Carole has thought about it. You dope."

"We'll see how it goes."

"Uh huh. I wonder what her parents think about all this?"

Wilf was trying to keep his patience. It was for Carole's sake. "I don't know. She doesn't want me to talk to them. I don't think her father was too excited. And her mother cried, but Carole says that's actually a good sign."

"And why do you think Carole didn't want you to talk to them?"

"I guess, because it's not the best time, with everything that's going on. You know. In town."

Clarence nodded.

Wilf could see that his father had decided not to pursue that line of questioning. It was too painful.

"Carole's nervous that you'll be angry." Wilf continued on, "That you'll think she's been disrespectful. That it will affect how you think about her and her work."

"Christ. I've liked Carole from the first day she stepped into my office and asked me if I had any openings." Clarence smiled at the memory. "As if I were running this huge law firm. There was only me and Dorothy Dale, and Dorothy had gone out for lunch. This is how I look at it. If she loves my son, that just makes her all the more valuable to McLauchlin and McLauchlin. Must mean she's even smarter than I thought."

"She'll be relieved to hear that."

Wilf could see, as the situation sank in, that relief was beginning to brighten his father's face as well. A person who cared for his son had arrived just in the nick of time. To share his burden, his worry.

"I'm glad for you, Wilf, I really am," his father had said.

Wilf pulled the car off the highway and into the restaurant's parking lot.

"I'm up for a steak," Clarence announced. "What do you think, Carole?"

"Oh, I don't know."

"Sirloin? T-bone? Rib-eye? Porterhouse? Filet?"

"Oh my god," Carole said.

Carole had the porterhouse. Clarence had his usual twelve-ounce t-bone. Wilf insisted on everyone ordering a Manhattan.

He'd never tasted one before but the name sounded appropriately celebratory.

Wilf chose the white fish.

Carole was sitting on Wilf's side of the table cutting her remarkably thick steak as neatly as she could and sipping her Manhattan. She'd swept her hair up in some kind of dramatic way and she was wearing an off the shoulder dress that showed off her good bones and slim waist. Wilf thought her neck and creamy white shoulders looked spectacular. Her whole person looked surprisingly spectacular, prettier than he'd ever seen her before.

To this point, no one had said anything about living together, not at work earlier that day, partly because Carole had set a new record for non-stop typing, and not through the first round of drinks and the appetizers.

Wilf looked around the restaurant, at the subdued lights, the rows of empty tables with their white shining linens, and he felt a kind of hallucinatory, drifting detachment. He'd been trying to get his mind around Chasson's news for the past five days. The injection. The plague. His mind wouldn't respond. It wouldn't go there.

He glanced over at Carole. How could she possibly eat her way through that steak, he thought to himself. She must be doing it to impress his father.

"I've always wanted to live in the country," Clarence said.

Carole's face went red.

"I've always thought that there'd be something very pleasant about it. All that air. Sky. Wind. A kind of freedom, you know. And no neighbours. No close neighbours anyway. That's a bonus."

Carole kept eating.

"Are there any close neighbours out where you two are going, I wonder?" Clarence asked.

Carole looked up from her steak. She glanced at Wilf. He was smiling at her as if he wasn't sure, as if she was the only one who would know the answer.

"I don't really know," she said. "There must be someone. There's a farm down the road on the other side."

"Are you on the river side of the road?"

"Yes. Aren't we, Wilf?" Carole gave him a desperate look.

Wilf reached over and took her hand. "I think I'm the luckiest man in the world. That's all I know."

"I'll second that," Clarence said.

※ ※ ※

Wilf and Clarence hadn't arrived back in the house for more than ten minutes when the phone rang. Wilf glanced at his father. Clarence had been doing all the phone answering lately but at that moment he seemed determined to ignore the insistent ringing. Maybe he thinks it's Carole, Wilf thought to himself. Or maybe, with Carole in the picture, he's decided to give up his job of deflection and protection. Or maybe he's just given up.

It was Andy. "Found you a truck. We can pick it up tonight if you want. I have tomorrow off. We can get an early start."

"We don't have that much stuff. It won't take all day."

Wilf looked across the room. Clarence was studying the statement Wilf had given to the OPP again. His brow began to furrow.

"All right, I wouldn't mind going out," Wilf said.

He got his coat back on, told his father where he was going and picked up Andy a few minutes later. They headed out of town.

"Uncle John says he doesn't use it all that often. Just to take hogs or cattle into market now and then. Things like that." Andy was lighting up a cigarette.

"To market?"

"Don't worry. He said he'd get my crazy cousins to clean it out if you wanted to use it. I just called him back and said, 'Order up that cleaning detail.' It'll be fine. We can put a tarp down if you like."

"Carole has a bed and stuff. She probably doesn't want it smelling like hogs and cattle."

"It won't," Andy said.

Andy's uncle didn't live all that far from Duncan Getty's place, just two concessions north and on the same side of the river. Wilf could see a full moon riding over the dark hills ahead of him. The sleet from earlier in the day was still lying across the fields in scattered ghostly patches. He rolled down his window and breathed in a frosty stream of air.

"I'm freezing," Andy said.

Wilf didn't hear him. He continued to drive along with the window open thinking of Carole. Her bare shoulders in the soft restaurant light.

He took another deep, frosty breath.

And something was moving inside, swimming through his bloodstream. Gone now though. According to Chasson.

To the one side of the car he could see a line of tall trees marching up a hill, still leafless, a darker dark against the sky. And all he wanted to do was to come alive. Feel joy like he once did. And natural affection. And harmless ambition.

"Try to stay on the road. It gets narrow through here," Andy said.

He was on the threshold of a new beginning. He could feel it. The stone cottage. Butterflies. All he had to do was concentrate on every breath. Get stronger somehow. Hold on to Carole. Keep everything else away. Cruikshank and dead airmen. Basil and a generation slaughtered. Sylvia and Bradley and mothers and children herded onto freight trains, all gone now, black clouds evaporating into a new day now.

"Watch out!"

Wilf corrected his trajectory and slowed the car down. He could hear dogs baying off in the distance somewhere.

Andy grinned. "Ralphie's out with his hounds again. Young Earl will be with him, too. Hope they cleaned up the truck first." He pointed out a lane up the road.

Wilf turned into it and tried to settle himself down. There was no settling himself down. "What are they after?"

"Anything that moves. Raccoons, mostly. They've got themselves a Blue Tick hound and a Black and Tan bitch. Ralphie's trying to breed them but they don't like each other. She's come into heat twice, but she won't stand still and after a bit of trying the Blue Tick just goes and lies down. Sounds like Linda and me, I said to Ralphie."

The car eased over a sharp knoll. "We have company," Wilf said.

Someone was standing in the middle of the lane holding up a lantern. Wilf came to a stop and Andy rolled down his window. "Ralphie. What are you doing? Are you lost?"

An excited-looking boy of about sixteen came up and peered in through the window. "I just felt like walking up the lane. Couldn't wait. Dad wants to see you."

"About the truck?"

Ralphie shook his head. "We just found something. Me and Earl. Dad wants to show you, you being a policeman and all." Ralphie looked over at Wilf. "Hi there."

"Ralphie, this is Wilf."

"Why do you need a policeman?" Wilf asked.

"You'll see. I'll hitch a ride on the running board." Ralphie grasped the top of the open window.

"Hold on," Andy called out to him, "Wilf's got his own peculiar way of driving." He looked over at Wilf and shrugged. "I guess we'll see."

The house was low slung and rambling and sitting in a frost-tinged valley. Every light was on in the place and a woman was looking out the side door.

"That's my Aunt Bess. Jesus, I hope Earl didn't get hurt or anything."

Wilf stopped the car. Ralphie jumped off the running board and Andy got out.

"Where's Uncle John?" Wilf could hear Andy asking Ralphie.

"Down in the woods. I'll show you."

Wilf got out of the car.

Andy was looking across the yard toward his aunt. "Where's Earl?"

"Mom won't let him come out. She says he's too young." Ralphie headed off into the dark. Andy waved toward his aunt. She didn't return his wave or change her expression. She just continued to stare. Ralphie was already halfway around the corner of the barn. "Come on. I'll show you!" he called back.

Andy started after him.

Wilf leaned against the car and looked back toward the house. The noise the dogs were making was deafening. He could see their dark shapes running up and down in the backyard now, leaping up against a chain-link fence. Aunt Bess was still standing at the door. Wilf knew who had switched on all the lights in the house. And as much as he wanted to resist the thought, he knew why.

Andy was already circling around the barn following Ralphie and his lantern when Wilf turned away from the woman. He walked across the yard, past the barn and out into a wet frosted pasture. Sleet lay in random patches in front of him. He could see fresh dog tracks crossing them here and there, streaking them with flying mud. The hounds had been out and running. He looked off toward Andy and his young cousin. The lantern had come to a stop. The edge of the woods stood out in darker relief against the sky.

"It gets steep," Ralphie said as Wilf limped up to him. He was eyeing the cane, taking Wilf's measure.

"Where's Andy?"

"He knows the way."

The woods behind Ralphie fell steeply down into a dark fold in the earth. They started the descent along a narrow dirt path, the lantern seeming as much a hindrance as a help as far as Wilf was concerned. He felt blinded by it.

Ralphie went first and Wilf found himself bracing against the boy's shoulder rather than trusting his cane on some of the steeper spots. Ralphie didn't say a word, just accepted Wilf's weight as if they'd been doing that descent every night of their lives. Wilf could see another pool of lantern light farther down.

"That's Dad," Ralphie said. "Blue found it first and then Dollie was all over it. I had to put them on their leads and haul them back up to the house. Me and Earl did. They were going crazy."

Wilf nodded. He didn't feel like asking a question.

The ground levelled off. Wilf could see the other light some small distance off the path. Ralphie went first, pushing through the branches and then holding them so they wouldn't whip back into Wilf's face.

Andy and an older man were standing in a grove of trees. The man looked Wilf's way as Wilf came into the light. He had a short grey growth of beard as if he'd been caught by surprise and hadn't had a chance to shave.

"This is Wilf," Andy said. "My uncle, John Moss."

The man nodded cordially enough and then turned to look at something on the ground. Wilf couldn't see anything at first in the shifting ring of light. He took a step forward and now he could see something, a large wire cage sitting beside a tree. There was something inside it but he couldn't make out what it was. He took another few steps. A small white hand came into view, and between each finger Wilf could see a faint pink membrane, like a webbing.

He knelt down and forced himself to look toward the face. Puckering lips, round eyes set wide apart, a slanting forehead. The child inside looked for all the world like a fish. A fish with a fringe of blonde silky hair.

"What the hell is it?" Andy whispered.

Curled up on its side it was as naked as the day it was born. A piteous rib cage pushed out, each small bone defined in the light of the lantern, each bone rippling under translucent skin.

"It's a boy," Wilf said.

"A water boy," John Moss added. "Looks like something that came up out of the river."

For the first time Wilf could hear a soft rush of water somewhere nearby. "Life unworthy of life," he said.

"What do you mean?" Andy was still whispering, as if the boy, clearly dead, might hear.

"That's what they called them."

"Who? What are you talking about?" Andy was sounding a little alarmed.

"Children."

"There's only one child here, Wilf," Andy said.

"How old do you figure it is?" John Moss had moved closer.

"He looks maybe seven," Andy said. "It's hard to tell."

"Who would do this?" Ralphie asked. He looked dazed in the lantern light. Frightened.

Hansel in the heart of the woods, Wilf thought.

"I'll have to call the Chief in again. Jesus Christ," Andy said.

"I'll wait here." Wilf struggled to his feet.

"You don't have to do that." Andy was already moving away.

"Someone should," Wilf said.

Ralphie was backing up into the trees. It wasn't going to be him.

"I'll just slow you down, anyway. Besides, I need a rest."

"I better check on Bess," John Moss said. "If I know her,

she'll be thinking we're all dead and buried by now. We'll get back here as soon as we can."

"I'll hold the fort." Wilf leaned on his cane.

"We'll leave you the lantern," the farmer said.

The men moved off. Wilf stepped outside the pool of light and watched the other lantern move away, slant upwards, break into separate fragile beams and disappear.

He turned back to the boy. A criss-cross of shadows lay over his small body. The longer Wilf stood there and the longer he stared, the more it seemed that the boy was floating in the air.

Wilf walked back to the cage and knelt down. A large closed padlock hung from a latch on the door. He looked around. He knew it was only a matter of time before they crept out of the shadows. The boy in his stripes. The man in his dark coat.

All Wilf could hear was the river moving restlessly, somewhere unseen.

All he could see were the surrounding trees.

CHAPTER NINETEEN

Wilf didn't go home that night. He didn't want to continue to torture his father. He chose to sleep on Andy's couch instead.

Another murder. Of course everyone was trying to convince themselves it was no such thing. Even the hard-bitten Chief of Police.

The kid had died of natural causes. A creature like that would be sickly anyway, wouldn't he? And an embarrassment. Whoever had been looking after him, no doubt someone from some distance away, had decided the best thing to do was to drop him off in the woods like an unwanted puppy. No involvement that way, whether it had been a private individual or some Dickensian institution for the retarded. No uncomfortable questions.

Even Andy's Aunt Bess had brightened at that theory. She made pots of tea and handed out pieces of pie to Bolton and the Chief and some curious neighbours. It was a stranger's problem. Strangers were driving by the farm and throwing out kittens and puppies and garbage all the time, Aunt Bess declared. It was becoming a disgrace.

Wilf sat at the kitchen table drinking tea and eating peach pie, and every once in a while when Aunt Bess bustled by they'd exchange glances. He could see that she hadn't been fooled, not even by herself. A deep unease haunted her eyes.

Wilf sat on Andy's couch and looked out the front window. The house was quiet. Andy and Linda and Davey and Carmen were fast asleep somewhere upstairs. It was comforting to know that they were just above his head, breathing softly, trusting, untroubled by his presence.

He looked at his watch. It was almost two o'clock. He looked out the window again. No lights in the house across the street.

He had no doubt that it was another murder. It fit the pattern. They were useless eaters. That's what the doctors had officially designated them, and then they had starved or injected or gassed them by the hundreds. Wilf had no doubt at all.

Five murders and a suicide in the space of two months in a town of less than four thousand people. How was that possible?

The bacterium hadn't worked, Chasson had said.

Wilf stretched out on the couch. He could feel the injection site high on his inner right thigh, though there was no mark left to see. He'd felt it there ever since he'd talked to Chasson.

"You're a bomb that failed to go off," Chasson had said.

Wilf looked up at the ceiling. He could feel something moving through his bloodstream. He could feel his body beginning to tremble.

When Wilf woke up the next morning, Linda was standing across the room clutching a tea towel and staring at him.

"What time is it?"

"It's after ten."

"Where's Andy?"

"He's gone to work. The kids have gone to school."

"They were quiet."

"I guess so. And you were really in a deep sleep."

Wilf pushed himself up to a sitting position. Though he'd left most of his clothes on, he thought Linda might leave the room and give him some privacy but she didn't.

"I'll put some coffee on," she finally said.

"Good."

She didn't move. "What happened last night. That little boy. Do you think Andy's going to get into any more trouble?"

"No. Why would he? He left the scene untouched. Called the Chief right away."

"That's what he said."

"There you are, then."

"I would appreciate it if you didn't get involved any more than you are, and don't get Andy involved this time, just stay out of it, okay? I don't say this to be mean, but Andy has a family."

"I know he does."

"Do you understand what I'm trying to say?"

"I'm not sure."

"I don't want him fired! There are terrible things going on. Everyone's frightened. You know that, don't you? The whole town is frightened. All we want is for everything to go back just the way it was."

"Before I came home, you mean?"

"No! I don't mean that, I mean these things! These awful things! I know I'm sounding stupid but everyone should just stop and not try to do too much. That's what I'm saying. Let's just everybody stay still and let things get back to normal. Like it was. That's all I'm saying." Linda's face looked blotched and pinched.

"Okay."

"I'm not saying you can't be friends."

"I know you're not."

"Anyway, that's fine then. I'll get you a coffee."

Linda would have cooked him up some eggs and sausages but Wilf said he wasn't all that hungry. He drank one coffee and ate a piece of toast and told Linda not to worry. Linda nodded her head but looked unconvinced. Wilf pushed out the side door. His father's Buick Roadmaster was still sitting there.

Wilf pulled out of the drive and wondered what his father was thinking. Dark thoughts, no doubt. He drove slowly toward the bridge that led to the downtown.

It had taken Andy about an hour to return to Wilf and that spot in the woods. Wilf had waited and watched all that time.

The man and the boy hadn't appeared. Only the wire cage and the child inside to keep him company.

Don't think about it, he commanded himself as he drove along. But he couldn't stop thinking about it. What kind of person would leave a dead boy in a cage in a woods and not expect it to be found? A city person? A stupid person? Of course it would be found. And anyone with a pair of eyes could see that he'd been starved to death. His rib cage looked to be as much on the outside of his skin as on the inside. His parched and swollen mouth.

He passed the office before he realized he'd gone too far. He circled around the cenotaph, came back and pulled into a parking spot. And what could he say to his father this time? How could he explain everything once again? Another dead body?

Father. I have a plague

Wilf closed his eyes. His breath had gone away somewhere. And Carole would be there, too. And it was a sure thing that Nancy Dearborn would have called.

Wilf pushed the car door open. He could hear a voice ringing through the cool air.

A man was preaching on the other side of the street.

"Jesus has given us a gift," he was calling out. "In our frailty, in our blindness. We have been given a gentle and surprising light."

The man had positioned himself in front of the town hall and was gathering quite a crowd. A few startled faces were peering down from the town-hall windows. Wilf crossed the street.

"We can see him clearly. We can see him in our mind's eye. This maimed one who has been given to us kindly, as a sign, as an instruction, as a guiding star."

A ragged boy seemed to be bobbing wildly through the crowd. As Wilf came closer he could see that the boy was limping in his dilapidated boots, his one foot turned completely over on an outside ankle. He was holding a sign up. *THE REVEREND GENE C. COONEY, NEW HOPE CHRISTIAN CHURCH, COME AND JOIN US.*

"We don't know which way to turn," the Reverend was preaching. "We are in the midst of catastrophe and confusion. We hear about a boy found in a woods and a blindness seems to overwhelm us, and not just in this, but in all the misfortunes that have lately befallen this town. But know that nothing under Heaven is by chance. Know that everything that happens is for our instruction and our salvation."

He was a powerfully built man, raw-boned and thinly dressed against the cold, his face bright with the unwavering certainty of his trade, Wilf thought.

Wilf stepped up on the sidewalk and looked around at the mix of men and women, young and old. Their faces looked not so much exalted as surly, begrudging, fearful, particularly fearful when anyone looked his way.

"This boy, found last night, dead and naked, like a revelation in the heart of a storm. Let's pray for a holy man who can read by lightning. Let's pray for a stranger who can interpret these miraculous works of the Lord."

Wilf turned away from the crowd and walked down the alley toward the police station. Ted Bolton looked up when he came in through the swinging doors and shook his head as if to say "Here we go again." Andy was helping Ralphie write out a statement.

Wilf could hear what sounded like the Chief of Police talking loudly to someone behind closed doors. "It's busy around here."

Andy glanced toward the Chief's office. "Upset citizens."

"Right now the rest of them are being entertained outside."

"By who?"

"By the Reverend Gene C. Cooney, I believe." Wilf came around the counter.

"I've already given him two warnings and a ticket."

"This morning?"

"No. Over the last few weeks."

"Hi, Wilf." Ralphie looked up from his composition. He seemed recovered from the night before. "Lots of excitement, eh?"

"You bet."

"There's a bunch of cops out at our house this morning."

"OPP," Andy said. "They're talking about opening up a branch office here in town."

Ted Bolton snorted out a laugh, "Could be."

Wilf sat down on a chair. "So what's happening? Are you still working on the theory that some strangers drove by, carried the cage a mile into the bush and dropped him off?"

Andy looked uncomfortable. "I'm not working on any theory. I'm getting Ralphie's statement and that's all I'm doing. Did Linda talk to you?"

"Yes."

"Oh."

"I'm not supposed to get you into any more trouble."

Bolton snorted again.

Andy's ruddy cheeks went a shade brighter. "Don't listen to her. She's just upset."

Wilf nodded. He liked Linda a lot. He liked Andy even more. He knew he should leave him alone. He should just get up and walk out. He couldn't. "That cage had a countrified look to it, didn't you think? It looked like two poultry cages welded together."

"It is two poultry cages welded together." Andy looked down at Ralphie's statement. "Ralphie's illiterate."

"No, I'm not."

"How do you spell 'discovered'?"

"The way I'm spelling it."

"Yeah, but how are you supposed to spell it?"

Ralphie winked at Wilf. "I don't know. That's a different question."

"*D I S*, not *D E S*, you idiot."

"Has Doc Robinson seen the boy?" Wilf asked. Andy remained silent. Wilf persisted. "What did Doc have to say?"

"Not much. Said he was probably closer to ten than six or seven. Just small for his age."

"Cause of death?"

"He's not sure yet."

"Starvation?"

"I must have missed something," Bolton said. "I didn't realize we'd taken another man on the force."

Wilf got up out of the chair. "Whoever it was, they were on their way to the river. That's why the padlock was on the cage, to make sure his body didn't float away, but Ralphie's dogs came running up before they could get that far and Ralphie and his brother were following. They dropped the cage and took off back through the woods."

"We all know they were headed for the river," Andy said. "Anyway, the OPP are on the case," He was looking a little wistful. "By the way, your father was in earlier wondering if I knew where you were. I explained everything, what we'd run into, all that. And that you'd spent the night at my place. I guess you should have called him."

Wilf nodded and went out the door.

※ ※ ※

Carole was sitting at her desk when Wilf came into the office. He stole a glance her way. She looked tense. "Morning. Where's the solicitor?"

"He's in court. He had to take a taxi to Brantford."

"Oh? That's too bad. I went out to get a truck last night for our move."

"That's what your dad was saying. With Andy."

Wilf pushed through the gate. He wanted to sit down at his desk but for some reason he couldn't. He stood there in the middle of the office. He felt marooned. "Have you talked to Nancy Dearborn?"

"Yes."

"There was more trouble."

Carole got up from her desk. She touched Wilf's face. Kissed his cheek.

Wilf didn't know whether he should pull away from her and save her life. He didn't know what to do. "We can use the car to move most things. We can start to move after work today. We can get the truck some other time."

The door opened and Reverend Cooney stepped in. "Morning," he said, a warm smile on his face.

Carole, caught and looking embarrassed, pulled away from Wilf. "Good morning. May I help you?"

Cooney pointed his Bible toward Wilf. "I think I saw you earlier, didn't I? I'm inviting everyone in town to a meeting tonight. A prayer meeting. To talk about that boy, the one they found in a cage. I know the answer to all that."

"Oh?" Wilf said.

Carole sat back down at her desk.

"All you have to know is how to read signs, which is a gift, like the prophets of old did. And you have to know your Bible. And most of all you have to be a prisoner of love. Captured by the Holy Spirit and lifted into Rapture!"

"I see," Wilf said.

Carole's rogue lock of hair slipped down. She didn't bother pushing it back up. She began to type.

The Reverend fixed his remarkably bright blue eyes on Wilf.

"Why don't you come out into the country tonight? Seven o'clock. All you have to do is drive out the Galt highway, turn east on Kipple Road and keep on until you come to the Cuthbert farm. That's where my son Josh and I now reside. That's where miracles are happening, my friend. Don't be shy." He turned to Carole. "You're invited as well, Miss."

Carole continued to type. "I don't know whether we can go. We're busy. Aren't we, Wilf?"

"I'll come out."

Carole stopped typing.

"Well, praise The Lord," the Reverend said. "I didn't ask your name."

"Wilf McLauchlin."

"The Reverend Gene C. Cooney. And yours, Miss?"

"Carole," Carole said.

"Honoured to meet you both." He smiled his practised smile once more, turned on his heels and went back out the door.

"I'm not going out there."

"His son has a club foot."

"Whose?"

"His."

"What does that mean?"

"I don't know. I'm just saying that he does. We could make a trip or two out to the cottage with some of our stuff. And then we could go to the meeting."

"It's on the other side of the river."

"We could cross at Glen Morris. There's a bridge there."

"Didn't you hear what I just said? No! I thought the idea was to get away from everything. Have some peace and rest and be by ourselves."

Wilf didn't seem to hear. He sat down at Dorothy Dale's desk and picked up the phone.

"Who are you calling?"

"Just Andy."

"Why?"

The operator came on the line and it wasn't Nancy. Wilf gave her the number and Ted Bolton answered. "Hi there, Ted. It's Wilf. Can I speak to Andy?"

Carole got up and pushed through the wooden gate. Wilf thought she might be going home but she just stood by the window looking blindly out on Main Street.

"Long time no see," Andy said.

"You said you'd given that Reverend Cooney a ticket. What was it for?"

"Unlawful assembly in a public place. Causing a disturbance."

"Did you get any information on him? How long he's been here? Where he's from?"

"He hasn't paid his fine yet. I know that."

"Is that all you know?"

"You don't quit, do you?"

"No."

There was a long silence. "I guess I could check my notes."

Wilf looked back at Carole. She hadn't moved from the window.

"I do want to go out to the cottage. That's what I want to do," Wilf said to her.

"Then why are you getting in the middle of everything? Again?"

"Someone did something to a helpless little boy, Carole. That's all." And I'm flying, Wilf thought to himself, careening through the sky. I'm at thirty thousand feet.

"He might have been sick," Carole was saying. "He might have died of natural causes."

"Heartless and neglectful then at the very least. But probably worse. Much worse." Because the doctors were anything but neglectful. Inspected every child. Recorded every name.

"I just have a couple of things," Andy was saying in Wilf's ear.

"Okay. What?"

"He lives out at the old Cuthbert place with his fourteen-year-old son. Only been there since just after Christmas. Rents the house but not the land. He's unemployed except for his ministry, such as it is. Comes from near Owen Sound. Last job was with the Grey County Children's Home. That's it."

"The Grey County Children's Home?"

"That's what I've got."

"What would that be?"

"A place for kids, I guess. Orphans, maybe."

"Unwanted children? That kind of thing?"

"I don't know. I guess."

"Did he say what he did there?"

"He said he was their minister. The chaplain."

"Okay. Thanks." Wilf hung up. "Reverend Cooney worked for a home for children. Orphans."

Carole was staring at him. "I don't know what to do." Tears were shining in her eyes.

"It'll be all right," Wilf said.

Carole shook her head.

"What do you mean, you don't know what to do?"

"For you," she whispered. "For you."

When Clarence returned from Brantford Wilf was standing beside the filing cabinets staring into space and trying to imagine how the bacterium worked. When did he have anything to do with that little boy? Or any of the others? Sylvia Young. Cruikshank. Basil. How was it possible? But he must have because the one thing he knew for certain, he was carrying a plague.

And where was the man with the rags on his feet? Where was the barefoot boy?

Nowhere to be seen. But their absence had to mean something, confirm something. They'd been wanting him to go somewhere, that's what it was, they'd been leading him somewhere. Which meant he'd finally arrived. In those trees. On that night.

As if the child in the cage held the answer to everything.

"Wilf?" Clarence was standing in the middle of the office holding two worn and bulging briefcases in his hands.

Wilf looked at him as if he were just waking up, and then he started to talk about the move out to the cottage and why he and Carole needed to have the use of the car that afternoon.

"I have to admit," Clarence interrupted, "that I am nonplussed. Andy told me about the events of last night."

Clarence looked at Carole. He looked back at Wilf.

Wilf just shook his head.

"Well, it's the damnedest thing." He began to walk toward his office. "If you and Carole want to move in today, why don't you take the rest of the afternoon off? It's Friday, anyway."

"We can wait until five," Carole said. She'd been working at her desk and trying not to see Wilf standing in a trance by the filing cabinets.

"But it's still getting dark by seven. Do you even have electricity out there?"

She hadn't thought about that. She could see the small white electric stove sitting beside the old wood one. "Yes."

Clarence stopped in the hallway. "Is it connected?"

"I'll call the landlord first," Wilf said.

"Good idea. And then, if you could work it in, you and I should have another chat about Scarfe Telfer. In the meanwhile I want you to promise to stay out of this latest mess. As your lawyer, I have to tell you that you are in no position to get further involved in anything. Will you do that for me?"

"What has Scarfe Telfer got to do with that boy in the cage?"

"I wish I knew," Clarence said.

Father and son stared at each other for a long moment, and then not hearing an answer and looking more than a little dismayed Clarence turned and headed back toward his office. The door closed behind him.

"You see? No further involvement. Your father thinks the same way I do," Carole said.

CHAPTER TWENTY

Duncan looked out his bedroom window. A police car was coming along the road. He thumped down the stairs.

His hands were free of the chain now. He'd spent all the previous day in the shop working with an old file he'd found, sawing away. The heavy metal bands on his wrists were still on, though. His wrists were sore enough before, but with all the effort just to get rid of the chain the bands had worn right through the skin. Now they were riding on wide circles of red flesh and yellow pus and both his arms had caught on fire.

He peered out between the boards that someone had nailed across the broken kitchen window. The car was coasting to a stop in the side yard. A lone policeman got out. Duncan didn't recognize him. He didn't look all that big. Not near as big as he was himself.

He looked around. He knew where he'd hide. There was a crawl space under the stairs. He'd hid in there lots of times when his father was still alive. That way he could listen to the radio too, without his father asking him why the hell he was sitting there gawking like a moron, and sometimes when he was hiding in there, even though he didn't want to, he'd have to listen to his mother getting cross at his father and his father saying, "He's dumber than Mortimer Snerd."

Duncan opened the little doorway under the stairs and looked in. His mother had kept her cleaning products in there ready for the next onslaught of mice. There wasn't much room at all among the bottles and the cartons, not nearly as much as he'd remembered when he was a boy.

He shoved everything to the one side and squeezed in with his feet first. His boots fit under the first step or two, his back dug into the next two steps and he still couldn't close the door. He put his fingers in the space between the floor and the door and pulled back as firmly as he could. A cramp began to shoot up one of his legs. His arms burned.

He could hear the back door open, then the kitchen door, and then the sound of boots coming across the floor. The policeman walked right by his hiding place and into the front room.

Duncan had been very cautious about going out to the shop the previous day because it had snowed and he didn't want to leave any tracks, but no matter how he'd twisted and weaved around it was impossible to miss all the patches of snow. He'd worried about that all that day, but though a few people had driven by luckily no one had turned in.

The snow was the reason why he hadn't gone searching for Babe and Dandy the previous night, too. He hadn't wanted to leave his tracks for everyone to see, leading from barn to barn. The snow was almost all melted today though, and he could tell the policeman hadn't seen any tracks. If he had he wouldn't have walked into the house as if he owned the place. He wouldn't have come in at all, he'd have been afraid.

This thought took away the pain in Duncan's arms and in his cramping leg. The man was all alone. There was just the man and himself. Alone in the house. He could hear his own breath panting faintly against the dusty floor. The policeman began to walk up the stairs right over his head. He was going up to check on the bedrooms. Too late. Why hadn't he done something about all the stealing? Why hadn't he stopped those people from having a party and tramping all over his mother's bed?

Duncan could see the man walking into his mother's room. He could see him standing there in front of her mirror in the afternoon light. *FREAK* it still said because for some reason he hadn't been able to wipe it off.

The man was looking through all the drawers in her dresser. He was touching the hair ribbons and the combs that were still there.

Touching her clothes. Underclothes.

Duncan could see himself as plain as day pushing the little door open and creeping up the stairs. He could see himself looking in through the bedroom door.

The man was naked on his mother's bed.

Soon there would be blood all over the walls and the ceiling, all over the floor.

He was coming down the stairs again. Duncan held the door tight. The man went right by his fingers and crossed the kitchen floor. A regular Mortimer Snerd, this cop. He wasn't even going to check down in the cellar.

Duncan could hear the kitchen door closing, the outside door slamming shut. He was probably going to look into the shop now. The stable. Too late.

Everything was gone.

He knew what he was going to do as soon as it got dark enough. He was going to look for Dandy and Babe. Search every barn within ten miles. Find them somewhere. Breathing softly. Great heads moving in the night.

"It's me," he'd say and he'd wrap his arms around their necks and they'd be so happy they'd lift him right up off his feet. And then what? What would he do?

He thought he could hear the police car starting up. He listened as hard as he could.

Duncan opened the little door and looked out.

By the time Wilf and Carole turned into the lane that led to the stone cottage with their first load of clothes and blankets and groceries, the sky had turned a darkening bruised purple. The landlord had said that the power would be on though. It better be, Carole thought to herself.

She looked out the window. The trees were already a mass of undifferentiated shadows, the house invisible although she was looking at exactly where it was supposed to be.

She thought of Duncan. Where was he? Hiding in a dark woods somewhere? In an abandoned barn? There had been talk that someone had seen him walking beside the river. It made sense that he'd try to make his way home. Where else would he go? But of course the police would be watching for him there.

She thought he must be hungry. And cold. Frightened, too. Angry. Why wouldn't he be angry? It was Wilf who had gone out there that night. It was Wilf who had tricked him into confessing in some way, some way she could hardly imagine.

She glanced over at Wilf. He was concentrating on driving up the narrow lane. She wondered if he even knew that Duncan Getty had escaped. Because of everything else that was going on she had decided not to tell him.

The headlights swept across the front of the cottage.

"We're home." Wilf said, pulling the car up.

When they got out the air felt colder than it had in town. The dark sky was moving west, squeezing a small strip of sunset into a long thin line. Carole looked off toward the sunset. Duncan's house was on the other side of the river

"Let's try the lights." Wilf walked toward the cottage.

Carole followed along.

Earlier, when Wilf had helped her gather up her clothes she'd thought he'd been overly polite with her mother. She knew it was just from tension though. His face was smiling but his body looked absolutely rigid. And then he turned to her father who was still sitting stubbornly in the front room. "Hello, Sir," he said, putting out his hand, "I assume Carole's told you about our plans. We're not going to move in tonight, but we thought we could get a jump on moving out some of her things."

Instead of standing up and shaking Wilf's extended hand, her father remained sitting in his easy chair, which was very unusual behaviour for him. "Is that right? And you're who? The famous Wilf McLauchlin?"

"Yes, Sir," Wilf replied and turned away and let her father sit there as if everything had been settled to everyone's satisfaction which was certainly not the case because her father had gotten up and had walked right out the front door without even putting on his coat.

Wilf felt around in the dark in the cottage and found a switch just inside the living room. The house lit up.

"Thank God," Carole said. It didn't take her long to make the cottage look like it might actually be inhabitable, just some of her clothes hanging in the little closet off the living room and a few dishes in the cupboards managed it. She began to feel encouraged. She surveyed the bedroom. Not having a closet was still a problem, though.

"We'll need a wardrobe," she called out to Wilf who was unpacking some of her mother's extra pots and pans. He had to do it with one arm of course, which made it look for the moment like he was taking everything, including the move, very casually.

"Oh?" Wilf replied.

Carole put her head around the kitchen door. "But I think the bedroom's too small for a wardrobe. Maybe, if we can find a nice enough one we could put it in the living room."

"How about this? Maybe we could sleep in the living room and give the bedroom to the wardrobe."

"I don't want to sleep in the living room. I want it to be nice."

"Me, too. Anyway, I don't care where I sleep, as long as it's with you."

"You know all the right things to say."

"That's because I think about them first and then I say them."

"I know you do."

"Actually, I don't. They just come out."

"I know." Carole's voice broke a little, though the last thing she wanted to do was show the confusion she was feeling.

Wilf turned to look at her.

"I just hope you'll be happy here," Carole said. "I hope you're not feeling pushed into anything."

"Carole, come on. Of course not. I was thinking the same thing about you. I hope you're not feeling that way. Being pushed."

"No."

"I want to be with you."

"Just say if you don't though, will you? I mean, if you change your mind anytime. Don't go on pretending. Don't surprise me."

"Do you know what I think?"

"What?"

"I think this was meant to be. I think we'll grow old together. That's what I think."

Carole made a face. "Let's not grow old too soon."

They drove back to town to pick up some things of Wilf's and some more clothes for Carole, because though it was still March and she'd need her winter things, spring wasn't far off and she'd soon require some lighter clothing and of course it could suddenly turn very hot so it wouldn't hurt to have a few summer things, and also there was the card table and four folding chairs her mother had volunteered until they had a chance to buy some furniture. Carole's bed and dresser and her grandmother's settee would have to wait for the truck.

It was completely dark by the time they arrived back at the cottage with the second load. They'd left the outside light on though, and Carole was relieved to see how welcoming the house looked glowing at the end of its lane. It was almost eight o'clock by the time they had the card table and chairs set up and the rest of Carole's clothes that needed to be hung up stuffed into the living room closet. Everything else would have to stay in cartons until the dresser arrived and a wardrobe was purchased or found.

Carole was hoping that by this time Wilf would have forgotten about the prayer meeting, but as soon as they were finished he looked at his watch and said in a determined way that he could run her back to town and go to the meeting himself or she could stay there and wait for him to pick her up on the way back, which would save time. Or she could go to the meeting with him.

"Why would it save time?"

"I can cross the river at Glen Morris."

"Well, I'm not staying here alone." Carole was standing by the door putting her coat back on, "It's freezing, for one thing."

They'd brought an electric heater with them on the first trip and actually the living room had grown quite warm.

Wilf hadn't moved. He was still sitting on one of the folding chairs watching her.

Carole knew that if he'd only get up and pull his coat on in as aggressive a manner as he'd just given her her three options, she'd ask him to drive her home. And if his face didn't look so tired. And if the flesh around his eyes didn't look so dark. And if he'd quit looking at her. And if she didn't love him so much.

"All right," she said, "I'll go."

❄ ❄ ❄

The Cuthbert place wasn't difficult to find. The old frame house sat on top of a knoll; there were cars parked all along the side of the gravel road and the implement shed beside it was radiating light.

As soon as Carole got out of the car she could hear shouts and amens and cries of exaltation coming from the assembled crowd. "I hate this kind of thing," she said, stumbling along the road.

Wilf caught up to her. "Have you been to one before?"

"Once. A whole gang of us went, just to make fun. I felt sick."

"Why?"

"It's upsetting, that's why. All the shouting and praying and rolling around. Like something was actually happening that a normal person couldn't see."

They'd reached a muddy lane and had just turned in when a figure came out of the dark. "Going to the meeting, I guess," the Reverend's son said.

"We were invited by your father." Wilf could feel Carole taking a firm grip on his arm. "Sorry we're late." He was trying to remember the boy's name.

He was a head shorter than either of them, his hair uncut and tangled, his slight body wrapped in a long winter coat. He held out a small cardboard box. His face looked wan and tired in the reflected light.

"I thought that would come later," Wilf said. And he remembered. "Josh."

"Two offerings." Josh's body tilted, shifting over on his twisted ankle. "One now. And one just before the Holy Spirit arrives."

"Really?" Carole said.

Josh smiled. He seemed more interested in Carole than he did in Wilf.

Wilf dropped a dollar bill in the box. "There you go."

"May God bless you forever and ever and ever," Josh said, not taking his eyes off Carole.

They walked on toward the noise and the light.

"I hate this," Carole said.

Wilf could hear Reverend Cooney's voice soaring above all the rest. "God has blessed me with a revelation!"

"Sounds like we're just in time," Wilf said, sounding cheerful enough. He led Carole into a crowd milling about by the large open doors.

"Hey there, Wilf!" Ralphie was shouting at him from a few people over and looking even more excited and full of mischief than he usually did. "The Rev just cured three people and a lame horse! You missed it!" He was being jostled by four or five other farm boys of about the same age.

"Holy Rollers!" one of them roared out as loud as he could to the delight of the crowd on the fringe. And then the boys began to howl like dogs.

"Come on, Carole," Wilf said.

They weaved into the crowd until they could see Reverend Cooney standing on top of a hay wagon, pacing up and down, his Bible in hand. He'd put on a bright necktie and he'd slicked down his hair, but other than that he looked the same as he had in town. He was easily ignoring the howls from the back.

"Sweet revelation!" he cried out.

Wilf led Carole up a wooden ramp toward the rafters. The shed was jammed full, some people standing on raised platforms, some sitting on improvised plank benches, others crowding in at the front, kneeling or sitting on the floor.

"I have a revelation!"

"Sweet revelation! Amen! Praise God! Go on!" the inner circle, the believers, called back, jumping up and sitting down.

Carole clung to Wilf and held his cane for him while Wilf snaked his arm around a roof joist for balance.

"The boy in the cage means something!" Cooney was pacing around faster now. "He means something! For those who have eyes to see. For those who have ears to hear. And not just him. No. Because it was a miracle. The whole picture. That's what you have to see. The cage. The padlock. The boy. They are one and the same. They are inseparable. They are the whole picture!"

"Praise God!" the believers said, jumping up and sitting down.

Wilf looked over the excited faces. The bobbing heads. Arms thrown up in the air.

Where is God, he wondered to himself.

"And what is this picture?" Cooney was going on. "This twisted boy? This half a boy? You've heard the stories. You can see him in your mind's eye. This little creature. Sin is what he is! Not him, no, but what made him. You see? And what made him was sin. Was he not the product of some hideously conceived union? Was he not the result of selfishness and backwardness and sinfulness and the hiding away from the light of God? And what is that cage but all our sins, our stubbornness, our pride, all the vices we can't let go, the vices we cling to with all our might. Remember your Bible. Remember the dog who vomits and turns back to his vomit and licks it up again. That's you, my friend. That's whoever is locked in sin, my friend, that is the cage, my friend. And the padlock is your heart." He began pointing out people. "And your heart. And yours! And yours! Locking God out. Locking salvation out. Locking everlasting glory out. Too proud. Too sinful. All out! And what is the key that will unlock all our hearts? What is this key? This mysterious broken man, this exalted son of God? Yes, only Jesus, my friends, only the Risen Christ, my friends. Only Jesus, yes, Jesus, yes, Jesus, yes! He is the key. He is the only one who can unlock your soul. He is the only one who can unlock you and save you from yourself. Praise God Almighty. Jesus, come! Jesus, come! Jesus, come to us all!"

The noise became tumultuous, joyful, deafening. Wails and exaltations and screams. The Spirit was descending and Josh was too late with his collection. Wilf could see him limping desperately through the crowd waving his cardboard box.

Cooney jumped down from the wagon. A middle-aged man stumbled toward him. Cooney opened up his arms. The man was crying, great wracking sobs. Cooney hugged him and both men collapsed to their knees.

Carole began dragging Wilf back down the ramp. "I'm going home," she said.

Wilf let her lead the way through the rapturous crowd, and when they'd reached the bottom of the ramp, through the jeering ring of doubters. She was being quite aggressive about it, bulling a pathway as if all the hallelujahs had dislodged something inside her, opened up some secret place, something that frightened her.

Ralphie was rolling on the ground, caught up in a religious spasm. Carole had to step over his legs.

"I want to talk to this young fellow," Wilf said.

Carole didn't reply. She let go of Wilf's arm and headed off into the dark.

"Hey, Ralphie," Wilf said.

Ralphie, frothing and mouthing some gibberish, his head rocking from side to side, sat up. "Oh hi, Wilf," he said.

His friends roared with laughter.

"I have a question for you." Wilf moved away a little from the rest of the boys. Ralphie got up and followed him, a lopsided grin on his face.

"I've been thinking about that cage, Ralphie. What do you suppose they were going to do with it?"

"Throw it in the river. Like you said."

"It was heavy, though." The sounds behind them rose to an ecstatic crescendo. Wilf had to shout against it. "They couldn't have managed to throw it very far and the river's relatively shallow along the shore."

"It's in flood."

"That's even worse. If it's over its banks, as soon as the water went back down the cage would be sitting there high and dry. Who would risk that? So I was thinking, maybe I was wrong. Maybe whoever left that little boy there was hoping you'd find it."

Ralphie came to a stop. "Why me? I don't know anything about it."

"Do you know Josh?"

Ralphie glanced back at his group of friends. He wasn't looking quite so sure of himself anymore. "Josh?"

"Yeah. The boy with the club foot. Reverend Cooney's boy."

"He's around here somewhere. I've seen him around."

"Does he know where you live? Does he know you have hounds? Does he know you hunt?"

"You think they left that cage there? The Rev and his son? Why would they do that? Holy Jesus, where would they get that little kid?"

"Out of his bed. Out of an institution. Out of a mortuary. For publicity, you see. To make a sensation. Create a show."

Ralphie was going a little bug-eyed.

"How well do you know Josh?"

"But it's not shallow," Ralphie said, "not down where that path leads. There's a drop-off there, it's deep as anything."

"Where?"

"Right there! It goes on for about a hundred yards. People used to swim there all the time. No one does anymore."

"Why not?"

"Afraid of getting sick. Polio and stuff. Anyway, that's crazy."

"What is?"

"What you just said. That they'd steal some little kid from somewhere and leave him out there for me to find." He looked at Wilf more closely. "That's really crazy."

When Wilf came limping up to the car Carole was sitting there staring down the road. He opened the driver's door.

"If I'd had the keys I would have driven away."

Wilf eased in. "And if you knew how to drive."

"That wouldn't have mattered. Revival meetings make me want to bring up."

Wilf started the car, switched on the headlights and began to pull away. "I take it you weren't saved then?"

"No."

"Thanks for coming, anyway."

"Once is enough though. We're not going again."

"No."

Carole looked out her side window. She couldn't see much of anything. "I'm glad you've given up on that idea."

"What idea?"

"That Reverend Cooney could have had anything to do with that boy."

"Maybe. Maybe not. Ralphie thought it sounded crazy. Or maybe it was me he thought was crazy."

"Who's Ralphie?" Carole finally asked.

"That kid who was lying on the ground."

"Oh."

"I think God is far away from here. Don't you?"

"I don't want to talk about it."

"According to my father, everything will be fine, though, so I suppose it doesn't really matter. Precedents have been set. Laws will be written. The United Nations has been established. My friends didn't die in vain."

Carole kept her face turned away.

"Do you think human beings are perfectible, Carole? Do you think we can save ourselves?"

"I worked all day and I'm tired," Carole said.

"Sorry." Wilf turned onto the highway that led into town and fell into a deep silence.

After a while Carole reached over and put her hand on his leg.

❋ ❋ ❋

When they reached Carole's street there was a strange truck backed into her family's driveway.

"Now what's going on?" she said.

It had wooden sides attached to the back and looked a bit battered and rusted under the light of the street lamp. Wilf pulled the car up in front of the house.

They'd already discussed, or at least Wilf had insisted that he wouldn't just let her off, that he'd come in too, in the hope that her father had returned and that they could have a more civilized talk. Carole had been secretly pleased and relieved that Wilf had wanted to do that but she hadn't let him see it. She had her pride.

They walked past the truck as they headed for the side door. Wilf thought he detected the faint aroma of manure. He looked at Carole. She didn't seem to notice.

Andy was sitting in the kitchen sipping on a coffee and eating a piece of cake. Mrs. Birley was sitting at the table with him. No sign of Mr. Birley.

"I guess you know Andy," Wilf said to Carole as they came in.

Andy stood up with a friendly grin. "Sure she does. Hi, Carole."

"Hi," Carole said.

"I told you Andy was going to borrow his uncle's truck."

"But it's late."

"It's not that late." Andy looked at his watch, "It's only, what, a little after ten. And the thing was, I knew you two were anxious and the truck was available, so I said to myself 'Why not?'"

"Who said we were anxious?"

"Wilf did."

"Where's Dad?" Carole looked hopefully toward her mother who was sitting there with a quiet smile on her face. She was round of body and bleach-blonde of hair and as far as Wilf could tell seemed to take everything that came her way with an unruffled and admirable calmness. Unlike her husband.

"I don't know," she said

"So let's get started." Andy finished off his coffee and picked up what was left of his piece of chocolate cake.

"Tonight?" Carole said.

"I think Uncle John has to go to market tomorrow."

"But if we take down my bed, where will I sleep?"

"In your new home, Dear," Mrs. Birley said.

"Oh. Right." Carole glanced at Wilf. She looked back at her mother. "We can leave Grandma's settee for later."

"Why? Take it now while you have the use of the truck."

"Where do you think Dad is?"

"He'll be fine," Mrs. Birley said.

Duncan stumbled through the bush. It was hard going because there was no moon and he'd had to circle around the houses at the one end of town and then follow along the smaller of the two rivers toward the mill dam. The air felt suddenly warmer though.

He began to think about which he'd like best if he could get to choose, a full moon but cold, or no light but warmer. It seemed lately that he could never have both at the same time. Never have just what he wanted. Never.

Earlier that night he'd started off intending to search for Dandy and Babe. He'd looked first through the windows of the barn to the west of his place because the farmer was still doing chores and the lights were on. He could see Old Man Wilson milking and his son dragging the full cans to the cooler, but it wasn't Babe and Dandy standing in the horse stalls. Or anyone else. They were empty.

He snuck right into the dark stables of the farm on the other side of the road. Four horses were thrashing around in box stalls there, their eyes rolling in the faint light coming in from the house. But none of them was Babe or Dandy.

At Eric's place he got chased off by the dog.

He ran along Eric's father's pasture and then he stopped. The dog came up to him, all stiff-legged and barking. He squatted down and talked to it real low. It stopped its noise and began to move its tail back and forth in a cautious sort of way. It sniffed at his hand, at the iron on his wrist, at the sleeve of one of his old windbreakers he'd found still hanging in the back kitchen.

Duncan reached out and began to scratch between its ears and along the side of its face. He stroked it under its jaw. He couldn't remember its name. Jasper or Jumper or some such thing. "There you are," he said, and in one swift move jammed his free hand down on its withers, brought his lower hand up and broke its neck.

The dog yelped once and then thrashed silently around on the wet ground. After a while it lay on its side and moved its legs like it wanted to run away. Duncan squatted there watching it. When it grew still he walked back along the edge of the pasture and went into the barn. Dandy and Babe weren't there. He circled around Eric's house, being especially careful not to walk through the patches of light thrown from the windows, cut across a field and came over the brow of a hill.

The countryside stretched out for miles and miles before him. He could see his own place not that far away, and some other ones that were lit up looking like candles on a big dark birthday cake. And he knew that there were unlit and unseen barns out there too, and unseen stables stretching out forever under the low, overcast sky. How could he search every one? He couldn't.

And then he thought of Carole.

She knew he had horses, she'd seen them clip-clopping down the street enough times and whenever he saw her he'd always wave and call out "Hi, Carole" and she'd always wave back. She never failed to wave. Never once. And he might even have told her their names. He was sure he had. She would know where they were. She would have thought about Babe and Dandy right as soon as he'd had to go away to jail to straighten things out.

What about Babe and Dandy, Carole would have said.

"Did you hurt that man?" That's what she had said, though, standing there looking frightened beside her back door. But by now she'd know why he'd had to do it. It was because they were going to get married someday. That was why.

And he knew then that he had to see her. See her window light up. See her hair tumbling down, see her slipping out of all her pretty clothes. One night she had come right up to her window and bent down a little to look out and he could see her breasts as clear as day and the curve of her hips and a little patch of darker hair.

Just the memory of it now made him shiver once again. So many things had changed, though. He knew they'd changed. His arms were on fire, for one thing. His wrists were red and wet. The police were chasing him with dogs. And as he thought about all these confusing things, he turned and turned on top of the hill behind Eric's place. Turned and turned.

He knew he had to see her.

Duncan heard the water splashing over the dam long before he saw it, and as he crept closer he could see that all the lights in the mill were on. It was just up from where Carole lived. The river was running high but not so deep or as swift as it had a few days before. When he reached the side of the mill, he stepped into the swirling water and waded along waist-deep trailing his hand for balance along the rough stones on the back wall. He came out on the other side, pulled himself up the bank, snuck behind four houses and finally reached his grove of famil-iar trees. Carole's window was dark. The windows downstairs were all lit up though.

Duncan's heart filled with gratitude. Something had gone

just right after all. He wasn't too late. He slumped down on the ground.

"Do you know where my horses are?" he was going to say, "Could you help me find my horses?"

And Carole would smile just like she always smiled, and she would get her coat on and lead him to where they'd been stabled and he'd help her up on the back of Babe, because Babe was more gentle, and he'd be surprised because she would hardly weigh anything at all, and he'd lead her and Babe and Dandy into the river valley through all the shaded glades he knew, and through all the ferny places. And they'd sleep together on a soft bed of moss and walk together along sun-dappled ridges and they'd live there together forever and ever.

Carole's light went on.

Duncan lurched to his feet. All the familiar feelings were rushing back in, the swooning delicious pulse of blood.

She crossed in front of the window, just as he'd wanted, just as he'd dreamed.

Let down your hair, Duncan thought to himself. Please Carole! Let down your hair.

She seemed to be looking across the room at something.

And then Wilf McLauchlin came into view.

❄ ❄ ❄

With Andy at the one end and Wilf and Carole at the other, they struggled to get the settee out the back door. It was the easiest route, out to the back stoop, down the stairs and cut across the backyard to the truck.

Wilf was struggling the most. Carole and Andy glanced at each other but neither one wanted to say, "Why don't you sit down and rest, Wilf, we can do it."

Andy had positioned a ramp leading into the truck which

made things easier. They teetered up it, placed the settee on its legs and sat down to rest.

"What smells?" Carole said.

"Wilf," Andy replied. "No. That's just good old straw. It's my Uncle John's truck. He has a farm."

"It smells stronger than straw."

"But not that much stronger," Andy said. "Anyway, I put a tarp down."

Carole looked at Wilf. He was sitting there smiling, his face gleaming with a sheen of sweat.

"Just the bed, the mattress, the dresser and the springs to go," Andy announced.

Wilf and Carole had already gone up to her bedroom and taken the bed apart. It seemed a strange thing to be doing. Unworldly, Carole thought, watching Wilf as he helped her haul off the mattress and pull up the springs. Unsettling in a way. Exhilarating in another way. Embarrassing, too, there were a few dust bunnies blowing across the floor. Suddenly she couldn't wait to get away.

Once the truck was loaded, Carole went inside to talk to her mother. Andy was standing out on the sidewalk having a smoke. Wilf walked up to him.

"So what happened out at Cooney's tonight?" Andy asked.

"He went on about the boy and the cage, all that. But in a prophetic mode. He didn't give anything away."

Andy lowered his voice. "The reason I came around with the truck tonight, I called someone earlier, just out of curiosity."

"Who was that?"

"The Grey County Children's Home. Cooney was employed there all right, but not as a minister, as a janitor. They had to fire him."

"Why?"

"Bothering people. Religious mumbo-jumbo. Trying to save

the souls of the kids there and anybody else who showed up at the door. Most of those kids can't talk anyway, most of them don't even know their own names, or so this woman was telling me. It's an asylum for children, really. And she said that he'd come in at night, too when he wasn't supposed to, him and his son, and wander around the building." Andy took a drag on his cigarette. "How big was the crowd?"

Wilf leaned against his father's car. "Jam-packed."

"He would have made himself a nice pile of money."

"Ralphie was there."

"Acting like a fool, no doubt."

"He told me an interesting thing though. There's deep water right off that river bank."

"I know. I used to go swimming there."

"How deep?"

"Fifteen, twenty feet at the most."

"So you could toss that cage in there somewhere and expect it to stay lost?"

"If you gave it a good toss. It wouldn't, though."

"Why not?"

"Because those kind of things always come back to haunt you. Someone would go fishing and snag it. Or some brave soul would go swimming and hit their head on it. And anyway, that poor kid wouldn't have done the Reverend much good underwater."

"No."

"To think he'd use a dead kid to draw a crowd." Andy dropped his cigarette and ground it out under his shoe. "We should do something about this."

"I thought you weren't supposed to get involved."

"I wasn't supposed to get involved with the war, either, remember? Just stand around here with a pop gun. I'm sick of it."

"You were in the Reserves."

Andy looked away.

"What have the OPP been doing?"

"Going out to the farms around Uncle John's. Asking questions. At least that's what I hear."

"What do you think?"

"About the neighbours? It's not one of them. It's the damn preacher. A kid died out at that institution and he stole him."

"And what? Kept him on ice?"

"Exactly. That's why the body looks the way it does."

Wilf glanced back toward the house. No sign of Carole. "Maybe. Then again, it could have something to do with a neighbour, when you think about it."

"Not possible. I know them all. The Ball family to the south have been there forever, same with Jerry Zakowski to the north. Everybody around there has been there forever. The Portmans. The Zigglers. The Kellys. Well, Mr. Kelly now. The Grahams."

"What do you mean, Mr. Kelly now?"

"His wife died. Aunt Bess was talking about it."

"When did that happen?"

"I don't know. A couple of weeks ago."

Carole came out of the house and hurried up to them. She looked determined. "I'm ready," she said.

Wilf and Carole got back in the car and began to drive out toward the cottage. Andy rattled along behind them in the truck.

"I'm just exhausted," Carole declared, leaning her head against the door.

"When did your mother think your father might come home?"

"After the hotels close."

"That would be about now."

"He didn't have his coat on but at least it seems to be turning warmer. It's because I'm their whole family. Sometimes I wish they'd had more kids."

"I'd feel the same way if you were leaving me."

"You always know the right thing to say."

"I stand in front of the mirror and practise. Are you happy?"

"Yes. Of course I am." And then she said, "Stupid."

Wilf smiled. "This feels like the start of something special." He longed to feel one of her hands on his leg again, or both of them, the warm reassurance of it but she looked distracted. She stayed by the door watching the headlights search along the road.

Andy helped them get their furniture into the cottage but they all agreed that it was too late and they were too tired to set up the bed. It could wait for the next day.

Wilf and Andy hauled the mattress into the bedroom and laid it on the floor. Carole busied herself putting her sheets and the blanket back on it, getting her pillow out of her laundry bag and Wilf's pillow out of the cardboard box he'd stuffed it into earlier.

Wilf walked Andy back to the empty truck.

"What do you think about going out to see Mr. Kelly early tomorrow morning?" Wilf asked.

Andy looked surprised. "Why?"

"Doc Robinson said the boy was about ten years old. If he did come from the neighbourhood, somebody must have been looking after him all that time. And then something must have changed."

"Like what?"

"Like somebody died."

Andy opened the truck's door. Wilf could tell that he was doing a calculation. The Chief of Police. Linda. His kids. The house. His future.

"Where do the Kellys live?" Wilf asked.

"Next door to my uncle's. But closer to the river."

The light over the front door of the cottage was making a

series of hazy rings in the dark. Andy was staring toward it, his broad face growing grim. "On a bit of land behind the Zakowski farm. Do you have a phone?"

"Not yet."

"I'll pick you up," he said.

❋ ❋ ❋

Carole couldn't get to sleep.

They'd snuggled together afterwards, the electric heater glowing beside them, but she remained restless. Wilf, on the other hand was fast asleep.

The mattress had proved to be a little too narrow but she hadn't cared because she'd really wanted to feel his warm nakedness anyway, his toasty body pressing up against her own from her breasts down to the tip of her toes.

He'd taken off his sling. He always took it off whenever they made love so that wasn't surprising, but she'd thought that since they were actually going to attempt a comfortable night's sleep together he might put it back on again. Now his scarred arm was under him somewhere, pinned down. She was worried that it wasn't getting enough blood and because it didn't have any feeling that he wouldn't know.

She looked toward the dark window. The glow from the electric heater was making red waves on the glass. She wished again that she'd taken the time to hang something over it. Wilf had teased her, saying there wasn't anyone around for miles and anyway it was dark in the room, but the heater was throwing some light and all the time they were making love her eyes had kept going back to the window.

She turned to Wilf again. His face looked peaceful in the heater's glow. At least he wasn't snoring. He looked younger in his sleep, she thought. He wasn't taking nearly as many pain pills as he had in the past. At least that's what he'd told her. Wilfred McLauchlin.

She touched his hair and vowed that from now on she would listen to everything he wanted to tell her, everything he needed to say, no matter how crazy or painful. She wouldn't shut him out.

She wondered if he were dreaming.

Wilf was walking through a cathedral. Light was pouring down from some glass somewhere. A rainbow of colours were drifting past as soft as mist. He was walking with a fixed intent but he didn't know to where or why. Searching for something but not able to see his way. Just the sound of his flight boots echoing on the floor. Looking for a way out. That was what it was. Feeling now along a damp wall. His face rubbing along the cold stones. Peering in through a hole, the smallest of apertures.

Adrienne O'Dell was standing by his hospital window. Duncan Getty was sitting in a chair. Scarfe Telfer was leaning by the door.

And then Michael Chasson's face came into view.

"Wilf, you can see," he said.

CHAPTER TWENTY-ONE

Wilf could see the boy like a small gentle light being carried through the dark. He could see a shadowy figure at each end of the cage sliding downhill toward the river. Hear the sound of Ralphie's hounds, their baying ringing through the frosty air. A change in tone. More excited, higher and sharper now.

The answer was there. The boy floating in his criss-cross of shadows. Amongst the trees. In the moonlight. Somewhere.

Wilf turned to look at Carole. She was still asleep, a worried expression on her face as if a row of figures weren't quite adding up or an important file had gone missing. Morning light was creeping in through the window.

She opened her eyes. "What time is it?"

"I don't know." Wilf looked at his watch. "Not quite seven."

Carole groaned and rolled away.

They stayed in bed until eight and had just finished their breakfast when Andy came down the lane in his old Ford, having managed to piece it together somehow.

"I have to go somewhere," Wilf announced, seeing the car pull up. "I'll be back soon."

Carole was standing at the sink washing dishes. "Where?"

Wilf crossed the living room and opened the front door. "Here's Andy now."

"But where are you going?" Carole came out of the kitchen, drying her hands and looking anxious.

Wilf started to pull on his coat. "I have to go out to his Uncle John's to pay for the use of the truck. And there's another farmer that lives near there. We thought we might drop in on him."

"Why?"

"I'll be right there!" Wilf yelled out the door. "It won't take long, Carole," he said.

"But why?"

"Well, it's just that Andy thinks that this farmer might know something about the boy in the cage."

Carole stood there clutching her tea towel. "Your father wanted to speak to you. Remember?"

"I just have a few questions. The boy deserves justice, Carole. Don't you think?"

Carole shook her head as if she didn't know what to think. She walked back into the kitchen.

Wilf waited to hear the encouraging clatter of dishes. He didn't hear a thing.

❋ ❋ ❋

"How much do I owe your uncle?"

They'd crossed the bridge at Glen Morris and were approaching Uncle John's farm from the upriver side.

"You don't know anything about farmers, do you?"

"I guess not."

"He'd be insulted if you tried to pay him. He wouldn't accept it because you're a friend of mine. And if he didn't know you, he'd overcharge you. That's just their way."

Wilf looked across the fields toward where he knew the river had to be but all he could see were the tops of trees. Mostly pine, some hardwood, a few standing dead and stark against the sky.

"What are we going to say to him?" Andy was beginning to look a little less aggressive than the previous night.

"To who?"

"Kelly."

"That we're on a secret mission to locate poultry cages. We want to see if he has any poultry cages."

"Jesus. The OPP would have asked about that already, and anyway every farmer around here has poultry cages."

"Okay. Then it might be suspicious if he doesn't have any." Andy rolled his eyes.

"Just tell him that we're doing a follow-up. You are, anyway. In case he'd thought of something since the OPP were talking to him yesterday. Kelly knows you, doesn't he? He knows you're a cop."

"He doesn't know me. I don't know him." Andy slowed and turned into a rough narrow side road. "That's Uncle John's field on the right. Jerry Zakowski's farm is on the left over there. Kelly's land is closer to the river. I don't know how much he has. Maybe twenty-five acres in all."

Wilf had to brace his hand against the dashboard. "Where's this road lead?"

"Nowhere. It goes past the Kellys' a hundred yards or so and stops."

"Why don't you know him? You know everyone else."

"No chance to know him, I guess."

"They didn't mix in?"

"No."

Andy turned down an even bumpier lane and pulled up at the side of a small, unpainted clapboard house. There were several ramshackle outbuildings scattered about, including a henhouse, but no main barn.

Wilf looked around. "What does he grow here?"

"I don't know. Vegetables."

"He keeps chickens."

"Everybody keeps chickens," Andy said.

A man was standing by a board fence holding a dusty pail in his hand. He looked toward the car as it pulled up. Wilf could see some pigs rooting around behind him. A great pink snout was sticking through the slats. The man put the pail down and began to walk toward the car.

"Okay. We're just following up on the OPP," Andy said, opening his door. "Let me do the talking."

Wilf got out of his side of the car. The air smelled of all sorts of barnyard things. He looked toward the approaching man. Before the farmer could get within twenty feet Wilf knew he'd seen him before.

"I'm Andy Creighton from the town police. Just helping with the OPP investigation. This is my associate Wilf McLauchlin."

The man's eyes looked ravished from sleeplessness and whatever hair he had left was standing up in thin grey tufts. "Daniel Kelly, pleased to meet you." Though he smiled just slightly he didn't offer his hand.

Another farming trait, Wilf wondered. Probably, because Andy hadn't offered his hand to the farmer either.

"Sorry to hear about your wife," Wilf said, though he wasn't supposed to do any talking.

Mr. Kelly nodded. He looked off. "I still can't grasp it."

Standing there in an old flannel shirt and caked rubber boots and staring across a rutted, half-frozen field, the man looked absolutely wrung-out, Wilf thought.

"We were just wondering if anything might have occurred to you since yesterday," Andy spoke up. "About that boy we found in the cage."

Kelly looked back at Andy. His eyes blinked. He seemed to be trying to bring Andy back into focus. "No. I didn't know anything about it yesterday. I don't know anything more about it today. Damnedest thing, boys."

"It is," Wilf said and turned to Andy. "It's not all that far from here, is it? Where Ralphie found him?"

The treetops along the valley had become a row of tall pines just beyond Kelly's buildings. They were all leaning easterly from years of prevailing winds. The river was down below somewhere.

"Not too far. About a half-mile downstream."

"Makes no rhyme or reason," Kelly said to no one in particular.

"What's that?" Andy said.

"Theresa's death. That she should go before me."

"I saw you last night," Wilf said.

The man turned his washed-out eyes on Wilf and held them steady.

"At Reverend Cooney's."

Daniel Kelly nodded. "I just can't get over it," he said.

Andy and Wilf drove back into town. Andy got off at the garage at the one end of Main Street where he could spend some time with the usual crowd that gathered there on a Saturday morning. Wilf got behind the wheel.

They'd agreed that it was worth another trip out to Cooney's, though Andy would have to stay behind because Cooney already knew that he was a cop. Wilf would report back, and in the meantime Andy would hide out from Linda.

Wilf sped out along the highway toward Kipple Road. It seemed to take no time at all. He turned onto the gravel road, rattled along, then aimed the old Ford up into Reverend Cooney's laneway and came to an abrupt stop.

The Reverend was nowhere in sight. Wilf could see Josh limping toward him though, wrapped in the same long coat he had on the night before and looking just the same too, perhaps he hadn't even bothered to go to sleep.

Wilf struggled out of the car.

"Morning," the boy said, settling down on his bad ankle at a distance and looking like some ragged bird.

"Morning. I was wondering if I might have a moment with your father."

"Why?"

"I was moved by the meeting last night. That's why. Quite taken up by the power of it all. I would really appreciate seeing your father."

Josh held out a dirty hand.

Wilf reached into his pocket and pulled out a two-dollar bill.

Josh's eyes lit up. He shuffled forward. "He's in the temple," he said, plucking up the bill.

"Up there?" Wilf pointed his cane toward the implement shed.

"We're putting in more benches."

Wilf limped up the slope toward the open doors. Josh limped along behind him. The march of the lepers, Wilf thought to himself.

The Reverend was building some extra seating behind the hay wagon, tiering it up on a series of old planks and oil drums.

"Expecting a larger crowd?"

Reverend Cooney turned around from his work. He smiled. "You were here last night."

"Standing at the top. Back row."

"I never miss a face."

"Amazing."

"You're from the law office in town."

"I am. And I have something of a private nature I'd like to ask." Wilf looked back toward Josh who was lurking in the aisle.

"Why don't you find us a few more boards?" The Reverend called out to him, "I believe there's some left in that pile behind the barn."

"He's paid for a blessing," Josh said. "Two dollars."

The Reverend stepped off the seat and onto the bed of the wagon. "Then a blessing he shall receive."

The boy turned and limped out the doors.

"A hard-working son you've got there, Mr. Cooney."

"The Reverend Cooney, actually, not that I make a big fuss about it. And yes, he is my great joy. His affliction is my great joy."

"How is that?"

"Because I cursed God. Why should I have a crippled son? Why has the Almighty imposed this on me, I cried out. But then, as God had planned, my son became the joy of my life and I knew that I had sinned and I knew that I had been, to the very bottom of my soul, a coward. Afflictions are how we find God's love in this life. Isn't that a wondrous thing?"

"No gulf too deep," Wilf said. "No distance too far."

"That's the mystery of it, isn't it? That's the wonder. If you like, I'll pray for you now."

"That's not why I'm here. It's not that."

"No?"

"I have a question for you. You know Daniel Kelly, don't you? He has a farm not too far from here."

Cooney's face clouded over a little. "What about Mr. Kelly?"

"He collapsed last night right about where I'm standing."

"He received the Holy Spirit last night."

"You should know that I'm working for the police."

"I see." Cooney took a step backwards.

"And they seem to think that that dead boy you've been speaking so eloquently about has something to do with Mr. Kelly and his late wife. They've sent me out here to ask you what you know about the Kelly family. In the strictest of confidence, of course. Tell me what you know, and if there's no criminal culpability on your part I'm sure you won't be in any further trouble."

The big man stared down at Wilf, his blue eyes blazing now. "Mister, I stand in amazement that anyone, much less a lawyer, would approach a man's minister and ask him to divulge anything at all. Don't you know you're treading on sacred ground?

Don't you know that what happens between a man, his God and his minister is a sacred trust?"

"But you're a janitor," Wilf said.

Cooney's handsome face went cold. He strode back across the wagon and stepped over the gap and onto a board suspended precariously between two oil drums.

"Why are you running away?"

"Who's running away? I have work to do."

"We talked to the Grey County Children's Home. You're not a Reverend anybody. You don't have any degree, licence, training. And you were fired for bothering the children. For being a bloody nuisance."

Cooney picked up a hammer and looked around for something to hit.

"How many people do you think are going to come out here when they find out the truth about you?"

"And what is a piece of paper but a piece of paper?" Cooney shouted out. "When a man is a lightning rod for God! When a man is ablaze with the Spirit! When a man is Truth! How far do you suppose people will come to see him, to touch and be touched, to be healed?" Cooney began to drive a large nail into a board. "They will come from miles and miles and miles."

"How far do you suppose they'll come from when they find out you knew all about that boy in the first place. Knew who had put him there, knew exactly why, but you were keeping it a secret just to drum up attention to benefit yourself?"

"Why don't you leave?"

"Because you're covering up a murder, Mr. Cooney. That's serious business."

Cooney was working on his knees. He stopped his hammering and looked back at Wilf. "The man told me something in absolute trust and faith." He looked around the implement shed, the tiers of benches, the painted sign that read *NEW HOPE CHRISTIAN CHURCH: THE REVEREND GENE C. COONEY PRESIDING.* "Why are you trying to ruin everything? Why don't you leave the poor man alone?"

"Somebody starved a boy to death. We're assuming, for the time being, it wasn't you."

"He wanted to know if he was making the right choice. That's all."

"What choice?"

Cooney was beginning to look in as much pain as Kelly had the night before. "I gave the man my word!"

"What choice?" Wilf said again.

"Between his daughter and his God." Cooney looked at Wilf, his eyes full of unmistakable anguish now. "Will you swear you won't make an arrest on the strength of what I tell you? Because I can't stand the thought of that. Then who am I?"

Wilf had gone as still and as rapt as any hunter in any woods. "I swear," he said.

Cooney stood up. He examined the hammer in his hand for a full half-minute. Wilf waited.

"God's Truth is," he finally said, "Mr. Kelly wanted to save them both. His daughter and that child. But he couldn't, not the way he saw it, so he wanted me to agree that God would understand his choice. And I kept telling him that he was exactly wrong, that only by saving them both could he truly and for all eternity set his daughter free. Mr. Kelly did not follow my counsel. And yes, his soul was wracked with the agonies of the damned. And yes, despite everything, the Lord had mercy on him last night. He was saved by the Grace of the Living God."

"You knew what was going on for some time then. Is that what you're saying? And you didn't do anything?"

"What could I have done?"

"You could have gone to the police."

"She was only twelve years old! Twelve!" He looked at Wilf as if just the mention of her age should elicit a sea of mercy.

"And?" Wilf said.

"And?" Cooney looked bewildered for a moment. "And you remember what it was like, don't you? Ten years back or so? They were terrible times. No jobs to be found anywhere. Men riding the rails, tramping the roads. And all this little girl did was go for a walk down by the river. There were some men camped down there, and there was this man, this afflicted individual who was travelling with them, as a kind of amusement I suppose, as a kind of mascot. And the men took her and made a spectacle of her and dragged her down into the water. And they put him on her, all of them laughing and shouting and urging him on. This soulless witless man and this terrified girl." Cooney looked away from Wilf, as if he were ashamed for himself and ashamed for the world. "When she made her way back home, all she said was that she'd fallen down. That's all she said. She scarcely knew what had happened anyway. And when she started to show the child she was carrying, and she did tell her story, her mother and father faced a choice. Keep her home, say nothing, shield her from shame. Or trust that everything is for a good purpose in God's Creation, that our fate is meant to free us, not imprison us. They chose to say that she was ill and kept her away from school, and when that hapless baby came and they saw what it was they were convinced that they'd been right. And in so doing, they trapped her in a lie and in darkness and in hatred for the rest of her life."

"Why do you say hatred?"

"Because she hated that child. Hated it with all her might. She went off on her own at sixteen, according to her father, found work in some city, came home only rarely. And when she returned for her mother's funeral and Mr. Kelly couldn't get that boy to eat she wouldn't even try. He wanted to take it somewhere, get it help. And she said, 'They'll ask questions, you'll destroy my life.' And she said, 'No.'"

"What was its name?"

"It didn't have a name."

"They must have called it something."

Cooney shook his head.

"Where's the daughter now?"

"Mr. Kelly said she's leaving today."

"She's out at the farm?"

"I suppose."

Wilf turned and headed for the open doors.

"You understand, don't you?" Cooney called out after him.

"Understand what?"

"That there are two victims here. She was a child, too. She was a victim, too."

"I understand," Wilf said.

Cooney's voice cut like a knife through the air. "Then why don't you leave her alone?"

Wilf drove back toward the Kelly farm. He turned into the muddy side road and coasted past their lane and pulled up behind a screen of trees.

His breath was coming too rapidly; it was threatening to disappear on him again. He got out of the car and walked into the edge of the trees. A wet urgent pungency was rising up out of the loamy earth. Random patches of snow were trickling away. Shafts of sunlight streaked down through the branches.

Wilf began to push his way deeper into the tangle. After a short struggle he came out at a snake fence running along the top of a slope. Kelly's outbuildings and a gleaming pig wallow were just below him. A muddy corral sheltered a few sleepy cattle and a sagging haymow. Chickens were pecking about here and there.

A door slammed shut and Kelly came out of the house. He crossed the yard toward an old pickup truck and slumped down on its running board. He sat there for a while looking back toward the house and then he got up and walked toward the largest of the outbuildings. He pushed through the door and disappeared inside.

Wilf came out of the trees and made his way down the slope.

He skirted around the henhouse, limped by an old rusting and padlocked gas pump and came up to the back of the truck. He looked toward the house. There was no one standing just inside the doorway; there was no movement behind any of the windows.

"Leave her alone," Cooney had said. Pity the father, who sat there night and day listening to the boy's cries grow weaker and weaker. Pity the mother, who is dead. And most of all, pity the daughter.

He couldn't. Every instinct, every muscle, every heartbeat told him that the answer to the boy in the cage was in that house. He couldn't stop.

Wilf crossed the yard, climbed up on the side porch and tried the door. It opened. Two suitcases were sitting on a linoleum floor. He stepped inside. The kitchen was long and shadowy, the ceiling so low it almost brushed his head.

He listened for a moment. Nothing but a muffled silence. No creaking floor above him, no sound of a door being drawn closed anywhere. A smaller door stood in front of him on the opposite wall. He crossed over to it and lifted the latch. It made a kind of scraping sound and swung open over a warped wooden step. There was a light switch on the wall.

Wilf turned it on and everything beneath his feet lit up.

He began to ease himself down step by step. He could smell musty air, feel its coolness move past his face. He could see the floor beneath, a red-coloured earth as smooth as clay. A tangle of vegetable and fruit baskets of every size and shape lay before him. A solid wall of preserves ran down the one side. A pile of ashes was mounded up in front of a furnace. And just past the furnace Wilf could see another door.

He made his way toward it and pulled it open. At first he couldn't see anything in the gloom and then he began to make out a stovepipe running up a rough rubble wall. A blanket was wrapped around something just beneath it. He pulled the blanket away. A small heating stove and a scuttle half-full of coal came into view.

The floor was the same reddish clay as in the larger room and Wilf could see that a woven pattern had been pressed into it, as if a rough mat had laid there not so long ago. A whitewashed post was holding up the swaying ceiling. A single nail was sticking out of its side.

"What are you doing?"

Wilf swung around.

A young woman was standing in the dusty light by the open door. "I'm Wilf McLauchlin," Wilf managed to say. "I'm with the town police. I'm investigating." There was a profound wildness in her bony face and a wildness to her eyes and in the way her hair cascaded down past her waist. "Perhaps you saw me earlier today. Are you Mr. Kelly's daughter?"

Her eyes moved to Wilf's cane, lingered on his left leg, landed on his left arm. "What are you investigating?"

"Why your father would need a stove in a root cellar."

"He needs to keep the potatoes from freezing."

"I thought that's what a root cellar was for."

"You don't know much, do you?"

"I don't even know your name."

The woman's feral eyes came up to meet Wilf's eyes and stayed there, remaining hard and motionless.

Wilf looked away. "I don't see any potatoes here."

"You broke in. You have no right."

"I have a search warrant."

"Let me see it."

Wilf just stood there.

"Get the hell out of our house," she said and disappeared from the door.

Wilf could hear her running up the stairs. He followed her,

hurrying along through the baskets and hauling himself up the steps into the kitchen. He could see her through the open side door. She was running toward the largest of the outbuildings.

Wilf headed across the yard toward the truck. He knew he had time to do that much. If the keys were in it he'd drive it away. Let Andy explain everything. Let Andy get a search warrant. He wrenched open the door.

A key ring was hanging down from the ignition. House keys, extra truck keys, padlock keys all shining in a patch of sunlight, suspended there. Wilf came to a stop.

He began to fumble one-handedly with the ring. He managed to slip off three keys and shut the clasp again. He eased the truck's door closed as quietly as he could. And then he ran, half-stumbling around the gas pump and past the henhouse, refusing to look behind him, hopping and puffing up the slope.

He reached the edge of the trees. He flung himself over the snake fence.

He looked back.

Mr. Kelly was nowhere in sight. Neither was his daughter.

※ ※ ※

Duncan was sitting in a tree. He could see the stone cottage and most of the yard that way. Carole had already come out and gone back in twice since Wilf had left earlier that morning. She seemed restless, afraid to be left alone.

She deserved to be left alone. He'd seen her the night before. He'd heard her, too. Her little mewing cries coming through the glass, moaning like any old barn cat in heat, her white legs waving in the air. He'd watched the whole thing and then he'd wandered half-blind toward the river.

Wilf McLauchlin and Carole. Just like his lawyer had said. Wake up, his lawyer had said. Wilf was never his wing man. Carole was never his friend.

Duncan had found the edge of the water in the pitch dark. He'd huddled under some bushes and wondered what he should do. He was on the wrong side of the river, for one thing. And he'd never find Babe and Dandy anyway. And the truth was, he was pretty much starved. He decided to finish the last jar of his mother's strawberry jam he'd been carrying around in his coat pocket. By some miracle the jar was still sitting on the shelf in his closet, the special jar he'd saved from when all the rest was used up, because he knew there would never be any more. Never again the sight of his mother working in the kitchen, never again the smell of berries and sugar, never again watching clouds billowing up from all the pots on the stove.

Duncan lay down on the ground and ate the whole thing, spooning it out with his finger. He didn't want to hurt Carole. But more and more, trying not to think about it, he kept thinking about it. He thought about it first when Wilf and Andy Creighton had started carrying out her furniture. And he thought about it after he'd snuck into the back of the truck. Her mattress was riding right there beside him all the way out into the countryside. He'd reached out and touched it. He was already sure she'd done the two-backed beast with Wilf McLauchlin. Already positive. And he'd been proved right.

But how would it all work out? What could he do?

He'd begun to shiver in the cold and the dark just thinking about it. He could wait for Wilf to leave the next day and then walk into the house. She'd look up from whatever she was doing. "I'm sorry, Duncan," she'd say, but she'd be lying because there'd be fresh jism running down her legs again. And he'd grab her by her throat, and by her hair, and he'd press her face up against his crotch.

No.

She was his friend. A long time ago. "Hi, Duncan. Hi!" In the park. And he was swinging back and forth in a sweet daze just for her. Swinging. Higher. And higher.

He really didn't want to hurt Carole.

He'd hang himself instead.

And he could see himself dragging her to that same mattress, ripping off all her clothes, her breasts loose once again, but this time he'd be able to touch them. Squeeze them.

Or wade out into the river. Hold his head under the water. He was brave enough to do that. He could do that for Carole. Take a deep breath and float away.

And she'd be screaming and screaming because she didn't like him at all. Never did. Screaming and fighting against him. Because he was a freak.

Or he could roll over right where he was and take the empty preserve jar and break it over a stone. He could cut himself with it.

And he was on top of her now, pushing in a jagged piece of glass. And blood was gushing from his hand and from the hole in her neck and the feeling was rushing into him now, just like that time with Basil, only a lot more, lifting, lifting him up. And the mattress was turning red as a rose.

Now it was the next morning. Duncan continued to sit in his tree and stare wide-eyed toward the cottage and think of Carole. And sometimes he had to cling to a branch just to keep from falling down.

✳ ✳ ✳

Wilf got out of the car in front of the garage and waved at Andy.

Andy was talking with some friends. He walked around the grease pit and came out into the sunlight. He smelled of whisky.

"What's up?"

"Where's the padlock?"

"What padlock?"

"The padlock that was on the cage that kid was in. Where is it?"

Andy stared at Wilf and didn't like what he saw. "Don't tell me you've got the key."

"I've got the key."

"From who? How the hell did you manage that?"

"Where's the cage? Where the hell's the lock, Andy?"

"The OPP have it."

"Where?"

"In our storage room. But just for now. They'll be taking it away."

Wilf was already hurrying back down Main Street.

Andy caught up to him. "I'm off duty."

"That's good. You smell like the Arlington Hotel. Can we get in without being seen?"

"Ted just drove by in the cruiser."

"Where's the Chief?"

"I don't know." Andy looked nervously along the street. "How did you get the key? From Cooney?"

"No. From Kelly."

"Kelly? Jesus, you didn't go back there, did you? Wilf? Tell me you didn't break into his house."

"I didn't break into his house."

"Oh, Jesus Christ! He wouldn't keep that key around anyway. He wouldn't be that stupid."

"How many keys do you get when you buy a padlock? You get at least a spare one, right, just in case you lose the first one. And who ever remembers where they put the extra key?"

"Me! If I was committing a murder!"

"But it wasn't exactly a murder. At least not a fast one. It was slow. And it wasn't planned. At least not by him."

"Then why bother with Kelly? I don't know what you're talking about."

"The boy had to come from somewhere, he had to have a mother. And Kelly has a daughter. She's out there right now."

Andy came to a halt. "Kelly has a daughter?"

"Cooney told me everything. It was her child. She hated it. And it was her decision to starve it to death. What we're hoping for is that in all his upset and confusion Kelly forgot the spare key."

"He has a daughter?" Andy said again, as if he were truly amazed.

The office was empty.

Andy gave Wilf an all clear sign and went back into the station. By the time he'd unlocked the storage room and was pushing the door open, Wilf was right behind him. The small room was windowless and narrow and cluttered with an assortment of stolen or abandoned bicycles and tricycles, a car tire, a kidnapped lawn ornament, a store mannequin, a wheelbarrow.

Wilf made his way to the far end. A space had been cleared away and in the harsh glare from the overhanging light he could see the wire cage again. "She hated him."

"I know." Andy came up beside him. "You already said that."

The padlock was still closed and dangling down from the latch on the door. Someone had cut a large hole in the back of the cage to take the body out.

Andy fished out a handkerchief. "Use this. They've already brushed everything for fingerprints but why be in deeper shit than we already are."

"I only have one hand."

"Right." Andy held the handkerchief around the padlock while Wilf pulled a key out of his pocket. He tried it. It didn't fit.

"We're screwed," Andy said.

"I have two more." Wilf tried another one. The key slipped in and turned. The padlock sprung open.

"Mother of God," Andy said.

They raced back out into the country, Andy driving and Wilf telling him what he knew about Kelly's daughter, how she came home for her mother's funeral, stayed long enough to deal with her son, in a manner of speaking, and now she was getting ready to leave again. And he told him what had happened to her when she was twelve years old.

Andy's expression began to change. "I don't know about this. Do you think we're doing the right thing?"

"Think about it. She sat in that house for over a week and didn't lift a finger. Neither did Kelly. And then, when her son was finally dead she stripped off all his clothes."

"This is so godawful, Wilf. She was only twelve."

Wilf watched a tree come up, race by.

The sun was so bright he could hardly see.

Another one came up. Raced by.

"She's older now," Wilf said.

They came to the muddy side road. Andy braked and turned into it and then swung into Kelly's lane. They were halfway to the house when Wilf said, "The truck's gone."

Andy made a bouncing U-turn in the yard. "We should have passed them on the way here if they're heading for the train station. Unless they left right after you did."

"Or drove straight west and took the highway into town. Or went somewhere else."

"You told me they didn't see you when you were searching the truck."

"They didn't. As far as I know."

"Shit," Andy said.

A passenger train was just pulling out from the town's station when they careened into the parking lot. They sat there watching the caboose begin to traverse the bridge that spanned the larger of the two rivers. Dark smoke was trailing up into the blue sky far ahead of it.

Wilf looked at Andy. "She won't be hard to find. She must have a job somewhere. A place she stays."

"Do you see Kelly's truck anywhere?"

Wilf looked around. "No."

Andy stared out the windshield. "You know what I think? I think I better hand that key over to the OPP."

"We could take one more drive out, just in case he came in on the highway and we missed him."

"I don't think so."

"The OPP are going to ask you how you came by it."

"That's easy. I'll just say you stole it. It's stolen property."

"Right."

"Trouble is, you'll be in a bigger mess than you already are."

"Do what you have to do, Andy. That's okay."

Andy sat there considering his options. Wilf expected to see him begin to pat himself down, looking for his cigarettes, but instead he said, "You know, I think I do remember seeing her out there. Years ago." He shook his head. "This little kid."

Andy turned the car around, drove out of the parking lot and headed out of town. After what seemed like a slow and reluctant ride to Wilf they finally reached Kelly's lane again. The truck was standing in the yard. Kelly was sitting on a kitchen chair on the front porch as if he were expecting company.

"I have a bad feeling," Andy said. He pulled the car up near the truck. He and Wilf got out.

"Hello again, boys," Kelly called over to them. His one arm was slung over the back of the chair as if he needed support. His eyes looked freshly bruised. His hair was still standing up in patches. "I guess this is one of those days."

"What kind of day is that, Mr. Kelly?" Andy said as he and Wilf walked up to the edge of the porch.

"The kind of day where men's souls are tested." Kelly turned his watery eyes on Wilf. "You were in my house. That's illegal."

Wilf glanced at Andy. Andy's face seemed as wretched as Kelly's.

"The Great Almighty was using you today, young man," Kelly continued on, "whether you know it or not."

"Oh?" Wilf replied.

"I'm afraid we're going to have to ask you a few more questions," Andy said.

"I was halfway to town before I remembered. You see, God has His own way." Kelly was keeping his eyes on Wilf. "Did one of those keys fit?"

"You tell us," Andy said.

"I'm going to have to ask you boys a favour. I'm going to have to ask you to look deep in your souls. And think about a little girl who was much much too young!" Tears as big as dimes began to roll down Kelly's cheeks.

Andy was beginning to look like he'd rather be in his car, rather be anywhere on earth than where he was. "You had a legal obligation to give a minor under your care the necessities of life and to protect him from harm. That's the law."

"Yes. I know that. But you don't understand. There were two lives at stake. I couldn't save both. I had to choose. Choose between my own daughter and that boy. God help me!" Kelly seemed to go deathly pale. He began to slide off the chair.

Andy reached up to steady him.

"My daughter!" the man cried out. "My daughter!"

"It's all right," Andy said, trying to get him back on the chair.

"No. It's not all right! It's not all right at all! She was misused. By this half-wit, this half-monster! When she was twelve years old! Oh God!"

A curtain in an upstairs window fell back into place as softly as a bird landing. Wilf saw it.

"We kept it a secret," Kelly was going on, "as anyone would have done, and when she gave birth to this helpless little creature we looked after it. Of course we did. But when Theresa died, you see, he wouldn't eat anymore. He wouldn't drink. We couldn't do anything for him. And how could we take him anywhere for help? What questions would people ask? What would people say? It would have been the ruination of my daughter's life!"

Wilf began to move away from the porch.

"I tried to do the right thing and my mind's coming apart. Just leave. Leave us alone."

"There's nothing we can do." Andy was sounding apologetic.

Wilf turned the corner and limped along the side the house. He stepped up on to the porch. When he pushed open the door the suitcases were nowhere to be seen.

He walked down a hallway. He began to climb a narrow flight of stairs. Before he reached the top he could see her through an open door. She was sitting on the edge of a bed watching him. The suitcases were on the floor beside her. Wilf moved closer. He could hear Kelly weeping. The bedroom window was open and the curtain stirred in the breeze.

"It was time to release that poor boy. It was time to set my daughter free," he was moaning.

Wilf stopped at the door. The woman's dark thick hair was fanning out all around her. Her eyes were gigantic and luminous in the curtained light.

"Hello," Wilf said.

She didn't reply. She didn't move.

"How long did it take your son to starve to death?"

"Not long enough."

"Reverend Cooney told me he didn't have a name."

"He didn't."

"You could have made that train today."

She kept her eyes on Wilf's eyes. "What would have been the point of that? You had the key."

Kelly's voice was sounding as close as if he'd somehow levitated himself and was just outside the open window. "We did everything we could. Theresa and I. She loved him. She called

him Paul. Took him for walks. Babied him. We didn't keep him
in that cage all the time, you know."

"He had a name," Wilf said.

"So did I," the woman said. "Listen to him. All he's proving
is how hopeless he is. To forget that other key."

Her father was whispering now, whispering in through the
window. "The cage was only there to hide him and to control
him when someone happened to drive in the lane. We cared for
him, we weren't bad people." He began to weep again.

"Do you think he's crying for me? He's crying for himself.
He thinks he's truly damned. Any moment now he'll start talking
about my walk down by the river again. And those awful men.
And that imbecile. And the very air will cry for him. All his pain."
She leaned forward a little. "He is damned, you know?"

"Is he?"

"No one has ever heard what you're about to hear. Ever."

"All right," Wilf said.

"He was crying just like that when he told my mother that
story. And it was almost true. Except that there were lots of
walks down by the river. Not just one. Except that there was no
drooling imbecile. There was only my father."

And it seemed to Wilf that all the faint light in the room
was falling into her eyes. And all the light in the house and all
the light in the world. And it seemed to him that any hope he'd
held that everything would be magically revealed if only he could
find the secret to the boy in the cage was simply laughable. There
was no light and he would never know.

He took one last glance at her face, flayed by her experience
and lost beyond all the telling of it, and he turned away and barely
able to see where he was going stumbled along the hall and back
down the stairs. By the time he reached the side door he knew
what he was going to do and it seemed to him that he should have
known right from the beginning. It was so obvious now.

He crossed over to Andy's car, climbed into it and turned the key. He could hear Andy shouting at him. He spun the car around and headed out the lane.

And he already felt free.

He raced out to the gravel road that ran past John Moss's place, turned on to it and headed in the opposite direction. He began to look for a substantial tree. A small turn of the wheel, one moment of flight and then nothing. What could be more wished for than nothing? It would end what he'd brought home inside himself, it would end the plague. Wouldn't it? Who could argue with that? Not the town. Not his father. Not Carole.

He roared by one likely tree.

He couldn't breathe. He was rocking back and forth. Where was the final detachment? The purposeful calm of the fighter pilot? He'd made his decision. Never get to the bottom of anything, never find out what was happening or how it was happening. Whatever it was. It was too huge, too amorphous, too close. Outside. And inside. Alive. In his blood.

He was approaching a second tree. He could see every bone in his hand as it clenched the steering wheel. It looked like one of Chasson's x-rays. He was getting ready for take-off. Somewhere.

The tree was racing closer, bounding toward him in great giant strides. He thought of Carole. She'd made him promise something. "Don't surprise me," she'd said. Wasn't that what she'd said?

Not like that other soldier had done. Her fiancé.

Poor Carole Birley.

Someone had just knocked at the door.

Carole was in the kitchen making herself some lunch from the few things she'd brought from her mother's and feeling angry and frustrated that Wilf could leave her alone for so long, that he could be so deaf to everything she'd said, so blind to what she'd been plainly feeling.

She stood there listening for whoever it was to knock again. There was only one door in the house. There'd been a back door at one time, but someone had taken it off and had covered the opening so there'd be room for the electric stove.

Another knock.

Carole walked across the living room and looked outside. Mr. McLauchlin's Buick was still sitting there, all shiny and dark. There was no other vehicle in sight. She tried to see the front stoop. She pressed her face to the window but she couldn't see.

Each time she'd returned that morning from wandering aimlessly around in the yard she'd locked the door. It was locked now.

A sharper knocking. It had a proprietary sound to it this time, as if it might be the owner of the cottage. Or perhaps Mr. McLauchlin. What if he'd come out by cab, frustrated that Wilf hadn't come into town to talk to him, angry that Wilf still had the car.

"Hello?" she called out, "Who is it?"

No one answered.

Carole unlocked the door. Duncan Getty was standing there. His great head looked even larger than it usually did with all of his hair shaved off. He looked half-starved. She could see pieces of chain dangling down from his wrists. She could see a large piece of broken glass in his hand.

"Carole," he said, "guess what? We're goin' to get married now."

She couldn't make her voice come out. She couldn't feel her legs.

Duncan seemed to take her silence as some kind of agreement. He stepped inside the house.

Carole backed up. "I don't know whether this is such a good time to get married, Duncan."

He stared down at her legs. She could see now that his whole body was trembling.

"It's just that it takes a lot of planning to get married. We'll have to invite people and rent a hall and everything like that. It's very complicated."

"But we don't need all that. We can get married by the river."

"Can we?" Carole turned away. Where are you, Wilf, her mind was racing, taking off, flying around and around, where are you?

Duncan trudged over to the bedroom door. He stared down at the mattress like he couldn't take his eyes off it. "Unless you want to get married here."

If I run out the door, how far will I get, Carole thought. Three steps? Four? "Getting married beside the river sounds a lot better, Duncan. Nicer. Maybe when it's warm. Maybe sometime this summer."

"We have to do it now." Duncan turned to look at her, "Because of Dandy and Babe. That's where they are. I'll show you all the best places, where moss grows soft as anythin'. Where fresh water comes right out on the bank and it's good to drink, where you can get out of the wind, where there's sunny spots. You can ride on Babe, because she's more gentle than Dandy. We can live there forever."

"But we can't live outside all the time. What if it snows?"

"It won't snow, Carole." Duncan reached out as if he wanted to touch her. His wrist looked mangled under its iron bracelet.

"Maybe we should think about it some more. If you could help me fix this place up, we could live here."

"There's somebody else livin' here already." His tawny eyes slid back to the mattress again. The jagged piece of glass was scraping restlessly against his trouser leg. "By the river or here."

Some woman began to cry in Carole's mind. She turned away and walked back toward the door. "All right then. You can show me if you like. We can go down by the river. Let's visit all those nice places." She picked up her coat and pulled it over her trembling shoulders. She stumbled outside and looked down the laneway. Wilf wasn't there.

Duncan came out behind her and walked toward the river. He motioned her to follow him. Carole trailed along behind. He turned and started walking backwards. "You didn't feed my horses when I had to go away. I thought you knew enough to look after them."

"I thought someone else had done that. I asked about them and someone said they were being looked after in a really nice place. I'm sorry, Duncan. I'm sorry!"

Duncan looked as if he didn't know whether to believe that she was sorry or not. "Anyway, they got away. They're livin' down in the valley now. I seen them."

"Oh, I'm glad."

They were approaching the trees. Carole's feet felt like wood, thumping uselessly against the ground. Dragging.

"You'll get up on Babe. I'll get on Dandy."

"All right."

She could hardly make her legs move. "You walk so fast, Duncan. Maybe we could rest for a while."

Duncan stopped and stared up at the tree he'd been sitting in. "I've seen your naked titties lots of times, you know."

Carole's mind went blank.

"Pressing them up against the window. Spreading them out. You were teasing me. I was too stupid to know, though."

Duncan turned toward her with a groan.

The first thing Wilf noticed was that the door had been left open. He'd been rehearsing his speech past every likely tree and rattling over the bridge at Glen Morris. "I didn't want to surprise you," he'd say, "so I have to tell you about Buchenwald and Michael Chasson and typhus," he'd say. "Not to upset you but if we could just talk. Maybe I could get through this, Carole." And they would have a grownup conversation. And then she would know. And if it didn't work, if her voice, her touch, her arms didn't work, at least when he drove away she wouldn't be surprised.

Wilf got out of Andy's car and stared at the open door and suddenly he wasn't thinking about himself anymore.

He walked into the house. "Carole," he called out. He looked through the rooms.

He went outside again.

Maybe she'd gotten so angry she'd walked back into town. But it was four miles away. Maybe she was off on a stroll. "Carole!"

It seemed to Wilf that everything had gone silent. He looked toward the river. No sparrows were twittering in the tangle of nearby bushes. No crows were cawing in the far distance. No sound of the wind, though the high branches in the pines that circled the cottage were moving back and forth.

"Carole!"

His eyes caught a flash of colour farther out in the waist-high grass. He waded out toward it. Carole's coat was lying there. A sleeve was stretched out and pointing off toward the river.

Panic came loose everywhere, in the sky, in the air.

Wilf pushed on toward the valley and came up to the edge of a ravine. He could see a flow of muddy water moving fast far below. He stepped off and plunged down. The steep slope was slimy and wet. He began to slide on his knees. A scream ricocheted up the ravine to meet him. He stopped.

Silence again. And then another scream, racing up from the

river, scattering and chattering past him like a flock of frightened birds. Wilf let himself go and began to slide again. He could hear the churn of the water clearly now; it continued to grow louder.

He saw Carole first. She was cresting against the flooding river, her hair, her face, her naked body wet and gleaming, clinging to a fallen tree, going under, surfing up again.

And then he could see Duncan Getty working his way out toward her, the muddy water swirling around his waist, hauling himself up, tipping the tree down.

Carole disappeared.

"Murder me first!" Wilf bellowed out.

Duncan turned, his round boy's face shining, his shirt open and floating in the current.

"Kill me!"

Duncan began to wade toward the shore. Carole's face came up out of the river. Wilf could see a glint of broken glass in Duncan's hand.

"That's right," Wilf whispered, barely able to hold himself up, bracing against his cane.

Duncan looked half in a daze rising up out of the water. Blood was running down his chest, streaming across his broad white belly, disappearing inside his soaking pants. He raised the broken glass and like a penitent and entranced monk, he punched it into his flesh again.

"Come on," Wilf whispered.

Duncan took a step up the slippery bank, looked down and when he looked up again the black handle of the cane was descending through the sky.

Wilf could hear Duncan's skull crack as he hit it. The shocking delight of the impact went right up his arm.

Duncan went down on his knees.

Wilf raised the cane again.

"Wilf," Carole screamed.

CHAPTER TWENTY-TWO

Wilf and Carole didn't stay on at the stone cottage. Carole went back to her parents' home. Wilf went back to his old room at his father's place.

Mr. McLauchlin told Carole that she could take as much time as she needed to recover. She insisted that she wasn't hurt, that nothing had happened to her, but it was clear to everyone who saw her that first day that this wasn't true. It took her two days to get out of her mother's bed. Her mother had put her there because Carole's own bed was still out in the country.

Wilf sat with her in her parents' house. When she felt like going outside, he sat with her on the front porch. He felt over-whelmed by guilt. They talked about everything they could think of except what had actually happened. Sometimes they were content enough just to sit together and not say a word.

Carole had half-swum, half-climbed back out of the river and Wilf had covered her up with his coat. They'd struggled up the ravine together, had climbed into Andy's car and had driven into town. By the time two OPP officers, the Chief of Police and Wilf had returned, Duncan had crawled about fifty yards away along the shore. He was lying there as still as death, covered in mud and looking like some unknown creature.

"He's dead," the one OPP officer had said.

The Chief had knelt down in the mud. "No. Unfortunately he's not," he'd said.

After ten days of rest Carole came back to the office, sat down at her desk and began to type. Wilf had been thinking in a desperate kind of way that it might help if she could talk about just what did happen, because it was clear to him that she was still struggling. He couldn't bring himself to ask though, and she didn't say.

He didn't tell her about the injection. The plague. He didn't say a word about Buchenwald. Or his search for a suitable tree.

Spring came and went and the heat of the summer settled over the town and no further mayhem or murder occurred. This didn't surprise Carole. She'd already told Wilf that she knew it was over. Whatever it was. Wilf had ended it himself that day on the river because instead of dying she'd lived. And by her intervention, and only by her intervention, Wilf knew, so had Duncan.

Wilf had to agree with her. There had been some kind of change that day. He'd left the group of men who were standing around Duncan and he'd walked into the dense trees and he'd felt something lift out of his body and out of his mind and float away, filtering through the ferny places, drifting along the shadowy corridors, up through the shafts of sunlight. He just didn't know what it was.

"Will the court be open to the public?"

Carole and Wilf were sitting on the porch steps in front of her parents' house late one airless August night. Duncan's trial was coming up and she'd been too embarrassed to ask Mr. McLauchlin.

"It doesn't matter. You won't have to go. They'll get him on Basil. They won't need you for a lesser charge. Just your statement. And Dad says he'll make sure it's read into the record and discussed in the judge's quarters, not in court."

Carole nodded and looked up at a white blur of moths chasing themselves around a street lamp. "He said he wanted me to take my clothes off. He said he'd seen me lots of time through my bedroom window."

"Oh?" Wilf continued to stare off into the dark, not daring

to move or look her way. "So I did. And then he started to touch me all over and then he picked up that piece of glass again. And I ran. Flew down the hill. Saw the tree in the river, and all I could think to do was climb out on it and the water was so icy cold and he was punching that glass into his chest and I screamed. And he punched it into his chest again. And I screamed again. And he came climbing through the branches like someone I didn't know, like someone I couldn't recognize no matter how much I tried. I didn't know who he was!"

Carole got up and walked out the front walk and stood there under the light.

"Are you all right?" Wilf asked.

"I don't know."

The next morning Wilf climbed into his father's car and without telling Carole or anyone else where he was going, drove to Hamilton. Duncan was being held there again waiting for his trial. Wilf was somewhat surprised that no questions were raised when he identified himself at the reception desk as a friend of Duncan's. He was early for visiting hours though and had to sit in a nearby coffee shop for most of the afternoon. He wasn't as surprised on his return because he had to empty out all his pockets and the area for visitors had a heavy wire mesh running between the prisoners and whoever came in to see them; a burly guard was standing at each end of the room.

If a person were contemplating revenge on a prisoner, Wilf thought to himself, a person wouldn't be able to act on it.

He handed the slip of paper he'd been given to one of the guards and was told to take a seat and wait. Three women, girlfriends or wives, Wilf guessed, were talking to three men sitting passively on the other side of the screen.

A door opened and Duncan came in.

He seemed pleased when his eyes found Wilf. He shuffled over in leg chains and sat down.

"How are you doing, Duncan?"

"I'm fine." He looked around at the other people and smiled a kind of shy smile.

"How's your head?" Wilf could see a long scar across his temple and fading suture marks.

"I get dizzy sometimes. I'm better right now."

"How's your chest?"

"All right."

"Do you like it here?"

"Better than freezing."

Wilf nodded and said more softly, "Do you know why I'm here?"

Duncan thought about it for a moment. He looked like he knew a secret, but he shook his head.

Wilf could feel the pain in his side and a heavy pain behind his eyes. "I just wanted to see you again. Have a closer look."

"At what?"

Wilf shook his head. "I really don't know."

"I just wanted the house."

"You what?"

"Because Carole's my friend. I wouldn't do nothin' to hurt her, Wilf. I just needed a house."

"You needed a house?"

"You went away, didn't you? If Carole went away too then I could have it. I needed a house to live in because I couldn't live in my own house no more. I was just chasin' her away. That's all."

"Who told you to say that?"

Duncan moved his face close, so close his nose almost touched the wire; his tawny eyes looked sly. "That's not why you're here," he said.

"It's not?"

"No. You nearly killed me. You came to see how you'd feel."

"Why?"

"Because you want to feel it again."

"I've killed a lot of people, Duncan."

"I know," Duncan said.

Wilf got in the car and began the thirty-mile drive back toward his hometown. And now he knew what the injection of that bacterium had caused. It had remained innocuously in his body, just as Michael Chasson had said, but it had changed everything. It had altered his consciousness; it had given him eyes to see.

He could see Adrienne. He could see Duncan and Scarfe. He could see Kelly's daughter, feel her quickening heart as she watched her father's face and listened to the weakening cries coming from the cellar. All the wild, ecstatic, unfathomable pleasure of it.

And he could see himself.

Wilf aimed the car down the busy highway.

Duncan needed a house.

It sounded like all the paltry defences and obfuscations at Nuremberg. They all needed a house. It sounded like every Council of War's explanation everywhere. Every revolution. Every domestic bloodbath. Every common thug.

Everyone needs a house.

Wilf sped along.

I was never motivated by base instincts, the good doctor said.

Of course not. Who but a madman would confess to serial acts of homicide because it feels so good? Beyond the reach of all social engineering, beyond all hope of enlightenment, all ideas of human progress.

A truck roared by. A long line of shining cars streamed toward him.

And now Wilf knew why that boy in the cage had held the answer. Because he was us. In his sad, half-formed face, in his incapacity, in his entrapment. He was us.

"But just think." Wilf was talking out loud now, "Think of all the tender people who wouldn't harm anyone, all the communities that get along, the co-operation, the goodwill. Isn't this true? Isn't this truer still?"

He could see Carole as clearly as if she were sitting there beside him. Her gentleness. Her gracefulness. Her unruly lock of hair that he loved.

Where is God, Wilf thought to himself.

The sun was beginning to set. It was truly beautiful flaming across the highway, it filled Wilf's eyes.

It filled his heart.

EPILOGUE

Hitting something, body instantly coming loose like a rag doll, hitting again.

And again.

And again.

A screech of sheering metal, a wing cartwheeling by, the canopy coming off and over on her side, spinning.

And pain. Something wrong somewhere. A warning coming down a telegraph wire, bicycling down a leafy small town street.

And stopping in a wash of petrol. And waiting for the whoosh and rush of flames.

It's snowing out.

Shapes moving around in all this black tumbling smoke. Going away. Coming again. Voices, foreign and excited-sounding. Coming closer this time.

Snowing. Feathery. Floating all around.

A man stands in a long dark coat. He has rags on his feet. I look down at him looking up at me.

Black snow. Landing on my hands. And on my mouth. Turning into soot and grime. Into bits of hair. And skin.

And we are both amazed. A boy climbs up on my solitary wing.

And I am flying.

Flying.

And the boy is balancing beside me, wing-walking in his striped shirt and pants at four hundred miles an hour.

In his bare feet and up on his toes.

Clothes fluttering,

Holding on in all this raging smoke.

ACKNOWLEDGMENTS

The genesis of *Death Spiral* can really be found in my previous novel, *Transgression*, which was about a young French girl who falls in love with a German soldier during the occupation of France, and who as a result was ostracized by her family, her community and all the world, or so it felt to her. It was about the harm we do to each other, both in small things such as this girl's somewhat innocent transgression, and in something as vast as a world war. The puzzling question as to why we continue to feel compelled to inflict mayhem on each other was left as a kind of ghost shimmering between the lines. In *Death Spiral* this ghost is now front and centre and so I think it makes sense, at least artistically, to acknowledge this previous novel first of all.

I found the creation and writing of *Death Spiral* a kind of no-holds-barred psychic wrestling match, and so it was wonderful, as always, to have my wife, Judi, in my corner. But she's much more than an excellent corner man. She's a great no-nonsense first reader with amazing instincts. She's a relentless editor. And quite simply, she is and has always been my one true and constant support.

There are also ghosts of the good kind hovering over this book, such as my grandfather who felt it necessary in 1916 with a wife and a young daughter and one glass eye to volunteer for the Canadian Expeditionary Forces, and who subsequently found himself fighting in Belgium where he was made a semi-invalid for the rest of his life. And my artist father who during the Second World War designed war bond posters and painted war scenes in front of my very young and impressionable eyes. And all the glamorous returning soldiers I looked up to after the war, the few exotic creatures that accompanied them called War Brides, the Displaced Persons that soon followed looking for any kind of employment. All very early influences, all crucial to this work.

I want to thank Kim McArthur for her immediate enthusiastic response on her first read of the manuscript, it made my heart do a back flip. Thanks to my editor Barbara Berson for all her insightful help, particularly around the deeper themes of the story. And thanks to Ted Boniface for once again bravely taking on the role of first outside reader and giving me back not only a welcome measure of confirmation but some key notes on places, times and facts.

And once again much gratitude to my representative Beverley Slopen, who trusts my instincts as a writer no matter where my mind goes, and who has worked and continues to work so effectively on my behalf.